Prologue

Sometimes I think that Mama Arnold named me Rain because she knew so many tears would fall from my eyes. Other children often teased me, singing *"Rain, rain, go away. Come again another day."* When I was older, boys would call out to me in the halls or in the street and say, *"You can Rain on me anytime, girl."* None of them would do it if my brother Roy was around, but he knew they often did when he wasn't, and he got so angry about it once, he raged at Mama Arnold, demanding why she named me Rain.

She looked at him with such innocence and confusion scribbled through the lines in her face.

"Where I come from," she replied calmly, "where my family comes from, rain is a good thing, an important thing. Without it, we would go hungry, Roy. You ain't known that kind of hunger, thank God, but I remember it. We called it bottom hunger because you were empty right to the bottom of your poor stomach.

"And I remember feeling that first blessed drop after days and days of lingering drought. My daddy and mama would be so happy, they'd just stand in the downpour and let themselves get soaked through the skin. I recall once," she continued, smiling, "how we all joined hands and danced in the storm, all of us gettin' soaked to the bone and not a one carin'. I guess we looked like a crazy bunch, but the rain meant hope and money enough to buy what we needed.

"Why, some people took to prayer sessions and rituals of all kinds to bring on the rain. I saw my first rainmaker when I was about ten. He was a small, dark man with eyes like shiny balls of black licorice. All the children thought he was charged with electricity from being hit by lightning so many times, and we were terrified of his touchin' us.

"The church paid for him. Nothing he did brought a drop and he left saying we must've angered the Lord somethin' awful to have Him be so unforgiving. You know what that does to a congregation, Roy? Everyone goes peerin' around at everyone else with eyes of accusation, blaming our troubles on their sins. I heard talk of one community drivin' a whole family out because they thought they were responsible for a prolonged drought.

"When your sister was born and I saw how beautiful she was, I thought to myself why she's as pretty and as full of hope for us as a good rain and that's when I decided it would be a good name."

Roy stared at her, obviously overwhelmed. Beneatha looked down, sullen because she had been named after some relative and that wasn't much compared to what Mama Arnold was saying about me, and I remember thinking I had a greater responsibility because of my name. Mama Arnold thought I would bring good luck.

VIRGINIA®
ANDREWS

EYE OF THE STORM

**POCKET
BOOKS**

LONDON • SYDNEY • NEW YORK • TOKYO • SINGAPORE • TORONTO

First published in Great Britain by Simon & Schuster UK Ltd, 2001
This edition first published by Pocket Books, 2002
An imprint of Simon & Schuster UK Ltd
A Viacom Company

The right of Virginia Andrews® to be identified as author of this work has been asserted by her in accordance with sections 77 and 78 of the Copyright, Designs and Patents Act, 1988.

1 3 5 7 9 10 8 6 4 2

Simon & Schuster UK Ltd
Africa House
64-78 Kingsway
London WC2B 6AH

www.simonsays.co.uk

Simon & Schuster Australia
Sydney

A CIP catalogue record for this book is available
from the British Library

This book is a work of fiction. Names, characters, places and incidents are either a product of the author's imagination or are used fictitiously. Any resemblance to actual people living or dead, events or locales is entirely coincidental.

Printed and bound in Great Britain by Bookmarque Ltd, Croydon

The Dollanganger Family Series:
Flowers in the Attic
Petals on the Wind
If There Be Thorns
Seeds of Yesterday
Garden of Shadows

The Casteel Family Series:
Heaven
Dark Angel
Fallen Hearts
Gates of Paradise
Web of Dreams

The Cutler Family Series:
Dawn
Secrets of the Morning
Twilight's Child
Midnight Whispers
Darkest Hour

The Landry Family Series:
Ruby
Pearl in the Mist
All That Glitters
Hidden Jewel
Tarnished Gold

The Logan Family Series:
Melody
Heart Song
Unfinished Symphony
Music in the Night
Olivia

The Orphans Miniseries:
Butterfly
Crystal
Brooke
Raven
Runaways (full-length novel)

The Wildflowers Miniseries:
Misty
Star
Jade
Cat
Into the Garden (full-length novel)

The Hudson Family Series:
Rain
Lightning Strikes
Eye of the Storm

My Sweet Audrina
  (does not belong to a series)

EYE OF THE STORM

Today, as I dressed to go to the cemetery to visit Grandmother Hudson's grave, I believed Mama Arnold couldn't have been more wrong. All I seemed to bring to anyone was bad luck. Of course, Grandmother Hudson didn't think that when she died. She might have thought it in the beginning when my real mother had arranged for me to live with her under the guise of my being some charity case. That way my real mother, Megan Hudson Randolph, could still keep secret her getting pregnant and giving birth to me when she was in college, even from her husband and especially from her two children, Brody and Alison. My grandparents had paid my stepfather Ken to take me as soon as I had been born. Years later, Grandmother Hudson would take me in reluctantly, like a parent who had to swallow the sins of her child.

Mama Arnold was much sicker than any of us knew, and after my younger sister Beneatha had been killed and Ken, my stepfather, had run off and been arrested for armed robbery, Mama Arnold wanted to be sure I would be safe. When I think back now to that day when she forced my real mother to meet us for lunch and then convinced her she had to take me back, I realize how strong a woman Mama Arnold really was. Grandmother Hudson and Mama Arnold weren't so different when it came to the importance of and the sacrifices for their families.

On first impression, people like Mama Arnold who scratch out an existence in their state of poverty and hard times don't look like very much. Mostly, they hobble along looking tired, aged beyond their years, cynical, hopeless, their eyes as vacant as blown lightbulbs. What people don't see is the great strength, courage and optimism it takes for women like Mama Arnold to do battle with all the evil around them in order to protect their children. Mama Arnold was our fortress.

It seems silly now to think of that fragile little lady as a power of any kind, but that's who and what she was. She and I weren't blood related, but she gave me the gift of grit. I stood taller because of her, and one of the things that had so endeared me to Grandmother Hudson was her recognition of that and her admiration for Mama Arnold.

Grandmother Hudson and I had grown so close so quickly. I really loved that woman and I know she loved me, despite her initial reluctance. After all, she was a woman born and bred in the Old South, formal and stern in her ways, and here I was a mulatto and her illegitimate granddaughter. She was a woman who wouldn't tolerate a stain on her dress, much less a stain on her family honor. However, in the end she proved her deep affection for me by arranging for my dramatics training in London and then, by leaving me so much of her estate: fifty-one percent of this house and property, fifty percent of the business and a two-million-dollar portfolio of investments that provided more than enough for my well-being.

Grandmother Hudson's older daughter, my aunt Victoria, was so outraged she vowed to fight the will in court. Still unmarried, running the family's investment and development business, overseeing projects, my aunt Victoria felt unappreciated and, from what I had witnessed during my short time with Grandmother Hudson, was always in some sort of conflict or other with her. Victoria resented her younger sister, my mother Megan, whom she thought their father favored over her, and whom she thought had a head full of air. Perhaps she resented my mother mostly though for having a husband like Grant, a handsome, intelligent, ambitious man, the kind of a man she wanted for herself and thought she could appreciate and satisfy far more than Megan could.

Toward the end of my senior year in high school, Grandmother Hudson had arranged for me to live with her sister Leonora and my great-uncle Richard in England when I attended the Richard Burbage School of Drama. Neither Great-aunt Leonora or Great-uncle Richard knew who I really was. They thought Grandmother Hudson was doing some sort of charity work, sponsoring a poor minority girl. They didn't learn the whole truth until Grandmother Hudson died.

When I was called back from England along with my great-uncle and great-aunt after Grandmother Hudson's death, my mother and her husband tried to get me to compromise and surrender much of what my grandmother had left me in the will. I think they both saw their offer as a way of paying me off and getting rid of me forever and ever, but I believed Grandmother Hudson had a purpose for what she had done, and I wasn't going to change anything in that will, not even a comma.

My aunt Victoria continued to rage about making legal challenges, something I knew was terrifying to Grant, who had political ambitions. The last thing he wanted out in the open was his wife's past affair with an African-American man and my existence. Even after the funeral and all, he and my mother had still not told their children the whole truth. Brody liked me, I know, but Alison couldn't understand why I was given so much and why I commanded so much of her family's attention. She despised me, but I wasn't sure the truth would make any difference when it came to that and so secrets and lies continued to swirl around this house and family like a maddened hive of bees.

Living in the mansion alone at the moment, I could practically hear those lies buzzing. Soon, they would sting us, sting us all and bring even greater pain, but everyone in this family was focused on his or her self-interests and had tunnel vision. They didn't see it. Mama Arnold always told me there were none so blind as those who refused to see, those who looked away or down or at some fantasy rather than the truth. This family took the prize when it came to doing just that, from my great-uncle's strange fantasies in his London cottage, to my mother's refusal to face reality, to go off and distract herself with new purchases at the least little drop of controversy or stress.

My aunt Victoria mumbled about her, complaining, calling her another Scarlett O'Hara because she was always saying "I'll worry about it tomorrow." Tomorrow, tomorrow—it never comes of course, Victoria liked to remind everyone.

Well, whether my mother was going to face it or not, tomorrow had come to this family. Grandmother Hudson in her last will and testament had insisted it come. Even in death, maybe especially in death, she hovered over her family, scowling down at them and demanding they finally take responsibility for their actions, for who they were and what they were.

I wasn't about to stop all that from happening, but I couldn't be more frightened of what the future held for me. I didn't have all that many choices. True, I had found Larry Ward my real father in England and met his family. He had achieved his dream: he had become a Shakespearean scholar and taught in a community college. He wanted me to visit and get to know his family and get them to know me better, including his wife Leanna, but Grandmother

Hudson's last bit of advice was not to push myself on them. She was afraid they would come to resent me. Maybe after a little more time, I thought, when I was more sure of myself, I would revisit him and his family.

Meanwhile, with my stepbrother Roy still in the army in Germany, the only friend I had here was Jake, Grandmother Hudson's driver. He and I had also grown very close during my time here, and one day before I left to study the performing arts in England, he surprised me by bringing me to see his new race horse that he had named after me.

Jake had history with this family and this property. It had once belonged to his family, but years ago, his family lost it and the Hudsons took it over. Jake had traveled a great deal in his life. He had been in the navy and he had never married and had no children or family of his own. I often felt like he was adopting me.

Today, he waited for me outside to drive me to the cemetery. I had been there before with everyone else of course, but this time I was going alone to say my own good-bye.

After the funeral and the reading of the will, I had moved myself into Grandmother Hudson's room. I didn't change anything, didn't move a picture or shift a chair. It helped me to feel she was still there, still watching over me.

Aunt Victoria had already been through Grandmother Hudson's things, making sure she had all her valuable jewelry, watches and even some clothing. Parts of the room, dresser drawers and closets looked absolutely pillaged. In fact the drawers were so empty there was not even a piece of lint left and the closets were full of gaping areas, even the hangers gone.

Of course, having lived here and helped take care of the house, I was quite familiar with everything, especially in the kitchen. I recalled the meals I had cooked for Grandmother Hudson and how much she had appreciated them. Her attorney provided me with all the information I needed to maintain the house and property. He said if I wanted, which I did, he would continue to manage and oversee that aspect of the estate. I had the feeling Grandmother Hudson had told him many nice things about me. He seemed very pleased that I had stood up to my mother, her husband and Victoria.

"Up to now," he said, "you're living up to your grandmother's expectations, Rain."

I thanked him for the compliment and told him even in the short time we had spent together, she had provided the example for me to follow. The only thing was, I wasn't confident about how much longer I could follow it.

I glanced at myself once more in the mirror and then started down the stairway to make the trip to the cemetery. It was a mostly cloudy day with a cooler breeze announcing the imminent arrival of fall. A perfect day for visiting graveyards, I thought as I stepped out of the house. Jake was leaning against Grandmother Hudson's Rolls-Royce, his arms folded, waiting for me. The moment I appeared, he smiled and stood straight.

"Mornin', Princess," he called as I crossed the drive toward him.

"Good morning, Jake."

"You sleep all right?" he asked.

I knew everyone was wondering if I would be able to live in a house this large all by myself. Aunt Victoria was hoping I would get spooked and go to her, practically begging to accept the deal she had offered through Grant Randolph.

"Yes, I did, Jake."

He smiled. Jake was a tall, lean, balding man whose bushy, thick eyebrows almost made up for his loss of hair. He had dark brown eyes which always seemed to have an impish glint, lighting up his narrow face. His chin was slightly cleft and his nose was just a little too long and too thin, but his smile for me was almost always warm, friendly, just as it was this morning.

Lately, he had a crimson tint in his cheeks. I knew he was drinking a little more than usual, but he called it his fuel and I could never say I saw him look or act drunk.

He opened the rear door of the Rolls for me. I hesitated, gazing in at the seat where Grandmother Hudson always sat firmly. I could still smell her perfume, the scent floating out to me. It made me hesitant.

"You all right with this, Rain?"

"Yes, Jake. Yes," I said and got in quickly. He closed the door and we started for the cemetery.

"Victoria called to tell me I'd be picking up Megan and Grant at the airport tomorrow," he said as we drove along. "Did you know about that?"

"No."

"Thought so," he said nodding and shaking his head. "Sneak attack."

"How did they even know I would be home?" I asked.

He shrugged.

"Victoria just assumes you will." He looked back at me, his eyes a little wide. "That woman is all confidence," he said. He laughed. "I can remember her as a little girl. She walked so straight and perfect and always looked like she was thinking. She was so serious, even back then, and I remember the way she would look at Megan, look down her

9

nose at her as if to say, 'How did this bug get into our house?'

"One thing about Megan though, she never seemed to pay her much attention. Victoria's comments slid off her back like ice cubes off a hot plate."

"Which had to drive Victoria crazy," I said.

"Exactly. Exactly." He laughed. "If Megan gave her much thought, she'd be upset, I suppose. Even back then, I nicknamed her Turtle. She'd get this far-off, dreamy look and crawl into her shell of fantasies to escape Victoria."

"Megan is like that with everyone," I muttered, more to myself than to him.

"Um," he said.

I hadn't told Jake anything about Megan being my real mother and I hadn't told him about my real father at all. Since the funeral and all that followed, he and I hadn't really spent much time together. This was the first trip, the first time he was driving me anywhere when I was by myself.

"So, have you decided to return to England, Princess?" he asked me.

"Probably," I said. "I'll stay in the dorms this time, of course."

"I understand. Leonora and Richard are two pieces of work, all right. Frances used to shake her head and laugh at how regal and how English Leonora had become."

I wanted to tell him there wasn't all that much that was funny about them. They had lost their little girl who had a defective heart valve and it had left my great-uncle rather bizarre. Shortly before I had left England, he had impregnated their maid, Mary Margaret, whom I discovered was the daughter of Great-uncle Richard's driver, Boggs, the man who ran his house. No one but Boggs, I and Mary

Margaret knew. Both my great-uncle and great-aunt were people who created their own imaginary world to replace the reality they couldn't face, and Mary Margaret had been forced to be part of Great-uncle Richard's fantasies.

"You didn't happen to find yourself a nice young Englishman while you were there now, did you, Princess?" Jake asked.

"No, Jake," I said.

He raised his eyebrows at the way I had replied. He could hear my audible sigh following. At the school I had met a handsome Canadian boy, Randall Glenn, the type of young man who could make every woman's heart flutter when he looked her way. We had become lovers for a while. Randall had a beautiful singing voice. I was sure he would be a great success, but in the end, he proved to be too immature for me.

"No one to go back to then?" Jake pursued.

"Shakespeare," I replied and he laughed.

The cemetery soon loomed before us. We passed through an arch and went to the right and then to the left to the Hudsons' plots. Grandmother Hudson had been buried beside her husband Everett and to his right were his parents and a brother.

Jake stopped the car and turned off the engine.

"Looks like there might be a little storm later," he said. "I was going to take Rain out for a little trot, but I'll wait until tomorrow. Hey," he said while I procrastinated, building up my courage in the rear seat, "maybe you can ride her from time to time. Until you return to England, that is."

"I haven't ridden for a while, Jake, not since school here."

"Yeah, well it's like ridin' a bike, Princess. You just get on and it comes back. Don't forget," he reminded me, "I've seen you riding. You're good."

"All right, Jake. I'll do it," I promised, took a deep breath and got out.

I didn't think as much about Grandmother Hudson during the funeral. There were so many people and so much tension between my aunt Victoria and my mother, I was often distracted. I kept expecting Grandmother Hudson would appear and be outraged by the ostentatious arrangements Victoria had made.

"How dare you conduct such a silly service in my name? All of you, get on with your own lives," she would command and then smile at me and we'd go home.

Dreaming seemed to be the best medicine for such deep, sickly sadness, I thought and walked toward her grave. Jake remained in the car, watching me.

"So here I am, Grandmother," I said to her stone, "right where you put me. I know you had your reasons for this. You know they all hate me because of what you have given me. Was it meant to be some sort of test?"

I stared at her stone. Of course, I didn't expect to hear any answers. The answers, she would say, are in you. Coming here I hoped would help me find them, hear them.

The wind grew more brisk. Clouds looked like they were galloping across the sky. Jake was right about the weather. I zipped up my jacket further.

"Maybe I should just do what they want, take their compromise money and go. I could return to England and never come back here, just like my real father. None of them would miss me and to tell you the truth, I don't believe I'd miss any of them.

"Somehow, I don't think that's what you would like, but what am I to accomplish here, Grandma? What can I do that you haven't already done?"

I knelt and put my hands on the earth that covered her coffin and then I closed my eyes and pictured her standing there in that doorway the day I had left for England. She didn't want to go to the airport with me. She said she hated good-byes, but she allowed me to hug her. I could see the hope in her eyes. I had come to be with her to take back my name, a name denied me as soon as I was born.

"Don't let them take it away again, Rain," I could hear her whisper in the wind.

"No matter what they do or say, don't let them take your name."

Maybe that was the answer, the only answer.

Maybe that was the reason to stay.

Much of her, of that, remained in the house. Her body rested in the graveyard a few miles away from it, but her spirit joined the spirits of the others who passed from room to room in a chain of memories lighter than smoke, looking for a way to resurrect some of the glory.

They were testing me, visiting me, challenging me by tinkering with my thoughts and feelings. They filled the shadows in the corners and whispered on the stairs, but I wasn't afraid even though I quickly began to have strange dreams, strange because they were about people I had never seen or met. Yet, despite that, there was something familiar about them, some laugh or wisp of a smile that filled me with even greater curiosity. I saw a little girl sitting all crunched up on a sofa, her eyes wide with surprise. I heard sobs through the walls. My eyes traveled down until they found two teenage girls listening, their mouths open with astonishment. Well-dressed people paraded through the hallways to rooms filled with displays of food and wine. There was the sound of violins and then a beautiful voice could be heard singing the famous aria from *Madama Butterfly*.

I could make little sense out of any of it, but I kept trying, searching for some clues, some answers. Even though I had lived in the house for a while before going to London, there was still much for me to look at and explore. I spent hours in the library perusing the books and then sifting through the old papers and some of the correspondence still kept in file cabinets and drawers. Most of it was about the various projects for development Grandfather Hudson had started. However, there were some personal letters, letters from old friends, people who had relocated to different states or even different countries, some of them old college friends.

I discovered that Grandmother Hudson had had a close girlfriend in finishing school who had married and moved to Savannah. Her name was Ariana Keely and her husband was an attorney. She had three children, two boys and a girl. The letters were filled with details about her children, but very little about herself and her husband. Occasionally, she would drift into something revealing and I would be able to read between the lines and understand that apparently neither she nor Grandmother Hudson believed they had found the happiness and the perfection both somehow had thought was inevitable for people who had been given all the advantages.

"As you say, Frances, we're privileged people," Ariana wrote in one letter, *"but all that seems to guarantee is a more comfortable world of disappointment full of more distractions, more ways to ignore reality."*

It all made me wonder that if someone wealthy, born with status and advantages couldn't be happy, what should I really expect?

I was thinking about all this as Jake drove me home from the cemetery. Neither of us had spoken for quite a while. I sat gazing out of the window, but really not looking at anything. The sky continued to darken.

"You all right, Princess?" Jake asked finally.

"What? Oh, yes, Jake. I'm fine. Looks like it is going to pour."

"Yes," he said. "I was going to go into Richmond tonight, but I think I'll wait until morning, get up early and make the airport pickup."

I sat back. The dreary sky and my rush of sad memories filled me with a cold loneliness. You're too young to have to do battle with a great family, I told myself. I didn't ask for any of this. Thoughts about my mother, her husband

18

and Aunt Victoria ganging up on me again tomorrow consumed me with dread.

"Maybe you oughta go to a movie or something, Princess," Jake said. "I can come by and take you, if you'd like."

"No thanks, Jake."

He nodded.

"Did you keep in contact with any of the friends you made when you went to school here?" he asked.

"No, Jake," I said smiling. He was trying hard, worrying about me. "I'm okay for a while. I'll keep myself busy by making myself dinner. Would you like to come to dinner?"

"Huh?" he asked.

"I've got a great recipe for chicken with peaches, something my mama used to make."

"Hmm. Sounds delicious," he said. "What time?"

"Come by about six."

"Should I bring anything?"

"Just your appetite, Jake," I said and he laughed. "You know how well stocked Mrs. Hudson kept the house."

Jake nodded, looking at me in the rearview mirror. Something in his eyes told me he knew I should be calling her Grandmother Hudson. It occurred to me that Grandmother Hudson herself might have told him the truth, but he never asked me any prying questions. Sometimes, I thought he seemed like someone on the sidelines who knew everything and was just waiting and watching to see how it would turn out.

"That I do. I took her shopping enough," he said. "No matter how I assured her, she always behaved as if she could never get me when she needed me. She'd always hit me with something like, 'Why add another worry to the

19

load you're already carrying on your shoulders?' That woman," he said shaking his head, "she never stopped trying to change me."

"She was very fond of you," I said.

He nodded, his eyes smaller, darker. Suddenly he was the one who grew quiet. Neither of us said another word until we pulled up to the house. The first drops began to fall.

"Thank you, Jake. I'll get my own door," I added before he could step out. "See you later, Jake."

"Okay, Princess," he called as I rushed up the steps and into the house.

I was excited. I had something nice to do. I was going to make us a wonderful meal, my first dinner in my own big house. Wouldn't Mama Arnold laugh if she saw me now?

About an hour before Jake arrived, however, the phone rang and my mood took a plunge back into the pool of depression. It was Grandmother Hudson's attorney, Mr. Sanger.

"I received a call from Grant, Megan and Victoria's attorney a little while ago, Rain. It looks like they're deciding to go forward with this challenge. They'll be requesting all Frances's medical records and they'll try to show she wasn't of competent mind when she changed the will and gave you so much. It still might all be just a tactic to get you to compromise."

"I know they're coming to see me tomorrow," I said. "Jake told me."

"I could be there if you'd like," he offered.

"That might just make it all nastier. I'll call you if I need you," I said.

"Sorry," he said, "but this is often the way these things can go."

With the wind picking up and whipping the rain at the windows and the roof of the house, and now the news of an impending legal war between me and my reluctant family, I couldn't keep the trembles from making my hands shake as I worked in the kitchen. I set the table and brought out the candelabra. I imagined Jake would like some wine. I didn't know anything about wine, so I decided to wait for him to make the choice. When I glanced at the grandfather clock in the hallway, I saw it was about three hours slow again.

That brought a smile to my face. I remembered how unconcerned Grandmother Hudson was about time. Most of the clocks in the house were off, even the electric ones in the bedrooms and kitchen. The fancy French clock in the office had a malfunction she never had fixed and her cuckoo clock in the breakfast nook sometimes worked, sometimes didn't. It could pop out at the most unexpected times. I asked her many times why she didn't get it and the other clocks repaired.

"At my age," she would say whenever I mentioned the clocks, "you don't want to be reminded how many hours have gone by."

I told her she wasn't that old. Jake was older than she was and didn't even think of slowing down.

"Jake," she said, "hasn't the sense to think about his age. If he did, he'd realize just how much of his life he's wasted."

I had to smile at that too. She sounded disapproving, but she never really criticized Jake. Her complaints were like whippings with wet noodles. I could see by the way they looked at each other that they had an endearing affection. It was just that whenever Grandmother Hudson smiled at him, she always looked away first as if smiling directly at him might shatter some essential glass wall they had to keep up between them. I thought it had something to do with employers and employees, but I could never be that way, no matter how rich I was.

Anyway, I would soon find out that there were other reasons.

I rushed to the door when the bell sounded. Jake surprised me by being dressed in a sports jacket and tie. He had a box of candy too.

"You didn't have to get dressed up, Jake," I said, laughing.

"I couldn't imagine coming to Frances's house for dinner without being properly attired," he said as he entered. "Sweets for the sweet." He handed me the candy.

"Thank you, Jake. Is it still raining pretty hard?"

"Slowing up. The front's moving north to get the Yankees now," he said.

When he saw the dinner table, he blew a low whistle.

"Very nice, Princess. Very nice. Looks like you learned a lot being an English maid, huh?"

"I know what bangers and mash is and I can speak some Cockney slang," I told him and he laughed. "I didn't know what to pick out for wine, Jake. I thought I'd leave that to you."

"Oh. Sure," he said.

"You know where the wine cellar is, right?" I asked him.

"I do, Princess," he said. "I even know which floorboards creak in this house."

I nodded. Of course he did. He had once lived here a long, long time ago.

"Okay, Jake. I'll get things started while you do that," I told him and went to the kitchen.

When I brought in our salads, he had already opened two bottles of wine and poured me a glass. It looked like he had poured himself a second already.

"One thing about Frances," he said. "She always had good wine, whether it be a good California wine or French. She was a very refined woman, classy," he added. "Let's have a toast to her." He held up his glass and I lifted mine and we tapped glasses after he said, "To Frances, who I'm sure is setting things right wherever she is."

We both took a long sip of our wine.

"Good-looking salad, Rain. Warm bread, too! I'm impressed already."

"Thank you, Jake."

"So," he said, "tell me about your time in London. I hope you were having some fun."

I described the school, told him about Randall Glenn, the talented boy from Canada who was studying to be a concert singer and how Randall and I had done a great deal of touring. I told him about Catherine and Leslie, the sisters from France, the showcase presentation I was in and all the encouragement I had received.

"It sounds like you should return then," he said. "I hope you don't get stuck here for some silly reason, Rain. Take advantage of your opportunities. Frances would want that. She'd be disappointed if you didn't," he said.

When Jake and I looked at each other, I couldn't help feeling there were things that were not being said. Every time he would mention Grandmother Hudson's name, he would get a misty glint in his eyes.

I brought out the main dish and he raved about it, saying someday I'd make a lucky man a wonderful wife.

"But you'll probably be one of these modern women who thinks the kitchen is beneath her," he added.

"I don't think so, Jake. Not the way I was brought up," I said.

He wanted to know more about my life growing up in Washington, D.C. He listened attentively, his face turning hard and his eyes cold when I described with more detail than ever before what exactly had happened to my stepsister Beneatha.

"No wonder your mother wanted to get you out of that world," he said.

Again, our eyes locked for a longer moment. I was surprised that Jake had already finished a bottle of wine himself and was well into the second. I had yet to finish my first glass. I looked down at my plate, pushed some of my food around with my fork and, without looking up, asked, "How much do you really know about me, Jake?" I lifted my eyes quickly. "How much did Mrs. Hudson tell you?"

He started to shake his head and stopped, a smile on his lips.

"She used to say you had a divining rod for the truth," Jake said softly.

"Divining rod?"

"You know, those things some people swear can find water."

"Oh." I nodded. "So what well of truth have I discovered, Jake?"

He laughed but then grew serious quickly.

"I know Megan is really your mother," he admitted. He fingered his wineglass. "I always knew."

"Grandmother Hudson told you?"

He nodded.

"What else did she tell you?"

He looked up.

"Not long before she died, she told me how you hunted down your real father in London," he said.

"I didn't exactly hunt him down."

"Those were her very words. I just knew she would do it, she said. Frances wasn't angry about it. She was impressed with your resourcefulness."

"Why did she trust you with all these deep family secrets, Jake?"

I fixed my eyes on him intently and he poured the remaining wine into his glass.

"Maybe because she had no one else she really trusted," he said and drank his wine.

"I didn't think she needed to tell anyone anything."

He looked surprised, his bushy eyebrows hoisted.

"Naw," he said. "That was just what she wanted everyone else to think. She wasn't really as much of the iron queen she pretended to be."

"Why did she leave me so much and make it so difficult for me with the family? Did she tell you that? Did she explain what she hoped would happen?"

He shook his head and shrugged.

"She thought a lot of you, Princess. You came crashing into her life like a wave of freshwater. She was very depressed about her family until you arrived on the scene. When you're that age and your family is disappointing, you start to wonder what it was all for and that can make you very sad. You took most of that sadness away. She wasn't going to check out without making sure you were strong."

"I'm not so strong, Jake, even with all she's left me. I'm

by myself again. Grandmother Hudson's attorney called me a short while ago to tell me that my mother, Grant and Victoria are pushing forward with the legal challenge even if it means dragging everything into the open, Grandma's health records, my mother's past, everything about me, too. She'll make me look like some fortune hunter taking advantage of an elderly lady. I'd be better off if I had inherited nothing," I moaned.

"Hey, hey, don't talk like that," he ordered, but I couldn't keep the tears behind the dam of my lids. They began to pour over and streak down my cheeks. "All the people I love are either dead or too far away to help me."

"I'm here," he boasted and rose from his seat. He came over to me and put his arm around my shoulders. "You're going to do fine, Princess. We owe it to Frances," he said.

"Sure," I muttered and flicked the tears away with the back of my hand.

"I'm going to help you," he insisted.

"Okay, Jake."

"I mean it. I can help you."

"Okay, Jake."

He stepped away and stared at the wall.

"I've got to believe she worked it so I would do this," he muttered, more to himself than to me.

"Do what, Jake?"

He was silent for a long moment. Then he turned and gazed at me, looking down at me as if he was high up on some mountain.

"Give you our secret."

"Whose secret?" I shook my head. "You're confusing me even more, Jake." I looked at the wine. Was he babbling now because he had drunk so much?

"Frances's and mine," he said. He smiled. "And now

yours, but you keep it like some last resort, some last bullet to put into your gun, okay?"

I stared at him. He still made no sense. Jake was nice. He was a kind man. I actually loved him, but it was best to just nod and finish up the dinner, I thought.

"You don't believe me, don't believe I can give you something to strengthen your position and your resolve, huh?"

"Sure I do, Jake."

He sat and turned to me.

"Frances and I were lovers once," he said quickly. "We had an affair. It lasted quite a while actually. We had lots of opportunity and we took advantage of it. We stopped when she became pregnant."

"Pregnant?"

"With Victoria," he said. "She's mine. I'm just about positive and so was she."

I shook my head to throw the words back out of my ears. Grandmother Hudson, unfaithful to her husband? She was my rock of morality.

"It wasn't anyone's fault. It just happened. Everett neglected Frances. He was obsessed with his business interests and rarely traveled or went to a social occasion unless there was a financial benefit or reason to do it.

"One day we started to spend more and more time with each other. I don't think it ever occurred to Everett that she might stray or have a romantic interest in anyone else, not that I ever believed she had any for him.

"Theirs was one of those Old South, old-fashioned marriages. You know, parents get together and decide wouldn't it be perfect if your daughter married our son. Parents always knew better in those days. So much for what they knew better, huh?"

He finished the wine in his glass.

"Did my grandfather know? I mean, about Victoria not being his daughter?"

"I think so, but he never said anything. He wasn't the sort who would," Jake said.

"What sort is that?" I asked, grimacing.

"Upper crust," Jake said. "One just couldn't conceive of such a thing in that world. Frances never said anything to him. As soon as she realized she was pregnant, she just decided that was it for us.

"When I returned from my years in the navy and knocking about, Victoria was already in her late twenties. I used to be afraid that anyone could take one look at her and see me in her face, but Victoria has one of those faces that seems to have created itself. She doesn't look much like Frances and I don't think she looks very much like me. Our noses are different, our mouths. Maybe we have similar eyes and ears," he conceded.

"Maybe she isn't your daughter then," I said.

"She didn't look much like Everett either. You've seen his pictures. What do you think?"

"Maybe there was someone else."

"What? Someone else?" He shook his head. "No, never."

"Why not? If my grandmother had an affair with you, she could have had one with someone else, too."

He stared at me a moment as if the idea had never occurred.

"Or are you upper crust, too, Jake, more upper crust than my grandfather, and can't even conceive of it?" I asked him.

He continued to stare and then he smiled and shook his head.

"No, Frances told me with an air of certainty that couldn't be challenged. We stood down by the dock late one afternoon, just before the sun set, and she said—I'll never forget it because of how she put it—she said, 'We've gone and done it up good, Jake.' Of course, I didn't know what she meant.

" 'What's that mean, Frances?' I asked.

" 'I've got a cake in my oven,' she said. That's what she said. Some cake. 'Too much unbridled passion,' she added, 'passion that makes you throw caution to the wind.'

"I was stunned. I just stood there playing with a stick in the water and watching the ripples and thinking, *What's going to be?*

" 'Of course, we won't see each other that way anymore, Jake. I'm sorry. I'm sorry I needed you so much,' she told me and walked away.

"I felt like everything had evaporated inside me. I felt like a shell. Any minute a wind would come sailing over the water, lift me like a kite, and blow me over the trees.

"I guess in a way it did because soon after that I joined the navy."

He sat there silently, staring down at his plate and his empty wineglass and then he closed his eyes.

"I never loved anyone but Frances," he continued. "I couldn't. It was like I was given just enough love fuel for one woman and I used it all on her. I returned to work for her just so I could be around her.

"Sometimes, when I drove her places, I'd pretend I wasn't her hired driver. I'd imagine we were man and wife and I was taking her somewhere just the way any husband would take his wife some place. If Victoria went along, I even imagined I was like any other husband and father."

Everyone spends time in his or her fantasies, I thought. Everyone.

"Does Victoria have any idea? Did Grandmother Hudson ever tell her?"

"Oh no, no," Jake said quickly. "But that's why I wanted you to know, to have this information. When and if she has you up against the wall, you can fling it at her and I'll be there to verify it.

"They got ways to test the blood and prove it beyond a doubt, you know. She'll know that so she won't be so sure of herself. It will knock her off that high pedestal," he promised.

"It would be revealing Grandmother Hudson's secret, too. I don't know if I could ever do that, Jake."

"Sure you can. If the time comes, you'll do it. You knew her well enough to know she wouldn't mind," he said confidently.

"Wow," I said shaking my head. "Talk about skeletons in the closet. The closets here should be rattling."

He laughed.

"I'd better get going," he said. "I got to get up early and head for Richmond to pick them up at the airport."

"Don't you want some coffee, first?" I wanted him to have coffee because he had drunk so much wine, but it didn't seem to faze him.

"No. Thanks. This was a great meal. You want me to help you clean up?"

"No, Jake. I'm very experienced at it, remember?" I said referring to my days at Grandmother Hudson's sister's home in London, as well as my days here.

"Right. Okay. Maybe I'll see you some time in the afternoon when I bring them around."

"Oh, are they staying overnight?" I asked quickly.

"No. I'm taking them back for a nine o'clock flight."

Good, I thought. Jake kissed me on the cheek and left. When the door closed behind him, the emptiness of the great house settled around me like some dark cloud. The thickness of the night still heavily overcast turned the windows into mirrors flashing my image back to me as I crossed through the rooms. The wind was still strong enough to make parts of the house creak and groan. Just to have other sounds floating through, I turned on the television set and found a music channel. I made it loud enough to hear while I cleaned up the dining room and then the kitchen.

Afterward, I returned to the den and watched some television until my eyelids felt heavy and I caught myself dozing on and off. I'll sleep well tonight, I thought, but the tension over tomorrow's family meeting slipped in beside me as I walked up the stairs. By the time my head hit the pillow, there was static in the air crackling around me, and with its tiny sparks of lightning, scorching my brain.

No matter how I turned or scrunched the pillow against my cheeks, I was soon uncomfortable, turning and tossing again and again until it was nearly morning. Then, I finally fell asleep the way someone would accidentally step into a poorly covered old well, descending in a panic down into the darkness, my screams rushing out above me as if they were tied to a hot red ribbon. The moment I hit bottom, my eyes clicked open. Sunlight was already streaming in, flooding the room with wave after wave of insistent, unrelenting illumination.

I groaned. Every part of me ached. I panicked with the possibility of my getting sick. If there was ever a wrong time for that, it was now, today of all days, I thought. When I rose, I poured some of Grandmother Hudson's sweet-smelling bath powder into a hot tub and soaked for nearly twenty minutes before I got dressed and went down to make myself some coffee.

The phone rang almost as soon as I entered the kitchen. It was Mr. MacWaine, the administrator of the Burbage School of Drama in London, the man who had discovered me and, with Grandmother Hudson's help, had brought me to England.

He wanted to know how I was doing and what I was planning for my immediate future.

"If I've had one inquiry concerning you, I've had ten," he told me. "We do hope you'll be returning, Rain," he said.

"Thank you. I expect I will. I was going to contact you about arrangements to live in the dorm this time, Mr. MacWaine."

"That won't be a problem," he assured me. "I am happy to see you will continue with us. I am sure Mrs. Hudson would have wanted that," he said.

I thanked him for his concern and interest.

"Oh, before I forget," he continued, "there was one inquiry I promised I would pass on to you. Apparently you won the admiration of a London professor, a Shakespearean scholar, Doctor Ward. He's an acquaintance of one of the board of trustee members and he's asked after you. Was he at our showcase?" Mr. MacWaine wondered.

"Yes," I said. I didn't know what else to say, but almost immediately after I said it, I regretted lying. Whenever I lied about my secret past, I just added to the deception, the false foundation beneath this family now, I thought. I hated being any part of that.

"Lovely," Mr. MacWaine said. "Do keep me informed

as to your arrangements. In the meantime, I'll see to the dormitory space," he promised.

Speaking with him lifted my spirits and reminded me that I did have a place to go, a future just waiting for me to fulfill it. I was certainly not stuck here. How wonderful that my real father was asking after me, thinking about me, looking forward to seeing me and getting to know me. Grandmother Hudson had been disappointed in people too often to believe there would be any value for me in pursuing my real father. I understood her cynicism, but I wasn't at all ready to accept it.

Buoyed, I discovered I was hungry and prepared myself some breakfast. Then I went through the house, dusting and cleaning some so that Victoria couldn't point to anything and say, "See, see how she is letting our property deteriorate."

As I was cleaning up after breakfast, the phone rang again. This time it was Aunt Victoria.

"Your mother," she said punctuating the word with such venom, she turned it into a curse word, "and Grant are flying in this morning. We will be at the house by two o'clock. We're meeting with our attorney for lunch first," she added, which was clearly meant to intimidate me.

"It seems like lawyer's day," I replied coolly.

"What's that supposed to mean?" she fired back.

"I'm meeting with my attorney for lunch here at the house, too," I said.

I wasn't, of course, but I wanted to do her one better and show her I could be just as intimidating. There was a long pause.

"You're making a big mistake being so obstinate," she said.

"Isn't that odd?" I countered.

"Isn't what odd?"

"I've been thinking you're making a big mistake being so obstinate."

If a moment of silence was ever packed full of explosive energy, this was it.

"We'll all be there at two," she repeated. "Make sure you're there as well."

"I have no place I'd rather be today," I said. "Thanks for the warning."

When I hung up, my heart was pounding.

But to me it sounded like all the ghosts in the house were clapping.

2

Fortune Hunter

When the doorbell sounded only a little after twelve, I knew it couldn't be my mother, Grant and Aunt Veronica. It was too early. My first thought was it might be Mr. Sanger, my lawyer, who must have decided he had to stop by and give me advice.

Instead, Corbette Adams stood there looking in at me after I opened the door. Corbette had played George Gibbs to my Emily Webb in the Dogwood High School production of *Our Town* that had earned me Mr. MacWaine's admiration and the invitation to study the performing arts at his school in London. Easily the most handsome boy at Sweet William—the sister school to Dogwood, the private school I had attended while living here with Grandmother Hudson—Corbette had moved like some soap opera star over our campus, basking in the swoons of so many of my classmates.

He was the first boy with whom I had made love, and

confronting him now filled me both with angry heat and guilt. Who could blame me, however, for falling beneath the power of his charm and good looks then, especially me, someone so overwhelmed by all the wealth and privilege he and all the others enjoyed? I had been lifted from one world and dropped into another with little or no preparation.

Corbette's familiar sapphire orbs brightened once again at the sight of me. He didn't look much different from the last time I had seen him. His brown hair with hints of copper was still unruly, curling upward at the nape of his neck, the only imperfection in his otherwise perfectly respectable appearance. Despite the position of esteem his family held in the community, there was always something defiant in Corbette, a danger which made him even more attractive and exciting to most girls, and admittedly, once to me.

His strong lips opened and fell back in a soft smile.

"You're even prettier now," he said. "Or else I have just forgotten how beautiful you were."

"Hello, Corbette," I said coldly.

I stood there in the doorway not backing up to let him in. He wore his Sweet William dark blue blazer over a light blue shirt, jeans and a pair of white tennis sneakers. In his right hand he carried a bouquet of white roses and quickly extended them toward me.

I didn't reach for them and the smirk of displeasure remained on my face. He shifted his weight from one foot to the other.

"Sorry about Mrs. Hudson's death," he said. "My family went to the funeral and I heard how beautiful and dignified you looked. Many people were impressed with how sad and upset you appeared for a girl who only had been

Mrs. Hudson's ward and for so short a time, too. There's a lot of gossip about you, about what she might have left you in her will," he added, still smiling with that unrestrained self-confidence that I had come to despise.

After all, once he had succeeded to have his way with me, he couldn't wait to brag and then treat me like some trophy he could cast off cavalierly.

I still didn't take the roses. Remaining unimpressed, I looked from them to him.

"What do you want, Corbette?" I asked briskly.

"Oh, I just came to see how you were doing and pay my respects."

"I didn't think you knew what respect meant," I snapped back.

Confronting him now, I realized that time had done little to diminish the embarrassment and belittlement I had felt that day he had brought some of his friends over from Sweet William to watch me horseback riding. From the lusty smiles on their faces, I knew immediately that he had told them everything about our intimate night after the play performance. He tried to get me to sleep with one of his friends, offering me up as if I belonged to him now and he could give me to whomever he wanted, whenever he wanted.

Seeing me continue to stand like a stone statue in the doorway, he nodded and lowered the roses.

"I know, I know," he said. "You've got every right to be angry at me."

"Thanks for giving me permission," I said.

"I was a jerk back then. I wanted to show off and it was wrong," he said. He shrugged. "You know how boys can be stupid sometimes. I was more in love with my own reputation and image than I was concerned about doing the right thing. Our male egos get us into more trouble," he bemoaned shaking his head. "That day I was just plain immature. I'd be the first to admit it. I wish I could go back in time and punch myself in the nose."

His eyes clouded with remorse.

I shook my head. How easily he could assume different attitudes, pretend different emotions. No wonder he had been his school's best actor for so long. When a girl looked at that handsome face with its perfect nose and beautiful eyes, it was difficult to be hard and cautious. You wanted to believe him. You wanted him to mean every sweet thing he said to you and you would deny all the signals and warnings to the contrary.

Men were always complaining about women using their good looks and sexuality to snare and trap them. Corbette Adams was a good example of the shoe being on the other foot. Catherine and Leslie, my two French girlfriends back in London, loved to think of themselves as *femme fatales,* I remembered. Corbette was about as fatal for a *femme* as any woman could be for any man.

"I'm happy you feel badly about that, Corbette. Maybe the next girl you seduce won't feel as low and dirty as you made me feel. Thanks for stopping by," I added and started to close the door on him.

"Wait," he cried putting out his hand to prevent it from shutting. "Can't I spend a little time with you, catch up on things? I'm leaving for college in another two weeks and won't be back for months."

"I really don't think we have much to say to each other, Corbette."

"Ah, but that's where you're wrong," he said. "I've had a couple of girlfriends this year, but I haven't known any girls as nice as you or as intelligent. It didn't take me long to realize how stupid I was to treat you badly. C'mon," he pleaded. "Let me at least apologize properly. Then, if you still want to throw me out, I'll even help."

He held out the roses again.

Everything inside me, including my too vulnerable heart, told me to toss them back in his face and shut the door, but I didn't. Maybe I was bored. Maybe I was just willing to think of something else beside the arrival of my mother; instead of closing the door, I took his roses and stepped back.

"All right. You can come in for a while, but I have people coming in about an hour for an important meeting."

"Thanks," he said entering. He gazed around with some surprise in his eyes as if he expected to see a house stripped of all of its valuables immediately after Grandmother Hudson's death.

"What?" I asked.

"Quite a house, quite a house. My mother always talks about this house. She'd love to buy it."

"Maybe she'll have the opportunity," I said dryly and led him into the drawing room. I set the flowers in a vase. They were beautiful, a creamy rich white with a strong, fresh scent.

"The word around is that you've inherited most everything. Is that so?" he asked without delay.

"So that's it," I said turning on him. "You're here to get all the good gossip to spread. I bet you bragged you could get me to tell you all the details, right, Corbette?"

He started to shake his head and I laughed.

"Go ahead, sit, Corbette," I said in the tone of voice I would use on a mischievous little boy. I nodded at the chair to his right.

He did and I sat across from him on the smaller settee.

For a moment I just looked at him, fixing my eyes on him intently. It made him a little uncomfortable.

"You are different," he said. "You seem very bitter. What happened to you in England?"

"I'm not any more or less bitter than I was before I went to England. What happened is I grew up a little more," I said. "You don't look like you have changed much." I didn't mean it to sound like a compliment, but that's the way he took it.

"Hey," he said holding out his arms, "why fix it if it ain't broke?"

"Who says it ain't broke?" I retorted, wiping the smug smile off his face.

He nodded.

"You were always a lot tougher than the other girls at Dogwood. I knew that right away and I liked it," he added with a wide-eyed smile. "You've got spunk. Who wanted just another Barbie doll?"

"Normally, that would be flattering, but coming from you, it almost sounds like an insult. Okay, Corbette," I said sitting back and folding my arms under my breasts, "catch me up on your life. How was your college year?"

"Oh, terrific. I was in a play and I won a big part, too. One of the first freshman to do so, it seems."

"What play?"

"*Death of a Salesman.* I played Biff. You know it, right?"

"Of course," I said. I nodded. "I can see you as Biff."

What I was referring to was someone whose ego had been blown up way out of proportion to what he really was and was able to accomplish, but again, Corbette saw only what he wanted to see. I was beginning to wonder if that wasn't a disease of the rich and privileged in our world.

"I received a lot of compliments for my performance.

I'm seriously thinking of going to Hollywood, maybe even before I finish college. A friend of mine at school has an uncle who's an agent and he told him about me. You might see me in the movies," Corbette predicted.

"Somehow, I think that would be very natural for you, Corbette."

He stared a moment, finally realizing that I wasn't being complimentary.

"You sure don't like me. I guess I can't blame anyone but myself."

"I don't think about you enough anymore to not like you, Corbette."

He brightened again, again deliberately missing the point.

"I was hoping we might bury the hatchet and maybe go out or something. I'd love to take you to dinner tonight." He lifted his hands quickly, palms to me. "Nothing bad, no plans to take you to my place. I won't even kiss you good night if you don't want me to," he promised.

I was almost tempted to say yes just to be with someone my age, just to get away from all this tension and turmoil. My hesitation gave him reason to hope.

"There's this great new Italian restaurant I've found. It's small, cozy. We could sit and talk and maybe get to know each other properly. We've got a lot more in common now, you know," he added.

"What's that supposed to mean?"

"Well, you're a significant landowner in the community. You've inherited some wealth. You're no longer some poor girl from the inner city dependent upon someone's charity. You're different—"

"I'm no different than I was before all this, Corbette. You think just having some money makes me a better person? Is that how you measure people?" I snapped back at him.

"No, of course not." He shook his head. "Damn, you make me think about every word I use as if we're in court or something. Maybe you should study to be an attorney."

"Maybe I will. It seems these days they're just as important as doctors used to be," I said thinking about all that was about to happen between me and my mother and aunt.

He laughed.

"Right. In a television advertisement they could say, 'Lawyers, don't leave home without one,' " he recited, writing the words in the air between us.

I couldn't help but smile.

"That's better. We don't have to be dueling with words."

Was I a fool to permit his sweet talk and smile to relax my defenses? Grandmother Hudson had taught me a saying early on: *Fool me once, shame on you; fool me twice, shame on me.*

An idea occurred to me, a quick test of Corbette's sincerity.

"Maybe I don't have as much money as you think, Corbette, and maybe I'm not a landowner. Maybe everything you've heard is just an exaggeration. Maybe I'm waiting to get my walking papers and be off, never to be seen or heard from again."

His smile froze and then slowly evaporated.

"What is the truth?" he asked.

I smiled to myself seeing how the look of uncertainty had entered those magnificent eyes and snuffed out some of their charm and glitter.

"Well," I said gazing around and lowering my voice,

"I'll tell you as long as you promise not to make this the news of the day."

"Hey, I'm not a gossip."

"Good. They said I could stay here awhile as long as I kept it clean."

"Huh?"

"They actually wanted me to stay awhile and maintain it. They'll pay me, of course, and they'll even pay for my train ticket to wherever I want to go afterward. They hope to sell it in about a month, I think. Someone's got to be here to watch over it all until then and no one in Mrs. Hudson's family is willing to live here."

"Are you saying she didn't leave you a wad of money?"

"Hardly," I said laughing. "Is that what people really think?"

He stared.

"Oh, she had arranged for me to return to England for another year and I'm hoping to win a scholarship for expenses, but if that doesn't happen..."

"What?"

"I have a cousin who manages a department store in Charlotte and she said she could give me a job, maybe in the cosmetic department."

"You mean you wouldn't even return to college?"

"Not for a while. I couldn't afford it," I said. "You know how expensive college can be, and I don't have a sugar daddy. I don't have any daddy," I added, my voice sharper, my eyes narrowing.

He nodded and stared. Suddenly, he looked very uncomfortable and shifted in his chair.

"What's this meeting you're having here in a little while?" he asked, still a little skeptical.

"Oh, just a meeting to get my instructions," I said, sounding as nonchalant about it as I could. Then I smiled. "So, you want to take me to dinner? About what time?" I asked.

"Huh? Oh, er...first I gotta see if I can get us reservations. It's a small place and it's gotten so popular lately."

"You want to use the phone? You can as long as it isn't a long-distance call. I promised them I wouldn't make any long-distance calls," I added.

"Really? Well, I think it would be long distance from here. Yes, yes it would. Why don't I just call from home and let you know," he said.

"Fine."

He was squirming now, glancing at the doorway.

"You know you were so right when you said I should let you apologize. It isn't right to hold a grudge and everyone should be given a second chance, don't you think?" I asked him.

"Yes, sure," he said.

"Boys will be boys, but you're older now and wiser. Something like that wouldn't happen again, I'm sure. I just know you're a more considerate person, Corbette. How's your brother, by the way?" I asked.

He was so ashamed about having a brother with Down's Syndrome that he had initially told me his brother was dead. I had found out he wasn't dead; when I had confronted him, he had blamed it all on his mother who couldn't face the facts. The truth was it was easier for him to simply say his brother was dead because to him he was dead.

"He's okay. No different," he quickly replied. He glanced at his watch. "Well, I'd better get a move on if I'm going to make any arrangement for tonight."

"So soon? We didn't really get a chance to catch up," I said.

"Well…well, we'll have plenty of time later," he offered.

"That's right, we will, won't we? Fine," I said standing. He practically jumped to his feet. "Thanks for the roses and for coming by."

"Sure."

"Please don't gossip about what I told you," I said, scowling at him.

He shook his head.

"I wouldn't."

"Good." I smiled at him and walked him to the front door.

"I'll call you in a few hours. Unless it's absolutely impossible," he said. "Then I'll call tomorrow or the next day, okay?"

"Sure," I said. "Don't forget. I'm so looking forward to getting to know you the right way, as you said before," I told him.

He nodded and walked out. I felt sure I wouldn't be seeing him again.

"I see you still have that sports car."

"Oh, yeah. I'm taking it to college with me this year," he said. "Freshmen weren't permitted to have cars on campus."

"See," I said. "There are truly some benefits to getting older. Everyone thinks you're wiser."

"Right."

"I know I am," I said as he hurried down to the automobile. I watched him get in and start the engine. Then I waved. "I know I am," I repeated, my eyes small.

He drove off and I went inside and closed the door behind me. For a moment I stood in the entry way and thought.

There's a lesson, a lesson about money and how important it really is.

I was grateful Corbette had come along to teach it to me. It made me feel stronger and even more determined for the meeting that was about to take place.

Of course, they didn't have to ring a doorbell. I should have realized that. Victoria had her own set of keys to this house. I was putting away my dishes and glass from my lunch when I heard her voice reverberate through the hallway, ricocheting off the walls like a hard thrown tennis ball.

"I want to have each and every art piece evaluated and some of the accent pieces in this house are valuable antiques. Mother never paid attention to what things cost. She had no idea, no idea at all what she was giving away."

I stepped out and looked down the hallway at the three of them. My mother looked smartly dressed in a black leather jacket, a tailored shirt and an ankle-length pleated skirt. Aunt Victoria wore her usual double-breasted business suit and Grant was in a dark blue, pin-striped suit.

Right from the moment I first met my real mother, I could see the resemblance between us. She was about my height, slim and small boned. We had the same color eyes and practically the same shape jaw. Her forehead wasn't as wide and her nose was smaller, but perfectly straight with just a slight sharpness at the tip.

The dimple in her cheek flashed on and off at will it seemed or else reacted to some thought flashing through her mind. I always wondered what my real mother saw when she looked at me. Did she see the resemblances between me and my father and did that bring back some romantic memory? Or did she merely see a living, breathing problem, a reminder of her big mistake? I had long since given up the hope that she would ever look at me the way a mother should look at a daughter: eyes filled with pride and love.

Today, her eyes were dark with worry. Every time she turned them to me, they would practically shout out with the plea for me to make all the stress disappear. I could hear her prayer: let me return to my fantasy world; let me continue to float through my happy illusions, ignoring anything and everything unpleasant and burying worry and concerns in some bottom drawer to be forgotten. Please, those eyes begged from the very second she turned to me in the hallway, please, Rain.

Grant was as calm and as distinguished as ever. His suit looked as though it had just come off the rack in the department store. He was a handsome man with thick, light brown hair that resembled the color of dry hay when the sunlight played through it. I saw that during the days of Grandmother Hudson's funeral and after. Somehow he managed to keep a tan all year long. I suspected he went to one of those tanning salons. His dark complexion brought out the blue in his blue-green eyes, eyes that always looked full of intelligence. When he gazed at me, I could feel his concentration, his search for every little hint of thought in my face. No wonder he was so successful in court and as a negotiator.

The moment I appeared, Victoria's stern, narrow and boney face flashed its fury at me. She pulled back her shoulders and stiffened her long neck. After what Jake had revealed, I couldn't help searching for some suggestion of him in her looks. Now that I was thinking about it, I did see similarities in their mouths and jaws and even in the shape of their eyes. However, she had nothing of his joviality, not even a hint of softness or compassion in her face. What brought laughter and smiles to Jake's lips brought only smirks and scowls to hers. I couldn't imagine her even considering the possibility of any relationship to him, much less being his daughter.

Jake was right: I could wound her deeply by telling her. She thought she was such a blue blood.

"We'll all go into the drawing room," she declared.

"I'll be right there," I said and deliberately returned to the kitchen to finish cleaning up. I wanted them to wait.

When I did enter the room, I could see my making her wait had raised Victoria's ire to explosive heights. Her normally pallid cheeks were crimson and her eyes looked like matches had been lit behind them.

"If you have the time for us, we'd like to have a sensible business conversation," she said.

My mother and Grant were sitting on the settee. Grant was sitting back with his legs crossed. My mother looked very uncomfortable, her shoulders turned in, her eyes down. She glanced up at me to see what I was going to do.

"Hello to all of you, too," I said and sat in the chair opposite Victoria.

She turned to Grant, who was obviously elected to conduct the meeting. I was sure they had practically rehearsed every word at lunch before arriving.

"You were expecting us, weren't you?" he began softly.

"No, not really. I learned about your coming only from Jake who informed me he was picking you up in Richmond. I had to guess as to why."

Grant turned to Victoria who sat back, her arms on the arms of the chair, looking like some queen about to pronounce sentence on one of her subjects. Her long, thin right finger moved up and down nervously.

"I thought you were calling her," he said.

"What difference did it make? She wasn't going anywhere," she said. Then, softening, she added, "I knew Jake would tell her."

She lifted her eyes and looked at Grant, obviously concerned he would be displeased.

"Okay. I apologize for what this looks like then, Rain. We didn't mean to come bursting in on you."

"You're not," I said.

"Good. Now that things have settled down somewhat, we all should stand back and take a clear, intelligent look at what's been done and what should be done, for the benefit of all concerned," he quickly added.

"It seems very late for that," I said directing myself at my mother who continued to avoid my eyes.

"Yes, well, reliving mistakes doesn't really do anyone any good. It's like opening wounds, tearing away scars, bleeding and bleeding. Healing is way overdue," he said.

Grant did have a strong, resonant voice that he could shape with sincerity and feeling. He will be a great political candidate, I thought.

I glanced at Victoria and saw how she was fixed intently on him. It was almost as if he was speaking to her and not to me. It was only when she looked at him, I realized, that her face showed any softness. That held my curiosity almost as much as the purpose of the meeting.

"Now, no one is here to deny you what is rightfully yours. No one here wants you to return to your previous, unfortunate state," he continued.

"No one?" I asked glancing at Victoria.

"No one," he insisted. "However," he said, "there is an obvious misappropriation of good intentions, an obvious lack of balance. I'm sure Mrs. Hudson saw all this as an opportunity for her to right the wrongs she believed had been inflicted on you. Like any mother she wanted to right the wrongs committed by her child," he explained.

While he spoke about me and what was my mother's affair with an African-American man, he didn't so much as glance at her. He could have been talking about anyone, any client. Always the professional apparently, he could distance himself even from his own wife.

My mother didn't lift her gaze from the floor, but her right hand rose to flutter at her throat as if it were seeking some string of pearls to fondle, while her left hand squeezed her thigh. She looked like she was holding onto a railing to keep from falling.

"I don't believe my grandmother did anything for me out of guilt," I said. "She wasn't the type. She did what she believed was right and she had her reasons. You can call it disproportionate or whatever fancy word you want to use, but it's what she decided and she wasn't crazy at the time. Her attorney is willing to swear on the stand about that."

"I know. I know," Grant said, still talking in reasonable tones, "but when these things reach courtroom stages, what seems clear and simple often turns out to be quite complicated. Mr. Sanger will be the first to admit on the stand that he is not qualified to evaluate someone's mental condition. He's not trained as a psychiatrist or any sort of doctor. He's only an attorney doing the bidding of his client."

Grant smiled.

"Another good attorney will make that quite clear and then, if there is, and I fear there is, some reason to believe that Mrs. Hudson was under great emotional and psychological strain at the time, things might suddenly have a different appearance, especially to objective third parties.

"Now look at the facts, Rain. You weren't living here with her all that long before you went off to London. Before you left, Mrs. Hudson had great difficulty keeping domestic help. They either couldn't tolerate her or she wouldn't tolerate them."

"There was nothing mentally wrong with her," I insisted. "Jake will swear about her too."

Victoria blew a laugh out of her stiff, thin lips.

"Jake! The chauffeur? Another expert on the witness stand," she said.

I almost shouted it out then, almost cried, "That man you belittle as nothing but a chauffeur is your father!" But I remembered Jake's caution to use it only as a last resort.

Grant glared at her with a look of reprimand anyway, and she shook her head and looked away.

"Be that as it may, Rain, you're obviously a very bright young lady," he went on. "You can see where this might all go. In the end the family will have suffered. Your life will be put on hold and you might very well end up with much less than you should or could if you agree to sit down with me and be reasonable.

"There's no reason why we all can't be very friendly about it and look after each other's interests now," he continued. "I'm sure that was what Mrs. Hudson wanted, right?"

My mother looked up quickly to see how I was reacting. Was I anything like her? she wondered, I'm sure. Would I welcome Grant's soft, concerned and reasonable tone of voice? Would I look for a way to avoid conflict and unpleasantness? How could my reactions be any different from hers, always choosing the easiest solution no matter what cost it was to your own self-respect?

I glanced at Victoria, smiling to myself as I recalled the way she had spoken about my mother to Grandmother Hudson.

"Megan is afraid she'll get a wrinkle if she has one mature thought," she had said.

Victoria had only to look at my face to see that was not my biggest fear.

"I believe," I said slowly, "that my grandmother did what she wanted and expected that her children would respect that."

Grant stared at me a moment. I could see the frustration start at the corners of his eyes in the form of tiny wrinkles moving like thin cracks down a glass pane.

"When I spoke ·with you last, I mentioned a figure around a half-million dollars. Lawyers are going to be very expensive, for both of us. I think if you walked away from this difficult mess with a million dollars, you'd have a wonderful chance to build a successful life for yourself," he said quickly. "Especially if it's invested intelligently for you. I could help with that."

Victoria looked like she had swallowed a peach pit and it was stuck in her throat. That's how red her face became. My mother looked surprised. I imagined that Grant had decided on his own to raise the offer from a half a million to a million dollars.

"It's a lot of money," my mother said, almost in a whisper, and smiled.

"It's not the money I care about so much," I said.

"Then what is it? Why would you want to remain here

and be involved in such an ugly, legal battle?" Grant practically demanded.

"It's what Grandmother Hudson wanted," I said. I knew it was something I was repeating until it was almost a mantra, a chant to help me get through the tension, but it was what I truly believed.

"You can't believe she wanted everyone snipping at everyone else, right? You can't believe she wanted her family name dragged through the mud and splattered on the front pages for everyone to see? You can't believe that she worked and her husband worked all their lives for that sort of thing, can you? If you really cared for her and if you're really concerned about her legacy, you wouldn't let that sort of thing happen."

"Neither would any of you," I fired back.

Now, Grant's face took on some crimson. He sat back and let the hot air in his lungs slip out his slightly open lips.

"Would anyone like anything cold to drink?" I offered with a smile.

Victoria looked satisfied when she turned to Grant this time. She looked like what she had predicted would happen had come true and she liked being right. Grant shook his head. Then he turned to my mother, which was obviously their predetermined signal for her to start.

"Don't you want to return to your studies in London?" she asked me.

"I'm thinking I will, yes. I'd like to get to know my father better, too."

"Well, how will you do all that if you're bogged down here in a legal swamp?" she asked. "You don't want any of that, Rain. You shouldn't have that in your life now. Go sit in the office with Grant and work out a compromise so we can put all this to rest and go back to being a family."

"A family? What kind of a family? You haven't even told your children who I really am. They looked at me at the funeral, wondering why I was crying more than they were!" I practically shouted.

"We're going to take care of that problem," she promised.

"Hmmm," Victoria muttered.

I knew she was thinking that this whole thing is a problem that shouldn't have begun.

"Good. You do that, Mother," I said. I stood up. "Mr. Sanger told me to tell you that if you have any questions about the will, you should refer them to him. I was just about to make some coffee before you all showed up. Would anyone else like some coffee?" I asked.

The three of them stared at me.

"Don't do this, Rain," my mother pleaded. "Your mama wouldn't have wanted this for you."

I felt the fire in my heart reach into my face, especially my eyes.

"You met my mama, Mother," I said slowly, each word stinging sharply as a dart. "You saw what she was like. Do you think she was a woman who ran from a battle?"

I turned before she could respond, and I walked out, feeling as if Grandmother Hudson's eyes had been on me the whole time. I could almost see her smiling.

Almost immediately, Victoria began her complaining.

I lingered in the hallway, listening.

"So much for how you were going to convince her, Megan. Your being here didn't add a thing to help us. None of this would be happening if it wasn't for what you did," she happily reminded her. "You've put Grant in a very difficult position. Now, what will we do, Grant?" she followed, her voice suddenly becoming the voice of a more desperate, feminine woman turning to her man for strength.

"We'll have to go see Marty Braunstein. I was hoping it would be for other reasons."

"Don't worry about it, Grant," Victoria assured him. "In time she will see how ridiculous it is for her to be a majority owner of the estate. She's young and she won't want to be bothered by all this responsibility. Believe me, after a while, she will compromise. You don't have to risk your reputation," she told him. "Let me handle things. She wants to be involved in our affairs. All right, I'll involve her."

"That's a determined young woman," he said. "If there wasn't so much at stake, I could let myself admire her."

He groaned and stood up. I could hear my mother sniffle.

"Too late for tears," Victoria spit at her.

I continued to the kitchen and started making the coffee. I heard the front door open and close and thought they had all just walked out, but a moment later, my mother appeared in the kitchen doorway.

She smiled and gazed around.

"It's so hard to come here and not see my mother," she said. Her dark eyes skipped nervously about the kitchen. "Even now, I expect her to appear, maybe come in through the French doors, wearing one of those ridiculous garden hats."

"I miss her," I said.

My mother nodded.

"I know you do."

Our eyes met. How I wished we could love each other like a mother and a daughter should.

"Why are you letting Victoria tell you what to do?" I asked her.

"Victoria has always been the practical one, the sensible one, Rain. Maybe that was because she had a different upbringing, a different kind of education. My father didn't send her to boarding school for the rich, nor did he have her sent to a girls' finishing school. She went to business college and learned about stocks and bonds and options and such stuff, whereas I was taught polite rules of social etiquette, things to prepare me for high society. Maybe that was why I was so rebellious in college. I wasn't taught anything practical. I was designed to marry someone like Grant and always have a husband to take care of me and make these sort of decisions.

"Please think more about all this, honey. We really could be something of a family you know." Her teary eyes were beseeching, her soft smile trying to assure me that a pot of gold waited at the end of this soon-to-be rainbow.

I sighed, for I would so much like to be the eternal optimist, but I didn't believe in the magic of rainbows, especially the ones she promised.

"You shouldn't have brought me here, Mother. Grandmother Hudson was one of the few people in my life who loved me and whom I loved. Love means honoring and respecting someone, too. She taught me that. I won't take her wishes and plans for me and tear it all up just to satisfy your sister. She never loved Grandmother Hudson as much as I did in the short time I was able to know her."

Unwilling to deny that, my mother nodded.

"I didn't need to see what she had done with her will to know how much she loved you, Rain."

"Then you should understand," I said. I turned away but she walked over to me.

"You're a good girl, Rain. I truly wish only good things for you. I want you to be happy and put all this behind you. Be sensible. You'd be better off away from all of us anyway," she said sadly.

She hugged me quickly and then started out, stopping in the doorway.

"Call me if you need me," she said.

I watched her walk down the hallway and out the door.

"That call was made a long time ago, Mother," I muttered after she had left.

"And you never answered."

3

Riding the Wind

The telephone rang so early the next morning, I thought it was ringing in my dreams. Whoever was calling didn't give up. Finally, my eyelids unglued and I realized I wasn't imagining it. As I reached over for the phone, I looked at the clock and saw it was only five-thirty.

"Hello," I said, my voice so groggy and deep, I thought someone else had said it for me.

"Rain?" I heard. "Is that you?"

I scrubbed my cheek with my palm and pulled myself up in the bed.

"Roy?"

"I'm sorry I'm calling you so early there, but it's the only chance I'll have, maybe for days," he said. "How are you?"

"Five minutes, Arnold," I heard someone growl behind him.

"Roy, where are you?"

"I'm here, in Germany, of course. What's happening

now? Are you going right back to England? Did you talk to your real mother? Does everyone know about you? I mean, who you really are and all?" He was rattling his questions off quickly, hoping to stuff a lot of information into those measly five minutes, I thought.

Of course, for most of our lives, Roy and I had believed we were brother and sister. Anyone who really cared to take the time and interest could have looked at him, at me and at Beneatha and challenge that, I guess. My features were so different from Roy's and Beneatha's, but for us the thought that Mama Arnold could have had me with a different man was just about as far-fetched as believing we had aliens from Mars or someplace living next door. And there was no way a poor black family would adopt another child. Ken, who never really wanted to be a father in the first place, often complained and said, 'The devil gives us children to drive us to drink.' Roy told him he didn't need any devil for that. He knew how to drive himself better than any devil could.

Ken and Roy fought a lot, and until Roy grew taller and stronger, Ken battered him around often. Toward the end of our lives in Washington, Roy began to stand up to him and then there were some really nasty fights, which nearly shattered Mama's fragile heart. Roy's love for her was about all that kept him in check—and his love for me.

Once Roy found out I wasn't his blood sister, he confessed his romantic love for me, but it was impossible for me to think of him as anything but my brother. I told him so many times. Up until the moment the truth about me was revealed, he was my big brother, my protector. I knew and Beneatha knew he favored me over her, but I tried to make light of all that and made excuses for him whenever I could. After Beneatha's violent death at the hands of gang members, Mama Arnold wanted to get both of us out of the projects more than anything. She encouraged Roy to enlist in the army and she left to live with her aunt, never telling Roy or me just how sick she really was.

Apart from each other for some time afterward, Roy and I met again when he came to visit me in London. For a while, lost and confused myself, I seriously considered that we could become man and wife. I let him make love to me almost as a way of testing the waters, but it still didn't feel right. I knew I was breaking his heart, but I couldn't get myself to change. Perhaps what fate had done to us was cruel, yet I also thought what we might do to each other could be worse.

"No, not everyone, not yet," I said. "My mother's husband knows, of course, but the community here doesn't know it all and my half brother and half sister still don't know."

"Why not?"

"I don't know, Roy. It's up to my mother and her husband to tell them."

"They're still ashamed of you, Rain. That's why," he said.

"Probably."

"Who's taking care of you? Is your mother doing that at least?"

"No," I said, "but remember I told you Grandmother Hudson put me in her will?"

"Yeah, sure. How much did she leave you?"

"A lot, Roy."

"A lot? How much?"

"It's in the millions, Roy," I said.

"Huh? Dollars?"

"Yes," I said laughing. "I own a majority share of the property, a portfolio and fifty percent of the business."

"Wow."

"But the family isn't happy about it and they're talking about taking me and the will to court. They want me to compromise and take a million dollars."

"They do? What are you going to do?"

"Fight," I said.

"Fight? Maybe you ought to just take the money and run, Rain. Why force yourself on a family that doesn't want you?" he asked.

It was a good question, of course. What did I want out of all this finally? Maybe what I wanted was to see the day when they had to accept me just so that day I could turn my back on them. Pride was rearing up like a magnificent horse.

"Okay, Arnold, hang up," I heard that person growl again.

"Where are you, Roy? Why is someone telling you to hang up? Roy?"

"I'm all right," he said.

"You did get in trouble for coming to see me in London, didn't you? You better tell me the truth, Roy Arnold," I ordered.

"All right, I did, but it doesn't mean nothing," he said.

"Are you in the clink?"

He laughed.

"Something like that. Don't worry about it. I'll put in my time and then I'll be coming home. I'll be coming back for you, Rain. I promise," he said.

"Roy..."

"That's it, hang up," I heard. "Now."

"Bye for now, Rain," he said quickly and the phone went dead in my hands. Thousands of miles away, Roy was being locked up in the stockade, a price he had been willing to pay just to spend another twenty-four hours with me. How I wished he didn't love me that much.

I dropped my head back to the pillow, but it was almost impossible to fall back to sleep. What was I going to do with my life now? How long would this controversy last? Was Roy right? Should I just pack up and return to England immediately? How I wished I had someone close to advise me, someone more than just an attorney who based everything on black-and-white pages and legal codes. I didn't even have a close girlfriend.

Loneliness was like rust, eating away inside you, weakening your resolve. I just wanted to pull the blanket up and over my head and close myself off from the day and what it might bring. Then I remembered how much Grandmother Hudson hated people who languished in self-pity and how angry she once got when I dared to pity her. I also recalled my stepfather whining about his life and how my mama hated it.

"Self-pity is just a fancy way of avoiding responsibility," Grandmother Hudson used to say. "Replace it with good old-fashioned raw anger and defiance and you'll get further in your life," she advised.

"I hear you Grandmother," I muttered under the blanket. Some people are so influential, their voices echo in your head years and years after they've gone. Grandmother Hudson was certainly one of them.

I threw the blanket back and rose to shower, dress and make myself some breakfast. While I sat there sipping coffee, I decided to write my real father a letter and see if he would write back and give me some advice.

Dear Daddy,

As you know I returned to Virginia to attend Grandmother Hudson's funeral. I told my mother I had met you and she was very interested in how you reacted. I also told her about your wonderful family.

She, my stepfather, and Aunt Victoria are very upset about the amount Grandmother Hudson has left me in her will. They want me to compromise and take less or they, mostly Victoria, I think, will take me and the will to court to challenge everything.

I don't believe Grandmother Hudson would want me to compromise. Maybe I'm just being stubborn about it and in the end, I'll regret it, but for now, I have said no. My attorney, Grandmother Hudson's attorney, doesn't think I have to compromise either, but I know that sometimes lawyers drag things into courts to make more money for themselves. At least, Grant, my mother's husband, who is a lawyer too, is saying that. He thinks the legal fees will be so big, we'd be better off compromising.

Anyway, all this could delay my return to London. What do you think about it? Do you think I should just take what they want to give me and run, leave them and this place forever and ever?

I suppose it's unfair to ask you anything and put you on the spot. I want you to know I'm not in any way expecting you to do anything for me. It's just nice to have someone I can trust to write to and listen to now.

I hope everyone is well. I'll let you know what I finally do decide and when I will be returning.

Love,
Rain

I considered signing it *your daughter, Rain,* but thought it was best to just write my name. I addressed it and got it ready to send.

Just before noon I heard the doorbell. Of course, Corbette hadn't even bothered to call me back to let me know about the restaurant and our dinner date, but I hadn't expected he would. Now, I wondered if he had decided to return in person, maybe thinking I was still worth seducing again.

My mouth opened with surprise when I discovered it was Aunt Victoria. Since when had she decided she would ring the doorbell instead of just burst right in?

"I'd like to speak with you," she said.

It was partly cloudy and cooler, so she wore a dark blue woolen knee-length coat over her gray business suit. She was wearing a pair of black leather gloves as well. Her hair, which normally was simply brushed back with a slight wave that looked like a last-minute thought, was neater, more styled. I noticed that she was wearing some makeup, including a brighter pink lipstick. It actually softened her face and when it did that, I did see more resemblances to Jake.

"I thought we had said everything yesterday," I replied.

"No. May I come in or are you just going to keep me out here?"

"Come in," I said with a slight shrug.

She entered and pulled off her gloves.

"Do you have any coffee on?"

"Coffee? Yes," I said, even more surprised.

"Good."

I just stood there for a moment and she raised her eyebrows.

"You want to have it in the breakfast nook?" I asked.

"Fine," she said and walked down the corridor quickly, her heavy, square-heeled shoes clicking like the taps of a tiny hammer. She was so long-legged that when she walked, her feet seemed to have a slight snap each time she took a step.

I hurried to the kitchen and got out a cup and saucer.

"What was it like working for my aunt and uncle in London?" she asked, taking off her coat and placing it on a chair.

"It wasn't very pleasant," I said. "They have this slave master, Mr. Boggs, who runs the house like a military operation. He actually has a drill with white gloves, checking on the dusting and polishing."

"It doesn't surprise me," she said. "The one time I was there, I couldn't wait to leave. Do they still have that silly little cottage in the back kept like some sort of a mausoleum filled with Heather's toys?"

I froze for a moment.

"You know all about that?"

"Of course," she said. "When I was there, I was almost burned at the stake for daring to enter it."

"Yes, it's still there," I said. I poured her a cup of coffee. "Milk?"

"Thank you," she said.

Was it my imagination or was dreadful Aunt Victoria behaving like a human being toward me?

I poured myself a cup and sat across from her.

"I know," she began, "that I look like the bad one here. It was always that way. Whenever a problem arose and a hard, but important, decision had to be made, your mother would go sailing off someplace and leave it all to me. So naturally, I was the one people resented. Even my own mother resented me," she complained, her voice cracking with uncharacteristic emotion.

It occurred to me that I hadn't seen her cry at Grandmother Hudson's funeral, not even a single tear. She was the one supervising the arrangements, making sure it was all perfectly coordinated down to where cars would be parked at the cemetery. My mother sobbed and with reddened eyes greeted people, hugged people and let people hug her. Victoria seemed aloof and in charge not only of the details of the funeral, but her own emotions as well.

"I loved her in my own way, when I was permitted to love her. As you know from the short time you were here, my mother was a very strong, domineering woman. She hated compromise and was intolerant of failure and stupidity. I thought she would love me more for being more like her than Megan was, but do you know what, Rain? I've come to the conclusion my mother didn't like herself very much. That's right," she said when I widened my eyes, "at the end of her life, she had decided she didn't and that's why she favored you so quickly and with such uncharacteristic charity.

"Maybe she saw you as a third daughter, someone not as weak as Megan, but someone not as strong as me. Maybe you were more like the daughter she wished she had. I thought about this all night last night, trying to understand why she had left you so much of our family's fortune and that's what I have concluded."

She sipped her coffee and gazed out the window for a long moment. Had I misjudged her? Was I as unfair and unsympathetic as I accused her of being?

"As you witnessed for yourself yesterday, my sister isn't going to be any great help to you or to this unpleasant situation we all find ourselves in," she continued. "Frankly, I'm tired of doing all the dirty work in this family. I have my own ambitions and interests, too.

"Therefore, I've decided to declare a truce between us, if you are amenable."

"A truce?"

"Grant's right. We don't need to fill the pockets of

lawyers, who in the end, will benefit the most from any family dispute," she explained. "For good or for worse, my mother decided that you and I would become partners of sorts. I will continue to make money for the family business and you will benefit from it. How does all this sound so far?"

"All right," I said cautiously. I felt like someone waiting for the second shoe to drop. "What do I have to do?"

"Do? There's nothing for you to do. You can return to the life you want. I imagine you want to go back to England, isn't that so?"

"Yes," I said.

"Well then, what we'll do is simply put up the house and property for sale and invest the profits."

"I don't know," I said.

"You don't know?"

"This house…I keep thinking how important it was to Grandmother Hudson."

"Yes, it was, but she's gone and there's the upkeep to think about now. How can a girl like you think about staying here indefinitely?"

"A girl like me?"

"Young with your whole life ahead of you," she replied. "You can't want all this worry, especially if you plan on being in England."

"I suppose that's true," I said.

"Of course, it's true. Everyone has his or her destiny to fulfill. Mine, for better or for worse, was to walk in my father's footsteps for a while and then fill those footsteps when he was gone. I've done well for the family. Mother never wanted to admit it and give me credit. She was old school and had this old fashioned idea that women don't belong in the world of business. In her day strong women were content subtly manipulating their husbands like puppets, remaining hidden in the background, behind the curtain of what was considered proper and what was not.

"I recall how she thought it was so unfeminine of me to be interested in stocks and bonds. Mother died not really knowing the difference between a junk bond and a municipal."

"I don't know the difference," I confessed.

"Just my point. And why it is so important we get along. I'm not asking you to learn the difference or change the direction of your life, but there's a considerable estate to protect and maintain. You can appreciate that, I'm sure."

"Yes," I said.

"Good. Well. I'm happy we had this little chat," she said. "There is some paperwork I'll bring over in the next day or so, some matters we have to resolve with the investments. Don't worry. I'll explain it all to you clearly. I have a feeling," she said standing and reaching for her coat, "that it will be easier talking to you about some of this than it would be talking with Megan.

"By the way," she added as she put on her coat, "I'm not surprised she hadn't told Brody and Alison the whole truth about you. Tomorrow, remember? Everything's put off until tomorrow. Tomorrow, she'll worry about it," she said, laughed and started out.

I followed her to the door. She turned back to me after she opened it.

"I'm so glad I decided to have this conversation with you. Who wants to be wrapped up in all this unpleasantness with all we have yet to do with our lives? And don't worry about Grant. I'll speak with him and make sure he understands it all," she added.

As she walked out, I wondered if that wasn't the real

reason she was being so nice and so reasonable: showing Grant she could handle things, handle me better than Megan could, and showing him how she was the one in the end who helped him protect his precious image.

Did she really hope to steal her sister's husband?

Knowing what I knew of them all now, I wasn't willing to bet a nickel on what any of them might do to each other, much less to me.

I closed the door, my head spinning.

What had just happened? What did it all mean? Was she sincere? Had she really thought about it all night?

I felt like running upstairs, packing and getting myself on the first plane to London.

Jake squinted suspiciously when I told him all that had happened, including Victoria's surprise visit and flag of truce. He had brought the Rolls-Royce back after having its scheduled service at the garage completed and I went out to talk to him.

"She just left," I concluded. "She says she's coming back with paperwork. Do you think I ought to have Mr. Sanger read it all first?"

"Of course," he replied quickly. "Don't ever relax and close your eyes around Victoria," he warned.

I smiled.

"I didn't need you to warn me about that, Jake, but I've got to say you don't exactly sound like a proud father."

He laughed and then grew serious.

"I didn't have anything to do with her upbringing. Everett was the biggest influence on her, a far bigger influence than Frances, despite what Victoria might have told you. Everett taught her how to be indifferent, analytical and cold when involved with business. I remember her telling Frances once that Everett had warned her she would be dealing mostly with men in the business world and that men in that world had little respect for women. They would always be looking to take advantage of her, cheat her, outsmart her. Everett's advice to Victoria was to pretend to be naive, innocent and weak, and when she got enough information to go for the jugular.

"She got so she enjoyed it. He taught her how to be a corporate hit woman, a hunter whose prey was good business opportunities and weak opponents. 'If Daddy were alive, he would be proud of what I've done,' she would say.

"She's a lot like my grandfather," Jake added. "The little I remember about him, that is.

"But don't misunderstand me, Rain. I give Victoria credit for being so successful in business. Everett wasn't wrong. Men would have eaten her for breakfast if she wasn't as firm and smart as she is. There's little compassion for your competitor when it comes to making money. The bigger the stakes, the less compassion. There are some good things to learn from Victoria.

"However," he said, "she views you as one of those competitors, so here's my advice: watch your back."

"Okay, Jake."

He nodded and looked around. The sky was cloudless. It was turning out to be one of the most beautiful days since my arrival. The breeze was warmer and the air was clear. Everything glittered.

"You know what you should do today," he said. "You should take my pony, Rain, for your first ride. She's ready and waiting. What'dya say?"

"I don't know."

"C'mon. You'll enjoy it. She's been asking for you," he said.

I laughed. I had enjoyed my riding classes at Dogwood and was looking forward to getting in the saddle again.

"Okay, Jake," I said and went in to change into my riding pants and boots, an outfit Grandmother Hudson had bought me for Dogwood.

"Very professional looking," Jake said when I returned. "Rain will be impressed."

"We'll see," I said and we drove off to the farm where Jake boarded his horse.

At the stable, I marveled at how beautiful Rain had become. She was a chestnut brown horse with an almost blond mane. She looked at me with curiosity when I drew closer and then lifted her left front leg and stomped the wooden floor.

"That's how she says hello," Jake told me. "She doesn't say hello to just anyone, so you're off to a great start."

I laughed and scratched her snout. Jake gave me some sugar cubes to feed her while he went for her saddle and bridle. I knew how to feed a horse, how to keep my palm flat and let her pluck the cubes out. She nodded.

"That's her thank you," Jake said as Rain backed up. Jake threw the saddle over her and fastened the girth. "You should be able to do this yourself, right?"

"It was one of the first things they taught us in class," I said.

"You do the bridle," he told me and I did. Rain put up no resistence.

I watched Jake clean her hooves with his hoof pick. He tightened the saddle and told me to get up so he could adjust the stirrups. That done, he led us out of the stable.

"Take her west. You'll see the beaten track. It will bring you to the crest of that hill," he said pointing. "From there, by the way, you can look down on your property, house and all. Continue following the track and it will bring you back here. It should take you about an hour and a half.

"Just squeeze her gently with your legs and lean a bit forward and she'll bust into a lope. She likes it, but she likes to test you and will resist when you pull back. Don't let her have her way once, not even a little bit. She's like a spoiled teenager. Once you establish you're in control, she'll be as gentle as a lamb. Okay?"

"All right, Jake," I said.

"Have a good ride. I'll be waiting for you," he said. "I've got to go see the guy who owns these stables."

He started away. My heart raced. I could feel the horse's great strength beneath me. She twisted her neck with impatience at my hesitation, but I held the reins tight for a moment to do just what Jake had prescribed.

"We'll go when I'm ready," I said and then I loosened my grip and squeezed her ever so gently. She started forward, her head up, prancing proudly toward the path. I looked back and saw Jake watching.

"That's it," he said. "You're sittin' up straight and perfect. I knew it," he called.

He was right. Minutes after I had begun, all I had learned and all my past riding experience returned. After I had conquered my initial fears at Dogwood, I grew to love being on horseback. The irony of a poor girl growing up in the streets of the inner city finding herself dressed in an expensive riding outfit being trained along with some of the wealthiest young women in the area never left me. Even now, it brought a smile to my face. I used to sit on the horse and think how Mama Arnold would just roar with laughter and tears of happiness.

I could feel Rain's desire to break into a lope. She pulled on the reins, tossed her head from side to side, snorted, whinnied, did everything but rear up and toss me off. I pulled her to a halt and made her stand still. She lowered her head and tossed it again and then lifted her head and stamped her right front foot. Finally, she settled down and I let her go forward, slowly. After five minutes or so, I gave her more head and she broke into that lope. It was beautiful, like riding on the wind. Then I was afraid I was giving her too much and pulled her back as we drew closer to the hill.

We went up slowly and at the top, I stopped and gazed out just as Jake had instructed. There was Grandmother Hudson's beautiful big house, mostly mine now, nestled in the valley. The lake looked painted silver. High above two crows circled. Seeing the property from this prospective filled my heart with joy.

How could we just sell it off as an investment, treat the land and the house like some stock or bond on the market? It had too much personality, history. It wasn't a piece of property; it was a home.

Victoria was going to have to battle with me about this, I concluded. Seeing it from this height, I was convinced it was Grandmother Hudson's purpose to give me the controlling interest, that I would know the meaning of home and want to protect and cherish it.

Rain looked out as if she, too, appreciated the view. She wasn't impatient. I stroked her neck.

"Someday soon, we'll ride over there, Rain. You can come visit me," I told her and then we continued over the path, through some woods, past a sparkling stream of water where the afternoon sunlight turned the river's stones into jewels and crystals as the light filtered through the surrounding trees.

I gave my four-footed namesake another chance to lope and then we slowed down, making our way back toward the stables where Jake waited. Sitting on a chair, reading a paper, he watched us approaching and then he stood up.

"Well?"

"It was wonderful, Jake. Thank you."

"She looks like she got a good workout, Princess. You did good."

After we walked her and cooled her down, I brushed her for about a half hour. At Dogwood, they always made us brush our horses. It was the best way for them to get used to you. By the time Jake and I left it was late in the afternoon.

"I'll see you soon, Rain," I told her. She twisted her neck and then nodded as if she understood.

"That you will," Jake said. "When you return to England, maybe you should do some riding," he suggested after we got into his car.

"Maybe," I said. I looked back at the horse ranch as we drove off. "It's really beautiful here, Jake. I made a decision up there. I'm not going to sell," I said. "For as long as I can, I'm going to keep the house."

He laughed.

"Good," he said.

"When I return to England, you should move in and take care of it," I added.

"I don't know about that, Princess."

"I do. Think about it, Jake. Someday, I'd like to come

back here and think of it as my home, too. I know you'll see that it's well maintained. Okay?"

"I don't know, Princess," he repeated. "It has a lot of memories for me. We'll see," he promised.

I sat back in deep thought. Was I just dreaming, creating my own world of fantasy to ignore the hard reality? How could I ever return here? What would I be returning to?

"Now who's this?" he asked when we drove up the driveway of my grandmother's estate. A silver Corvette convertible was parked in front of the house.

Could Corbette have another sports car? I wondered.

I got out and approached the car. Then I heard his voice, calling from the dock. My half brother Brody waved.

Jake had waited to see if I needed him.

"Who is it?" he asked, squinting.

"It's Brody," I said.

"Oh."

"Megan must have finally told him the truth about me," I said.

Jake nodded.

"I guess you two should have some privacy. I'll be by tomorrow. You know where I am if you need me. Thanks for giving Rain her exercise," he added and drove off as Brody hurriedly approached.

I stood there, anticipating.

"I've been waiting here for nearly an hour. I almost gave up. I thought you might have gone away, maybe back to England or something. My mother didn't seem to know anything about your plans when I asked," he continued.

"Oh?"

"I knew she and my father had been out here, but she didn't want to talk about it.

"So," he said shrugging and looking about, "I decided I'd give my new car its first big ride. Do you like it? Dad bought it for me a week ago for my good grades in class and my achievements on the football field—I made a record number of touchdown passes this year, you know," he said proudly.

He spoke quickly, obviously nervous, which was uncharacteristic of Brody from the few times I had been with him. He always seemed so self-assured, so confident, almost arrogant. He had some reason to be. He was a very good-looking young man, tall—six feet two or more—and his shoulders were so wide they almost filled most doorways. Today, just like the first time I had met him, he wore his blue and gold varsity jacket and a pair of black slacks with soft looking black leather loafers. His hair was as ebony as mine but his eyes were more green than brown, although I saw hazel specks in them. He had a mouth like mine but a firm, tight jawbone. His complexion was athletic with a rosy tint in his cheeks and full, dark crimson lips.

"You mean your parents don't know you've come here?" I asked.

"By now they probably do. I left a note in the kitchen. Last time I did that, though, my bitchy brat sister got to it first and threw it in the garbage can to get me into trouble. I figured out she did something like that when I got home to an angry father. On a hunch, I went into the kitchen's garbage disposal and found the note. When I showed it to Dad, he grounded Alison for a month. Still, as usual, she got her sentence commuted and was out in a week."

"Your parents are not going to like that you came here, Brody," I said.

"Why not?" he asked, his eyes full of innocence.

So much for my mother's promise to tell him and Alison the truth finally, I thought. Had they even told Brody about Grandmother Hudson's will and its controversy?

"You've been horseback riding, huh?" he asked.

"Jake asked me to exercise his horse for him."

"I haven't done much of that myself, but I'd like to," he said.

He glanced at the house.

"I keep thinking I'll see Grandmother Hudson. It's hard to think of this place without her."

"Yes."

"So," he said. "Why don't I take you someplace nice for dinner?".

"Don't you have to start for home? I know it's a long ride," I said.

"What do you think I intended on doing, driving down here, touching the property and then turning around and rushing home?" He laughed. "It was a long ride. You're right. I've got to do something more to make it worth it," he said, flashing that charming smile at me.

"I'm a little tired, Brody," I said. "I haven't been horseback riding for quite a while and it takes a lot out of you, especially when you've got to start with a new horse. You can't help being very tense and that wears on you, too."

"Oh, sure," he said. He looked down and then he looked up, his eyes brightening. "So you won't have much desire to cook anyway. Here's what I'll do. I know a great Chinese takeout not too far from here. I'll go get us a couple of dishes, some soups, egg rolls, and fortune cookies. What do you say?"

"You really should start for home, Brody."

"Don't be silly. Come on. We've really never gotten a good chance to get to know each other and my grandmother was very, very fond of you obviously. If she liked you, you must be special. She didn't like all that many people."

"Brody, listen…"

"What do you like, chicken, shrimp, lobster? Forget it. I'll get all three and you can have some leftovers," he said excitedly.

"Brody…"

"I insist," he said. He looked at the house. "Technically, I guess, I have a little ownership in this place through my mother, right?"

I stared at him. He was so exuberant and in some ways so innocent compared to me. What was I to do? Just blurt the truth in his face and make more trouble in this family? Why didn't my mother have the courage to do the right thing so something like this wouldn't happen? If she hadn't, Grant should have, I thought, or is his fear of staining his precious public image so great, he could live with all the lies in his own home, too?

"Are you expecting someone else? Is that it? That guy you were in the play with last year, maybe?"

"No," I said quickly. I should have thought about it and seized on the opportunity, but I didn't think fast enough.

"I know you don't have any other hot date. You said you were tired. Right?"

"No, I don't have another date," I admitted.

"So? Then, it's okay, right?" he asked. He lifted his

arms. "You've run out of all the possible excuses, Rain. Unless you're afraid to say you can't stand me."

"Of course that's not it, Brody."

"So?"

"Okay," I relented.

"Great."

He literally leaped into his car.

"I've got to take you for a ride in this. It's like a little airplane," he said. He started the engine and smiled as he gunned it. "I'll get you some moo goo gai pan," he said and spun the car around me. "Be back before you can say kung fu in Chinese."

I couldn't help but laugh at him. After all, why should I be mean to him or unfriendly?

He waved and shot down the driveway too fast, slamming the brakes on at the end to let a slow, late-model station wagon go by. He looked back at me, smiled, raised his hands and then turned back to driving off.

"This is a mistake," I said. "But it's not all my fault. In fact, none of it is my fault."

I went into the house, my emotions twisting and turning in torment and confusion. Just when and how would truth come by and finally sweep all the lies from this family?

4

Secret Pain

After I took a shower and quickly washed my hair, I put on
a plain white blouse and a light blue skirt with a pair of blue
and white tennis sneakers. It was all right to do exactly what
Brody proposed, I told myself. It was fine to get to know
each other better, but I had to be very careful about the level
of expectations I encouraged. Under no circumstances
could I permit him to leave this house tonight still believing
he and I could become romantically involved. He might
leave disappointed or even angry, but when his parents finally told him the truth about all of us, he would understand.

As I ran a brush through my hair, I admitted to myself
that if the situation were different, if Brody were just another young man, it would be easy to fall in love with
him—and not only because he was so good-looking. He
had sincerity and sensitivity. He was perceptive, too. He
didn't pretend his family was something other than it was.
He knew our mother's weaknesses and he was certainly

objective about Alison. I thought that took maturity. How I wished my secret was out and he and I could truly become brother and sister. I felt confident that when that occurred, I would have a wonderful new friend.

Despite my self-imposed restrictions and concern, I couldn't leave my vanity table without putting on a little lipstick. I smiled to myself, recalling a conversation that had grown into a little argument with Leslie and Catherine, the two precocious sisters from France who had eventually seduced my boyfriend, Randall Glenn.

"Women are *always* conscious of their appearance, *chérie*," Leslie insisted.

"We are always on a stage," Catherine added. They laughed. "That is why we are more natural in the theater, eh?"

"Men can be just as vain," I countered. It was annoying how they would giggle and hide their faces after some of the things I said as if I was so naive about sex.

"You're not such experts," I snapped at them.

They stopped smiling.

"Even as little girls, we worry about our looks," Catherine said. "We want our papa to think we are lovely. We flirt before we can talk."

"*Oui.* We know natural—is that how you say?" Leslie asked her sister.

"Naturally," she corrected.

"Naturally, yes. It's who we are...*la femme,*" she cried and laughed. "You cannot be ashamed, *chérie.* No, no, you cannot help it," she asserted. "Even those men you don't like, even those you still don't want to see you...how do you say?" She looked to her sister.

"Before breakfast," Catherine said laughing.

"Oui, before breakfast."

"That's silly. You're both just...obsessed with sex," I accused. That made them laugh harder.

"Oui, oui, but of course," Leslie said.

Afterward, often, when I caught some man looking at me, even a teenage boy, I felt the heat rise to my face. My posture improved, my eyes shifted away and then back. Then I would growl at myself for being so...so French.

Maybe it was time to admit to myself that it felt good to be appreciated, admired, to simply be a woman. I would never admit it to those irritating, confident sisters, but I didn't have to admit it to them for them to know.

Just be careful, I warned my image in the mirror when I finished putting on the lipstick.

I went down and set the table for us and then waited in the sitting room. Brody was taking so long I began to wonder if he hadn't changed his mind or called our mother and been told to get back immediately. I couldn't help but wish that was true. It would make it all so much easier.

Ten minutes later, however, his car pulled up. I looked out the window and saw him hugging the bags as he made his way to the front door. For a few seconds, I actually considered not opening it. If only...

"Sorry I took so long," he said when I let him in. "They were so busy. No one cooks anymore, just like my father tells his friends about my mother." He charged down the hallway toward the kitchen, excited and happy, as though he were being carried along on some magic carpet. He turned back to me. "My mother's favorite meal is reservations. Get it?" he asked when I didn't burst into laughter. "Reservations?"

"Yes, Brody, I get it," I said shaking my head.

He set the bags down on the kitchen counter.

"The table is already set for us," I told him.

"Oh. Sure. Great." He brought the bags into the dining room, setting them on the table so he could take out the containers.

"I can make some tea," I suggested.

"Tea? What have my English great-aunt and great-uncle done to you? Naw. I bought some good Chinese beer," he said and plucked two six-packs from the second bag. "It's all still hot," he said, nodding at the containers of food. "I'll serve it."

He started, dipping the big spoons into the containers and filling up a plate for me.

"I didn't buy any soup. I thought it might be too much."

Seeing the amount of food he had bought, I could only laugh.

"I'll say."

"So you'll have lunch tomorrow. Big deal. You're supposed to have leftovers with Chinese food. It's expected. Dig in," he ordered.

It was good and I said so.

"Yeah, I remember enjoying a meal at that place. We had come down to see grandmother and my father decided we should all go out to eat. Grandmother didn't want to, but he talked her into it and she enjoyed herself." He laughed. "Aunt Victoria checked the bill at the end of the evening and found where they had charged us for a full dinner when it was supposed to be à la carte. She's got an adding machine in her head, I think."

I smiled. It was as if some sort of dam holding back his childhood memories had broken and all of the images, words and events were rushing out.

"Want one of these beers?" he asked.

"No, thank you."

"They're good." He poured a whole bottle into his glass.

"Did you always like coming here?" I asked.

"We didn't come that often. Most of the time, Aunt Victoria would insist we come because she had to discuss some business problem or something. My mother hates talking about business. She doesn't even run her own checking account. My parents have a business manager who calls her when she's overdrawn or something and then she moans and groans about it to my father, claiming it's their business manager's fault for not warning her soon enough."

"Is she really that irresponsible?" I asked. I couldn't help but be interested in what my mother was really like and what Brody's family life had been and was like.

He stopped eating and smiled.

"Naw. She just knows how to manipulate my father. He's supposed to be the politician in the family, but my mother's the champ. I never saw her not get what she wanted."

"If your father didn't want to give things to her, he wouldn't," I charged.

He thought a moment then nodded.

"Probably true. The only advice he ever gave me about women was never to underestimate them. 'When it comes to women, things are rarely what they seem,' he said."

"Men can be just as conniving, Brody."

"We try," he said chewing on his egg roll, smiling, "but we're amateurs compared to the supposedly weaker sex."

"We are weaker," I insisted.

"Oh sure," he said, losing the smile. "Look at Queen Elizabeth. You lived in England. You should know all about her in history."

"That's different. She was a queen. She had to be strong."

"All women are queens in their own homes," he said. "Hey, don't get me wrong. That's the way it should be. You're right. If my father didn't want it to be that way, it wouldn't. Lately, though, I think he agrees to things and does things more out of a need to avoid any controversy. He doesn't want to be distracted. My father's an ambitious man, but that's only because other people recognize he's very capable. You know, he could end up being president of the United States," he said proudly.

"So you have a good relationship with him?"

"Oh, sure. We're buddies. He comes to all the games when I'm starting quarterback. Once he even took a red-eye flight to get there in time and paid for a high-premium ticket, too."

"That's very nice, Brody. I'm happy for you."

He nodded and poured himself another beer.

"Don't drink too much," I warned.

"Hey, if you saw how much beer we consume in school, you wouldn't worry. You develop an immunity or something, I think. I've downed a six-pack on my own lots of times."

"I just don't want you to get sick or be unable to drive," I said.

"I've been thinking about that. If you don't mind, I'll stay over tonight. Sleep in my usual room, of course."

My heart pounded out its warnings like drums sending messages about impending disaster.

"I don't think your mother is going to be happy about that, Brody."

"She hasn't called yet?" he asked.

"No."

"That Alison. If she found that note and dumped it again so I would get into trouble, I'll wring her spoiled neck."

"You'd better call your mother, Brody. Please."

"Sure. I'll call," he promised. He took another long sip of his beer and sat back, studying me.

"What?" I asked.

"There's something I've always wondered about. My mother never gives me a straight answer."

"Oh." I looked down quickly, pretending interest in my food.

"How did Mother get to know you, to recommend you for that program that set you up here with Grandmother Hudson? I never even knew my mother was involved in anything like that. The closest she gets to minority problems is attending the Young Republican teas."

I continued to look down. I felt like a spider, weaving a web of lies. Only instead of some innocent fly being caught, I would surely catch myself. How much longer did I have to weave?

"I don't know what she has told you," I said cautiously.

"Practically nothing. I know she convinced Grandmother to give you a try and Grandmother apparently liked you from the start."

"It was just a program at the school for students who exhibited promise," I began. "One day I was called into the principal's office and your mother interviewed me. I guess you can call it that. Next thing I knew, I was recommended. The rest you know."

"I just can't figure out when my mother did all that. She actually went to a school?"

"Maybe it wasn't all that much to do. Maybe some friend of hers told her about the program and she thought it would be a good idea."

"Too many maybe's," Brody shot back at me. He opened another beer. I glanced at him, my heart pounding. Some lies are so thin you can see right through them, I thought.

"I remember how surprised my father was about it," he continued. He practically gulped his beer now; it obviously made him nervous to talk about me, too. "What surprised him the most was how quickly my mother had made all the arrangements for you, and how easily she had talked my grandmother into taking you in.

"My grandmother was very particular about people coming to see her, much less live with her. I think she held a record for firing maids. No salesperson would dare come within one hundred yards of this property."

"She was sick. She needed someone else in the house," I explained.

"A teenager? I know how Grandmother Hudson thought about today's teenagers. She used to say she would have had to hire a lion tamer if she was a mother of a young person today."

I laughed.

He shook his head.

"It's too mysterious, all of it. Lately, my parents are behind closed doors more than ever, too. I know grandmother left you money in her will, but I still don't know how much. No one will talk about it. My father says, it's being discussed and my mother just shakes her head and says, it's a difficult situation. That's her way of saying I don't want to talk about it. It will make me sad or sick or too depressed. What exactly did my grandmother leave you?"

"It's being discussed," I said smiling.

"I'm serious."

"Brody, it's all in the hands of lawyers. I don't know all the details of it myself," I offered.

He shook his head.

"I'm thinking of becoming a lawyer someday. I'm smart enough to read between the lines and pick up on some of the comments dropped around the house. Grandmother Hudson left you a considerable amount, enough for Aunt Victoria to bust a blood vessel, right? And since you're not a member of the family, they want to challenge it and stop it from happening, right?"

"Brody..."

"Jeez, I'm not here as a spy or anything. Just tell me something!"

"You guessed right," I said, "but I think it's all going to work out just fine."

"Just fine?" He laughed. "If I know Aunt Victoria, that means you get thrown out on your rear end. What are you planning to do with yourself now anyway, Rain? Are you really going back to England?"

"Yes," I said.

"Did you meet someone over there?"

I realized this might be the door of escape I had been desperately searching for. I nodded.

"Yes, Brody, I did. I met someone I can love very much. Someone who will love me," I said. I was really talking about my father, but Brody misunderstood just the way I hoped he would.

"Oh," he said. "Well, I'm not surprised or anything. You're a pretty girl. Anyone would want to have you as his girlfriend," he said.

I smiled at him, and gestured to our feast.

"This was all very good, Brody. Thanks for getting it."

"Huh? Sure," he said. I stood up and started to collect the dishes. He watched me closely.

"It really is getting late for you, Brody. Maybe you should think of starting for home?"

"Maybe," he said. He suddenly looked bitter, angry and hurt. I felt sorry for him, but what could I do?

I brought the dishes into the kitchen and put them next to the sink. When I returned, he was opening another bottle of beer.

"Brody, I believe you when you say you can drink a lot of that, but if you're going to drive tonight…"

"I'll be fine," he said impatiently. "You know, I've been thinking. I remember when you told me about your life, all the trouble, how you lost your sister through some gang and all. You've got to be careful about people, Rain. You're an orphan, really. You're out there hoping to find someone who will love you. You could be too vulnerable. You could jump into something too quickly."

"I know all that, Brody. Thank you."

"No, really. You should step back and give everything deep and serious consideration. Who is this guy in England? Is he much older?"

Before I had a chance to add to my web of deceit, the phone rang. I took it in the kitchen. It was my mother and their was a note of hysteria in her voice.

"Rain, is Brody there? Did he really drive down there?"

"Yes," I said.

"What is he doing there?"

"I didn't invite him," I told her immediately. It occurred to me that they might think I was encouraging him, just as a way to stop them from challenging the will. "He just appeared on the doorstep. I tried to talk him out of remaining here any longer, but he insisted he stay for dinner. He brought some Chinese takeout and we've just finished eating," I said.

"And?"

"That's all," I replied. "Nothing has been said," I added, knowing she really was primarily interested in that.

"Well, what's he doing there?" Her voice rang strident and thin.

"You can speak with him yourself," I said and called him to the phone. "It's your mother."

"I guess my sister didn't throw away the note after all." He took the receiver, and I returned to cleaning up the dinner dishes.

"I just felt like taking a ride, Mom. What's the big deal?" He listened a moment. "You weren't home and I didn't know where you were. Dad's in New York. I don't know," he said. "It's getting late. Maybe I better just spend the night and leave in the morning. Motel? What for? I've got my usual room here. Why are you getting so uptight? We're just having a very nice time."

He listened again, shaking his head and raising his eyes from me to the ceiling.

"Mom, I've never stayed with Aunt Victoria and I don't intend to pop over there tonight. She hasn't so much as said twenty words to me this year. I'm all right. Stop worrying about it," he insisted. "Right, right. Okay, here she is. She wants to speak with you again," he said. "Promise her I'll brush my teeth, will you? I've got to go to the bathroom," he said.

I took the receiver.

"Yes?"

"He drove there because he's got a terrible crush on you,"

she blurted. "He's always asking about you, even when you were in England. You've got to be careful about it."

"I understand," I said.

"You have to be careful with him," she continued. "Brody is a very mature young man and very charming. Don't forget who you are and who you are to him, Rain."

"I don't need you to remind me of that, but if you would just put it to an end already, we wouldn't have these worries. If he's so intelligent and so mature, he should be able to handle it."

"I will. Grant and I will definitely talk to him right after he comes home," she promised. I had heard that promise before and didn't have any reason to believe it would be fulfilled now.

I heard Brody return to the dining room.

"Tell her I'm behaving like a real Southern gentleman," he called.

"I'm nervous about his staying there. I'm going to call Victoria," my mother said.

"Fine with me," I said.

"I wish Grant were home," she muttered. "He'd get him to leave."

I wanted to say maybe it was time for you to take full responsibility and not put everything on your husband's shoulders, even your own past mistakes. Maybe it was time you really tried to make us all a family. Maybe Brody's actions have made it painfully clear and you should lift your head out of the sand. Maybe tomorrow was here, Mother. That's what I wanted to say, but instead, I just said good-bye.

"Sorry about all that," Brody said as soon as I entered

the dining room. He had, indeed, finished a whole six-pack and was into the second.

"She's very worried about you. Why don't you just go over to your aunt's house?"

"What is she so worried about?" He smiled. "What do they know about you that I don't know?" he asked with a lustful smile. "Are you a seductress? Will you put a spell on me? I might not resist," he said.

"Brody, listen…"

"I'm just kidding, just kidding. So, where were we? Oh yes, you were telling me about your love life in England. Where did you meet this guy? At school?"

"Yes," I said.

"Well, what's he like? Is he English?"

"No." I decided to use Randall. It had almost been true. "He's Canadian and he's a very talented singer."

"Oh. Well, you shouldn't get too involved with someone who wants to be in show business. Look at the lives they have to lead."

"I'm thinking of being involved in show business, too. I certainly am not interested in settling down with a husband and a troupe of children," I said.

He laughed.

"Someday, though, you will, right?"

"I don't know. Right now, I think it's better I just think about my career and not about any romance or relationship. I might not ever marry. I might just marry my career," I said.

I was trying to say anything I thought might make me less attractive to him. He nodded thoughtfully, but his eyes were beginning to look more and more glassy.

"Maybe I'll be more like Aunt Victoria," I said.

He blew out his lips and laughed.

"Now I know you're just fooling with me. You're about as similar to Aunt Victoria as I am. You're actually more like my mother. You even resemble her in some ways," he said pouring beer into his glass. "I don't mean you manipulate men or anything. I mean you're just as pretty as she is, prettier even," he said.

"I'd better put the leftovers away so they don't spoil," I said and reached for a container. He seized my wrist and looked up at me.

"You are, you know. You're prettier."

"Brody, please," I said pulling my wrist free.

"Is it because I'm nearly two years younger than you?" he asked. "Because I'm much older than other guys my age. Really. I am."

"Is what because of that, Brody?"

"Is that why you're trying to ignore me, ignore the way I feel about you?"

I stared at him and once again, the phone rang.

"Oh no," he said. "She's calling back. Let me get it," he said shooting up from his chair. He marched back to the kitchen and nearly ripped the phone off the wall seizing the receiver.

"Yes, Mother?" he said. "Oh," he quickly followed. "Hello, Aunt Victoria. No, I thought my mother was calling back. She did?"

He covered the mouthpiece.

"My mother called her. Can you imagine?" he whispered. "No, Aunt Victoria. I've decided not to stay at all. Thanks for the invitation, however. It's very nice of you."

He winked at me.

"Yes. Next time I do this, I certainly will call you first. Absolutely. Good-bye."

He hung up and laughed. Then he looked at me so intently, I had to stop what I was doing.

"What?" I asked him.

"You must have a reputation or something for both of them to be so concerned. I'm intrigued."

"I don't have any such reputation," I fired back at him.

He wobbled and shrugged.

"Okay," he said. "Let's get back to our conversation."

He started for the dining room.

"I'm putting everything away," I said. "Why don't you go rest a while on the sofa in the sitting room."

"No rest for the wary," he said—instead of the weary. "Get it?"

He laughed and left the kitchen.

He's getting drunk, I thought. It's not good. Suddenly, my mother's worries had become my own.

When I returned to the dining room, I saw he had taken my advice and gone to the sitting room. He had taken his one remaining beer. I cleaned the table, put everything away and in the dishwasher and then went to look for him. He was sprawled on the sofa, shoes off, eyes closed and a soft, contented smile on his lips. For a few moments I was able to look at him without his being aware.

I remembered once trying to imagine what it was like to be a boy. I was about seven or eight at the time and I had been looking at Roy just the way I was now looking at Brody. Roy was asleep on the sofa in the living room. I sat across from him and watched his chest lift and fall. I saw the very slight flutter in his lower lip as he exhaled. All of his features seemed to settle into a mold formed by his facial bones.

Boys have to look harder, I thought. Their bones have to be thicker so all their features are wider, longer. That's why he looks so different from me. If I were a boy, I'd look like that, too.

It was different gazing on Brody. When I saw a resemblance to my mother, I saw a resemblance, ever so vague and slight, to myself. Of course, he had inherited many of his father's features, too, and they seemed to overpower my mother's and mine. There was no mystery as to why Brody didn't look at me and think, could she be my mother's child, too?

He stirred, the corner of his lips dipping. Then he opened his eyes and looked at me without speaking. His expression suggested he thought he was dreaming and was waiting to see if I would remain there or pop like a bubble when he blinked.

"Hi," he said.

"Hi."

"Maybe I drank too much," he confessed.

"Maybe you did."

"My head started spinning so I lay down."

"I see you managed to bring your beer, however."

"If you'd had some, I wouldn't have drunk so much."

"Just like every man I know: looking for a way to pass the blame onto a woman."

He laughed.

"Are you really going to head for home?" I asked. "Or was that just something you told your aunt?"

"Just something I told," he replied.

"Well, I'm going to bed early tonight. My body aches

from my ride today. You turn and twist and get bounced in ways you never imagined when you're riding a horse for the first time in a long time."

"I could rub you down," he offered. "As a football player, I know exactly what needs to be done. The trainer does me almost twice a week during the season."

"No thank you," I said.

"I'm good at it," he bragged.

"I don't doubt that, but I think I'll pass and just get a good night's sleep, which I suggest you do, too. I'll be up early and make you some breakfast before you go."

"Anxious to get rid of me, huh?"

"No, but I don't want you to get into more trouble with your family, and I certainly don't want any more trouble with them," I said standing.

He remained prone, his hands now behind his head as he looked up at me.

"You are one pretty woman, Rain."

"I don't feel very pretty right at the moment," I said.

"I can't imagine you ever being caught by surprise. I bet you're even more gorgeous in the morning when you first open those big beautiful eyes."

I laughed.

"Where are you learning this fancy talk, Brody Randolph?"

"My heart," he said. "It comes right from here," he added and put his right palm over his heart.

"Okay," I said. "You know where everything is you might need. Good night."

I started out of the living room.

"There's more in my heart, more than needs to be brought out," he called.

I smiled to myself. Our mother was right. He was a charmer.

I didn't risk a reply. I mounted the stairs and went up to what was now my room, almost fleeing. After I had changed into my nightgown and prepared for bed, I heard music downstairs. He made it louder and louder and then he lowered it; eventually, he turned it off. I lay in the darkness listening. My heart began to pound when I heard his footsteps on the stairway.

"Sleep tight," he cried passing my closed door. Of course, I didn't respond. He went to the guest room he always used. I heard him knocking about, the water running, and then the house grew as silent as it ever did.

He'll sleep it off, I thought. After breakfast, he'll go home and finally, finally my mother will reveal our deepest secret.

I thought about that scene for a while and it made me feel sad for him. It wasn't just the disappointment about me either. I think for a son it must be deeply tragic to learn such scandalous things about your own mother. I recalled how high in his thinking Roy had held Mama Arnold. For a son, no woman could be as perfect as his mother. Brody was the type who would resent not having been told all these years, especially this last year.

Alison would be more embarrassed and angry, but she would direct it straight at me; I was confident of that. Now that I considered all the turmoil and tension that was about to explode in that otherwise perfect home, I could almost sympathize with my mother for trying to keep it a secret as long as possible. Wouldn't it really be so much easier for them all if I just disappeared?

I returned to that argument, considering my discussion with Victoria. She was right, I decided. In the days to come, I would cooperate and make my return to England easier for myself and for everyone else.

All this worry and thought had exhausted me. The moment I decided to close my eyes and go to sleep, I did. I was in such a deep sleep, too, so deep that I didn't realize Brody was in my room and beside my bed for quite a while. He must have kissed me once on the cheek before my eyes opened with the next kiss. At first, I was confused. I had forgotten for the moment that he was even in the house.

I felt his breath close to my ear and I spun around, barely smothering a scream. With the moonlight now coming through the window, his body gleamed and I quickly realized he was standing there completely naked.

"Don't be afraid," he said.

"What are you doing here?"

"I couldn't sleep. All I could do was lie there and think about you. Don't go back to England. I don't care what that guy promised you. He won't be as good to you as I will. I'll treat you even better than my father treats my mother."

"What are you talking about, Brody? You're not making any sense. Go back to bed."

"I'm talking about us, Rain. All this year you were right here," he said putting his hand over his forehead. "Many times I would stop listening in class or even to people talking to me, and I would picture you, hear you, even smell your hair and it filled me with such a longing, I was in pain. That's love, right? It can't be anything else."

"Brody, no..."

"You like me. You'll even fall in love with me if you're not already. I just know it will happen. I have enough love in my heart for both of us anyway," he declared.

He sat on the bed.

"You've just got to give us a chance," he pleaded. "Please."

He reached out to touch my face and I pulled myself back and sat up in the bed, holding the blanket against my body.

"You're still drunk," I said. "Otherwise, you wouldn't be in here saying these things, Brody. Go sleep it off."

"No. I'm as sober as I'll ever be."

He leaned toward me to kiss me and I put my hand against his cheek and pushed him away. He resisted, pushing himself forward until he forced my hand away and brought his lips to mine. I screamed and, using both my hands on his shoulders, shoved him away.

"What, do I have bad breath or something?" he asked. "Take it easy."

"We can't do this. You've got to get out of this room," I said.

"Why?"

"We'll never be lovers, Brody. Forget the whole idea," I said as firmly as I could.

"Why don't you like me? Do you think I'm some sort of spoiled brat like my sister? I work hard. I don't take anything for granted and I'll never take you for granted, Rain."

"That's not it, Brody. I like you."

"You think my family will be opposed? You think because they're from white Southern families, they'll object to you because you're African-American? If they did that, I wouldn't care. They'd lose me," he promised.

I shook my head.

"Brody, please stop."

He grabbed my left hand and started to bring it to his lips.

"Stop it, Brody!" I shouted, pulling my hand roughly from his.

"What? You think you're better than me or something? Is that it?"

"Think what you want. Only get out," I said sharply.

"There are lots of girls who wouldn't throw me out of their bedrooms," he bragged, his ego bruised.

"Good. Go to them," I said.

I hated being this mean, but I had to, I told myself. I had to be meaner still.

"You're too young for me," I continued. "And you're still a boy. The years between us don't even begin to suggest the differences. I'm worlds older than you and I don't want any relationships. I told you that. I don't know what gave you the idea we could be lovers."

"Me neither," he said angrily.

"So then, go to sleep. Let me sleep," I cried.

In the darkness he couldn't see the tears streaming down my cheeks. If he had, he would not have understood what really poured them over my lids.

"Sure. Go back to England," he said. "You'll be sorry. I sure had you pegged wrong."

"That's right," I said. You pegged me wrong." I covered my face with my hands.

He stood there staring at me for a few moments and then he left my bedroom, slamming the door closed behind him.

"Oh Mother," I cried, "you don't know how much pain you continue to put into your own children."

I fell back to the pillow and turned to smother my tears in it. I couldn't fall back to sleep. About twenty or so minutes later, I heard Brody stomp past my room.

"Have a good life," he cried and pounded down the stairs.

"Brody!" I shouted.

I got up and charged after him. The front door slammed shut as I hurried down the stairs. By the time I got outside, he was in his car, revving it up angrily. He spun it around, the tires squealing, and shot down the driveway.

"Brody!" I called after him, running down the steps.

A few seconds later, the taillights of his car disappeared in the darkness

He was gone.

5

Unburied Sins

It was a nightmare so powerful it became real. People are afraid of their dreams, not because they will toss and turn in their sleep and wake up sweating, even crying. No, they are afraid of their dreams because they believe their dreams might be predictions, turning their imaginings into terrible prophesies.

I didn't fall back to sleep for hours after Brody had left in that wild, angry rage. When I finally did, I saw those two red taillights growing in my mind, first into furious eyes and then merging into one large ball of fire that exploded along with the ringing of the telephone, raining down hot embers out of a thunderous, black sky above me.

After waking to the phone's ringing, I felt my heart pounding like a tom-tom, stealing my breath and filling my lungs with vibrations that reverberated down my spine to the ends of my feet. The phone rang and rang. I sat up, turned and lifted the receiver.

"Hello," I said.

Silence, deep and ominous followed without anyone speaking.

"Brody? Is that you?"

I heard a great, deep groan.

"Brody?"

"He's dead!" she screamed. It was the most chilling scream I had ever heard, piercing my heart, slicing it to the point where it stopped and then started. Every part of me wanted to pull away, explode like the light in my nightmare and send my arms and my legs, my head and my feet and my hands in different directions.

"He's dead!"

My stomach twisted. I felt my throat close as my blood drained down my body. I could barely hold the phone. It seemed to gain more weight every passing second.

"What? Mother? Who's dead? What are you saying?"

"Grant just phoned me from the scene of the accident. He sounded like a dead man himself. I didn't recognize his voice. I kept asking, Grant, is that you? Finally, he just screamed at me, screamed that Brody was gone. WHAT DID YOU DO?" she shouted so loud herself that my ear rang.

"Brody? What happened? He can't be dead," I barely uttered.

"I don't know. I don't know. They said he lost control at a turn an hour from my mother's house, went off the road and hit a tree. Why was he driving home so late? I thought he was going to stay over, if not with you, then with Victoria. What happened? What did you do? What did you tell him?"

A terrible shivering began in my body. My bones were rattling, my teeth chattering.

"I told him we couldn't be lovers. He wanted that and I had to be hard and mean to him to stop him."

"Oh God," she said. "It's my fault. All this is my fault."

I didn't say no. I couldn't make excuses for her because in my heart and soul I believed she was responsible. Not being sympathetic with her had an unexpected result, however. She suddenly turned angry at me.

"Couldn't you make something up, string him along so he didn't get so upset? Why did you do this so late at night and send him out like that? Why did he stay there if he told Victoria he wasn't going to stay? Did you encourage him? You did, didn't you? You're getting even with me, is that it?"

"Of course not."

"Why did he leave like that then? Why didn't you stop him?"

"What did you want me to tell him, Mother? Should I have been the one to tell him the truth because you didn't have the courage? This isn't my fault!"

"You could have been less mean, maybe," she moaned. "Why didn't you just ignore him?"

"He came to me in the middle of the night, Mother. He came to my bedroom naked. He wanted to have sex with me."

"Stop it! You're making this up. Stop it!"

"He wanted me to be his girlfriend. He said he was deeply in love with me and that no matter what anyone thought, he would still love me."

"I won't listen to this. Brody's dead. My son...Grant will hate me," she said in a mad loud whisper. "He'll blame me. They'll all blame me. Do you understand what's happened?"

"I'm sorry," I said, through my tears. "I wanted him to be my brother. I wanted him to be my friend."

"Was he drinking? Did you and he drink my mother's liquor? You had a wild party! That's why he tried to make love to you."

"Mother, nothing like that happened. He brought some beer, but he wasn't drunk when he left," I said.

"He brought beer," she muttered as if she had discovered the real murderer. "Grant will want to know. He brought beer."

I could envision her maddened, her eyes wide.

"He drank it at dinner, hours and hours before he left, Mother."

"Well then, maybe this is all a mistake," she said in a much lighter, more hopeful voice. "Maybe Grant's confused. It's another young man in a similar car. I'll call him back on his car phone. That might be true."

"I don't think so," I said softly.

"Alison's still asleep. She'll be destroyed. They argued like any brother and sister all the time, but she loved him and he loved her. He's going to be a lawyer like Grant, you know," she said, her voice changing, sounding younger, even childish. She fluttered a thin laugh. "He'll be a great lawyer. Everyone says so. He's articulate, bright and he makes a very impressive appearance. You should see him in his tuxedo. Juries will fall over themselves trying to satisfy him.

"Grant says the same thing," she continued, following it with another little laugh. "He's not dead," she said through her tears. "God wouldn't take him now. It's a mistake. Grant was just overwhelmed with the sight of this terrible accident. He called too quickly. He'll call back any moment and say, Megan, Megan, I made a big mistake."

I didn't reply. Brody had been killed. Suddenly, I couldn't breathe. My chest froze, my lungs locked. I was getting dizzy.

"I don't feel good, Mother. I can't talk anymore."

"What? Hello? Mother," she said.

"What? What did you say?"

"MOTHER!" she screamed.

I dropped the receiver and grabbed my stomach. Just before everything in it came rushing up and out, I made it to the bathroom and fell to my knees. I vomited and vomited into the toilet until I was in terrific pain. Then I fell on my side and lay there on the cold bathroom floor. I brought my knees up tight against my stomach, and in moments I was asleep.

With the phone off the cradle, no one could call me. Bad news was electric, even from great distances. Jake heard the horrible news from Victoria, who informed him she had tried to call me and was told by the operator that the line was not working. He drove up to the house quickly and rang the bell. When I didn't respond, he got the spare key hidden in the garage and let himself in. I didn't hear him calling my name downstairs, but moments later, he came charging up and discovered me on the bathroom floor.

"Rain!" he cried shaking me.

I opened my eyes. The lids felt like they were made of iron. My eyeballs ached.

"What happened?" he asked.

"Whaaa…"

I looked around, confused, forgetting why I was in the bathroom.

"Victoria called. Brody was killed last night in a car accident. Do you know about that?"

I closed my eyes again—closed them hard and wished that this wasn't happening, that Jake wasn't here, that when I opened them again I'd be in bed, and that it was all just a nightmare. I'll be forever grateful, I thought. I'll do anything God wants me to do.

"Rain," Jake pursued. "What exactly happened here? Why are you on the floor in the bathroom with the phone off the hook?"

I groaned and sat up slowly. He went to soak a wash cloth and then he put it against my forehead. I held it there myself.

"I feel so sick," I said.

"Can you stand up?" he asked.

"I don't know," I said.

He helped me to my feet and guided me back to the bed. When I was lying down with the blanket around me, I looked up at him and told him my mother had called. Yes, I know it all. Then I started to cry, but no tears came. All I could do was shake. My well of sorrow had run dry for now.

"He must have been going like a bat out of hell," Jake said. "The car is totaled, squashed like a smashed pumpkin. He wasn't wearing his seat belt either, so he got thrown and slammed. They think he died immediately. They hope," he added. "Maybe I should have hung around after I saw he had come, huh?"

Everyone was looking to share the blame, I thought.

"It wouldn't have mattered, Jake."

"Did you two have a fight or something?" he asked and I told him what had happened. I spoke slowly, like someone in a trance. He just listened and then slowly shook his head.

"You can't blame yourself for this, Rain" he said. "You did the right thing. They had no right leaving the burden on your shoulders. Don't you go blaming yourself, Rain. Hear me?"

"Yes, Jake."

"I gotta call Victoria and tell her the house isn't on fire or anything. I'll make you some tea, okay?"

"That's a switch," I said laughing. It wasn't really a laugh. It was a different sort of cry, a sob disguised. "Someone making me tea. I'm a MIF," I called after him.

He stuck his head back in the door.

"Pardon?"

"Milk in first," I said.

"Oh. Right," he said and I laughed again and again until I was gasping with those dry sobs. I finally ran out of energy even for that and lay still, staring up at the ceiling.

"Mama," I whispered. "Still think I'm going to bring good luck? Still think you should have named me Rain for good things, for blossoming and growing good things?"

I'm a mistake, I thought. I was created in error and my whole life is just a mistake.

Jake practically spoon fed me the tea. My body didn't want to cooperate. It didn't want to be a body anymore. It wanted to disappear and the best way to do that was to stop eating and drinking and caring, but Jake was persistent.

"You're not going to do this, Rain," he said. "You're not going to fall apart now. This family, for better or worse, needs strength, not weakness around it. No one is going to blame you. No one who knows the truth is going to hold you responsible for anything."

"Except me," I said.

"What could you do? Submit, pretend? You wouldn't have had any easier time living with yourself. I want you to get yourself up, get showered and dressed. Victoria will be here this afternoon and you'll have to deal with everything that's coming."

He looked around.

"This was Frances's room. Just think about your Grand-mother Hudson. Imagine what she would want you to do and do it," he urged.

"I'm tired, Jake."

"You're far too young to be tired," he replied. "Me, I can say that. Not you. You've got too much living to do.

"MIF," he said smiling and shaking his head. "Some MIF."

He got up from the bed and took the empty teacup with him.

"I'll be downstairs, waiting for you," he said. "I'm hungry and I expect you are too. Let's make us both something to eat."

I watched him leave and then I glanced at Grandmother Hudson's picture on the dresser, the one where she was standing by the lake pointing to something and smiling. I could almost hear her say, "Jake's right. Get a hold of yourself and help me deal with my ridiculous family.

"Remember what I told you about self-pity. Remember that now, more than ever."

I lifted myself out of bed, my body running on reflex and memory alone. I did what Jake had told me to do. I showered and dressed and went downstairs to make us something to eat. I prepared some tomato soup and toasted cheese sandwiches. I was surprised I was able to hold any of it down, but I did. Jake and I sat at the kitchen table and talked softly about what had happened.

Before we finished, Victoria charged into the house, her eyes full of shock, anger and confusion. She glanced sharply at Jake, who rose to put his dishes in the sink.

"I'll be out front if you need me," he said, more or less to both of us.

"What happened, Rain?" Victoria demanded after he walked out. "I can't make any sense out of what Megan is saying and by now, she's probably sedated. Grant won't come to the phone. They tell me he's beside himself, locked in his office."

I stared at the floor. No matter what had been done to me and what this family would like to do to me now, I couldn't stand hearing about their terrible burden of sadness. It brought back vivid memories of Mama after Beneatha's violent murder.

"Grant is destroyed," Victoria declared, sitting at the table. "I don't know if he'll be able to come back to himself. Megan will be of no help. She's worse than a lead weight around his ankle now."

I lifted my head and looked at her. She was angry at me not because of what had happened to Brody, but because of how it affected Grant.

"I didn't do anything deliberately to harm him," I began. I told her how Brody had been so insistent about having dinner with me. I told her about his expressions of love for me and how it was getting far too serious and I had to do something to end it.

"And you never told him who you really are?"

"Maybe I should have. Maybe he would have been calmer and understood and not been in such a rage against me, but I was frightened. I didn't want to cause any more trouble."

She stared at me a moment and then nodded.

"It's not your fault," she said with surprising firmness.

"It's been Megan's fault from day one. And my parents' fault for always making excuses for her, doing things to cover up her mistakes, permitting her to live in a rose-colored world.

"If she did poorly in school, they blamed it on the teachers or the subject. If she spent money unwisely, it was because someone scammed her. Always the victim. Poor Megan this, poor Megan that.

"Grant shouldn't have been so understanding once the truth about you was out," she continued, talking mostly to herself now. "She plays that game all too well, getting people to feel sorrier for her all the time. Men are so weak when it comes to someone like Megan. My father was blind and stupid whenever he looked at her, listened to her, saw the things she had done. She's a snake charmer.

"Grant is in a different situation," she said, catching herself, her eyes nearly clicking with the change in her tone of voice. "He was trapped this time. Of course, he couldn't just heave her out and let the world know what he had married. He has a great future. I understand that. You compromise to get what you want. That's good business sense.

"Grant has wonderful business sense. He admires that in me, too, you know. I can tell."

She pressed her thin lips together firmly and nodded.

"I've got to go to him to see what I can do to help him. My sister won't be able to help him one iota. She'll play the role of a tragic woman so no one dares blame her for any of this."

She fixed her eyes on me, the pupils smaller, her eyelids trembling with her fury, "But you and I know the truth, don't we? One day, we'll force her to face it.

"All right," she said standing, "don't do anything or say anything about this to anyone. I'll be in touch.

"As you can see," she said smiling coolly, "I'm really the only one you can trust in this family."

Before I could say anything, she pivoted on her heels like some marionette and marched out of the house to carry out her self-imposed mission.

My God, I thought, she's actually happy. She's going to use me as a wedge to drive my mother and Grant further and further apart, believing he will just spin around and fall gratefully into her waiting arms.

I got up slowly and followed her out to tell her I wouldn't be part of any plan to destroy my mother, but she was already gone, her car's engine a distant hum. Jake crossed the driveway.

"What'd she say?" he asked.

I looked at him.

"You're wrong, Jake," I told him.

"About what?"

"There's no way she could be your daughter."

Except for Aunt Victoria calling to tell me she had taken charge of the arrangements for Brody's funeral, I didn't hear from anyone over the next few days. Every day I expected my mother might call and babble incoherently, moving from self-blame to accusations. I was afraid of the phone ringing.

"It's lucky I decided to come here to help," Aunt Victoria told me. "Grant is still not in any condition to help himself and Megan is practically comatose most of the time. She's milking this for all it's worth."

"I doubt a mother losing her son would be milking for sympathy, Aunt Victoria," I told her.

"You don't know her like I know her. I can see that

Grant is disgusted with her. He hasn't said anything to anyone, but when I talk to him, I see it in his eyes.

"We're going to have the funeral at their local church and Brody will be buried in the Hudsons' portion of the cemetery. My mother would want that, don't you agree?" she asked.

Why was she trying to get me to be her ally in all this? I didn't want to agree with her about anything, not even the weather. I was silent.

"You're coming, of course," she said. "I've already discussed it with Jake."

"I don't know if I should," I nearly sobbed. Just the thought put ice in my blood.

"That wouldn't be nice," she said. "You are Brody's sister," she reminded me with relish.

"I don't think they'd want me there," I said.

"No one has said such a thing. If you don't come, you'll look like you are responsible," she emphasized.

That terrible thought curled up in my heart like a vicious, evil worm.

"It will generate more nasty gossip about you and the family and will hurt Grant even more," she continued. "You come, stay in the background, but show your face and express your sympathies," she ordered. "It's all arranged. Just dress properly.

"I've got to go. I'm the only one who can get Grant to take in a morsel of food. He's a shadow of himself. The house is full of mourners, most of them very important people. The story has been in all the papers. As dreadful as it all is, in the end, Grant will emerge even larger."

"How horrible," was all I could say to her, but she

wasn't prepared to hear anything that she didn't want to hear, especially from me.

"Out of tragedy, the truly great emerge. Make every setback a lesson and search for something to gain from it," she recited. "My father taught me that and I have never forgotten it. If you're wise, you'll listen to me."

"I've got to go. Good-bye," she said.

Mama would say, "That woman's got a chunk of coal in her chest where her heart should be."

Without Jake I wouldn't have been able to make it through the funeral. As we drove to the church that day, he talked about my grandmother and her ability to maintain her stature and class regardless of the situation.

"I must say," he told me, "I rarely, if ever, saw her flustered. Even when she told me she was pregnant, she spoke from strength."

I know he was telling me all this so that I wouldn't be afraid or panic, but when we approached the church, I couldn't believe the size of the crowd. Brody's former high-school teammates had all come down, dressed in their varsity blazers. Those closest to him were now his pallbearers.

Aunt Victoria greeted me and took me down the aisle to sit in the pews reserved for the immediate family. All eyes in that church had turned to me. I could feel the curiosity, the questions, the surprise pouring from them and washing over me. I tried to keep my own eyes locked on the altar, but the sight of Brody's coffin choked me up. I couldn't swallow; I could barely breathe.

Oh God, I thought, please don't let me faint or do anything to bring any more attention to me.

Grant did look gaunt, thinner, with dark circles around his eyes. My mother was obviously packed full of drugs.

She wavered, barely moving under her own strength. Victoria told me the woman beside her was a special duty nurse she, Victoria, had decided to hire.

"Grant thought it was a very good idea," she whispered as we moved into the row.

I must admit Alison looked terribly afraid and smaller to me. When she gazed at me, at first she didn't react. She watched Aunt Victoria and me settle in and then she turned away, gazed at the coffin, and finally looked back at me, her eyes now full of daggers.

My mother never lifted her head. The minister didn't attempt to make any sense of the tragedy. He confined his remarks to how lucky we all were to have had Brody with us for as long as we had. Except for Alison who smirked throughout the sermon, no one showed any reaction or emotion. Grant stared stoically ahead and my mother kept her head down, her eyes closed like someone just enduring, waiting for the pain to end.

The pallbearers took the coffin out of a side entrance and the funeral procession continued on to the cemetery. After Beneatha's death, when Mama and I had some quiet time together, she told me that you really don't believe someone you love is gone until the moment you see them lowered into the ground.

"It's that dust unto dust," she said. "That's what brings it home here," she explained slapping her palm against her breast so hard I winced anticipating her pain. "In church you keep thinking it's just a ceremony for someone else, but once you gaze into that grave, all denial falls away like some fortress wall you had built around yourself."

How those words rang true for me when we drove through the marble arches and stopped at the Hudsons' section. My mother crumbled, Grant fell to his knees and Alison became hysterical. Brody's teammates stood by, stunned by the reality, every young man's face turned back into a boy's face full of fear and shock. It couldn't end fast enough.

Aunt Victoria stood behind Grant. When his friends helped him to his feet, she was there trying to hold his hand. My mother had to be carried to the car. Finally, the worst was over. The long trip back to their home was a blessing. They could sleep in their limousine and restore some strength.

I wanted to go back home, but once again, Aunt Victoria insisted I go with the rest of the family.

"Either you're going to be a part of this family or you're not," she snapped at me when I started to protest. "You pay your respects decently."

I felt like I was being whipped around, but she made sure to add more guilt on my conscience.

Of course, I had never been to my mother's home. It wasn't as large as Grandmother Hudson's, nor was it on anywhere near as big a tract of land, but it was a very impressive estate of nearly seventy-five hundred square feet with a pool that had water cascading over fieldstone. There was a large gazebo and a long circular driveway lined with hedges and old-fashioned lamps. The house itself was a three-story Georgian. The entryway opened to a curved staircase on the left. To the right was a large living room, filled now with mourners. Aunt Victoria had arranged for the food and service. Grant had a large office toward the rear of the house and that was where he was greeting his friends. My mother was upstairs in bed.

I saw no point to my being here. I didn't know anyone,

and most people had no idea who I was. They didn't even know I had been living with Grandmother Hudson. I imagined they thought I was one of Alison's friends. She had a group from her school gathered around her in the den-library. I glanced in at them and quickly went by before Alison saw me. I didn't want to speak with her, if I could help it.

I wasn't sure I should say anything to Grant, but Victoria seized my hand and told me I should.

"Tell him how sorry you are," she instructed.

"What does he know about Brody's visiting me?"

"Megan didn't tell him much. I had to fill in the details," she said, closing her eyes as if it had given her great pain.

"What details?" I asked, my heart pounding. What did she tell him about me and about what had happened?

"The difficult situation you were in, of course," she said. "And not because of any fault of your own," she added, her eyes shifting toward the ceiling. I knew it was a gesture meant to point up to my mother's room and point the finger of accusation at her.

"Grant kept Brody in the dark, too," I snapped at Aunt Victoria.

"Not because he wanted to. Believe me," she said. "The poor man, the poor, poor man."

She stopped at the office doorway and practically turned me into the room. Grant was out of view, surrounded by his associates and friends. Some of them turned to look our way and then they parted and I saw Grant seated on a nailhead red leather sofa, a drink in his hand, his tie undone, his hair disheveled. He fixed his eyes on me, but didn't show any emotion or interest.

"Rain would like to express her deep sympathy to you, Grant," Victoria said approaching with me.

His eyebrows lifted and he studied my face, looking for proof of my sincerity.

"I'm sorry for your loss," I said. "I'm sorry that I didn't get to know Brody better."

He nodded, his eyes softening and then he closed them and leaned back.

"Do you need anything, Grant?" Aunt Victoria asked him.

He just shook his head.

She and I turned and left the room. On the way out she muttered, "He doesn't need anything except for a wife who can stand by him when he needs her the most."

I couldn't leave without seeing my mother, regardless of what Aunt Victoria told me about her being completely under sedation. I told Victoria.

"She won't even know you're there," she said. "Why waste your time?"

"It's far from a waste of time," I spit back at her and headed for the stairway. Aunt Victoria watched me a moment and then turned to go back to her self-appointed duties as surrogate wife.

I didn't know where to go upstairs, but I didn't have to because my mother's nurse was just coming out of the bedroom. She paused to greet me.

"May I help you?" she asked.

"I'd like to see Mrs. Randolph," I said.

"She's not seeing anyone just yet," she told me. "I'm sorry. I'm sure you understand." She gave me a plastic smile.

I flashed her a similar smile, turned and pretended to follow her down the stairs. When she walked into the living room, I stopped and went back up. I slowly opened my mother's bedroom door and peered in.

It was a very large bedroom with a sitting area that had a small sofa and reclining chair facing a television set. The large windows had light blue velvet drapes and gauzelike white curtains. The floor was covered in a butter-soft, thick dark blue carpet.

At first I didn't even see my mother. Her bed was custom made and larger than the ordinary king-size bed. It had tall, round posts, a footboard with an embossed rose and a headboard with two more roses crossing each other to symbolize lovers. Almost lost in the oversized pillows was my mother, her dark hair loose around her milky white face. The comforter was up to her chin. Her head was turned slightly away from me.

I closed the door softly behind me and walked to her. Her eyes were wide open, but even so she still looked like she was asleep.

"Mother," I said softly. "Mother."

She slowly turned to me and just stared with that blank look in her eyes.

"I want you to understand how I am really very sorry and sad about Brody."

I didn't think she was going to answer or that she had even heard me, but she suddenly shook her head and nearly smiled, her lips folding inward.

"Our sins," she whispered, "come back. You can try to bury them, to burn them, but they're out there, just waiting for an opportunity. Remember that. Remember."

I shook my head in opposition. She widened her eyes.

"You're the opportunity," she declared. "You came

back. It's in you. The darkness, the evil," she whispered. "It's in you."

Tears burned under my eyelids. I swallowed and shook my head.

"Yes, yes, you came out of the night. It's my fault, of course. It all started with Larry and my father. I heard you cry when you were born. Don't you think I've heard that cry again and again?

"I don't know where it will end," she said. "All I can do is wait. What did the minister know? If he knew the past, he would have shaken his finger at me and pointed to the coffin. I should be in that coffin, not Brody.

"The baby was crying," she said. "When they took the baby, she was crying. I knew it was wrong, but my daddy wouldn't listen."

"Mother, you're not making any sense. Listen to me…"

"All I can do is wait," she muttered and turned her head away. "Wait."

"Mother, you've got to get stronger," I told her. "Think about Grandmother Hudson. Think about Grant and Alison."

She closed her eyes. I stood there, looking at her for a few long moments and then decided it would be better if I spoke to her after some time had gone by. I reached out and touched her hair.

She smiled with her eyes closed.

"Mommy, is that you?" she asked. "I'm not afraid now. You can go back to sleep. It was just a bad dream. I boomed it just like Daddy said and it's gone."

"Good-bye," I whispered and left her room.

As I was descending the stairs, Alison appeared at the foot of them and gaped up at me with her hands on her hips, two of her girlfriends at side. One of them said, "I told you."

"What were you doing up there?" she demanded.

"Talking to your mother," I said. "You should be up there holding her hand and not visiting with your friends," I added and started for the front door.

She reached out and seized my arm, spinning me around.

"Why did you come here? You don't belong here. If Brody hadn't gone to see you, he'd still be alive."

"Think what you want." I pulled my arm free and walked out, but she followed me onto the portico, her girlfriends practically attached. Jake stepped forward from the Rolls in anticipation.

"You brain-washed my grandmother to give you so much," she spit at me, "but we'll get it all back. You'll see. We're getting it all back!"

I didn't respond, continuing toward the car.

"You're some kind of freak, you know that? Just some kind of freak! You don't belong anywhere near our family. My daddy will get rid of you, just wait.

"That's my grandmother's car," she shouted when Jake opened the door for me. "You don't belong in it. You belong in the back of a pickup truck. You belong in hell!"

I turned and looked back at her. Her braces glittered in the sunlight that slipped through the narrow opening in the increasingly overcast sky, and her eyes looked like two little marble balls with little black circles at the centers. She had her hands clenched into fists and she had stiffened her body in defiance.

The blood that we shared surely was in retreat in both our bodies, I thought. I couldn't imagine ever having a warm moment between us.

Whose fault was that? Mine? My mother's? My grandfather's? Ken's?

Maybe it was a combination of everyone tossing his or her self-interest into the fragile boat of love, sinking it in the sea of tragedy we were destined to cross together.

We might all drown.

At this point I didn't care. I didn't care at all.

6

Never the Same

The weather, which had been threatening all day, finally changed for the worse. About an hour or so before we had reached home, the rain came. The sky burst open. Sheets of wind-swept drops whipped across Jake's windshield. The wipers were barely able to provide Jake with a clear enough view of the highway. All around me, the deluge of water streaked the windows, carving streams of tears in the glass. I could almost hear the sky crying over the monotonous sweep of the wipers and the hum of the tires on the wet pavement. Other cars rushed by, their headlights on, everyone looking like he or she was driving in a panic.

"We're getting a big one," Jake muttered.

I had curled up in a corner of the rear seat and closed my eyes, opening them only when we heard the clap of thunder rolling over the roof of the car. The fast-falling drops sounded more like pebbles being heaved on us. A streak of thick lightning on our right seemed to singe the very air. Low clouds resembled smoke rising out of the trees and meadows, even rising from the houses that we rushed by.

Maybe it was the end of the world, I thought. Maybe the events in my life were so severe, Nature decided to throw in the towel and start someplace else, on another planet, perhaps, where life would evolve into people far less cruel to each other and themselves, and especially Nature.

Jake tried to cheer me up by describing some of the fun he had had in storms when he was younger, especially a time when he was once caught in a sailboat with a girl-friend he had told he was an expert sailor just so she would go out with him.

"Ever hear the expression, *Caught in the web of your own deceit?* Well, I turned that sunfish over three times, soaking us both, until finally I had to confess I didn't know how to get us back to shore. She bawled the hell out of me and finally when we were in shallow enough water, we walked the boat in. You wouldn't think a kid so awkward in the water like that would end up in the navy, would you? But I did.

"Every time that girl saw me afterward, her eyes would get wide and crazy, she'd hunch up her shoulders and scream, 'Who are you trying to drown these days, Captain Marvin?' "

I felt myself smile, but I didn't laugh. Jake was watching me in the rearview mirror.

"I guess I was never exactly a candidate for the Don Juan award. The female animal has always been a mystery to me."

"It's all a mystery to me, Jake," I finally said.

"Well, maybe the trick is not to spend so much time worrying about it, Princess. Maybe the trick is to just push forward and leave those questions to priests, philosophers and teachers, huh?"

"Maybe," I admitted. After a long silence between us, I said, "Next time Victoria comes around, I think I'll just give in to everything, Jake. There's no mystery about that. I don't belong here."

"Hey, forget that idea. You belong here just as much as anyone."

"I don't think I belong anywhere at the moment, Jake."

"You'll change your mind in the morning," he said. "When this storm clears, we'll take Rain out. She's overdue. She's been asking after you," he continued. That brought another smile to my face. "She lifts that hoof and stomps and neighs and twists her head and peers out of the stable looking for you. I can tell. I speak horse."

"Okay, Jake," I said laughing. "Until I leave, I'll ride her for you."

"For you, too. And for her," he corrected.

The rain didn't let up before we reached the house. In fact, the storm seemed to grow stronger. Trees were being bent in the wind to the point just before they would snap. Many branches had broken and were already scattered over the driveway and the street. Jake said he would call the grounds people in the morning and have them come up as soon as the weather permitted.

"You want me to do anything for you, Princess?" he asked when he came to a stop in front of the house.

"No, Jake. There's nothing to do. I just want to get some rest."

"Have some of that hot tea you call MIF," he suggested.

"Right."

"I'll call in the morning," he said. "You know how to reach me if you need me."

"Thanks, Jake. Don't get out and get wet for me. Just take the car home," I said. "I'm not going anywhere for a while. That's for sure," I said. I opened the door, but I didn't try to open the umbrella. I was confident the wind would take it out of my hands or break it if I did.

Instead, I charged out, slammed the door behind me and ran up to the portico. I turned at the door and saw Jake take a swig from his silver liquor flask before starting away. Everyone has his or her own way to face loneliness, I thought, but I wished Jake had found some other way.

It was terribly dark and cold in the house. I went from room to room turning on all the lights and then I went to the kitchen and heated some soup for myself. I started a fire in the fireplace in the sitting room, brought in my bowl of soup, and stared into the flames.

The wind howled around the house, twisting and turning itself to slam at the shutters and windows and make itself sound like hundreds of horses stampeding on the roof. I got a blanket and sprawled out on the sofa, permitting the fire to throw its warmth on my face. One question loomed above all others for me. Why? Why had I been brought to this house? For me it had yet to prove to be a safe harbor, a refuge, a sanctuary. Was fate just playing with me now? Was I being used to tease and torment this family, a family I certainly didn't ask to be born into? I fell asleep, haunted by the questions.

The storm lingered over the next few days and except for Jake checking in on me from time to time, I heard from no one. The days dragged by monotonously as I waited for the skies to clear and events to work themselves out. It was hard. What do you do with yourself, with time when you have it in superabundance? What direction should your thoughts take when daydreams could lead you into so much sad territory?

I tried to occupy myself with reading, watching television, listening to music. Finally, the storm moved away and the ground began to dry. A day later I heard from Aunt Victoria, who told me she had been very busy helping Grant make a transition from tragedy back to a productive life. When I asked her about my mother, she simply said she's unchanged.

"We're deciding how to handle that. I don't know if private therapy will be enough and neither does Grant," she told me with an ominous undertone.

What new plot was she hatching? Should I care?

She told me she would be by in two days with the paperwork she had promised earlier. I didn't tell her that I had come to a decision she would like very much. I had finally decided to leave and give them all what they had wanted. I told Jake I shouldn't have been so stubborn about it. I should have accepted the compromise and gone back to England. Brody would still be alive.

He hated that talk and told me I was not right to blame myself again and again. Finally, he stopped arguing about it. Instead, he talked me into taking Rain for a ride, now that the weather permitted it. I could see clearly what he hoped would happen and I didn't deny that I hoped it myself: his beautiful horse would bring me some peace and contentment.

The rides were practically the only thing I looked forward to doing. Rain became more and more comfortable with me and I started to believe in Jake's descriptions of the horse anxiously anticipating my arrival. As strange as it might seem, she was the only living thing that really seemed to love me now and riding her was the best way to escape from my dark depression.

Every time we reached the crest of that hill, Rain would expect me to stop and dismount. She would graze on some grass and I would sit on a rock and look out at the land, Grandmother Hudson's house, and the beautiful horizon. I would tell myself that ordinarily, considering where I had come from and what I had been through growing up, I should feel lucky. I should cherish all this and fight hard not to lose it, but the wall of tragedy was too tall and too wide and too heavy.

It's just not meant to be, I told myself. Run away. Stop fighting it.

As she had promised, Aunt Victoria came to see me with a stack of papers. I sat listening numbly when she described the different investments, legal documents, the reissuing of certificates, on and on, a gobbledygook of business information that clouded my tired and confused brain. Maybe I was more like my mother than I had imagined. Maybe, like her, I just wanted someone to do all this for me and not bother with anything practical.

In the middle of her endless stream of financial information, I put up my hands like someone seeking to surrender.

"I don't care about all that," I said. "I want to go back to England as soon as possible. You were right."

She stared at me a moment and then she nodded and smiled.

"So, you want me to go ahead and sell the property?"

"Do whatever has to be done," I said.

"What about all this?" she said nodding at the pile of papers.

"I don't want to be part of it. Tell Grant I'll accept his offer."

She didn't speak, but I could see from the way her face blossomed, her eyes filling with glee, that she was overwhelmed with happiness. Now she could go to him and say, "See how good I am for you. See how I do what I promise."

I didn't care. If Grant was going to be snared by her conniving ways, he deserved it. I wanted to be as far away and as uninvolved in this family as I could be so I couldn't be blamed for that, too.

She took a breath and started to gather up all the documents.

"Very well. I'll go back to our attorney and inform him of this change," she said. "You're being very sensible, sensible indeed. In the end you'll be far happier."

"I'm already happier," I told her.

She looked like she was going to laugh, but just nodded and smiled instead.

The next day I received a letter from my father in England. It was the most exciting thing that had happened to me in a long time. I just sat there staring at the envelope, terrified and yet exhilarated. What would I do if he had written that after thinking it all over, he and his wife had decided it was probably best for all involved if I didn't contact them anymore? After all, look at all the new and complicated problems I was bringing along in my luggage? Yet, who else did I have?

My fingers trembled as I tore open the envelope and slipped the letter out. He had written it on his school stationery, most likely while he was at work. Did he do it there because he didn't want Leanna to know?

* * *

Dear Rain,

What a wonderful surprise it was to hear from you, even though I could see from your letter that you are very troubled. I'm glad you wrote to me at such a time. I have no reason to expect it and I certainly don't deserve it.

How presumptuous it would be for me to offer you any advice at all. I don't know all the details about your situation back there. I can't even begin to imagine what it all must be like for you. Is the secret of your birth completely revealed, for example? Or is it still some skeleton hanging in a closed Hudson family closet?

Maybe none of that matters anyway. The point is you are obviously not being accepted with open arms. I suppose you are like a small boat adrift in a wild sea, being tossed and turned and desperate for some sanctuary.

Long ago, I decided that there were things more important to me than just making a lot of money. I suppose that was a consequence of all my rebellion and protest. Corporations, big successful businesses and businessmen and women were the enemy willing to sacrifice and destroy the smaller and weaker to pursue the almighty dollar.

So you have the opportunity to be very wealthy, even wealthier if you defy the family. Still what happiness will you gain after defeating them? I suppose that should be your guiding principle. Will Megan ever accept you fully? Will her husband? Will your aunt Victoria? Any of them?

Most likely they will resent you even more.

You ask me to give you advice. I'll dare to do so. Compromise and come back. Pursue your interests here and give me the opportunity to become the father I never was. Leanna agrees. It will be strange for my children at first, but in time, I think they'll learn to accept you and understand.

You can always return to America and another life.

If you take this letter, crumble it up and throw it in the garbage, I'll understand. If I never hear from you again, I'll understand. As I said, I have no right to any expectations.

In Julius Caesar, *Shakespeare wrote that the eye sees not itself but by reflection. Find a way to look into yourself, Rain. The answers are all there, waiting.*

Just like me.

> *Love,*
> *Your father*

I didn't even feel the tears streaming down my cheeks. They surprised me when they reached my chin. I wiped them aside and sat back, thinking of my father. It was the first time in weeks that I had felt any hope. I decided to write back immediately and tell him I had decided, even before his letter had arrived, to return as quickly as I could. I had decided to turn my back on this family and take what some would rightfully call reparations, compensation and restitution for the pain and suffering I endured and still endured. Without shame, I would complete the negotiation for my money and I would leave. The only one I would truly miss was Jake and, of course, riding Rain.

While I waited for Aunt Victoria to get all the business papers in order with the family's attorney, I spent more time doing just that. Jake brought me to the stables earlier and I helped feed and care for Rain. I took longer rides, deciding to go off right and make our own paths through the woods and then through other meadows, nearly reaching my grandmother's property line before starting back.

Jake said I was doing wonderfully and Rain was getting stronger, leaner.

"You two are really a pair now," he told me. He brought Mick Nelsen, the trainer, around to watch us and once I joined Mick while he rode his horse. Rain seemed unhappy, maybe jealous. She twisted and turned her neck and seemed to pout, trotting with her head down and only occasionally stealing a glance of the other horse, who was indifferent.

When Rain and I parted from Mick and his horse before returning to the stables, a change came over Rain. She lifted her head proudly and regained her energy. Reluctant to end the ride now, she actually tried to get me to start again. Jake laughed later when I described her behavior.

"Just like a woman," he said. "She wants your undivided attention."

That night Aunt Victoria called to tell me she would be over late the next afternoon and she would bring their attorney along to explain every detail.

"We don't want you to think anything is being done surreptitiously," she said. "No lawsuits five years down the road, if you please."

"Fine," I told her. "I'll be here."

I told Jake I had to be back by two. It was a day I shall never forget. I relive each detail like some meticulous detective searching for a clue, an answer, a reason. What could I have done differently? If I had lingered ten more minutes over my breakfast or not been so efficient when I had gotten to the stables, would the events of the day have been changed? Could I have prevented what happened?

Was I being punished for defying Fate or Grandmother Hudson's wishes? Who was I to dare to think I was master of my own destiny? I was forced into this world, into this body and soul, given this name and all these thoughts, and pulled out of the great body of God to be born unwanted. And now, I had the audacity to think I could make it all right?

And then of course, there was Brody, lingering in my mind like an extra shadow, a soul for whom I bore eternal responsibility, a soul that demanded satisfaction.

As soon as we drove up to the stables, Mick approached.

"Your horse Rain—she's anxious today," he said. "Hyper as I've ever seen her. You're going to have to move in with her," he told me, jokingly. "She don't like you not being here when she wants you."

"Is she all right?" Jake asked suspiciously.

"Yeah. Just give her a little longer warmup. It might be the crisp air. Makes 'em impatient to get those muscles flexed, their blood movin'."

I walked Rain around the track. She snorted and whinnied and tugged at me moving her head toward her rear to say, get that saddle on and let's stop this nonsense. It made Mick laugh, but Jake kept his eyes small, his face full of concern.

"She is more rambunctious. Let Mick take her out today, Rain," he told me.

"What? Why?"

"I don't like the way she's acting. Mick?"

"Okay by me," he said.

Disappointed, I watched him saddle and put the bridle on. Rain kept her eyes on me. Even Mick noticed.

"She knows somethin's up, Jake."

"Yeah," he said finally smiling.

When Mick sat in the saddle, she actually bucked. It took Mick by surprise and he nearly spilled. Embarrassed, he pulled up on the reins firmly. She snorted, twisted and pounded the ground with her left hoof. Mick turned her and made her trot forward, but she kept stopping, fighting him and trying to turn back toward me.

"I'll be damned," he said.

Jake looked at me and then at Rain. Finally he nodded.

"All right. You can take her out," he relented.

Those words would later drive him into the darkness of excessive drink and eventually an early grave.

Happy, I hurried to get into the saddle. The moment I did so, Rain calmed down and waited obediently.

"Make it a short one," Jake instructed. "Just once around the smaller circle, okay?"

"Okay, Jake." We started out. "I'm going to miss you, Rain," I told her as we moved gracefully onto the path. "If I come back to visit, will you remember me?"

Whenever I spoke to her, Rain had a way of rocking her head from side to side as if she really understood. It brought a smile back to my face. I ran my hand through my hair, closed my eyes to feel the wind, and let her have her head. She broke into a run and we were off. As always, I felt like she and I had become one animal, our movements coordinated. We established a graceful rhythm. I was sure that Jake and Mick were smiling and nodding their heads as well. I knew they were watching me longer than they usually did. Jake was still nervous when I had left.

The heavy storm we had the days before had scattered some leaves and twigs over the meadow. Some of the dampness brought out rodents and other creatures excited with the sudden unexpected rebirth of bugs. Just at the foot of the crest where we would either go forward, up and then down to complete what Jake called the smaller circle, the path now forked to the right as well because of the rides I had taken with Rain in that direction. Marking the cross-roads was a small scattering of rocks and some dead treetrunks.

Once Mick had told me about keeping an eye out for snakes, especially copperheads.

"They are almost impossible to see anyway," he said, "because their coloring allows them to blend in, especially with fallen trees. But," he assured me, "like almost all snakes, they are not aggressive. Live and let live is their motto. The problem is horses don't know that. So try to steer clear of places where snakes might house them-selves."

He meant rocks and logs. Usually, I stayed pretty far to the right or to the left of the markers, but I was distracted myself and in deep thought about my decisions. Normally, Rain would steer clear on her own, but copperheads, as Mick told me in his colorful language, "make their living being practically invisible. They won't move until they have to. You could step right on a copperhhead and not know it."

Rain's hoof did exactly that. Copperheads, especially the young ones, leave their tails out so other animals they pursue as prey will be attracted, thinking the tail is a lizard or something and come close enough for the copperhead to strike. Rain stepped on the tail and the snake spun around. It didn't strike Rain, but the sight of it, put a panic through her that vibrated right up my legs and into my heart.

She bucked and twisted in a frantic effort to stay clear of the snake's thrusting head and the turn she made was so abrupt and sharp, I lost my grip and flew out of the saddle. I don't even remember hitting the ground.

All I remember is a whack on my head and lower back and then, all was dark.

When I opened my eyes again, I was looking up at a bright ceiling fixture in a hospital emergency room. I heard people moving around me, the sound of running water, a pan being placed on a sink counter. A whirl of white uniforms went by before I saw the face of a concerned middle-aged doctor. He had very thin, gray hair and eyes that looked swollen with worry. There was a small red spot on the bridge of his nose, probably made by his reading glasses.

"Hello there," he said and smiled.

"Where am I?" I whispered. It sounded far away, like a voice in a tunnel.

"You're at the hospital. You had an accident. Can you remember anything about it?" he asked.

I told him as much as I knew, but I felt groggy and nauseated. My body felt distant, too.

"Well, that blow to your head gave you a concussion. It's not a serious one. It will get better," he promised.

He lingered over me, his smile sliding off his face.

"I'd like you to lift your left leg for me," he said.

"Lift it?"

He nodded and I tried to lift my leg, but I didn't feel anything. Nothing happened.

"Now try your right," he said and I did the same thing. He nodded. "Can you feel that?" he asked.

"What?"

He straightened up.

"What's wrong with me?"

"When you fell from the horse, you also struck your

lower back. We're going to have to transport you to Richmond where they have the medical facilities to properly evaluate and treat spinal cord injuries."

"Spinal cord?"

"The faster we get you moved, the better chance you'll have for some recovery," he added.

The word *some* hung in the air like a soap bubble threatening to pop and disappear.

"No," I cried.

"Just relax," he said. "I'll send in your father," he added.

My father? Was I hearing things?

Seconds later, Jake stepped into the room, his hat in his hands, his face looking like he had aged years. Every crevice was deeper, his eyes dark and full of pain, the folds in his forehead thick.

"How you doin', Princess?" he asked.

"Jake, I can't move my legs."

He nodded.

"I don't know why I let you get on her. Every instinct told me it was going to be bad," he muttered.

"Now, who's blaming himself for things beyond his control?" I tossed back at him. I had to keep closing my eyes because the room wanted to spin.

"I should have known better. I'm older, more experienced."

"Don't, Jake." I thought a moment. "Did you tell the doctor you were my father?"

"Yeah. It made all the paperwork easier for now. These places..." he mumbled.

I opened my eyes and reached up for his hand.

"You are already more of a father to me than I've ever had, Jake," I said.

He pressed his lower lip under his upper, tightening his jaw. There is something about tears coming into the eyes of a grown man that makes me feel even deeper sadness. I know that no one should be beyond feeling and crying if he or she needs to, but someone like Jake who has seen a great many things in his life and survived so much trouble just looked like he was too rock solid to mourn anything in public.

"I'll go see about the ambulance," he said and quickly left but not before I saw a fugitive tear travel down those toughened cheeks.

It was a very uncomfortable ride. I had to be strapped tightly to keep my movement to a minimum, not that I was about to get up and dance. Even lifting my head an inch off the pillow put me on a merry-go-round. I welcomed my intermittent naps.

The trauma center in Richmond was busy, but efficient. Once I was handed over to the doctors there, they quickly made a diagnosis. They evaluated my lungs and then concentrated on my spinal injury. I was given a neurological examination, tests of my reflexes and then put through a series of other tests and machines to determine just how bad the injury was.

It all seemed like a blur and before I knew it, I was in a hospital room, waiting. Two doctors appeared in the doorway. They conversed softly with each other first and then approached the bed. One was much older than the other, gray-haired but with bright blue eyes and a kind face. The younger man had dark brown hair and hazel eyes. He looked more like a scientist than a doctor. I didn't feel he was looking at me as much as he was looking at a medical problem.

"I'm Doctor Eisner," the older man said. "This is Doctor Casey, my assistant." He smiled and looked at his clipboard. "So your name is Rain?"

"Yes," I said. I felt my lips move, but I spoke so softly, I didn't hear myself.

"Interesting name," he remarked. "Well, my dear, here's what we know about your injury. You've had damage to an area on your spinal cord we describe as L3 and L4." He turned the clipboard revealing a diagram of the human spine.

"As you see," he continued, his voice sounding like that of a teacher, "the spinal cord is about eighteen inches long and extends from the base of the brain, down the middle of the back, to about the waist. There are nerves that lie within the spinal cord. We call them UMNs, upper motor neurons, and their function is to carry the messages back and forth from the brain to the spinal nerves along the spinal tract. These nerves that branch out from the spinal cord to the other parts of the body are called LMNs." He smiled. "Lower motor neurons. They communicate with the various areas of the body, send messages to initiate actions, like muscle movement. Understand so far?"

I nodded, holding my breath.

"The spinal cord," he said pointing to it, "is surrounded by rings of bone called vertebra. In general, the higher the injury in the spinal cord, the more dysfunction a person will experience. So, if you follow down with me," he said running his pen along the diagram, "you can see that your injury is thankfully below the areas that would have negative impact on your breathing, your upper body. Your injury is confined to your legs.

"Now," he said quickly, before I could ask anything, "we have determined that what you have is what we call an incomplete injury, which means there is some function

139

below the primary level of the injury. We believe you will be able to move your right leg some. You will, in time, be able to put some weight on it and help yourself in and out of your wheelchair."

"Wheelchair?" I cried.

"Yes," he said holding that kind, soft smile. His assistant just stared at me, making me feel more uncomfortable.

"Why? Did I break my spinal cord?"

"Well," Dr. Eisner said widening his smile, "it isn't necessary to break it to have problems. Usually we find them crushed or badly bruised. Doctor Casey can explain it to you," he said looking at the younger doctor.

The younger man cleared his throat and smirked instead of smiling. He spoke very nasally, as if the words came out of his nostrils rather than his mouth.

"The spinal cord swells. Blood pressure drops sharply in the damaged area, starving cells of their blood supply. Hemorrhaging begins in the center of the cord and spreads outward. Dying nerve cells produce scar tissue and the connections in the cord are broken. The result is paralysis," he concluded emotionlessly.

"I'm permanently paralyzed?"

"Below the waist," Doctor Eisner said. I guessed that to him that sounded like it was better than it could have been. "We are still evaluating your bladder," he concluded.

I didn't speak. I could see he was watching me carefully for my reaction.

"Will I die?" I asked him finally.

"Oh no, no," he assured me.

I wished he had said, "Of course."

* * *

For days afterward, I was poked and prodded and explored with electrical impulses. Doctors studied every part of me. I felt like a lump of meat, but I didn't complain nor did I speak very much. If I was asked about a feeling and I did feel it, I told them; if I didn't, I told them, too. That was all. I didn't carry on conversations with the nurses or the interns. They tried to get me to talk, but I just stared.

My concussion improved and I was soon able to lift my head with more ease. I could feed myself, not that I had much of an appetite. They always turned on the television set for me, but I didn't really listen or look. It was like a big bulb with shadows.

Jake came to see me every day. He was staying with a friend in Richmond. He brought me candy and magazines. The sudden aging that had come into his face right after my accident got a strong foothold. I even thought his hair was graying faster. His shoulders were always stooped some and he had trouble looking directly at me. It was as if he expected I would turn my eyes on him with accusations.

The only thing that attracted my curiosity was what my reluctant family was doing and how they were reacting to these surprising events.

"Victoria is frustrated and confused, of course. All her plans are put on hold now, maybe forever," Jake told me.

"I don't care about that," I told him.

"Yeah, well, until you're better, you have to care. You'll need all the financial support you have and you can't give up a nickel, understand? I've taken the liberty of speaking to Mr. Sanger and he's on top of it."

"Get better? I won't get better, Jake. Didn't you talk to the doctors?"

"Sure you've got some work ahead of you, but therapy will get you stronger and…"

"And I'll always be in a wheelchair," I said.

I knew why he had to pretend, but I couldn't.

"Don't blame Rain," I told him. He looked at me. I could see something had changed. "What did you do, Jake? You didn't hurt her, did you?"

"Of course not, but I decided to sell her," he told me. "What am I doing with a horse like that anyway?"

I looked away. Maybe my name was a curse. Giving that beautiful horse my name had doomed her, too. Now, she would suffer without fault, suffer just because she had been born. No wonder we had gotten along so well.

"You shouldn't do that, Jake."

He continued to look down for a moment and then he lifted his eyes. They were so bloodshot, the tiny veins in them crisscrossing brightly.

"I got a call from Grant," he said.

"Oh?"

"He asked after you. They haven't told Megan anything yet."

"It won't make any difference to her. Tell them not to bother. Tell them…it doesn't make any difference to me anymore either," I said.

Jake looked at me, then out the window.

"You don't have to keep coming here, Jake. I know you'd rather go home."

"Hey, don't tell me that," he said. "I'm not leaving you here by yourself."

"I've got to get used to that, Jake. Who's going to want to be with me now?"

"Now don't talk like that," he ordered. "Frances would be very..."

"Sorry she had ever taken me in," I finished for him. "If I ever was a burden before, I'm a burden now."

Jake stepped closer to the bed and seized my hand. He squeezed it firmly.

"You're going to get better, Princess. I'm not going to let you fade away. You'd better get used to having me on your back," he threatened.

I stared up at him. His eyes brightened and then grew dim. I felt sorry for him.

"Okay, Jake," I offered. "Do what you want."

"Right," he said. "I'll be back with more information tomorrow. You just make up your mind we're going to beat this," he said.

He smiled.

"I mean, how can you disappoint Victoria? If you don't get better, she can't go after your fortune, right? How would that look now? She's stuck. Have some pity on her, will you," he joked.

I had to smile.

It felt good, almost like cracking open a surprise package.

Then they wheeled in my chair.

Reminding me that smiles and laughter were like precious antiques. You could dust them off, but they had no more function except to lie there on the shelves to help us recall a time more beautiful, a time when there was still something called hope.

7

Going Home

A week later, the stone-faced Doctor Casey appeared with a mousy nurse. When he spoke to her, she didn't face him, but held her head straight so that it seemed like she was gazing at me while her eyes lifted until they were almost under her lids and then turned toward him. It was as if she had to sneak a look or as if he was someone of great royalty who couldn't be looked upon directly.

He went through his usual examination. His wearing those plastic gloves when he touched me made me feel contaminated enough, but when he finished and stepped back from the bed abruptly as if he had been in and out of a bed of disease, I felt absolutely infectious.

"Doctor Eisner and I have completed our evaluation of your condition," he began with that thin, nasal tone. He held his narrow neck stiffly when he spoke, his hazel eyes unmoving. He made me think of a life-size puppet as his jaw worked the words *fate* itself wove over that dark pink tongue. "Therapy will enable you to strengthen your legs and keep the musculature from atrophying. However, until a new, more promising treatment for spinal injuries is discovered, you will be at your threshold of recovery.

"As you know, you will have occasional painful muscle spasms. If you are not properly active, pressure sores will develop. Reduced mobility and poorer blood circulation can give rise to troublesome skin ulcers. You'll have to get into the habit of inspecting your skin daily.

"Bathe daily and dry throughly, especially between your toes and in the groin area. The therapist will give you a self-care handbook with instructions to follow. Be sure you understand it all before you are discharged," he said.

"I'm being discharged?"

"From this section of the hospital, yes," he said. "There isn't much more we can do for you here. We're going to transfer you to the physical therapy department. They'll start you on a program that you will continue for the rest of your life," he added dryly. It sounded like a jail sentence falling from the lips of some severe judge.

He made notes on my chart and then handed it back to the nurse. She glanced at me, smiled, and waited.

"Do you have any questions?" he asked.

Questions? That's all I had, I thought. For example, what would have happened if Ken Arnold had taken us to a different city to live after I was born? What would have happened to me if Beneatha had not gotten involved with gang members and been killed and Mama had not gotten so sick? What would have happened if I had never learned the truth about myself? What would have happened if I had overslept and missed that last ride on Rain?

I looked at the doctor. He seemed anxious to have a

question thrown at him, as anxious as some whiz kid who wanted to prove his intelligence.

"When do I wake up?" I asked.

"Excuse me?" The doctor looked puzzled.

His nurse raised her thin, dark brown eyebrows and relaxed her small mouth.

"Forget it," I said. "You can't get answers from people in your nightmares."

"Oh," he said making a small circle with those pale lips. He had only just realized my suffering went deeper than the places he could prod and poke, even with his x-ray machines. "Doctor Snyder will be in to see you in a little while. She's our psychologist," he said. "Good luck," he added and turned.

His nurse patted my hand. I gazed at her with a look that made her pivot faster than a marionette and follow the doctor quickly out of my room. I stared at the bland, egg white wall. Since the accident, I wasn't sleeping well. I would doze off and wake up constantly. I did that now and when I woke this time, I heard a female voice, say, "Hi."

Slowly, I turned my head, expecting the nurse to be adjusting something and was surprised to see that the woman speaking to me was seated...in a wheelchair.

"I'm Doctor Snyder," she said.

She held out her hand for me to shake. I just looked at it and her. She pulled it back.

"I see from the look of surprise on your face that Doctor Casey neglected to tell you anything about me. I don't know why I should be astonished about that. Actually," she continued, changing her expression as if she was talking to her own therapist in a session, "I should be happy about that. He doesn't see me as anything more or less than who

I am…a psychologist, not a paraplegic psychologist, and that's what we all want, isn't it?

"You will want people to see you for you too. Someday," she added.

"No one could see the real me, even before the accident. Why should I expect they will now?" I replied.

She lifted her right eyebrow like an exclamation point and smiled.

Actually, she had a very pretty face framed in strawberry red hair, cut and styled so it swept up around her small chin. Despite her condition, her blue-green eyes were dazzling, full of life and excitement. Tiny freckles peppered the crests of her cheeks and then dripped down very slightly toward her jaw bone, but she had a rich creamy complexion. Her lips were so ruby, she didn't need any lipstick. Looking at her face, anyone would think this is one of the healthiest, happiest people he or she had ever seen.

She wore a robin's egg blue sweater with a white blouse and a dark blue skirt. Heart-shaped diamond studs twinkled in her lobes. A gold locket rested comfortably between her small breasts.

"I know it's of little consolation to you right now, but a few inches higher and that injury you sustained would have left you far worse off than you are." She smiled again and gazed past me, toward her own memories and thoughts. "My father once told me we should measure ourselves against our own actions and fate and not against someone else's. Instead of thinking there are so many people better off than you are, he said, think how much better off you are now than you could have been if…

"That *If* hangs above everyone's head, Ainsley," he said.

She lowered her chin and dropped her voice in an imitation of her father.

"Ainsley?"

"Yes. My father insisted that my mother and he find an uncommon name. Looks like your mother and father did the same. Rain?"

"It was supposed to mean good things," I said.

"So it will; it can. Let me take a wild stab," she said leaning back and pretending to think hard, "you've been lying here wondering why me? What did I do?"

"Not exactly," I replied.

"Oh? That's a switch. Finally, someone who thinks she deserves it?"

"I didn't say that. I'm just not all that surprised," I added.

She had a wonderful intense look. Her eyes just filled with interest, but not the way Doctor Casey's did. Hers were warm, excited in a way that made me feel like I was someone important, a discovery.

"Care to tell me why?" she asked.

"I don't know if I have the time," I said. "I'll check my appointment book."

She laughed.

"What happened to you?" I asked her. "And don't tell me you fell off a horse."

"No. I've never really ridden a horse. I've gotten on ponies at fairs is all. I'm a city girl. I was in a bad car accident. A tractor-trailer ran over my car nearly four years ago. They had to cut me out of it. Remember what I said about the big *If?*"

"Are you sure you're better off than you could have been?" I asked dryly.

"I'm still happily married. I have two teenage daughters

who keep me from feeling sorry for myself, and I have a successful career. Also, I love pizza, and from what I've been told by psychics, there isn't any on the other side. You don't even want it!"

I stared at her a moment and then I laughed. The sound of it was so surprising, I just let it go on a little longer.

"So," she said settling in her wheelchair. "Tell me your story."

She was a good listener, never looking like her thoughts were wandering or like she was thinking why did I start with this girl in the first place? She asked many questions and made some notes in a small pad. Maybe I was starved for conversation. Maybe I had been shut up in my own mental dungeon too long, but I found what seemed like un-limited verbal energy. It felt good, too, good to get it all out. It was like puncturing a swollen spot on my body and watching all the pus leak out. I skipped around, of course, and tried to include only the events and people that had the most significance.

Finally I paused and looked at her. The smile was gone and in its place was the dark, serious expression of some-one who had just heard she had lost her best friend.

"Sorry you asked?" I questioned.

"No. Actually, I'm grateful you're so forthcoming. Most of my patients make me feel like a dentist. Pulling teeth," she added when I looked puzzled.

"Oh."

"You know, sometimes, often, it's much, much harder for someone who has a relatively easy life, to contend with such a difficult setback. You've been through so much, I feel confident you're going to do well."

"Sure," I said. "I'm just a chip off the old tragedy."

She laughed.

"You're already ahead. You've got a sense of humor."

"It's not humor. It's disguised disgust," I said. Suddenly, I was feeling tired. I closed my eyes.

"I'll let you rest now, but I'll be back to see you tomorrow and we'll talk again. They're moving you to the physical therapy department, you know."

"Right. I'll be remade."

"The most difficult thing for us is the realization that our once whole and healthy bodies are no longer fully functional and we're now plagued with a myriad of secondary problems with which to contend."

"Don't just give me the good news," I said. She laughed.

"I won't. What you're doing now, your reaction to all this is your self-defense. Learning to accept this condition and coping is almost as devastating as the actual accident was. No one wants to be dependent on other people."

"Me especially," I muttered.

"But believe me, the rehabilitation program will help you become independent. Just don't fight it. Learn, listen, be willing to try and you'll regain your self-confidence and become a productive member of society again, Rain. I know dozens and dozens of paraplegics who are."

"Jeez, I'm so lucky. I just don't realize it yet, huh?"

She smiled.

"No, you don't. Remember my father's *If*," she reminded me and turned around in her chair.

I watched her roll herself out and away.

That's me, I thought. That's me from now on until the day I die.

I turned my face into the pillow, wishing I could hold myself down and stop myself from breathing.

They moved me to rehabilitation that evening. Early the next morning, a team of therapists greeted me and explained their roles in my program. They kept me so busy, I almost didn't have time to feel sorry for myself. There were other patients with similar injuries around me, most as Doctor Synder had said, with far more severe damage. Seeing the quadriplegic patients brought that home clearly. I was amazed at how most of them continued and worked on their therapy activities.

When Doctor Synder returned, we talked about it and she seemed almost proud of them. It was as though we were a people unto ourselves now, and what each individual accomplished reflected on the whole group of us.

"Every time you feel like giving up," she said, "think about them. The truth, Rain, is that the vast majority of paraplegics do adjust well, as you will," she predicted with confidence. "You'll drive a car, you'll have a full social life and if you want, you'll have a family, too."

"A family?" I had to laugh at that. "Who'd want me for a wife?"

"Someone who falls in love with you," she said simply.

"Sure."

I had yet to write and tell my father in London or Roy what had happened to me. Deep down I think I was hoping I would pass away during the night and I wouldn't have to tell anyone, but as more and more time went by, I realized it would have to be done soon. What I didn't want was their pity. Doctor Synder and I talked about that and she said, "Just make sure you tell them how well you're doing in therapy and you won't get their pity. Of course," she added, "you'd better make sure you do well."

"That sounds like blackmail," I told her and she laughed and said whatever works for you.

I grew to like her. Just the thought of leaving her made me afraid of leaving the rehabilitation center. When I expressed that, she said it was flattering, but she didn't want me to feel that way.

"Don't become dependent on anyone, Rain. Fight that and you'll always have your self-respect. I've got a van I drive. The side goes down and I can roll myself in and out. I don't even need anyone to open the door for me. Guess what happened to me last week," she said with a proud smile.

"What?"

"I got a speeding ticket. The officer pulled me over, told me I was going fifty in a thirty-five. I told him I missed the sign, but he said I should be more alert and he was giving me a ticket more because of that than the actual speeding. He was writing it out and then he looked down and saw I was sitting in a wheelchair. He stopped and looked like he was going to rip it up out of pity. That just infuriated me.

"If you're going to give me a ticket, do it," I said. "I have a lunch date.

"He turned beet red and quickly finished writing it. I thanked him and drove off with a smile on my face. Here," she said opening her purse and plucking it out, "look for yourself. I made a copy to hang on my wall in the office."

I stared at her a moment and then I laughed harder than I had since the accident.

Eventually, I got to the point where I could move in and out of my wheelchair on my own. Jake still visited often. He watched me in therapy. If I looked at him suddenly, I caught a sad, glum expression darkening his eyes and deepening every wrinkle in his tired face. He was stooping more, not taking as good care of himself either. His hair was unruly and often he looked like he needed a shave. When he was close, I could see the tiny bloody veins in his eyes were more prominent than ever. The moment he saw me looking at him, he brightened as best he could. He would tell me about the house and how it was being well looked after. He brought me mail, too. I had a letter from Roy telling me he was out of the clink and counting the days. Another letter from my father included a flyer announcing the upcoming production at the Burbage School. Of course, he didn't know I was severely injured, but it was so painful to see that flyer and know I would never go back to that school.

One afternoon after I was back in bed, resting, Jake came to tell me I was getting a visitor.

"Victoria will be here tomorrow," he said. "If you want, I'll stick around while she's visiting."

"It's all right, Jake. She couldn't frighten me before all this. She certainly can't now."

He smiled, yet he still looked so tired.

"Jake, you're not taking care of yourself," I said. "Grandmother Hudson would be upset."

He nodded.

"I'm all right."

"I'll be out of here soon and I'll need your help," I told him.

That raised his head and revived his eyes.

"Anything you need, of course," he said.

"I need you to be well," I said. "One invalid on the property is all we're permitted. I read the zoning ordinances."

He nodded, laughing silently.

"Okay, Princess," he said. "I'll shape up."

"Good."

After he was gone, I was left to ponder and anticipate my Aunt Victoria's visit and intentions. There was no doubt in my mind she believed she had the upper hand. I was sure she had been plotting with Grant against me, but I couldn't help being curious about them all, especially my mother, despite how much I wished I could put them out of my mind forever and ever.

Just as I returned to my room after a therapy session, Victoria appeared. I wasn't even in my bed. I was sitting in the wheelchair and I had just turned on the television set to continue with the soap opera I had been following. I heard the familiar click of her heels on the corridor floor and then she was there, pouncing on the entrance as though someone had dared forbid her coming. For a moment she was confused. I wasn't in the bed. Then she saw me and straightened up quickly into her usual ironing-board posture.

"Well, how are you?" she asked.

"How do I look?" I countered.

She was clutching her purse under her right arm, pressing it against her hip like a pistol and holster. Dressed in her usual gray skirt suit and blouse with those thick-heeled shoes, she looked as firm and as formal as ever. However, I could see she wasn't comfortable in the hospital setting. Her eyes shifted about like a frightened chicken. She had put on a dab of lipstick and what looked like a touch of rouge.

"You look remarkably well," she replied. She spotted the chair and went to it. For a moment we just looked at each other. "When I was a teenager, I had a temporary fascination with horseback riding. I started to take lessons, but I was never graceful or relaxed enough and always came away with an ache here or an ache there," she said indicating her lower back and her thighs.

"Megan was very good at it. My father bought her a horse. A beautiful Arabian. It cost a fortune to maintain it for her occasional rides. She soon grew bored with it, of course, and finally my father had the sense to sell it. It was months before Megan even knew he had, months before she even asked about her horse. She never told you?"

"We didn't have a long enough mother-daughter conversation for any of that," I said dryly.

"I suppose not. You know, her taking you back, bringing you to our mother and forgetting about you is just in character for her. She has no attention span, whether it be new clothes, children, horseback riding, golf, anything, even her own husband."

"How is she?" I asked.

"She's actually...as much of an invalid as you are these days. She's out of her room, but she doesn't get about anywhere near what she used to; she's of absolutely no use socially and politically to Grant. They don't have any dinner parties and he's had to attend most functions by himself. I happened to have been there to escort him to one affair," she added.

"How kind of you to make such a sacrifice," I said. She either deliberately or actually missed my sarcasm.

"I do what I can. I still have all my responsibilities here. She knows what's happened to you," she added after a short pause during which she looked at me. "Has she bothered to call?"

"No."

"I'm not surprised."

"I'm not either, but not for the same reasons," I said.

"Oh stop that," she snapped. It felt like a slap. It was so unexpected, I could only raise my eyebrows. "There's no reason for this self-immolation. You're not being punished for something you've done to Megan, believe me. What happened to Brody was all her fault. Her not calling you is just her way to find a scapegoat. She's always been like that. She's never accepted responsibility for her actions before this. She certainly won't now.

"Anyway, I've come to tell you that I'm seeing to everything."

"What do you mean?" I asked, expecting her to drop her bombs now.

"Everything that has to be done for you will be done," she declared in her characteristic take-charge manner. "Once again, I have to fill in for Megan, do what she should be doing. I've done it so much, I don't even mind it anymore."

"What exactly are you doing?"

"I've had a downstairs bedroom prepared for you at the house. I've had the medical equipment company provide what is needed. I've hired a full-time maid who has had experience as a nurse's aide. Her name is Mrs. Bogart. She'll be there when you arrive."

"Arrive?"

"I've been in continuous contact with your doctors and therapists here. You're going to be discharged from this facility in two days."

"Two days!"

Just the thought of leaving and going back into the real world was terrifying.

"That's what they're telling me. I've arranged for a therapist to be at the house three times a week at minimum."

"Why are you doing all this?" I asked.

"Why?" She smiled. It was more like a silent laugh. "Why? Because it has to be done and there's no one else to do it, especially not your mother.

"Oh, I've kept her abreast of it all, and Grant, of course," she added. "He wants you to know he harbors no ill feelings toward you. I assure you, he doesn't blame you one iota for what happened to Brody," she emphasized. "Now that he has had time to consider the why's and wherefor's," she added.

She crossed her long, thin legs and sat back with a look of grand satisfaction rippling across her thin face. Her eyes were almost electric with glee. So that's what she's doing, I thought. She's using me like a thorn to keep between Grant and my mother. She's finally found a purpose for me in her overall design.

I thought about the advice Doctor Synder had given me. It was essential not to become dependent upon anyone. That was doubly true in regards to Victoria.

"How do you know I even want to return to that house?" I asked.

She tilted her head as though the thought weighed down her brain on one side and threw it off balance.

"Where else would you go now?"

"I could go back to England," I said. It was such a pipe dream that even I had trouble saying it convincingly. She stared for a moment.

"And do what?" she asked.

"Whatever I'll be doing here."

"Nonsense. For one thing, you wouldn't have the support system you'll have here. Everything's more expensive there. You're not a citizen. You're not going to benefit from their health programs.

"I've decided not to sell the house anyway," she said. "With all that's happened to you, you can't think clearly and sensibly. You'll have to rely on me and that's that. My mother would be furious if I deserted you now."

She stood up.

I didn't know whether to laugh or not. Since when did she worry about what Grandmother Hudson would think? Didn't she think I could see through this false new sense of responsibility? Didn't she think I knew exactly what she wanted and what she was doing?

Yet, what choice did I really have? Take advantage of it, I thought. Take advantage of them all.

"All right," I said. "For a while anyway."

"It will be more than a while, Rain," she said. "There's no point in being like your mother and living in a world of dreams and illusions. When you face up to facts and reality, you get stronger and in the end, you're happier."

"Are you happy, Aunt Victoria?" I shot back at her.

Her smile came out as if it was actually a blooming flower stored too long under that hard shell of a face.

"I'm getting there," she said. "Finally."

She looked like her eyes were filled with all sorts of pleasing images. Then she blinked, looked down at me, and straightened up again.

"I'll see to the transporting of you back to your home the day after tomorrow. I understand Jake visits you frequently. Convey any requests through him and I'll see that whatever is within reason will be achieved.

"Is there anything you need or want at the moment?"

"Just my legs again," I said.

"Yes, well each of us has a burden to carry."

"What's yours, Aunt Victoria?" I asked.

"This family," she said without a beat. "It's always been."

She said goodbye and marched out, her heels clicking away and fading as she went down the corridor and out the door.

That night I wrote my two hardest letters, one to Roy and one to my real father, telling them both what had happened to me and what I had been doing as a result. I followed Doctor Snyder's advice and filled my letter with optimism, almost making my tragic accident sound like a little fall.

"For a while," I concluded in both letters, *"I want to remain at home completing my therapy. Some day in the near future, I'll reconsider my plans to return to England."*

I told them both not to worry about me and I promised them both I would stay in touch.

I had the hardest time falling asleep that night. Writing the letters had stimulated happier memories. My father had filled me with such hope and promise and I had been looking forward to seeing him again and becoming part of his family more than I had looked forward to anything in my whole life. Now that seemed impossible.

I thought about how terrible Roy was going to feel and how he would somehow blame it on himself that he wasn't here protecting me. I was afraid he might do something else to get himself in trouble and I had warned him in my letter not to do anything that would make me feel worse. I hoped he would listen, but I knew how headstrong he could be.

Everyone came back to me that night. I saw myself with Beneatha at dances. I saw myself walking with Mama and listening to her happy chatter. I recalled my long walks with Randall Glenn in London, our touring of the city and our strolls along the Thames. My memories were all memories of me moving. How terrible it is to lose something we all take so much for granted, I thought.

Before long my pillow was soaked with my tears and I had to turn it over to try to sleep on it. I didn't fall asleep until almost morning and I wasn't very good in my therapy sessions. Doctor Synder came to see me to talk about it.

"I'm glad you're moping about and crying about yourself," she said, which surprised me. "Hate yourself for what and who you think you are and that will give you more motivation to improve and change and become the woman I expect you to become."

She reached out and seized my wheelchair wheels, turning them around so I had to look at myself in the mirror.

"Go on, stare at that girl. Is that who you are, Rain?"

"I don't know who that is," I said.

"Exactly. Drive away this stranger who has taken over your body. Drive her out through your therapy and your determination to take control of your destiny again."

"I'll never hold a man's hand and walk again. I'll never dance."

"You will."

"How?"

"You will hold his hand and roll along with him and you will dance in your mind and you'll be so strong, he won't see you as anything but standing beside him. That's the way it is between my husband and me and that's the way it will be for you," she assured me.

"Go on, get out of here and take charge of your life, Rain Arnold."

I smiled at her.

"Will you come to see me?"

"No," she said. I lost my smile. "You'll come to see me," she corrected and I laughed. "That's more like it. I've got to go to see some patients who really need me now," she concluded and started out.

"Doctor Snyder."

"What?" she asked turning.

"Thank you."

"Thank you," she returned.

"Why?"

"Every time I see determination in a patient's face, I get stronger myself. You'll understand. In time, you'll understand," she said.

I watched her wheel herself out and then I sucked back my renegade tears and reached deep down inside myself to dip into that well of grit Mama Arnold had created in me.

I will get stronger, I chanted. I will.

Early the next morning Jake appeared. I was already dressed and in my chair.

"Well now," he said, "don't you look pretty?"

I had taken some time with my hair and put on some lipstick. I was so nervous my hand shook and I had to wipe the lipstick off and do it again. As I sat there waiting for Jake, my stomach had filled with goldfish swimming in mad circles and tickling my insides.

"What's it like outside?" I asked him.

"It's a beautiful summer day. The sky was a pink pearl color when I woke this morning. I woke early in anticipation," he said.

"I didn't sleep in anticipation."

He laughed.

"Well, it's time to go home, Princess."

"You know all that Victoria has arranged for me?"

"Yes. I have to admit she did a great job on preparing your bedroom. If there is anything invented for someone in your condition, she's got it there. I met your aide," he added with an impish smile. "She's got bigger arms than me and bigger shoulders and she looks like she could wipe up the devil with just a scowl. Victoria must have gone to great lengths to find her. She's no nonsense."

He got behind my chair and started to wheel me out of the room.

"Wait, Jake," I said and turned to look at the room that had become something of a sanctuary.

"You don't belong here, Princess," Jake whispered. "Let's get out of here."

He put his hand over mine and I nodded, closed my eyes and lay back in the chair. On the way out, all my nurses and some of the therapists made sure to say good-bye and wish me luck. I looked for Doctor Synder, but she wasn't around. She had said her good-bye and left me without fanfare. Was it just part of her treatment or was it because she couldn't bring herself to say good-bye? I liked to think we had become far more than doctor and patient. Visiting her would be a top priority for me, I thought.

Grandmother Hudson's Rolls-Royce was parked at the curb. For the first time ever in my life, I had to be helped into the backseat. The doctors wanted me to put more confidence in my right leg, use it more to move myself from the wheelchair to another chair and especially into a car, but it was a bit awkward and Jake didn't want me to feel embarrassed. He didn't wait for me to adjust myself. Instead, he scooped me up and put me in as if I were a baby.

"Let's just get you out of here and home," he said avoiding my eyes.

He folded up the chair and put it in the trunk and then he got behind the wheel.

"Got your safety belt on?" he asked.

"I can sit fine, Jake. Stop treating me like a cripple."

He laughed. It brought relief to both of us.

"Home James," I ordered.

"Right, right."

He started away and I looked back at the hospital. Had I really been there all this time? Was I really paralyzed? When will you wake up, Rain Arnold? Can't you shake off this nightmare?

Jake hated every moment of silence. He talked and talked, describing the smallest, simpliest things about the house, the maintenance, the grounds, the changing foliage. He babbled, even describing the plot of a television movie he had watched.

"Where is Rain now, Jake?" I asked, interrupting him.

"Rain? Oh, she's at a real horse farm north of Virginia. They'll treat her right, don't worry. I got a good price for her."

"You're a liar, Jake," I said.

"No, no, I did."

"I really wish you hadn't sold her, Jake. She'll always feel lonely."

"I just couldn't give her the attention she needed, Princess. That was it. Really."

"Sure, Jake. Will you take me to see her some day?"

"Oh, absolutely," he promised.

He tried to change the subject. After a while, he accepted the silence and drove on. I dozed and when I woke again, we were close enough to the house that my heart began to pound. I don't know why I was so nervous about returning.

"You're doing the right thing to come back here," Jake assured me. He was watching me in the rearview mirror and I was sure he could see the hesitation in my face. "You'll get good care and you're familiar with the place, which makes it easier. You'll be just fine, Princess. Just fine."

"I know," I said softly.

Then the house came into view. It loomed taller and larger than I remembered it.

"What's that off the portico?" I asked Jake.

"That? Victoria had Miles Hollinger construct a ramp for you. You can wheel yourself in and out of the house now. I was surprised she thought of it. You never know what she's going to do, but she does get the right things done," he said.

"A ramp?"

"Wait until you see some of the other changes she has made inside. Things are designed for your comfort now."

"Maybe I'll be too comfortable," I muttered. Jake didn't hear. Will the house become my new prison? I asked myself. Doctor Snyder had warned against becoming too dependent on people. Did she realize you could become too dependent on your surroundings as well?

Beware of crutches, I warned myself.

A thousand years ago it seemed Grandmother Hudson waved good-bye to me from those front steps. There was so much sadness and darkness in her face that day. Maybe she somehow knew how hard it was going to be one day for me to return.

8

Prisoner of My Body

Jake pushed my wheelchair up the ramp to the front door.

"I should be doing this myself, Jake."

"Next time, Princess," he said.

I wasn't that heavy, but I could hear him huffing and puffing.

"You're smoking too much, Jake," I told him. He laughed and agreed. I wanted to add drinking, too, because I could smell it on his breath, but I didn't.

Before he could come around to open the front door, a large African-American woman opened it for us so abruptly I was almost sucked into the house by the rush of air. Imposing looking, there were enough traces of gray in her short hair to suggest she was at least in her mid- to late fifties. Jake was right about her arms looking big and powerful. They put a strain on the short sleeves of her blue and white uniform. When she moved those arms, however, I could see that they weren't flabby. She was tall, at least

Jake's height, and she had a small bosom but wide hips. There were rolls of flesh up the back of her neck making it look like a spring upon which her large round head bobbed as she gazed down at me with a look of surprise. I imagined she had been expecting a lily-white Southern girl. Who else would Victoria Randolph have for a niece?

"I'm Mrs. Bogart," she said raising her voice on Mrs. Her stern expression, cold ashen eyes clearly telegraphed her insistence on being addressed that way. There would be no familiarity, no use of Christian names. This was no mammy out of *Gone with the Wind,* and there was no question in that face about who I was and wasn't.

Looking from me to Jake, she brought her thick lower lip over her upper, stretching the skin on her chin until I could see her jawbone clearly outlined.

"I'll take her from here," she told him.

If he had any intention of arguing with her, her quick, decisive move to seize the handles of my chair ended it. She practically knocked him out of her way and shoved me and my chair into the house. Once inside, she paused and looked back at him. "Put anything of hers right here," she ordered nodding at the table in the entryway.

"Yes sir," Jake said and saluted.

I laughed, but before I could thank him, she moved me forward.

"Wait," I said. "I want to thank Jake."

"You can thank him later. We've got to get you acclimated as soon as possible," she said.

"This is my home. I'm acclimated already."

Instead of replying she pushed me along, past the sitting room and the formal dining room and the kitchen to what was once considered the maid's quarters. I was amazed to see all the changes. The old four-poster dark maple bed, which I imagined was something of an antique, had been replaced with an aseptic-looking, metal-frame hospital bed, mechanized to be raised and lowered by the inhabitant pressing a button. Lamps with cold gray metal shades had been installed in the wall around the bed. The pretty brass ceiling light fixture had been supplanted by a strip of neon lights, and set on the wall facing the bed was a sizable television set.

The remainder of the room had been changed as well. The small chair and table in the corner were gone as was the soft-cushioned recliner. In their place were a number of therapeutic machines and other equipment I recognized from the hospital. When I glanced into the bathroom, I saw it had been completly refitted for a handicapped person. It had railings and braces around the toilet and the bathtub.

"I imagine you're very tired from your trip," Mrs. Bogart said.

"No," I told her. "Not really."

I caught a little twitch in her right eye as she stiffened her posture.

"You are," she insisted. "You just don't realize it. These journeys that are taken for granted by the rest of us," she said as if I was some sort of alien creature, "take a subtle toll on a handicapped person. Believe me, Miss Arnold, I speak from years and years of experience."

"You can call me Rain," I said. She ignored it and went to the bed to pull back the blanket. "I'm not getting into bed just yet," I said more firmly.

She stopped and looked at me, that twitch flashing once again.

"If you cooperate, things will be much easier for you and you'll be much more comfortable. Believe me."

"Why do you keep saying, believe me?" I asked.

She stared and then nodded. Her eyes blinked once with her conclusions about me.

"Very well. I'll see to your things. You can do as you want and call me when you're ready to get into bed."

She rolled the blanket back toward the pillow.

"I can do that myself anyway," I said.

She straightened up. Her lips seemed to go back and back, cutting deeper and deeper into her bloated cheeks until I could see the white of her teeth in dramatic contrast to her coal black complexion.

"Ms. Randolph hired me to assist you because I've spent the last twenty years taking care of the handicapped in hospitals and homes. I've worked closely with therapists and doctors and nurses. I've had a half-dozen patients like you.

"You've got some high mountains to climb, girl," she continued her eyes blazing with indignation at my audacity in challenging her suggestions and orders. "Mountains you don't even know are out there yet. Up to now, you've been in a hospital with round-the-clock attention, people pawing over you, making you feel like you're the center of the world.

"Here, you're all alone with your aches and pains, your spasms, your skin problems and your bathroom difficulties. Just getting in and out of this bed is going to seem like a ten mile hike, believe—

"Take my word for it," she interrupted herself. "Take my word for it because I've lived through it and seen it."

She nodded with a cold smile settling in her face and then continued.

"You think because you're home here, everything's

going to get back to the way it was. Well, it won't, ever, so you got to work on making the best of it all and that's why I'm here: to show you the way and to give you the benefit of my experience.

"Now that's the one and only time I'll give you a lecture. If you want me around, I'll stay and I'll do my job. If you fight me and contradict me and make me work double, I'll pack my bag and go off to take care of someone else whose family's knocking on my door and who will be more appreciative.

"I don't mean to sound harsh, but if we don't face reality right off, we're going to have a harder time tomorrow. That you can believe whether I say believe me or not."

"We?"

"What's hard for you is hard for me because I got to help you through it," she said without hesitation. "This isn't like taking care of some patient in a home who can't remember her name and age and when she went to the bathroom last. You've got an active mind in a broken body. I have seen what that can do and what that means.

"So you can sit in that chair now and not rest, and even wheel yourself up and down the hallway until your arms ache, but you'll have a better time of it if you lay down here a while, get some strength back, have something warm to eat and then start to readjust.

"That's my piece. Do what you want," she added and started out. "I got to get your stuff."

Her harsh, frank words brought tears to my eyes. Doctor Synder had warned me that tears would come far more often and easily now. She told me not to pay as much attention to them as I ordinarily would, but it was difficult to feel those hot drops zigzagging down my cheeks and pretend it was nothing. My heart ached more with every heavy beat. I didn't feel broken as much as empty. Everything warm and good inside me had been knocked out when I fell off Rain and onto those rocks.

I sat there staring at the starched white sheets and pillowcases of my bed. When Jake was driving me home, I had been looking forward to the soft, cushiony pillows with their scent of lilacs and the wonderful down comforter that made me feel snug and safe. Looking around the room that Aunt Victoria had remade for me left me feeling she had brought the hospital in here and I hadn't returned to Grandmother Hudson's home and my home after all.

The small raft of optimism I had tied to the dock in my harbor of hope seemed to fizzle and sink in the cold, dark waves again. In fact, I could feel my body slumping in the chair, my shoulders dipping.

Mrs. Bogart was right, I thought. Why bother pretending nothing terrible had happened? I wheeled up to the bed, reached out and pressed the button to lower it more just like I had been taught to do in the hospital. Then, following the steps I had learned at the therapy center, pulled myself up in the chair, braced myself on my right leg and swung myself onto the mattress. But I had not pulled the blanket far enough down and I was lying on top of it. Awkwardly, I rolled myself over and then worked it away. Now, I had to take off my shoes. Cupping my thigh, I pulled my leg up and strained to get the shoe off. It was suddenly so exhausting, I lost my breath and fell back against the pillow. My leg dropped like a leaden pipe, sending a spasm of pain up the sides of my back. I held down my scream and sucked in my moan.

A moment later I heard Mrs. Bogart return with my things and put them down. She came to the bed.

"Well, that's good," she said. Without asking if I needed her or wanted her to. She proceeded to take off my shoes and help me sit up, moving me around as if I was nothing more than an inflatable doll. She brought the blanket up, straightened the pillow, and lowered me to it. "Get some rest. I'll make you some lunch.

"Oh, that driver said he'd be back to see you, but I told him to wait a day or two," she said.

"A day or two? Why?"

"You got to get into a schedule before you start hosting visitors. The therapist is coming in the morning. I don't know what his schedule will be with you yet and we don't want your rest to be disturbed. You need to save strength for the therapy. I don't have to say believe me," she added, not letting me forget I had dared to criticize her expression. "You already know that from being in the hospital."

"Have I had any mail or any phone calls?" I asked her quickly before she left.

"I only been here a day before you come," she said. "No mail or calls yesterday and nothing yet today. Get some rest," she dictated and walked out, her footsteps echoing behind her. The great house seemed to swallow every sound until it was terribly silent.

I closed my eyes and then opened them and looked up at the ceiling. I had dreamed of being upstairs, returning to Grandmother Hudson's room. I thought I'd feel safe and happy there again. This was nothing like any sort of home-coming. I couldn't even have the illusion of getting back to some normality. Everything here and everything done for me was constantly designed to remind me about who I was and what I had become: an inmate, shifted from one prison to another.

Of course, I was forever incarcerated in the worst prison of all now, I thought, no matter where I was at the time.

My own body.

In moments—despite my determination to prove Mrs. Bogart wrong—I fell asleep exhausted.

When I woke, I was surprised to discover I had slept for over two hours. Almost as soon as my eyelids fluttered open and I glanced at the clock, Mrs. Bogart was in the room with a tray on which she had a bowl of tomato soup and a toasted cheese sandwich. I had to believe she was looking in on me continually and knew I was stirring. How could I help but be impressed with such attentiveness, despite her poor bedside manners? I was equally amazed by what she had brought me to eat. She saw that in my face immediately.

"I spoke to your nurses at the hospital and found out what you like" she explained briskly. "It saves waste and time."

She put the tray table over my legs, pulled me into a sitting position and patted down two pillows behind me so quickly and efficiently, I barely had time to take a breath. Then she stepped back and suggested I start eating before my soup got cold.

"Thank you," I muttered. She stood watching me for a moment. I half-expected her to begin criticizing the way I ate and telling me how she knew a better way because of her experience with paraplegics.

"Have you lost much weight since the accident?" she asked.

"Seven or eight pounds, I suppose," I said.

"You're better off being lighter," she said, "not that I imagine you were ever heavy. You don't look like the type."

"What type is that?"

"The type who would let her figure go," she explained. "I've had to deal with patients nearly twice your size. It's no picnic, believe me," she said. The moment she said it, she paused. I looked at her and I thought for a moment, she would smile or laugh and the ice wall between us would finally crack.

But just at that moment instead, we heard the front door open and close and the unmistakable click, clack of Aunt Victoria's heavy-heeled shoes as she came marching into the house and down the corridor toward us. Mrs. Bogart spun around to greet her.

"How's she doing?" I heard Aunt Victoria ask.

"As well as could be expected," Mrs. Bogart replied in a rather noncommittal voice. She glanced through the door at me and then walked away as Aunt Victoria turned into my room.

She wore a much more stylish blue skirt suit and again surprised me with some makeup on her face. I even thought she had taken greater pains with her normally dull, clipped hair. It had been blown dried and styled.

"Rain, I'm sorry I wasn't here to help settle you in, but I had a very important meeting with a group of developers out of New York who are thinking of building a theme park much like a Disney World on one of our properties. It could be a very, very big deal. It's actually exciting. I'll tell you more about it as the details develop. Go on, finish eating your lunch," she said with a wave of her hand.

I was hungry so I returned to it.

"Well," she said moving closer as she inspected the equipment, "I hope you're happy with what I've had done. I consulted with a therapist first, of course. We didn't spare any expense."

"What did you do with the furniture that was here?" I asked.

"Oh, I've turned it over to a consignment company. Maybe we'll get something back on it."

"I wished you had left it. I'd much rather have had that precious old bed than this."

"Nonsense, my dear. It wouldn't have been half as practical. Why make things more difficult for you than they already are?

"Of course, I've discussed most of this with Grant. I wanted to talk to Megan and get her involved in the events and actions that concern you, but she's now worse than ever when it comes to facing difficulties. She couldn't stand even hearing about you," she gleefully reported. "Grant's beside himself about it all, of course. As a matter of fact, I was just on the phone with him. He may even come here and pay you a visit. By himself!" she added.

"What for?" I asked quickly.

"What for?" She laughed. "Why, to do the responsible thing. He feels he has to take up the slack Megan has left and continues to leave."

She smiled, really very happy about all this.

"I'm surprised to hear he would worry about me," I said skeptically.

"Don't be. You know that vow husbands and wives take when they get married—that for better or worse one? Well, Grant is the type of man who takes such things seriously. He's inherited Megan's mistakes and he's not the sort who runs away from obligations.

"Mistakes? If I heard that word used one more time in reference to me, I'll scream loud enough for my mother to hear," I threatened.

"Sometimes," she said ignoring me and running her right forefinger along the top of my wheelchair, "I wish my father would have had a son like Grant. Why, if I had a brother with those qualities Grant possesses, the family business would be so much greater than it is. It's not easy for a woman in the business world, no matter what sort of facade I present.

"My mother was right about that," she said looking up quickly, "but I didn't want to admit it so I pretended I was having no problems when I was always fighting an uphill battle. I really needed someone like Grant at my side."

"Didn't you ever have anyone at your side?" I asked her, half out of curiosity and half out of a desire to press a needle into that self-contented smile.

She stopped moving her finger, straightening up, the soft, wistful look flying off her face as if I had seized her shoulders and shaken her.

"No. But not because I didn't want to," she added firmly. Her expression soured. "While my sister was off playing with her rebellious college friends, I was helping my father. He had far more health problems than anyone knew, especially Megan. He wanted it that way. It was always, 'Don't tell Megan. Protect Megan—precious, fragile Megan.

"Do you know where she was the day he died? Modeling clothes for a charity at a yacht party. She knew he was seriously ill, but she wouldn't accept it. I had to call her at that party and get her back here. Grant was in court, but he came as soon as he was able. I was there at my father's side when he took his last breath, not Megan, not his favorite.

"And then, all of it fell on my shoulders. Who had time to develop romances?

"But why are we talking about all this?" She cried, realizing she was being too honest and revealing. "Let's talk about your situation and what has to be done now," she insisted and began to rattle everything off in her usual indifferent manner of cataloguing.

"First, I've contracted with a private therapy company and they are sending their best man over tomorrow. He should be here by ten and he will know your condition thoroughly before he arrives. Second, I've spoken with Jake about the Rolls-Royce. It's superfluous and ostentatious now. Actually, I thought it always was, but Mother liked to hold onto those vestigial organs of high social standing.

"Jake is going to see about trading it in on a van that we'll have specially equipped for you."

"I don't want us to sell that car. It's Grandmother Hudson's car. It's…"

"Rain, dear," she said smiling, "as painful as it is for all of us continually to face it, the fact is my mother is dead and buried. There's no point in holding onto the car. I thought you were set on a more reasonable road these days. Why do you want to hold onto a car that you will have to be carried into every time you want to go somewhere, not to mention carried out of. How will that make you feel to see people watching you delivered like an infant from place to place?

"Well?" she pursued.

"You're right," I said reluctantly. She was, of course, especially when I envisioned myself being held like a baby or guided into my chair at street corners and curbs and parking lots.

"Good." She walked to the closet and opened it for me. "Third, as you can see, all of your clothing has been brought down for you. Everything you will need is here, shoes, undergarments, everything."

She turned and looked around, nodding with pleasure.

"Is there anything else you'd like in your room?"

"I don't have a telephone, I noticed," I said.

"Oh. That's right. I didn't think of that. I'll look into it ASAP. I wasn't sure if you would be too tired to discuss business with me, so I left the papers at the office. I'll bring it all around by the end of the week. How's that?"

"Fine," I said.

"Okay. I'm going to go talk with Mrs. Bogart to make sure she understands what's expected of her. I don't want the upstairs to go to pot just because you're not using it," she said. "I'll check on you again tomorrow."

She gave me a flashbulb smile and left. I finished my sandwich and sat back, my mind flooding with regrets. I wanted to defy everything in this room: the mechanized bed, the equipment, the railings, all that reaffirmed my state of invalidism, but whatever rebellion was left in me was muted and cowering in some dark corner of my tired heart.

Instead, I reached for the television remote and like a good veteran of hospital wars, I turned on the set and let the screen light up with distractions, images and words, music and stories to keep me from thinking about myself, video Valium to ease the pain of reality and welcome me to some cloudlike existence in the Land of Forget.

My first day at home was close to being over. Netted like some wild bird, I was now left to perch in my cage and look out at the world through bars, wondering what I had left to look forward to and how I would ever retrieve the song that had once come so easily from my now silent tongue.

Mrs. Bogart had a way of keeping me aware of her proximity. From time to time, I could hear her moving things about in other rooms, clanking dishes and silverware as if we had just finished serving a houseful of guests, vacuuming, polishing and dusting. Even when she was upstairs, I could hear her feet thumping into the rugs and on the wood. Furniture squealed when she moved it. Drawers were banged so hard, they sounded like they had exploded.

Periodically, that first day and night, she looked in on me. Sometimes, she just appeared in the doorway, glanced at me and moved on. Sometimes, she asked if I wanted something to drink, had gone to the bathroom, needed help in moving about, anything, it seemed to keep her voice in the air like some kite that looked like it was losing wind and would float down if it wasn't jerked and pulled.

I requested very little. My curiosity about the house, my initial desire to wheel myself through the downstairs, gazing at the rooms and the furniture dissipated like a balloon with a slow leak. I felt myself fold up in bed, close my eyes, and with the television running a stream of low noise and flickering shadows on the walls, I'd fall in and out of sleep until the first light of morning trickled through the curtains, parting the darkness as if I was being unearthed and discovered once again.

Who'd want to be discovered like this? I thought. I was certainly no treasure.

Mrs. Bogart was there almost as soon as I opened my eyes. I knew she had been installed upstairs in one of the guest bedrooms. What was she doing, sleeping with her ear on the floor waiting for my waking groans?

"Good morning," she said barely looking at me as she crossed the room to open the curtains wider. She went into the bathroom and started to run my tub. When she returned, she carried something green in a jar.

"What's that?" I asked.

"I was just going to explain it to you. Ms. Randolph let me order a case of it for you. It's an herbal bath powder that all my patients enjoy. It helps keep your skin healthy. The water will look green, but don't mind that."

"Oh. Thank you," I said. She nodded and started to help me out of bed.

I went into the wheelchair to the bathroom where she practically pulled off my nightgown. I quickly covered myself and then realized there was no point to my modesty. That's one of the first things that goes for someone in my condition, I thought. My body no longer felt like it belonged to me anyway.

She glanced at me while she continued to prepare my bath.

"You're a pretty girl," she said surprising me. "I've seen pretty girls wilt like sun-starved flowers in hospitals. They lose that glow, but you haven't. Yet," she added. Then she considered me again and nodded. "Maybe you won't, but you got to care about yourself."

"I don't know if I can," I admitted.

"If you can't, you can't," she said with a shrug. "No one's going to be hurt more than you."

"Thanks for the encouragement," I muttered.

Finally, she smiled, but it wasn't a warm smile. It was a smile of irony and self-satisfaction.

"Hell, girl, I'm not hired here to be your cheerleader. I'm here to help you help yourself and keep this place looking decent so folks will not feel disgusted when they come. Most of it is up to you and your doctor and therapist. I'm just telling you what I've seen over the years, what I know."

"Why do you want to do this kind of work? It seems so hard," I said as she helped me get out of the chair and into the tub.

"Pay's good," she said. "Besides," she continued as I began to enjoy the soak, "I had early experience at it. My father was crippled early with arthritis and in a wheelchair and my mother was..."

"What?" I asked when she hesitated.

She looked down at me.

"No damn good," she said and left me to bathe.

She took so long to return, I wondered if she expected I would get myself out and dried and in the chair. I've got to get to where I can anyway, I thought and started to do just that.

"Just hold on there, Miss Impatience," she said charging back into the bathroom. "You're not ready for that yet and if you go and fall and break something else, guess who's going to be blamed?"

She was efficient about getting me out, dry and dressed. She opened the closet and asked me what I wanted to wear.

"Don't forget," she reminded me, "the physical therapist will be here this morning."

I chose a sweat suit outfit. After I put it on, she stepped back and looked at me.

"You going to just leave your hair a mess after we worked so hard getting you clean and smelling good? Run a brush through it at least," she told me. "After that, wheel yourself down to the kitchen for breakfast."

I felt almost like a kid being told she could take the family car for a ride herself. Maybe her sassiness worked, I thought, because I did get myself over to the vanity table and brushed my hair. Then, surprised at how hungry I was, I wheeled out of the room and down the corridor.

Finally, I felt like I was home.

Perhaps it was because we were in the kitchen and not in my hospital-like bedroom, but while I ate my breakfast, Mrs. Bogart became more talkative, especially about herself. She ate her breakfast with me and told me about some of her former patients. One was particularly sad: a twelve-year-old boy with multiple sclerosis who died while she was caring for him.

She came from a small town north of Richmond and had never left the state of Virginia. She told me she had spent most of her teenage years and early twenties caring for her father; the men with whom she did develop some sort of romantic relationship eventually grew tired of sharing her energy and attention with him.

"Some people are just meant to spend their whole lives taking care of other people, I guess," she concluded. "At least, I'm not ashamed of it."

"Why should you be?" I asked her.

She looked at me with those ebony eyes flashing with heat and fired back, "Would you like to be doing this your whole life, child?"

I hesitated and decided this was a woman who only wanted to hear the truth. In some ways that was refreshing.

"No, ma'am," I said with conviction.

She stared a moment. Was the wall of ice cracking?

"So who's your mama? Not Ms. Victoria, I imagine," she said, folding her rolling-pin arms under her small bosom.

"No. Her younger sister, Megan."

"She's not married to your daddy, right?" she asked, tilting her head in expectation.

"Hardly," I said. She nodded, understanding only too well.

I told her about Grandmother Hudson and how I had come to live here. She listened, clicking her tongue and pressing her lips together once in a while. Her face grew solemn when I described what had happened to Brody. Then she rose in silence to clear off the dishes. My story seemed to take all thought from her mind. She was so silent for so long. Finally, she wiped her hand on a dishtowel and turned back to me.

"Ain't no point in asking yourself why all the time," she said. "The answers to those questions don't rest here with the living. We will find out later what the purpose was to all our burdens. That's what they mean by the promise in the Promised Land.

"My daddy used to say that," she added smiling softly to herself. Then, as if she realized she had left her character role on some stage, she snapped her lips, clapped her hands and scowled at me.

"You go on and get back to your room and get yourself ready for your therapy. He'll be here any minute. Go on, wheel on out of here on your own," she charged.

I turned from the table and started away. When I looked back, I saw her wipe something out of the corner of her right eye.

Only someone who has cried a great deal knows why someone else wants to stop the tears, I thought.

The physical therapist was right on time. I heard the doorbell ring at exactly ten A.M. I waited nervously in my chair facing the door. After all, this was someone with whom I was going to spend a great deal of time and most of my physical energy. I had liked all my therapists at the hospital. They were kind, patient and very knowledgeable people. Most of them were in their mid-thirties and forties and very experienced. That had helped instill some confidence in me.

I heard Mrs. Bogart's voice. She always spoke with authority, overpowering. I could barely hear the therapist as they came down the corridor. My heart raced. I gripped the sides of my wheelchair and sat as firmly as I could. Even so, I was not prepared for the man who appeared.

He had bright carrot short hair, small freckles on his forehead, nearly luminous turquoise eyes, a perfectly straight nose with a sensual mouth and a strong jaw. He was easily six feet two and slim like a gymnast with wide shoulders and a narrow waist.

He was dressed in white pants, sneakers and a light blue jacket under which he wore a tight T-shirt. The jacket was open so I could see some of his muscle development, especially his chest.

What surprised me the most was I didn't think he was older than his mid-twenties, yet Aunt Victoria had described him as the best therapist in his company. I wasn't prepared to turn my broken body over to a man who didn't look much older than I. I hoped I wasn't going to be someone's guinea pig or the subject of someone's internship.

The look on his face when he confronted me told me I was not exactly what he expected either. He stared for a moment, his lips softening into a soft, amused smile of surprise. Finally, he realized we were both staring dumbly at each other and he practically jumped toward me, his hand extended.

"Hi," he said, "I'm Austin Clarke."

I lifted my hand slowly and he pulled it into his impatiently, holding it longer than I expected.

Mrs. Bogart stood back in the doorway watching a moment.

"If you need anything, just shout," she said. "I won't be far."

"Thank you," he said and turned back to me, his eyes narrowing and his lips now forming a slightly sly smile, almost impish. "You're disappointed I'm not some older guy, huh?"

"Yes," I said, pulling my hand from his.

"They tell me I'll always look like a teenager. I have that complexion or maybe it's just this carrot top. I was thinking about dying it black, but then I'd have to dye my eyebrows and do something about these freckles. It's easier to tell everyone I take Dick Clark pills." He widened his smile in anticipation of my laughter. "They think we're related. Austin Clarke, Dick Clark?" I didn't react. "Dick Clark, 'Teenage Bandstand,' the guy who never seems to age?"

"I know who he is," I said.

He nodded and looked around the room.

"Good. You've got it all here."

He put down his small gym bag and approached the first machine.

"This is a leg pump. You know why we want you to use it?"

"Stop atrophy," I recited dryly.

"Yeah, that's one thing. When the muscles of the calves and thighs are in contraction, blood low in oxygen, what we call venous blood, is pumped through the leg muscle pump from the legs to the heart.

"The veins of the legs have valves which are similar to

those of the heart. They allow blood to pass through towards the heart while they prevent the blood flowing backwards towards the foot. In this way they only allow blood flow in one direction: toward the heart.

"During the pumping phase or muscle contraction, the pressure within the veins is increased, pumping the venous blood towards the heart.

"During the filling phase or muscle relaxation, the pressure within the veins is reduced and the veins fill themselves with blood in preparation for the next pumping phase. This prevents thrombosis, blood clotting, and increases peripheral circulation which is necessary for tissue nutrition, oxygenation and removal of metabolic waste. And yes, muscle strength, prevention of atrophy.

"Well?" he said standing back with his hands on his hips.

"Well what?"

"Aren't you impressed yet?"

"Overwhelmed," I said and he laughed.

"Okay. Let's just start and see where we go, okay?"

He went over to the equipment and brought out a rolled thick mat that he undid and spread on the floor. Then he looked at me.

"We'll go through a very basic evaluation. You know what I want you to do first?"

"Warm up and then some stretching," I said.

"Terrific. Maybe you should be the therapist."

"Believe me," I said, "I wish I could."

His smile widened and he stepped toward me. With tentative hands, waiting for my cooperation, he urged me to lift myself from the wheelchair. I knew he was waiting to see just what I could do with my right leg. I started and he came around behind me and put his hands on my hips.

"Don't worry," he said. "I have you."

His face was so close to my hair, I could feel his breath on my neck. I put all my weight on my right leg and started up. Then he took over and with ease gently lowered me to the mat. He had me lay flat and then he hovered over me a moment.

"You okay?" he asked.

"Yes." I closed my eyes and pressed my lips together and kept myself from screaming. I opened them and looked up. He was on his knees beside me.

"We're going to rotate every joint in your body and what you can't do yourself, I'll help you do," he said.

"Why am I doing this?" I muttered to myself.

He smiled down at me, those beautiful eyes full of laughter.

"So I can have work, why else?" he said.

Even if I wanted to, I couldn't stop a smile from settling on my face.

"Oh, one other thing," he said rising and going to his gym bag. He unzipped it and took out a small tape recorder. "I like to work with music. Is that okay?"

"Yes," I said.

He turned it on.

I was expecting elevator music, soothing, soft melodic tones like they had at the hospital.

Instead, there was a wham and a bam and the rock music began.

He shrugged.

"You can take the kid out of rock and roll, but you can't take rock and roll out of the kid."

My smile turned into a laugh.

"It's okay?"

"Yes," I said. "It's fine."

A moment later I saw Mrs. Bogart look in on us. The music had drawn her back. Austin saw her, too. She glared a moment, smirked, shook her head and walked away.

"Maybe she's not a rock music fan," he said.

I laughed.

"Hardly."

He started me on rotating my neck muscles and he worked me down my body until we reached the places I couldn't move and then he leaned over me and gently, gracefully began to rotate them himself.

He started to sing along with the music and I groaned.

"Okay, okay," he said. "Now you know why I'm a therapist and not a rock star."

"Did Aunt Victoria meet you?" I asked him, suddenly very curious about this whole arrangement.

"Who's your Aunt Victoria? I just was given my assignment and showed up."

"She prides herself on being right about every decision she makes. She was told you were the best in your company. The owner told her so himself."

He leaned forward until he was only inches from my face and he winked.

"My uncle owns it," he said.

Then he laughed.

I did too. I laughed so hard those familiar tears came again, only this time, I didn't seem to mind them.

Not at all.

9

Pills to Kill Pain

Austin Clarke was actually twenty-eight years old, even though he could probably pass for a senior in high school or at least a freshman in college. His uncle really did own the physical therapy company, but Austin told me his father wasn't happy he was working for his uncle, his mother's brother.

"My father wanted me to follow in his footsteps instead," Austin explained. "He owns an electric switch company in New Jersey, but I never found it very interesting or challenging to spend your life trying to manipulate costs so you could be more competitive in your bidding for jobs.

"My uncle Byron was always into health and physical fitness. He was a runner up in one of those Mr. Olympia contests, body builders, you know? My father thought he was wasting his time, but while my uncle was at the health clubs, he got interested in physical therapy and went to school for it. Then, he started his own company. I guess he was a big influence on me because I began working out and studying health foods and everything. Eventually, I got into it, too.

"Needless to say, my father's not going around bragging about my accomplishments."

"Why not? You're helping people who need you," I said. "Why wouldn't he boast?"

"It's a father-son thing, I guess. Manly pride stuff. Every father hopes his son wants to be like him and be as interested in his business, the things that interest him. Parents are always trying to make themselves over in their children, forgetting their children are individuals too," he said. "Sorry," he quickly added. "I don't mean to on a soapbox my first day."

"That's all right. I agree with you anyway."

We were outside. After a little over an hour of warm-up, stretching and some strengthening exercises, Austin decided I should always include fresh air as part of my therapy. It was a warm summer day, even a little humid, but I didn't mind. He pushed me along the path toward the lake. When we got down to the shore and the small dock, he dipped his hand in the water and nodded.

"Not as cold as I thought it would be," he said. "Anyone ever swim in this?"

"Not for a long time. Why?"

"Aqua therapy is very effective," he said.

"You mean you expect me to go swimming?" I asked, astonished.

"Sure, why not? It's still summer and the days are hot enough, aren't they?"

I shook my head.

"No way. I wasn't much of a swimmer before I got injured. I didn't have all that much opportunity. I'm a city girl and my school didn't have an outdoor or indoor pool. I didn't even go swimming until I started school here in my senior year."

"Hey, we all came from the ocean, don't you remember? It comes natural to us. We'll see. I think this could do you a world of good, especially these dog days."

"Dog days?" I laughed.

"Isn't that the way you Southern girls would put it?"

"I'm no Southern girl and you don't have much of a Southern accent. Where are you from?" I asked him.

He smiled and stood up.

"Trenton, New Jersey. My mother's the Southerner. She was born and raised in Norfolk. I have a younger sister who loves to sound like a Southern belle, honey," he said overacting a Southern accent. "Her name is Heather Sue Clarke and she always goes by Heather Sue. If someone calls her just Heather, she'll correct them and say, it's Heather Sue. She's been doing that ever since she was three.

"What about you?" he asked. "You have any brothers or sisters?" He looked back at the house. "This is a pretty big house to be in all by yourself. Where are your parents? Both working? Why is your aunt in charge of all this?"

I stared up at him and he just broke out into laughter.

"Sorry, sorry," he said holding up his hand. "Didn't mean to overwhelm you with my nosiness and hit you with a shotgun of questions."

"That's all right," I said. Then I sat back enjoying the air cooling over the water for a moment before I started.

Here I go again, I thought.

"I have a stepbrother and a half sister."

He nodded like someone waiting for the punch line of a joke.

"And I don't live with my mother. I live in this big house all by myself. With Mrs. Bogart, too, now. She was just hired. Not that she's much company," I added.

"Really?" He turned to look at the lake.

"I thought you would have had to know all about me before starting to work with me," I said.

"Well, I do know how you got injured. Sorry about that. You know," he said looking at me again, "I've done some interesting therapy work with children using horseback riding. Maybe someday you'll get back in the saddle."

"I doubt that."

"Don't underestimate yourself, Rain," he said, his eyes small, intense. "Don't live in a world of fantasy either, but before you come to any ironclad conclusions about your future, about what you will and will not do, give your recuperation and rehabilitation a chance. End of lecture," he quickly added and pretended to zip his mouth shut.

I gazed up at him. With the midday sun beaming down, its rays slipping between two puffy, lazy clouds over us, it looked like we were both in spotlights. My nose was filled with the fresh fragrances of wild flowers mixing with all the scents that rose from the water: the dampness of the wooden dock, the redolent smell of wet earth.

Austin's face was radiant even without the glow of sunshine on it. In broad daylight, his turquoise eyes showed some specks of green. He looked healthy and strong, young and vibrant, everything I was and dreamed I'd be again. Whenever he looked at me, he had laughter on his lips, a kind, happy laughter that followed interesting discoveries.

How could anyone look at me and think of anything else but pity and sorrow? I wondered. What secret did he possess? What magic potion did he drink every day that gave him the power to see beauty and goodness, hope and promise in a world that I saw only as dark and foreboding now? Was it just his good fortune with health and fitness?

"Are you married or engaged or anything?" I asked him, assuming this radiance in his eyes, this glow in his face had something to do with being in love. Someone out there filled his heart with great joy.

Days and days of memorizing *Romeo and Juliet* for class in London had kept it in my bank account of sweet thoughts and some of the lines came quickly to my mind: *"Love is a smoke made with the fume of sighs, Being purged, a fire sparkling in lovers' eyes..."*

"I'm not anything at the moment. Not too long ago, I thought I was in love and someone was in love with me, but while my back was turned, because I was busy with patients, one of my buddies stepped into the available moment, should I say, and the love I thought was so strong, turned to mush."

He stepped up on the small dock, raised his hands and cried, *"She's gone. I am abused, and my relief must be to loathe her."*

Then he laughed. My mouth dropped open.

"That's from *Othello*," I declared. He nodded.

"Seemed to fit at the time, so I borrowed it. It's a passion of mine. I have all these tapes of plays, dramatic readings, and I listen to them while I make myself dinner or when I'm just relaxing, lying on my sofa, my eyes closed." He stepped down again and in a loud whisper said, "I'm a frustrated actor."

I narrowed my eyes, suspiciously.

"Did my aunt tell you about me?"

"I never met your aunt, remember? My uncle gave me the assignment. I've read all your medical records. I told you I know how you were injured, but I wasn't given your autobiography, no. Why?"

"I spent most of the year in London at a school for performing arts, training to become an actress," I said.

"You're kidding! Well, we'll just have to get you up to speed so you can start auditioning for all the female wheelchair parts."

I stared at him and then, seeing the impish gleam in his eye, I laughed. It was as if a weight was being lifted from my shoulders. Who would have thought that I would be laughing at myself in this condition? Who would have thought I could find the slightest thing funny about myself?

He smiled.

"That's it," he said. "That's the secret. You've got to laugh at everything eventually. Only those who take themselves too seriously suffer, really suffer. You're going to get better in a thousand different ways, Rain. I just know it," he insisted. He put his hand over mine on the side of the wheelchair and looked into my eyes, forcing me to look deeply into his eyes so I could see his sincerity.

Was it my imagination or did I see something else there, something I wanted to see? Could a man ever look at me again and think of me as beautiful? If you saw yourself as being only half a person, surely everyone else would see you the same way.

He closed his eyes and pulled back quickly like someone who knew he had stepped over some boundary.

"I guess we should head back to the house. Mrs. Bogart gave strict instructions as to when lunch would be served. That's a woman I don't want to cross."

"Are you staying for lunch?" I quickly asked.

"Are you inviting me?"

"If you'd like to stay, you can stay," I said, retreating from any show of feeling. Being wounded so many times in relationships when I was completely healthy made me hesitant. Now I had even more reason to be.

"That's not much of an invitation. My ego's bruised, but," he added grasping the handles of my chair and starting me around, "I'm starving so I'll bear it."

He couldn't see the smile on my face as we started back toward the house, but it was there, sitting firmly on my lips like the memory of some wonderful soft kiss.

I had to believe Austin had at least one ulterior motive to his wanting to be at lunch. He spent most of the time talking about different foods with Mrs. Bogart. He believed the diet I followed was important. I could see she wasn't happy about having her menus challenged or him dictating anything to her, but Austin had an unobtrusive way about him and complimented her on so many different things that by the time lunch was over, she was smiling at him, albeit reluctantly, nodding her head and looking at him with approval.

"That young man knows his stuff," she told me afterward. "I've seen some pretty poor excuses for therapists in my time. Believe me, it's important to have a good one."

Austin had left instructions for activities I should follow when he wasn't here. He wanted me on the leg machine for at least ten minutes, three times a day. Mrs. Bogart hovered over me when I got myself from the chair to the machine, but I insisted on doing whatever I could do myself, by myself. Nothing haunted my thoughts as much as Doctor Snyder's warning not to become dependant on anyone. Independence was the key to the doorway of any real recovery, I thought.

Even if it meant it would take me ten times as long to get something done for myself, I would do it myself. I quickly learned how to get myself out of bed every morning, how to dress myself, and even as painful and as awkward as it was, to put on my own shoes and socks.

Sometimes, I would get so exhausted, I would fall asleep in my chair, my head down, my arms dangling, and when I woke, either after twenty minutes or an hour, I would ache in new places. Mrs. Bogart retreated, waited in the wings, or sometimes, I think, just stood there outside my doorway, listening. Maybe she was hoping I would scream for her and be more dependent on her, but I wouldn't call her unless it was absolutely necessary. I was still timid about some things, like getting myself in and out of a bathtub and had to have her assist me there.

Austin was to come every weekday for the first two weeks. It got so I looked forward to his arrival more than anything else. Gradually, he increased my activities. I exercised to his music and grew stronger and stronger. He spent lots of time just going through the basic movements of everyday life, showing me ways to get out of bed easier, move my body better to avoid pressure sores, and how to manipulate my wheelchair to get the most efficient use of it. It took a few attempts, but I was finally able to get myself up the ramp outside.

During our frequent breaks, Austin would tell me about some of his other clients, two of whom were at a rest home.

"Both of them still have pretty young minds. There are a lot of similarities between them and young people handicapped in one way or another. I just look past the wrinkles and gray hair and think of them the same as anyone else trying to regain mobility or movement to accompany their youthful mentality. I was thinking that it would be perfect if we all went brain dead first, like some switch..." he said looking away and smiling. "Yes, a switch would be flipped and our bodies would shut down instead of our bodies weakening or sickening and then leaving us..."

"Looking out of windows?" I suggested.

"Yeah." His smile became a flag of firm resolution. "I'm going to get you out of here, Rain. You won't be stuck behind any window. You're doing terrific. What do you say tomorrow we try some of that aqua therapy. It's supposed to be close to ninety-five degrees and sunny. I bet it would be fun."

"I don't know." I shook my head fearfully.

"C'mon, take a chance," he urged.

I laughed.

"Not much really of a chance for me to take, is it?" I asked.

"What do you mean?"

"I don't have much to risk anymore, right?"

"Wrong. You've got more to risk. You have all this extra experience and knowledge to hand down."

"What extra knowledge?" I asked, turning my eyebrows in toward each other.

"You know how to defeat tragedy," he told me.

I wasn't sure if everything he was doing was contrived, planned, right down to his smiles and laughs, but for now, I didn't care. It all made me feel too good and hopeful and that was something I wasn't about to surrender, even in the face of deceit.

"Okay," I said. "We'll go swimming. Or rather, you'll go swimming and I'll be a float."

"No you won't. You'll see," he said.

After he left I went through my wardrobe, searching for my bathing suits. I had the one I used as a uniform at Dogwood and I had two others, but they were both two-piece, one so abbreviated it was technically a bikini. I laid them all on the bed and pondered. It would take me hours to try them all on, I thought, but my fear of looking bad was motivation enough to give me the strength.

Mrs. Bogart looked in on me while I was struggling with the school suit.

"Why are you putting that on?" she asked and I told her Austin's plan.

She looked at me askance but didn't say anything. Without waiting, she helped me pull up the suit and zippered it.

"Thank you," I said. She shrugged and left. I stared in the mirror. My legs looked bony and thin to me and I thought my hips had widened. It brought hot tears to my eyes.

"What am I doing?" I muttered. "This is stupid. What am I doing?"

I started to rip the bathing suit off, pulling and tugging at it so viciously that I tore the zipper away from the material on one side. Then I felt my shoulders start to shake and a strange rippling through my stomach. Looking in the mirror, I saw I was crying hysterically. I was just doing it silently.

Maybe I had been working at my therapy too hard. Maybe I didn't listen to Mrs. Bogart enough and take enough rest time. Maybe I had permitted myself to drift through some world of fantasy in a bubble that finally burst. Whatever the reason, I suddenly felt a deep exhaustion. Both fatigue and depression went to the very bottom of my being, turning me into a limp lump of defeat. Half-naked, I sagged in the chair, devoid of the strength to remove the swimsuit completely and get myself dressed again.

A low moan began at the base of my throat and began to vibrate to the back of my neck and up behind my head. Suddenly, I had a terrific spasm in my stomach, too. My moan got louder and Mrs. Bogart came running. When she looked at me, I was shaking so hard, the chair was rattling.

"Okay," she said, "okay. Take it easy." She moved me quickly to the side of the bed and then she helped me out of the chair and under the covers. My teeth were clicking together. I was so chilled. She put another blanket on and then another before she went to call the doctor. Then she returned to tell me I was being taken to the hospital.

"No!" I cried.

"The doctor wants you brought in for some test or other. You got to go. Your driver's on his way. Let me get something on you," she said and put a sweatshirt and sweatpants on me while I continued to tremble.

Less then fifteen minutes later, Jake was at my bedside. He looked gray and tired, his face was so drawn. Was it my condition that was making me see him that way?

"How you doing, Princess?" he asked.

My trembling had subsided some, but the spasm in my abdomen was still severe.

"I don't know, Jake. Something happened. I'm sick."

"Okay, let's get moving," he said. Mrs. Bogart wheeled the chair toward us, but Jake lifted me out of the bed and carried me out of the house in his arms. My head rested against his chest.

"You can wheel her," Mrs. Bogart said.

"This is faster," he said.

"Don't you drop that girl on my watch, hear? I'm not being blamed."

"Nobody's dropping nobody," he assured her. "Stop worrying and open the door for us," he ordered with firmness. She moved quickly to get ahead of us and do it. Jake carried me out and put me gently into the back of the Rolls. Then he got behind the wheel and started away.

"I guess Victoria's right about the car," he said. "I should have had it sold and a van out here for you. Sorry, Princess."

"I don't want a van. I like the Rolls," I muttered. I had my eyes closed. "I want Grandmother Hudson's Rolls."

At the hospital they put me on a gurney and wheeled me into the emergency room. Tests were run and hours later, Doctor Morton, the physician on call, came to my bedside to tell me I had developed a severe bladder infection.

"It's not uncommon for people in your condition," he assured me. "We'll clear it up quickly and get you back on your feet."

I started to laugh and he stared a moment.

"Back on my feet? Take all the time you need, doctor."

That brought a smile to his face.

"Just an expression," he said.

"I know. Boy, do I know," I said.

They took me to a private room and gave me something to help me sleep.

Late in the morning the next day my eyelids fluttered open and I saw Aunt Victoria gazing at me, her face full of anger, her eyes wide and blazing. When she realized I was looking at her, she cooled and cleared her throat.

"I'm going to have to fire Jake," she said. "I told him specifically to go out and get that van and what do you think he's been doing? Loitering in the local tavern. I found out that he had to be taken home in a taxi two nights in a row because he was too drunk to drive himself. He was probably drunk when he came for you yesterday.

"We can't have someone like that for your driver. I don't want someone like that associated with the family name."

"No," I said, shaking my head vigorously. "He wasn't drunk. He was perfect. Don't you dare fire him. He's not your driver. He's mine."

"What's the matter with you? The man's an inebriate. He always was. I told my mother time after time that she should hire herself a decent, well-trained and respectable chauffeur and not someone without any ambition or class."

"Jake is my best friend in the world," I said. "Don't you even think of saying anything like that to him."

She saw the resistence in my face and softened her shoulders.

"I spoke with the doctor. He thinks your physical therapist might be working you too quickly, too strenuously. I've called the firm and asked for an older, more experienced therapist for you."

"It's not the therapist's fault. It's a common problem for paraplegics. I want Austin."

"Austin?" she said twisting her mouth into her cheek.

"I won't cooperate with anyone else. I won't," I assured her.

She studied me a moment and then shook her head slowly.

"You're not developing an attachment to this therapist, are you? That's a dangerous thing. I've been told so by people who know."

"No," I said too quickly. "I just feel comfortable with

him and we are making progress. Call them back and tell them he's all right."

"We'll see," she said.

"If you don't, I won't cooperate with you and sign any of your papers," I threatened. "I mean it."

She stared, her anger firing up her eyes again before she quickly quenched the flames and smiled.

"Don't get yourself so upset, Rain. I was just thinking of what was best for you. If that's the way you want it for now, that's fine. I'll take care of it. What I want you to do is rest and recuperate quickly so you can go home after the weekend. On Tuesday now, I'll be at the house with Grant to help explain some of the things we have to do with the estate. Okay?"

"Okay," I said, still not trusting her.

"Let me see to the van at least. I'll do that today myself," she said.

"Don't sell the Rolls-Royce," I told her.

She smiled that cold, sharp smile, stretching her lips into thin, pencil lines slashed across her narrow face.

"All right. We'll keep it for now. It's one of those things that can gain in value if kept up properly anyway," she said, determined to turn every disagreement into a victory for herself one way or another.

She rose and patted me gently on the back of my hand.

"Just get better and don't worry about the other matters. I'll keep in touch with the doctors. Is there anything you want right now?"

"No," I said. I closed my eyes. When I opened them, she was gone.

Later, while I was eating lunch, Austin came to see me.

"Talk about finding ways to avoid going for a swim," he said smiling. He had a bouquet of red roses for me.

"Thank you," I said smelling them. He put them in a vase and pulled a chair closer to my bed.

"This is a minor setback," he said. "Don't let it get to you. You'll just watch your medication and you'll be fine. We'll be back at work in a few days. Don't think that you've gotten away with anything. There are plenty of other days ahead when it will be ideal to go swimming."

"I'm really not worried about that," I said laughing.

"My uncle said your aunt was upset with me and wanted me replaced," he said after a moment.

"I've already spoken to her about that. You're not going to be replaced."

He smiled.

"I really don't think anything we've done has anything to do with this, Rain. If I did, I would tell you and I would change the therapy."

"I believe you, Austin. Please don't pay any attention to my aunt. We don't exactly belong to a mutual admiration society. I'm the relative who was shoved down her throat. We have what you might call a precarious truce."

"None of that is any of my business," he said quickly.

"It's all right. I don't mind you knowing more about me. Maybe, if you understand me better, you will change some of the therapy," I said.

He sat back and I began to tell him my story. I was interrupted only when the nurse came in to give me some medication. The rest of the time, he sat, transfixed, his reactions revealed in the movements of his eyes and the way they brightened and darkened.

"So that was why you told me you had a stepbrother and a half sister. I thought you were joking."

"I wish I were," I said.

My eyelids felt so heavy that no matter how hard I tried, I couldn't keep them from shutting.

"I'd better let you rest," I heard him say. "I'll check up on you and as soon as you're able, we'll start the therapy again."

My head nodded as if a powerful invisible hand had moved it. Then, I was asleep.

On Sunday, when they wheeled me out of the hospital, Jake stood by a brand-new van, equipped with an electric lift. All they had to do was wheel me onto it and it brought me up so I could wheel into place in the van. It seemed quite luxurious for what it was.

"Victoria wasn't happy about the deal I got. I put in a lot of options," he added in a whisper, "but there wasn't much she could do about it. Your attorney took care of it, and guess what," he continued as he got behind the wheel. "It's equipped so when the time comes, you can drive it yourself."

"What? How?"

"This seat comes out and your wheelchair goes right here," he explained. "All the controls are finger controls, even the brakes. It's easy. You'll be going wherever you want in no time, Princess."

I was impressed and a bit frightened at the prospect, but on top of a beautiful, bright summer day, the promise of a more fulfilling future reinvigorated me.

However, Mrs. Bogart greeted me with a whole new list of restrictions and orders.

"You got sick because you tried to do to much too fast

on your own," she said. "Believe me, I've seen it before. Maybe now you'll listen to people who know more."

I was too happy about being out of the hospital to permit even her sour face to upset me.

Just before I settled in for an afternoon rest, she remembered I had received a letter and brought it to me. It was from my father. The news of my accident and injury greatly disturbed him, and as he explained, added tremendously to his personal frustration.

> *I feel so helpless because I can do nothing for you even now, even when you need a parent more than ever, need a family more than ever. How strong a person you must be to fight all this alone, now that you explained what has happened to Megan, too.*
>
> *I can only promise you that as soon as I have the opportunity, I will come to America to see you. Leanna feels terrible about it all and wishes you could be brought here. She's a wonderful person. I'm sure you are wondering why someone who has no blood relationship to you would be so concerned and caring. Perhaps love among people who have no obligation to love is the strongest love after all.*
>
> *Please, please write to me and keep me up on your progress.*
>
> *Love,*
> *Dad*

Tears threatened to wash the words into oblivion. I folded the letter neatly and put it in my nightstand drawer. I would take it out and reread it. It was the next best thing to hearing his voice and seeing him.

What worried me was that I hadn't heard a word from Roy. By now he had received my letter and knew what had happened to me. It was impossible to believe he would have decided to have nothing more to do with me because of it, although I wouldn't blame him. I almost wished that were true for his sake.

"No one called me while I was in the hospital, Mrs. Bogart?" I asked her when she brought me some cold water with which to take my medication.

"Not while I was in the house," she said. "I did leave to do some shopping for us."

"Oh." I thought a moment. "Where is my phone? My aunt was supposed to see to that."

"I don't know. I've got lots else to worry about here," she added.

Furious about it now, I tried to reach Aunt Victoria. She had a phone service like some doctor when her office was closed. The indifferent operator said she would pass along the message. I told her it was very important.

Hours later, while I was having dinner, the phone rang and Mrs. Bogart told me it was Aunt Victoria. I wheeled myself over to it and she handed me the receiver.

"I need that phone installed," I began before I even said hello. "You promised to take care of it and I…"

"We have some other, far more demanding concerns at the moment, Rain. I'll see about the phone when I get back."

"Get back? Where are you?"

"I'm in Washington, with Grant. Your mother, my sister," she added, her voice dripping with disgust, "made a pathetic attempt to take her own life."

"What?"

"She swallowed a dozen or so sleeping pills. Grant is beside himself. We've had to contain the news, of course, keep the disgrace out of the press."

"Is she all right?" I asked.

"All right?" She laughed. "Hardly. She's not dying now, if that's what you mean. The maid found her in time, which was probably what she expected would happen, and they rushed here to the hospital and pumped her stomach. The doctors and I believe she will have to be committed to the psychiatric clinic for a while, maybe quite a while.

"They're nominating Grant for Congress next week, too. He certainly doesn't need this just when his dreams are coming true."

She paused, letting out a deep sigh like someone enduring a great burden.

"As soon as I can, I'll return and we'll do what has to be done for you. For now, I'm afraid you'll be on your own."

"Where do you think I've been?" I snapped back at her. She didn't reply and I calmed myself. "What about Alison?" I asked.

"What about her?"

"How is she taking all this?"

"Fortunately, she's not here. She's in Italy, traveling with a group of students. Grant isn't telling her anything about it. Why spoil her trip?"

"Yes," I said. "Why do that?"

What had Alison ever done to be blessed with a world of happiness and pleasure, a world where sadness was stopped in its tracks and when it rained, it rained lollipops and jelly beans?

And what had I done to live in a world where smiles

and laughter were mined like diamonds and cherished more than rare jewels?

"If you can," I said, "tell my mother I'm sorry to hear about her trouble and I wish she would get better."

Aunt Victoria grunted.

Even someone as insensitive as my aunt knew how I had wanted my mother to have sent similar good wishes to me after my accident.

But she never had.

Now I wondered if she ever would.

10

Giving Up

Austin returned on Monday to continue my therapy. My doctors had told him to keep my exercise light and easy and gradually build back up to the program we had been following. Consequently, we spent a lot more time just talking and being outside. He told me about himself and his family, revealing that he never really liked the way his father treated his mother.

"She works with him at the plant. Actually, I should say she works for him. He acts like she's just another employee. There's no change in tone of voice, no warmth, no real sharing. She doesn't even know how much money they have.

"For as long as I can remember, she asks him for things the way my sister Heather Sue and I do. I mean, she needs his permission to spend any of their money, even on her own things. My father has a business manager who reviews their household expenditures as well as their business expenses and gives him a monthly report. God help my mother if the categories have gone up in any dramatic way. Then we have the Spanish Inquisition at my house!"

"Doesn't she complain?" I asked.

"She likes it that way."

I knitted my eyebrows together.

"I swear. She's one of these old-fashioned women who believes the man should be totally in charge of these things. She likes being dependent, I think."

We were outside, under the sprawling old oak tree to the right of the house. A pair of squirrels watched us suspiciously. They seemed to freeze in midair when they stood up or turned, their eyes always on us.

The sky was strewn with thin long clouds that the wind spread like cream cheese over the deep blue. For us it was a welcome breeze coming out of the northwest, driving the humidity away.

Austin was on the grass, sprawled on his back beside my wheelchair, chewing on a blade and looking up with his hands behind his head. Suddenly, that looked so inviting to me.

"I want to lie on the ground, too," I said.

"Do it," he challenged. "You don't need anyone's permission or help."

I lifted myself out of the chair, mostly with my arm strength, leaned on my right leg that he had been strengthening with our exercises and then tried to lower myself gracefully, but I toppled to my left and fell over him instead. He screamed with pretended pain and threw his arms around me, holding me there for a few seconds. I turned and our faces were inches apart. Our eyes locked. He smiled.

"Nice try," he said and lifted his head just enough for

his lips to reach the tip of my nose. He kissed it and started to lower his head again.

"Nice try," I retorted.

His smile widened and then his eyes drew something deep and strong from inside him as he raised his head once more and this time brought his lips to my lips. It was a very soft, gentle kiss, but a kiss electric with expectation. It stirred feelings in me that I thought were gone, trampled and forever crippled by my injuries. My breath quickened as my heart began to pound.

"Oh boy," he said after he pulled back. "I'm sorry. I didn't mean to do that."

"You mean that's not part of my therapy?"

He laughed and shook his head.

"I thought I was the one with the sense of humor here."

"Maybe I'm not joking," I said.

His smile tightened and then he moved me gracefully off him and I lay back on the grass. He sat up and took the pillow I had on the wheelchair off and put it under my head.

"Comfortable?"

"Yes," I said.

He sat, looking down at me for a long moment, playing a blade of grass over his lips as he thought. The breeze lifted some strands of his hair and made them dance about his forehead.

"I'm not supposed to get emotionally involved with any of my clients," he said. "It's not fair and it isn't very professional. I can't let something like that happen again. Seriously," he insisted. "If I did, I'd have to ask my uncle to have me replaced.

"Not that you're not a very pretty girl, Rain. You are. If I wasn't your therapist, I could fall in love with you."

"Right," I fired back up at him. "You would see me wheeling myself down some street and say, there's a girl I'd like to know."

I turned away, fuming, frustrated, an arrow of anger looking for a target and finding nothing but air.

"You're making a mistake thinking you're not still very attractive."

I turned back to him.

"What kind of a lover would I be?"

"A good lover. You're still capable of having children, you know. It's a little more involved, but it can happen. I have a client in fact, a woman in her twenties, who recently gave birth. I've been helping her regain her strength. She has a lovely little girl."

"Really?"

"Absolutely," he said. "Didn't your doctors discuss all this with you?"

"No," I said.

"They should have."

He looked up sharply at the sound of an automobile coming up the drive.

"Someone's here," he said.

"Help me up," I asked him and he did so.

"It's Aunt Victoria," I said when she stepped out of her car. She started for the house and then caught sight of us. "You'd better get me back," I said. "She's bringing news about my mother."

"Right."

He helped me into the wheelchair and then started to wheel me back to the house. Victoria waited at the ramp. As we approached, she stepped toward us.

"What sort of therapy can you conduct out there?"

she demanded of Austin before I could introduce them.

"It's important she gets a good dose of fresh air every day," he said.

"Mrs. Bogart could wheel her about for fresh air. It seems a high price to pay a therapist for menial work."

"We do exercises out here, too, Aunt Victoria. And I wheel myself about most of the time. Anyway, why don't we leave my therapy up to the physical therapist, okay? More important, how's my mother?"

"I don't intend to conduct a conversation about that out here with a stranger present," she said. "Wheel her back to her room," she ordered Austin and went to the front door.

"Sorry," he whispered in my ear. "Imagine what would have happened if she had come a few moments earlier."

The thought of that set my heart racing and brought heat to my face.

In my room, Austin picked up his bag and told me he would be back the same time tomorrow.

"I hope I didn't make any new trouble for you."

"Don't worry about it," I told him, but he left with a deep look of concern on his face.

I impatiently waited for Aunt Victoria for nearly fifteen minutes after Austin left. Finally, I heard her distinctive heels coming down the hallway.

"I'm gone for a few days and all hell breaks loose at the office," she moaned as she came into my room. "I swear it's getting more and more difficult to find competent people. Just getting someone who can answer the phone properly is a major task these days. I spend more and more time applying Band Aids on unnecessary complications."

She caught her breath and gazed around.

"Where is your therapist?" she asked, pronouncing the word *therapist* as if it was a profanity.

"He's gone. I think you frightened him off," I said.

She raised her eyebrows.

"Maybe he should be frightened off. It's common knowledge these days that you are an heiress, Rain. Did you ever think of that? Here you are living in this mansion with this magnificent property, too. You've got to be careful. Fortune hunters will be coming out of the woodwork to take advantage of you in your weakened condition."

"Austin is no fortune hunter."

"How do you know? You can't possibly know him well enough to make such a conclusion," she concluded herself before I could reply. "You've known him for a rather short period. I'm sorry I have to speak to you like this, but your mother's not here to give you firm guidance.

"Just another thing Megan has left for me to do," she mumbled and surprised me by flopping rather ungracefully into the one and only chair. She let her head fall back, closed her eyes, squeezed her temples with her forefinger and thumb and sighed. "I'm so tired," she said. Then she sat straighter and looked at me.

"Your mother's been committed to a psychiatric institution until the doctors feel she is emotionally and mentally well-balanced enough to be back in society and not attempt to take her life every other day. Grant is very distraught. We finally told Alison, but there was no point in having her return. She can't do anything."

"She could visit her, help her care about herself and her future," I suggested.

Aunt Victoria tilted her head down and looked up at me with a smirk.

"Alison Randolph? Help someone else?"

"Well, why did they spoil her so?"

"Why? The apple doesn't fall far from the tree. Look at her mother."

"You really hate her, don't you? You hate your own sister," I accused.

"I don't hate her. I should, but I don't." She contemplated me for a moment. "It's easy for you now to pass judgment on me. You come swooping into this house and family, take a nibble here, a taste there and think you've digested our entire history, who we are and what we've all endured.

"Yes, I'm firm and I'm strong and I'm different from Megan, but that's not entirely a fault of my own. She never knew my father as I did, as I had to know him. He made all sorts of demands on me that he never made on her. He expected more from me.

"Don't think I didn't ask myself why a thousand times," she continued before I could even think to ask.

Actually, I was afraid to speak, afraid to utter a sound that would break the spell of this self-revelation. Her eyes became distant, dark.

"I could see the way he looked at Megan, how his eyes just flooded with warmth and love and pride. I never once saw him look at me that way, even when I made great profits for his company. I received a simple pat on the back or a nod while he practically swooned over her every smile and laugh.

"How can a father treat two of his children so differently?" she wondered aloud.

I was tempted to tell her, to give her Jake's secret. Maybe it would be better for her. Maybe she would weigh the disgrace of having him as her father against the terrible pain of not winning her stepfather's love and admiration the way she wanted. That understanding might make her a kinder, gentler woman, a woman who could come to terms with herself and live with herself and not be so bitter toward everyone else.

"Oh, I know how pretty Megan is. How could I not know it, right from the start? When your younger sister is so attractive and so popular, it's not easy. Everyone looks at you and wonders why you aren't the same. She was even invited to parties my peers made and failed to invite me to!

"And was Megan ever grateful? Hardly. She took everything for granted, even my father's love, especially my father's love."

Her eyes clicked shut and then open. She looked at me hard.

"So don't judge me and accuse me of hating her. I hate what she's become, yes. I'm not ashamed to admit that. I'm proud of that.

"I'm proud," she whispered and stared at the floor for a moment.

I was hardly breathing.

I saw her eyes blink again and then she looked up at me sharply.

"Let's get back to you. I still think it would be wiser for you to have a different therapist, an older, more experienced person, perhaps a woman. For a therapist to be effective, he or she has to remain more aloof, more impersonal. Just like a doctor."

"I appreciate your concern, but things are fine the way they are," I said.

She stared at me, her lips pursed so hard, it drained the blood from her chin.

"Okay. I see you have to make your own mistakes.

You've got your mother in you, all right. In more ways than one, you remind me of Megan.

"Let's move on." She opened her briefcase and pulled out some papers. "I have some things I need to have you sign. Since my mother in her infinite wisdom gave you so large a piece of our investments, you would have to be involved with each and every transaction on a daily basis. To expedite it all, I need you to sign a power of attorney over to me. You won't be worth any less," she quickly added. "In fact, you'll probably be worth more because I'll be able to act on opportunities before they disappear. This will make it possible for me to carry on and continue to build our net worth."

She handed me the papers. I looked at them. After reading the first few sentences, I thought they might as well have been written in Chinese. Should I just sign them or should I tell her I had to have my attorney study them first?

"My attorney might get angry at me for signing anything without his approval," I suggested as quietly as I could.

"Oh, for God's sakes," she cried snatching the document out of my hand. "It's a boilerplate document, a standard power of attorney giving me the right to sign papers for us both. I'll have your attorney," she said out of the corner of her mouth, "review it and then you can sign it and feel safe from the claws of the big bad aunt."

"You wouldn't sign anything without your attorney, would you?" I charged.

She stared at me.

"No," she admitted. "But I also wouldn't look a gift horse in the mouth. If I had an aunt like me, responsible, dedicated, concerned, watching over my property, I wouldn't be so uncooperative either."

"I don't mean to seem ungrateful. This is all just too much for me," I admitted.

She nodded.

"Yes, you are your mother's daughter. Megan was never ashamed to confess her weaknesses."

"I'm not confessing weaknesses," I cried. She could be so infuriating, making me feel like a twisted rubber band.

"Whatever," she said standing and flicking her hand in my direction as if I were a mere fly. "I have a lot to do. I was hoping you would help make it easier for me, but I'll just plod on and get through it all, as I have always done. I'll be back as soon as I can," she added as she walked toward the door. She paused there with her back to me for a long moment as if she was deciding whether or not she should tell me something. Finally, she turned.

"There is one more thing," she said. "I nearly forgot or, rather, I didn't want to create any more problems at the moment."

"What is it?" I asked in a tired voice.

"It concerns your stepbrother Roy."

"What? What about him?"

"Oh well, I suppose you've got a right to know everything that concerns you, whether you're in a wheelchair or not."

She opened her briefcase again and sifted through some papers, making me wait anxiously.

"My mother's name was on the envelope so they just forwarded it to me without noticing your name written after *ATTENTION*. My secretary tore it open and put it on my desk as she does with every piece of correspondence. Where did I put...oh, here it is."

She held it up.

"It's from his army attorney on his behalf, informing

you that he has been courtmartialed for violating a probation period."

"What? What probation period?"

"I'm sure I don't know the details," she said.

She handed me the paper. I read it quickly, my right hand at the base of my throat, my breath trapped right at the spot. Roy had tried to run away from the army and had been caught and placed under arrest.

"Oh no," I moaned. "He probably did this after he found out about me. I shouldn't have written to him and told him about the accident."

"No. Maybe not. Maybe if you had asked my advice, I would have made some other suggestions. Just like Megan," she repeated shaking her head, "acting impulsively. Always take a step back before deciding on something, no matter what," she lectured. She shook her head and then closed her briefcase sharply. "I have to go."

She turned and left me there, holding the terrible paper in my hands, wondering when I would stop hurting the people I loved.

Fortunately for me, Austin surprised me. Maybe it was because he had called and Mrs. Bogart told him I couldn't eat a thing at dinner that he decided to come over again. After learning about Roy, just the thought of food made my stomach tighten like a fist. Finally, I had turned from the table and wheeled myself from the table, Mrs. Bogart's orders, threats and warnings falling away. At first I was going to just go to sleep, but my frustration and anger had built to a point of exploding. It was twilight and still quite warm outside. I went to the front door, opened it and wheeled myself out.

"Where do you think you're going this time of the day, girl?" she demanded.

"Just outside for a while. I want to be alone," I emphasized and shut the door on her. I rolled myself down the ramp and then turned and went over the driveway toward the lake. I stopped at the foot of the path and gazed down at the water and thought about Roy, locked up again in some military prison, almost as frustrated as I was because he was trapped, too.

Of course, I should have realized he would have done something like that, I told myself. What was I thinking when I wrote that letter? Didn't I know him well enough to realize he would think only about getting to me, consider that more important than anything else? He always thought about me first and put me ahead of himself.

I should have thought about him first and not been so anxious to let everyone know my tragedy. I was just looking for sympathy. It was my fault, all my fault. I hated what happened to me. I hated being in this chair. I wished it was years back and I was still living in the projects. We used to think it was so terrible, but we were better off. I'd trade a hundred big houses and a hundred fancy cars and all this money if I could get up and walk away.

"Mama!" I screamed. "Look at what's happened to us and is still happening to us!"

My voice traveled over the lake and echoed in the trees. I saw a crow lift off a dead branch and flee into the darkness.

Good, I thought. Every living thing should flee from me. Even I should flee from myself.

My arms suddenly felt electric with new power. I gripped the wheels of my chair firmly and turned them, moving the chair forward, off the macadam and onto the gravel and dirt pathway that led toward the dock and the lake. The chair bounced and the wheels got caught in grooves, bringing me to a sudden stop, but I leaned back and pushed harder, lifting the chair up and out and onward again. Tears streamed down my face. My hands ached.

Midway, I picked up momentum and no longer had to push. The chair rolled onward, but it hit a rock and spun. It slowly tilted. I tried to keep it level, but my weight shifted too quickly and I went over with it, barely having time to utter a single cry. I fell onto a soft, grassy area. The right wheel continued to spin. I wasn't completely out of the chair, but I was twisted.

It seemed to take hours to move myself and get enough momentum out of my leg so I could get myself and the chair upright again. Finally, I did so and just sat there, breathing hard, sweating so much the strands of my hair stuck to my forehead.

The sun had fallen behind the tree line. Darkness drew the shadows out of the surrounding woods. Stars appeared and the lake itself turned an inky dark blue and gray.

I had only frightened myself with the spill. I wasn't scraped or bleeding, nor did I hit any part of my body hard, but there was some mud and dirt on my arms and my clothes. Once my breathing became regular again, I felt the same dark red ball of frustration and anger building inside me. I couldn't even do this right. The red ball swelled until it pressed on my heart and made it pound.

What a mess I am, I thought. Where's that independence I was supposed to be developing? I'll always be a pathetic invalid, kept here on this earth just to make life miserable for someone else.

I wheeled myself forward again, taking more care, holding the chair back from lunging in either direction too quickly. Darkness was closing in around me much more quickly than I had anticipated. I struggled to see exactly where I was going. Suddenly, I felt a horrible spasm of pain in my hip. It took the breath out of me and I had to release my grip on the wheels.

Again the chair picked up momentum. I held onto the sides and closed my eyes and told myself to relax.

I was heading right for the dock. The chair bounced hard and then hit the dock, wheeling me first to the right and then, after I leaned to the left, turned far too sharply and spilled me out, this time nearly knocking the wind out of me when I hit. However, I didn't realize how close I was to the edge. With what I was sure was a look of terror and surprise on my face, I went over and hit the water mostly with my back.

In seconds, I was sinking. I waved my hands and arms frantically and brought myself back up. I gasped again and again, never getting enough oxygen.

Wait, Rain, why are you fighting so hard? I heard a voice within me ask. Just let your arms fall to your sides and your weight and your dead limbs will draw you down to where you belong. I actually started to lower my arms when I heard the second splash and a moment later, felt Austin's strong arm around my waist. He elevated half my body out of the water and drove me toward the dock.

"Easy," he cried. "I've got you."

He lifted me out and placed me on the dock. I fell back, gasping with spasms. He was out of the water and beside me, holding my head against him.

"Did you swallow any water? How you doing?"

I felt my body start to relax and my breathing grew more regular.

"No," I finally said.

"What the heck were you doing down here by yourself? Just as I drove up I saw you hit the dock and I came running. Did you lose control of the chair? I wanted to take you swimming, but I didn't think you were this anxious," he kidded.

I didn't reply. I was shivering now, even though it was still quite warm.

"I've got to get you out of these wet clothes," he said.

He scooped me into his arms and started up the pathway. My eyes closed, I could feel his strength, the power in his legs as he practically ran up the small incline toward the house. It seemed, just seconds before we were at the front door. The moment Mrs. Bogart saw us she gasped and cried out.

"What happened to her?"

"She fell in the lake. Let's get her out of these wet clothes and into a warm bath," he ordered.

Mrs. Bogart charged ahead and he followed to my room. He set me down gently on the bed. She was already running the hot water. He pulled off my shoes and socks. My teeth chattered.

"I'll take care of her," Mrs. Bogart said coming out of the bathroom. You better get yourself out of those wet clothes, too. There are some large towels and a bathrobe in the downstairs closet near the powder room. I'll throw your clothes in the dryer," she added.

"Thanks," he said. He put his hand on my cheek. "You all right?"

I nodded.

"You feel any pain anywhere?"

"No," I managed to whisper. Except in my heart, I wanted to say—but I didn't have the strength.

"As soon as you get warmed up, you'll feel better," he said. "I'll be right back. I'll go fetch the wheelchair, too."

"Why'd you go and do something stupid like this?" Mrs. Bogart asked me as she pealed off my wet clothing. "After you were so sick, too. I knew I shouldn't have let you go outside yourself. I knew it. Now she'll blame me."

"I'm not a child," I muttered. "And stop worrying about being blamed."

"No," she said. "You're not a child. A child would have more sense."

I almost laughed. Tired and weak, I let her take control. Moments later, I was soaking in a hot tub, my body starting to revive. I closed my eyes and felt myself drift.

"How's she doing?" I heard Austin ask Mrs. Bogart. I thought it was part of some dream until I opened my eyes and remembered everything.

I called for her and she came in to help me get out of the tub and put on a nightgown. She brought in my wheelchair and wheeled me back to my bedroom, where Austin was waiting. He was wearing a terry cloth robe and was barefoot.

"How are you doing?" he asked me.

"Better," I said.

Mrs. Bogart looked from me to him and said she would see about his clothes. We watched her leave and then Austin rose and sat on my bed.

"What were you really trying to do, Rain?"

"Drown myself," I admitted.

"I guess I made trouble for you with your aunt, was that it?" he asked.

"Hardly," I said. "No, I was upset about something else.

My stepbrother got in trouble with the army again. I wrote and told him about myself, and he tried to come back here and was arrested and will be courtmartialed. It's all my fault."

"Why? He was the one who tried to go AWOL."

"Because of me! Because of my writing to him," I emphasized.

He shook his head.

"I don't buy that. We're all responsible for ourselves. There were other things he could have done. If he makes you feel guilty…"

"He hasn't. I haven't heard directly from him," I said. "My aunt just as an afterthought managed to give me the information earlier. Everyone I touch," I muttered, "and everyone who touches me…"

"Look, Rain. It's easy for me to tell you what to do and what to think, I know. I'm not the one in the wheelchair, but despite what's happened to you, there's no curse on you. Bad things happen to people. That's life. You know from being in the hospital's physical therapy department that there are people worse off than you."

"And better," I reminded him.

"And better," he agreed nodding, "but we're all vulnerable to the whims of fickle fate and we've got to do the best we can with the hand we're dealt. That's the only responsibility we have. Giving up doesn't gain us anything but some momentary pity from people who will quickly forget us."

I looked up at him, sharply.

"What makes you so wise?" I asked.

He shrugged.

"You think you would have been better off at the bottom of the lake?"

"I would have brought people less misery," I said.

"And less pleasure," he retorted.

He looked at me so intently, his eyes moving over my face so slowly and with such a look of appreciation, I felt my skin tingle. He was looking hard at my lips—lips that were slightly parted and waiting to be kissed, which was what he did, so gracefully and softly, I thought I must have imagined it. When he pulled back, his eyes remained closed as if he was savoring the delicious moment.

Before I could speak, we heard Mrs. Bogart coming and he straightened up.

"Here you go," she said bringing him his clothes, dry and neatly folded.

"Thank you. I'll just go in here and dress," he said nodding at the bathroom.

She stood there, her eyes narrowing as she gazed at me and then at him.

"Thank you, Mrs. Bogart," I said to put a period to her suspicions.

She nodded.

"I'll be nearby if you need me," she said and left.

Moments later, Austin stepped out of the bathroom. We just stared at each other.

"Tired?" he finally asked.

"More like numb."

He smiled.

"Would you like me to help you into bed?"

"Yes," I said even though both of us knew I could do it without him.

He took my hand and guided me up, holding me at the waist. His face was close to mine, his lips practically touching my cheek. His breath felt so warm and sweet. As

I moved onto the bed, his hands traveled down my thighs and helped raise my legs. I lay there, looking up at him.

"You're beautiful, Rain," he said. "Even when I'm working with you, I don't think of you as handicapped or injured. That's never happened to me before with a patient. Don't ever, ever again think you're not worth the effort."

He leaned over and kissed me softly, holding my hand as he did so.

He straightened up and backed away, but I held onto him.

"Don't leave," I whispered.

His eyes widened and he gazed at the doorway.

"What about Mrs. Bogart?" he asked.

"She'll go to bed soon," I said.

"Yeah, but not until she sees me leave."

"She's not my boss. I'm her boss."

"That's not what I'm afraid of. See you later," he said.

He confused me because he didn't say good night. I heard him go down the hall, say good night to Mrs. Bogart and leave. She came by to check on me and I asked her to put out the light and close the door. She did so and I lay there, confused by my mixed emotions. I was disappointed, yet excited, afraid, yet full of longing.

A few minutes later, I heard a noise at my window. I turned and watched it go up.

Seconds later, Austin was back in my room.

And only moments after that, he was beside me in my bed.

11

Can I Be a Woman?

"Don't worry," he whispered afer he put his arm around me. "All I came back to do was hold you until you fall asleep."

"That's exactly what worries me," I said and he smiled. In the warm glow of the moonlight that spilled through my open curtains, his face was radiant, his eyes capturing the glitter like two small precious stones.

I nestled my head against his shoulder and chest and he kissed my forehead and stoked my hair.

"Doctor Synder and I talked about all this," I said. "She tried to assure me someone could still love me, but I wrote it off as just something cheery a therapist has to say, especially since she was also a paraplegic. She wanted to believe it as much or even more than I did.

"I was suspicious about you, too," I said, "about all the nice things you've been saying to me."

"You mean you're not anymore?"

"I don't know. Still, it's pretty crazy for you to come sneaking back in here."

"And risk my career," he added nodding.

"You sure you want to?" I asked, lifting my head from his chest.

"There's only one way to answer," he replied and kissed me, this time harder. Then he lowered my head to the pillow and sat up so he could take off his clothes.

It was like watching it all in a dream, aloof, apart, above my own bed, floating. Perhaps I had died in the lake and all this was wishful thinking in the afterlife. My heart wasn't just pounding. It was hammering and throbbing against my breastbone, rushing blood to my head, making me dizzy. I was afraid, not of making love, but of not being able to, of not being capable of returning his love and affection.

There were so many more reasons why we shouldn't be doing this than there were why we should. Why was it that more often than not the men in my life were forbidden for one reason or another?

When he was naked, he lifted my nightgown, bringing it up. Then he waited for me to raise my arms.

"Don't be afraid," he said.

Of course he would understand my fears, I thought. Who better?

I raised my arms slowly and he took my nightgown off. Then he brought his body to mine and kissed me and held me. He took such special care with each caress, each kiss, I felt we were making love in slow motion. Seconds and minutes were glued together. The hands of the clock struggled and strained to move an iota forward. All the tingling and all the warmth that blossomed under his fingers and beneath every place that his body touched mine returned to me like memories long lost and forgotten, now traveling back over vast chasms of darkness to reach my aroused brain charged with expectations and promise.

Can I do this? Can I be a woman again? Can I feel him grow hot with anticipation and pleasure? Would we turn our separate selves into some magical conjoined living, breathing creatures of ecstasy? Or would I fumble and moan, be clumsy and awkward and as unsatisfactory to him and myself as would a promise undelivered, my kisses turning to smoke, my embrace nothing more than wishful thinking?

My name was on his lips. When he cupped my breasts and then brought his mouth to them, my head fell back on the pillow. I closed my eyes so I could feel myself drift deeper and deeper into the warmth built around me by my own hot blood and tingling skin.

"You're so beautiful," he said.

His words were like some kind of perfume sweetening the darkness. I moaned with pleasure I had believed was gone forever, and just like some old friend shaking her head at my skepticism and disillusionment, my body chastised me for my doubt, teasing me with each rush of warmth that flowed down to my thighs.

He was there almost as quickly to greet them. I flinched and he paused.

"Do you want me to stop now?" he asked.

Should I have said yes, stop, don't make me believe I can be a complete woman again, don't fill me with false hope and promise, don't help me up and then leave me to fall again? Should I have turned away from him?

And turned to what, though? Everlasting disappointment, acceptance of defeat and tragedy? Like a swimmer who had gone too far out, I could not refuse any extended helpful hand, but surely Austin's hand wasn't just any. The way we had first looked at each other, the warm feelings we both had when we were together, the comfort and ease with which we moved in and out our most intimate thoughts and memories certainly all meant that this was something special, that together we were something special.

"Don't stop," I said and lifted my head to kiss him.

I was surprised and rapturous when I felt him inside me, filling me with so much exhilaration, I couldn't breath. I clung to him as if I was dangling in the air and if I let go, I would fall forever and ever. The rush that followed our climaxes flowed up my stomach, around my heart and then into my brain. Maybe I passed out for a moment, maybe I just reached some point beyond mere consciousness, but I found myself surprised I was still clinging to him and he was still there, holding me, catching his breath, pressing his lips to my neck and then, with one quick peck on my own lips, lifting himself away and falling back beside me.

Neither of us spoke for a long moment.

"Are you all right?" he asked.

"I don't know. I have the feeling I could get up and walk away," I said and he laughed.

"If that's all it took, I'd be the most successful therapist in the business."

We were both silent again. Then he leaned on his elbow and turned to me.

"When I saw you go into the lake, Rain, my heart did flip-flops and not just because I was watching someone drown. It was more than that. I panicked. I was going into that lake, too. I was going to drown with you. I was going to lose you."

"Really?"

"Really," he said, his eyes as innocent and honest as a little boy's. "Ever since I began working with you, you're all that's on my mind. Sometimes, I'm drifting so badly when I'm with other patients, they practically have to yell to get my attention. All I do is apologize all day and wait for the time I can come back to you. It's like your face has been printed indelibly on the insides of my eyelids. Close my eyes to rest them or go to sleep, and guess who I see?"

I smiled and touched his lips. He kissed the tips of my fingers. Then he sighed and sat up.

"I'd better be going," he said. "I can't be here when Mrs. Bogart comes around, that's for sure." He put on his shirt. "Now, we are like *Romeo and Juliet*, forbidden lovers. I'll have to reread it."

"It doesn't have a happy ending, Austin," I reminded him.

"We will," he promised.

He dressed as quietly as he could. Then he kissed me good night and slipped out the window.

He was gone so quickly I was sure it had all been a dream.

I curled up as best I could, snuggled against my plush pillow, and closed my eyes.

In moments, I was asleep. The darkness, trouble and pain of the day fell back like ashes consumed in the fire of our wonderful passion.

For the first time in a long time, I actually looked forward to tomorrow.

The energy and excitement with which I greeted each new day astonished me almost as much as it did Mrs. Bogart, who—no fool herself—glanced at me and then at Austin with a knowing look, confirmed by a small nod or a gleam in her eyes. Yet she said nothing nor made any derogatory comment. However, the first time I invited him to stay for dinner, she shook her head disapprovingly. I soon found out, she had become Aunt Victoria's little spy, not out of any displeasure or anger, but because Aunt Victoria had convinced her I was vulnerable to so-called fortune hunters.

The next day Aunt Victoria rushed in like a guard dog, growling and barking, seething with anger at the trespasser.

"What's this I hear that your therapist is now having dinner with you and visiting you at all hours as well as spending far more time than he's been hired to spend on your therapy?" she demanded without even a hello.

I was in the den-office writing a letter back to Mr. MacWaine from England who had been told of my accident and had written to express his regrets and sympathy. I had yet to hear anything from Roy, despite my attempts to contact him. I was going to write another letter to his army attorney.

I sat back in my chair.

"Well?" she demanded. "What's going on here?"

"I don't see where this is any business of yours, Aunt Victoria. I don't mean to be insolent or nasty, but I am in charge of my life, even if I am stuck in this wheelchair."

"That's ridiculous," she said. "No one's suggesting you can't be in charge of your own life, but you are obviously not listening to good advice. I don't give you this advice on my own. I've spoken with a number of experts on the subject and they all agree that in your condition, especially so fresh in it, you are absolutely defenseless. If someone like me doesn't stand up for you, you'll be—"

"Hurt?"

"In more ways than you can imagine." She paused, approached the desk, folded her arms under her small bosom and stiffened her neck. "Now," she said firmly, her lips tight, "I want to know just how far this whole thing has gone. Are you having a romantic episode with this...this so-called therapist?"

"Romantic episode?"

"You know exactly what I mean."

We stared at each other. I didn't know whether to laugh or just shout her out. Suddenly, her face softened.

"Believe me," she continued, her voice far more gentle, "men are first and foremost sexual predators. They sneak up on you and pounce when you're most weak and vulnerable, and I'm not just referring to someone like you. They circle even the strongest and healthiest women with their smile and their soft talk and their promises and then they take your...self-respect. It doesn't even occur to them that they're doing that and even if it did, I don't think it would matter much."

"What are you talking about?" I asked, grimacing with some confusion. It was hard to accept Aunt Victoria as someone who gave advice to lovelorn women. She glanced at me and then she turned and walked to the window.

"I know you think I'm someone without any experience in these sort of matters, but that's not true. I'm just good at keeping it all under lock and key." She turned to me. "I do have some wisdom, womanly wisdom to share with you. My sister," she said almost spitting the words, "never cared to listen to anything I would tell her in that regard. She was always more experienced. Who was I to tell her anything? Well, having more experiences, sleeping with more men, doesn't mean you've become wiser about it. You have to have the right stuff up here," she said pointing to her temple, actually poking it with the tip of her finger so hard, I had to wince. "You have to be able to make use of the experiences.

"She never had it and never will. But you do, Rain. I know you do," she said, sounding like she was pleading for us to be good friends. "And I can give you some advice that you will appreciate.

"Listen to me," she said angrily. "Men are predators, fortune hunters, ready to pounce. I've been victimized myself," she revealed and then looked away.

The silence was so deep and thick, I could hear water running through a pipe on the other side of the house.

"What do you mean you were victimized?" I finally asked.

She pealed a laugh that sounded maddening. "He pretended I was more important to him than she was. He even went so far as to…as to act as if he needed me near him, needed my comfort. I felt sorry for him and I cared for him. Who do you think has made the biggest campaign contribution?"

"You mean Grant? Did something happen between you and Grant?"

She didn't nod, but her eyes said yes.

"Does my mother know about this?"

She laughed again.

"Your mother doesn't even know what room she's in. She never knew about Grant and I. I'm sure that Grant has strayed often."

"How can you respect a man who cheats and deceives and has no honor and no integrity?" I asked.

"How could he not be bored to death with a woman as shallow as she is?" she countered. "It would strain any man's patience and integrity."

"But with his wife's own sister!"

"I don't want to think about it anymore," she replied instead of answering. She looked alarmed, her eyes fleeing from mine.

Was she telling me the truth or was she vocalizing some fantasy? Stranger things have certainly happened in my life and around me, I thought.

"Now listen to me," she continued, returning to her original vigorous attack, "I want you to have a different therapist, a responsible older person immediately."

"We've already had this discussion, Aunt Victoria."

"You're being foolish, Rain." She paused, stared a moment and then nodded. "Think, look at yourself in the mirror. What good looking, healthy man is going to become devoted to you for you and not for your wealth? Don't be blind and stupid."

Cold tears froze over my eyes, clouding my vision. I had these fears always under the surface of my hopes. I didn't need her to remind me of them.

"It's not your problem," I said, my voice cracking.

"Of course, it's my problem. Thanks to my mother, we're partners now. If you become involved with someone, I become involved with him as well."

"Oh, so that's it. You're worried about the bottom line again, that net worth statement you wave like a flag around here, those documents you slip under my door behind my lawyer's back."

"I do nothing of the sort. I'm sorry you haven't signed the power of attorney. That would make it all so much easier and you wouldn't be bothered by all the paperwork. You know that all you've been given, your attorney's seen and approved and it's all occurring like I predicted. I'm living up to my responsibilities, for both our sakes. You should have more faith and trust in me. Why last week, I made an investment for us…"

"I don't care about it," I said quickly. "My lawyer doesn't want me to sign the power of attorney."

She shook her head.

"Every time I think there's a chance you might be more like me than Megan, you go and shatter the idea. I'm warning you, Rain, if this man, this therapist is pursuing you romantically than with or without the power of attorney privilege I will take whatever action is necessary."

"Please stop," I begged, my tears coming faster now. "Just stop."

She nodded.

"Okay." She paused, took a deep breath which raised and lowered her narrow, thin shoulders, and then she spoke. "Now there's another bit of news to deliver," she said.

"What?"

"Don't bother to send for Jake."

"What? I told you not to fire him!" I screamed at her. "I told you he works for me, not you! I told you…"

"I didn't have to fire him. He's in the hospital," she said gleefully.

"In the hospital? Why? What happened?"

"He's suffering from cirrhosis. That's a liver ailment caused by excessive alcohol."

"I know what it is. How is he?"

"Very sick," she said and spun around to leave.

"I want to see him," I cried.

"Don't ask me to take you," she warned before I could even think of it. "It's a waste of time," she said at the doorway. "And I certainly haven't any time to waste."

She walked out, her footsteps tapping on my heart as much as they did the hallway floor.

As soon as I could, I called Austin's pager. He called back to tell me he was with a patient, but he said he would be over the moment after he was finished and promised he would get me to the hospital to visit Jake. In the meantime, I tried calling Jake at the hospital, but they said he was unable to use the phone.

It was all too much. I broke into a crying jag that I didn't think I could stop. Mrs. Bogart came quickly and in between my sobs, I told her how ill Jake was. When she heard the reason, she smirked and nodded and said she wasn't surprised.

"I often smelled whiskey on his breath," she told me. "People have enough trouble in their lives without going out and making more on their own," she declared. "If they do, they deserve what they get."

"I'm sure he doesn't want to be sick," I fired back at her. "Why are you so cruel?"

She huffed up, her face swelling and filling like a balloon.

"I'm not cruel, but I've seen what drinking does to people. My own daddy killed himself and an innocent woman in a drunk-driving accident," she revealed.

With that, she turned and left me. I was sorry now that I hadn't spent time learning how to drive my van yet. It underscored the futility of wallowing in self-pity. I should be taking advantage of every opportunity I had to restore my independence. I vowed to do so from now on, with or without Mrs. Bogart and Aunt Victoria's help.

Finally, Austin arrived and we immediately set out for the hospital.

"Where you taking that girl?" Mrs. Bogart demanded when she heard us in the hallway.

"I'm going to visit Jake," I said.

She looked at Austin reproachfully, but he ignored her and wheeled me out. He got me securely in the van and we drove off.

"I'm sure she's on the phone with Aunt Victoria by now," I told him. "What I hate the most about my paralysis is that it makes everyone treat me like a child. Even my housekeeper thinks she can order me around."

"You're right. The way others view handicapped people often hurts their self-image and slows their rehabilitation," Austin said. "It's a pet peeve of mine. Ironically, the more privileges handicapped people earn, the more they are belittled. Friends of mine are always joking and calling handicap parking spots, handicrap spots. I've nearly gotten into fistfights over it."

His face turned crimson just by his talking about the problem. He realized it and smiled at me.

"I guess I'm just one of those people who can't help himself from getting too involved with his patients," he said.

"Just as long as you're not as involved with any other as much as you are with me," I responded and he laughed.

He looked at me and shook his head. "Hardly."

When we arrived at the hospital, he wheeled me into the lobby and we went to the information desk to find out where Jake was. Minutes later we were in the elevator going up to the third floor. It was very quiet, nearly the end of visiting hours.

"Oh, I was wondering where his family was," the nurse on duty told us when we asked for his room. "He has been in and out of consciousness and asking for his daughter.

Doctor Hamman is with him at the moment and I'm sure he'll want to have a word with you."

Austin was about to tell her that I wasn't Jake's daughter, but I put my hand over his quickly and he looked at me and saw I didn't want that.

We approached Jake's room slowly. Just before we reached the doorway, Doctor Hamman stepped out with another nurse.

"Better move him to ICU," he told her. She nodded and then saw us standing there and touched the doctor's arm. He turned.

"Oh," he said. "Are you related to Mr. Marvin?" he asked.

"Yes," I said.

He nodded, regarding me with a somber look.

"I'm afraid his liver disease has moved into a very serious stage. It's affected his kidneys and they are failing."

"How could this happen so quickly?" I asked in a broken voice.

"Quickly? Oh, this hasn't happened quickly. Mr. Marvin has been recieving treatment for cirrhosis for some time now. He's been repeatedly warned about his alcohol consumption. For some reason his consumption dramatically increased recently and that has led to serious complications. The disease can be subtle. Sometimes it is discovered, sometimes not. Such cases are called cryptogenic cirrhosis. Some may have only subtle physical changes, such as red palms, red spots that blanch on their upper body which we call spider angioma or fibrosis of tendons in the palms. Some suffer from jaundice, or have memory problems. Every case is different.

"I'm sorry," he said. "I have to move him to intensive care. Without a kidney transplant, he must go onto dialysis immediately and with the continued degeneration..." His voice trailed off.

He waited to see if I had any more questions, but I couldn't speak. He nodded and then continued down the corridor. Austin held my hand. Then, I wheeled myself into Jake's room. He looked unconscious, but when I reached his bed, he turned and smiled.

"Hey, Princess....what are you doing here?"

"Oh Jake, it's better I ask what are you doing here?" I countered. "I just spoke with the doctor. You knew you were sick and you kept on drinking."

"Doctors," he said grimacing. He closed his eyes. "I'll be all right. I'll be out of here in no time. Don't worry about me," he said. He opened his eyes. "Say, how did you get here?"

"Austin drove me in the van," I said.

"Oh. You better learn how to drive yourself," he said softly.

"I will. Austin will help me immediately," I said looking up at him. He nodded.

"Sure."

"Good," Jake said as if that was the last thing he had to be sure would happen before he left this world. He closed his eyes again and fell immediately into a deep sleep that looked like a coma. I waited to see if he would waken, but he was still sleeping when they came to move him to the intensive care unit. Austin and I watched them prepare him for the move and then wheel him away on a gurney.

"Still wonder why I think everyone who cares for me suffers?" I asked Austin.

"Stop it, Rain," he snapped. "Don't start berating yourself. You're not responsible for this. You heard the doctor.

Jake knew he shouldn't drink and yet he continued to do so."

"Just take me home, Austin. Take me home and leave me there," I told him.

On the way home I talked about Jake and told Austin much of what I knew and understood about his relationship with Grandmother Hudson. I described how right from the start he had been my best friend.

"I know he blames himself for what happened to me, Austin. I know that drove him to drink more. Don't you see? That's why I say anyone who gets too close to me, suffers.

"Aunt Victoria is right, but not for the reason she thinks. Don't come back here, Austin," I begged him. "You're better off just forgetting about me. I'll go get another therapist."

We had pulled up to the house and he had turned off the engine.

"Stop that silly talk," he ordered.

I started to cry and he seized me by the shoulders and shook me, harder than I anticipated. I looked up at him.

"Stop it!" he cried. "You're not going to wallow in this self-pity, Rain. I won't let you. I know you can return to a good, productive life and I'm not going anywhere, so get that out of your foolish head," he insisted, his eyes steely. "Tomorrow, we'll start your driving lessons, but right now let's get you inside and comfortable."

He got out and helped me out of the van. Then he wheeled me up the ramp and into the house. Mrs. Bogart was nowhere around. She had either left for some reason or was in her own room. I didn't call for her. Austin took me to my room and closed the door behind us. I sat there feeling stunned and helpless. He kissed me on the cheek and began to help me undress and get ready for bed. I let him do everything. For the moment I enjoyed being helpless.

After he carried me to my bed and lay me down, he brought the blanket up around me snugly and kissed me. I felt like a little girl again, back in the projects with Mama tucking me in and wishing me sweet dreams.

Austin didn't leave. He sat for a while and just watched me sleeping. I heard him rise and go to the bathroom, but I didn't open my eyes. I drifted in and out of sleep and each time I opened my eyes, he was still sitting there. Finally, I groaned and looked at the clock. It was nearly two in the morning.

"Why don't you go home, Austin?"

"I'm fine," he said.

"You can't be comfortable," I said. "If you insist on staying here tonight then come to bed," I said.

He smiled.

"Okay."

He rose, got undressed and slipped in beside me. I turned my torso to him and we embraced. Snuggled in his arms, I felt safe again, safe and content. He kissed me softly on the lips and we both finally, fell asleep.

I woke with a jolt when my bedroom door was opened and the air just seemed to rush over me. Austin was still asleep.

"Well, this is a fine sight!" Mrs. Bogart cried. She stood there with her hands on her hips. "A fine sight."

Austin opened his eyes and looked at me and then at her. He dropped his head back to the pillow and groaned.

"Close the door, Mrs. Bogart, and never, never come bursting into my room again," I told her.

"You don't need to worry about me doing that," she threatened. "I won't stand by and just watch this sinfulness and be talked to like that."

She slammed the door hard as she left.

"Uh-oh," Austin said.

"Don't worry. My grandmother was famous for rotating household help. I'm just following in her tradition," I said and he laughed.

Mrs. Bogart didn't leave immediately, but she gave notice to Aunt Victoria, who used it as another excuse for one of her fiery lectures about the pitfalls of being involved with men. I paid even less attention to her than before; when she moaned about how difficult it was going to be to find someone else as qualified as Mrs. Bogart, I told her not to worry about it. I'd find someone myself.

"That's absolutely ridiculous," she declared and marched out of the house, grumbling under her breath about how this was all happening at the wrong time. She had too much to do and was too busy to babysit for a reckless invalid.

During the next two weeks, Austin continued my therapy and often stayed overnight with me. Every chance we had, we drove over to the hospital to visit Jake. Sometimes he knew I was there, sometimes he didn't. On occasion he babbled what to other people sounded like nonsense, but to me it was a weaving of all the secrets that made up the cocoon that had enveloped him at the end of his life.

Austin gave me driving lessons with the van and expanded my therapy to include other daily activities, all designed to ensure my growing independence. I couldn't help but be a little terrified the first time I drove somewhere by myself, but the mechanized van made all of it possible. I even went to the supermarket and shopped. That night I told Mrs. Bogart to take the evening off and I made Austin and myself dinner.

He raved about the food so much, I thought he was deliberately overdoing it, but he swore everything was truly delicious. When I challenged that, he put down his fork and looked at me reproachfully.

"Were you a good cook before your accident?" he asked.

"I was often told so," I admitted.

"Did you cook and bake with your feet?"

"No," I said laughing.

"Then how could your accident have any effect on your ability to cook?" he cross-examined me. "Well?"

"I guess it couldn't," I confessed.

"If I compliment you on your jogging, you can doubt me," he told me. "Until then, I insist that my honesty not be challenged."

I laughed. How wonderful he could make me feel. He toasted me with another glass of wine and then he rose and kissed me.

"Let's leave the dishes for Mrs. Bogart," he whispered, his lips grazing my ear. "It's the least she can do."

I turned to him and smiled.

"Oh? And what will we do?"

His eyes told me what he wanted. Mine spoke just as clearly and as loudly. He wheeled me from the table and gently lifted me out of my chair and onto my bed where we made love more passionately—yet more lovingly—than we ever had before.

Afterward, I felt complete and contented. I only hoped and prayed it wasn't a will-o'-the-wisp dream that would fade and turn dry and crisp like an old leaf and finally crumble to dust.

I could be happy. I could be happy again, I told myself.

We were nearly asleep when the phone rang. My heart knew why before my brain heard the words.

Doctor Hamman was calling to say he was sorry.

"Mr. Marvin has expired," he said.

Austin held me as I cried for Jake. Then I caught my breath, wiped my cheeks and turned to him.

"The person who should be getting this call has no idea why she should be the one getting it, Austin. That's almost as horrible as what's happened to Jake. His daughter wasn't at his side."

"You were there, Rain," he reminded me. "And Jake loved you as he would a daughter."

"I'll take care of him," I vowed. "I'll see that he has a proper funeral."

I lay back in Austin's arms. He held me as pictures of Jake ran through my mind, his smile, his laughter, his encouragement and even that look of sadness on his face when he had taken me to the airport for my trip to London.

"It's so important to have someone whose eyes fill with tears when they say good-bye to you, Austin," I whispered.

"Mine certainly won't," he said. "Because I won't ever say good-bye."

Oh please, I prayed, let those words never turn to dry leaves and crumble into dust.

12

Reflections in a Broken Mirror

With Austin's help, I made the arrangements for Jake's funeral. He was to be buried in his family plot in the same cemetery where Grandmother Hudson was buried. Mrs. Bogart left the day before the funeral. I could see she was now feeling a little guilty about leaving me. When she came to me after breakfast to say good-bye, she had trouble lifting her gaze from the floor and looking at me directly.

"I'm sorry about that man's dying and bringing you more sorrow," she began.

"His name was Jake," I corrected. "Not that man."

She looked up quickly, her neck stiffening.

"Yes, well I don't like to see bad things happen to anyone, even when they bring it on themselves. I'd stay with you a little longer to help you get through your bad time," she added, her conscience rising to the surface like some stubborn memory refusing to rest quietly under the heavy surface of her anger and her ego. "But I have a new position with someone who needs me more and I promised to be there this afternoon."

"Don't break your promises," I muttered dryly.

"You're being a bad girl, not listening to your aunt. Victoria's a very wise woman and you're going to be a sorry soul if you don't listen."

"You mean sorrier soul, don't you? I'm already a sorry soul."

She shook her head and pressed her lips together blowing out her cheeks and making her eyes retreat into small dark orbs.

"I cleaned the house and I left you plenty to eat. You'll be fine if you get someone soon."

"Thank you," I said, "but I'll be fine even without someone new."

"I doubt that," she muttered. She started to turn away and I pivoted my chair toward her. My sudden move surprised her and made her flinch.

"Mrs. Bogart you are a competent assistant. I'm sure you're going to be of great value to your next client. But handicapped people such as myself have needs other than just food and water and shelter.

"I hope you take some of that understanding with you to your next assignment and not be such a stern judge just because you can walk."

She shook her head with a look that nearly resembled appreciation, not just amazement.

"Where'd you get all this obstinacy and stubbornness?" she asked. "Even in your injured state."

I smiled.

"My stepmama never looked down on anyone, no matter how low they seemed to be."

She wiggled her shoulders like some big bird fluffing up its feathers and gripped her bags. Then she marched herself out of the house. The sound of the door closing reverberated through the corridor and died in some corner. I took a deep breath, closed my eyes and told myself I really would be fine. I was able to do whatever I had to do for myself.

Austin phoned to see how I was. He knew Mrs. Bogart was leaving. I assured him I was fine, and he promised he would be over as soon as he could after his work. I spent most of my day organizing the house for easier access, taking an inventory of my supplies. And then, because it was an exceptionally beautiful afternoon, I wheeled to the back patio. Sipping some lemonade, I watched the birds that flitted from tree to tree. They seemed so active, so busy preparing for the change of seasons. Mama used to say she bet birds were just full of gossip, sitting on telephone lines all day and hearing all those conversations. I laughed, remembering how the two of us would gaze out of the apartment window down at the street.

It struck me as odd that I had never sat here before to watch the birds and appreciate their grace and beauty. There were so many more than there were back in the city. As I observed them, I realized that movement was so much a part of whom and what they were. A bird that lost its power to fly was no longer a bird. It was something else, I thought, something much less.

Was I something else? Was I much less? Were Mrs. Bogart and Aunt Victoria right to think I couldn't act on my own behalf properly just because my movement was restricted? I refused to believe that now. Thanks to Austin, I had confidence in myself again. I could write and think and cook and clean and take care of my basic necessities. I could drive and I could go most anywhere. Most of all, I could love and be loved.

No, they were wrong. In fact now that Mrs. Bogart was gone, I felt good again. I felt in charge of myself and that gave me back my dignity and identity. Good riddance to you all, I thought defiantly. I'll be like the birds again, free, graceful, content.

When I heard someone drive up and enter the house, I thought it was Austin so I hurried to get back inside and greet him, but it was Aunt Victoria. She looked quite harried, her hair a little messy, her suit creased. She had been calling for me and looking in various rooms. When she finally saw me wheeling in from the rear of the house, she stopped and waited, an expression of surprise on her face.

"What are you doing?" she demanded. "Why are you out there by yourself?"

"Just getting some air."

She absorbed my answer as if it was something hard to digest and then she put on a scowl.

"So now you are satisfied? Mrs. Bogart is gone. Whose idea was it really?" she asked, her eyes getting smaller. "It was his idea, wasn't it? That therapist wanted you alone here, right? That's his plan."

"No. She decided to quit on her own, Aunt Victoria," I said calmly. "You know that."

"She was driven to quit. That's what I know. All right, all right," she muttered. She looked around, her eyes moving wildly in her head. "I won't spend any more time on that." She pressed her right palm against her heart as if she was having some pain and took a deep breath, her thin, narrow shoulders rising and falling hard.

"What's wrong with you? Aren't you well?" I asked.

She spun on me as if she was going to spit at me and then paused and smiled coldly, her lips stretching and becoming pale, her eyes wide.

"She's coming home today. Her doctors claim she's well enough and Grant's taking her back with open arms. Open arms, even after all this!" she cried, her own arms out as if she was referring to the house. "The doctors say her depression has receded enough for her to resume a normal life. Can you imagine such drivel? She's never had a normal life. It was all her plan, all her conniving little plan. How can he want her back? You see what I'm saying about men? You see how right I am?

"They're going on holiday," she continued and laughed a short, maddening little laugh that sounded more like the tinkling of glass. "A little well-deserved R and R he calls it. How does she deserve it?"

"She lost her son, Aunt Victoria. She's suffered horribly. No matter what you think of her, she's your own sister. How can you be so hard?"

"What? You say that? You ask that? You whom she's abused more than anyone you want to know how I can be so hard?" she asked, pointing down at me.

"I don't want to be angry or upset or hate anyone anymore, Aunt Victoria. If you thought I would become your ally against my mother, you were mistaken. I want to get on with my life and make the best of everything. Hating, wanting revenge, all that just eats away at you until you've turned yourself inside out and you're a stranger to yourself and anyone who could or would love you."

"Oh, such wisdom and from a teenager in a wheelchair," she muttered, throwing her hand back as if she was tossing away some rotten fruit.

"I'm not a teenager in a wheelchair," I said. "I'm a young woman with a handicap who's doing just fine, thank you."

"Right, right, that's it, young Megan, bury your head in some sand, put on the rose-colored glasses, shut your ears and your eyes to anything that makes you unhappy, giggle like a fool at dinner tables and travel everywhere with blinders on. All you are now to me is my sister in a wheelchair," she said disdainfully. "I can't look at you without seeing her face."

I shook my head.

"Think what you want. I'm tired of fighting with you or anyone else," I said.

She sighed, looking away and then back at me with a more familiar expression: her businesswoman face.

"You paid for Jake's funeral, I understand."

"That's right. I called your office and left all the details for you. The funeral is at ten tomorrow at the church."

"I have a very important meeting with the directors of an equity group tomorrow morning. I won't be there."

"You've got to be there," I said sharply.

"What? I've got to be at the funeral of my mother's chauffeur instead of attending an important business meeting?" She laughed. "Hardly," she said. She started to turn away.

I couldn't stand the thought of her belittling Jake. I wouldn't permit it.

"He's not just your mother's chauffeur. Wait!" I shouted with insistence.

"What is it?" she said impatiently. "I have important calls to make and I've wasted enough of this day already."

"Jake...wasn't just your mother's chauffeur. Jake was your father," I said.

For a moment she didn't speak. Then she took a few steps back toward me and laughed.

"Are you mad? Is that a consequence of your being crippled, these distorted, ridiculous thoughts? My father— Jake the family chauffeur?"

"He told me so himself. He and Grandmother Hudson were lovers and she got pregnant with you. That's why the man you thought was your father, treated Megan differently than he treated you. He knew."

Her cold smile was replaced with the hardest look of anger and hate I had yet seen on the screen of her face. This venomous expression rose from some well of enmity that surely went as deep back in time as Cain. A veil of darkness fell across her as she stepped closer. She seemed to grow taller, her shoulders rising until she loomed above me like the angel of death about to pounce.

"How dare you distort things I've told you in confidence? How dare you create some disgusting, ridiculous tale of sin? Is it to cover your own guilt? Is that it? Do you hope that by doing this, the fingers of blame will no longer point at you?"

"No, of course not. I'm telling you what Jake told me and what you should have been told years and years ago. He was proud of you, Aunt Victoria. He often spoke of your strengths and accomplishments and—"

"Stop it!" she screamed. Her eyes shot daggers down at me as she slapped her palms over her ears so hard it had to have stung. "I won't listen to another syllable! If you should as much as dare to even suggest such a thing to any-one, I'll...I'll make you think that being in this chair was wonderful compared to what will follow."

"I don't care if you believe it," I said quietly. "But you should attend the funeral."

She just fumed for a moment. Then she lowered her hands from her ears and nodded.

"All this rebellion, this nonsense, it's his doing, the fortune hunter's," she said. "I'll see about that." She turned and started toward the front door.

"Austin has nothing to do with any of this," I shouted. "Don't you even think of doing anything that would harm him. I'm warning you."

She didn't hesitate.

"Aunt Victoria, I'm warning you! Aunt Victoria!" I cried.

With firmness in her steps, she pounded down the hallway and out of the house, slamming the front door behind her and leaving me shaking in my chair.

There weren't many people at Jake's funeral. Aside from the friends he had at the local tavern and a few old friends who knew him before he had left and enlisted in the navy, there was just Austin and myself and Mick Nelsen, the horse trainer who had helped me with Rain. At the cemetery Mick told me how much Jake had talked about me and how much he had loved and had admired me.

"I used to kid him and say you sure she ain't your daughter, Jake? He said no, but you were the closest he'd ever have to a daughter. He just loved the way you rode that horse and the way the horse took to you."

I asked him exactly where Rain was and he told me and assured me the horse was in good hands. I mused aloud that I might take a ride to see her someday and Mick promised he would call ahead for me and make the arrangements whenever I wanted. He stood beside us as we listened to the minister and then watched Jake's coffin being lowered. Afterward, Austin took me over to Grandmother Hudson's grave where I sat for quite a while. Austin waited at the van so I could have my private time. He hurried back when he saw my shoulders quaking from my heavy sobs.

"It's time to go, Rain," he said handing me his handkerchief.

I wiped my eyes, nodded and lay back, letting him do all the work wheeling me through the cemetery and into the van. Shortly afterward, he was wheeling me up the ramp and into the house. With Mrs. Bogart gone and no replacement hired yet, the long corridor and large rooms seemed even more empty and dark. Austin suggested we go out to dinner.

"That's something we haven't done yet," he said. "Why don't you get dressed up and I'll go put on a jacket and tie and we'll go to a really nice place I know. It's got a patio overlooking water. How's that sound?"

"Nice," I said smiling.

"Need any help getting ready?"

"No," I replied firmly and with confidence and determination added, "I want to do it all myself tonight."

"That's what I thought. I'll be back in about two hours, okay?"

"Yes," I said. He kissed me and left.

Undaunted, I turned toward my room to see just how strong I would be and how high I could rise from the fires of sadness that burned around me. I chose one of my prettiest dresses to wear. It occurred to me that I hadn't bought a single garment since my accident. I had lost all interest in how I looked, whether I was in style or not. That's going to change, I thought. Here Grandmother Hudson left me all this money and I haven't spent a nickel on anything that wasn't a medical necessity. Even though I was in a wheelchair, people still saw my feet. It was still important to have nice shoes, and my hair should be attractive.

I vowed in front of my mirror that I would change my appearance. I would replace this sickly, weak and pitiful look with a vibrant, hopeful one. I could be pretty again. Austin wasn't just saying nice things to make me feel better. I saw it in his eyes, in the way he looked at me when he thought I wasn't watching him. He did treasure me. I'd lost my ability to walk, but not to be attractive.

I couldn't deny that I wasn't somewhat afraid of being in charge of my own bathing. I had done most everything else for myself at one time or another, but Mrs. Bogart had always been around when I bathed. I ran the water for my bath and I set out my clothes and then I got undressed and manipulated myself out of the chair and into the tub, but once I was in, I suddenly had this terrible fear I wouldn't be able to get myself out. It made enjoying the bath impossible. In minutes I needed to get out, just to be sure I could. What if I was still here when Austin arrived? How embarrassing.

In my panic and haste to get out, I slipped and banged my arm so hard against the ceramic tile it took my breath away. I started to cry, but then I got myself under control and went about getting out of the tub with more purpose. Moments later, I was sitting on the side, drying myself. I got back into the chair and wheeled myself to the bedroom. With the pain in my arm, it took at least three times as long to put on my clothes, but at least I could do it. However, when I looked at myself in the mirror, I saw how twisted and creased my dress was. I did what I could to straighten it, and then I worked on putting on my shoes. By the time I started on my hair, I was exhausted.

A noise in the bathroom startled me. In shock, I saw I had left the water trickling in the tub and it had finally begun to run over.

"Oh no!" I screamed and wheeled myself back as quickly as I could. I struggled to turn the chair in the small puddle that had already formed. When I reached over to shut off the faucet completely, in my haste, I slipped. Before I could prevent it, I fell into the puddle, soaking one side of my dress.

I screamed and pounded the side of the tub until my right hand ached. Then I caught my breath and pulled myself back into the wheelchair. The wheels tracked water into the bedroom. For a long moment I just sat before the mirror gazing at my rumpled dress and tousled hair. Exhausted, aching and disgusted with myself, I dropped my arms down the side of my wheelchair and lay my head back, feeling a wave of defeat and nausea wash over me. It didn't bring tears; it brought an ugly fury. I lunged at my cosmetics and flung lipsticks and eye shadow tubes in every direction. I swept the vanity table clean and then, in an even wilder rush of madness and frenzy, I hurled my hair brush at the mirror and the blow cracked the glass from top to bottom. Then I let my head fall forward and sat there like a twisted sack of potatoes.

I never heard the doorbell. Finally, Austin who had been ringing and ringing came around the house, looked in the window, saw me and tapped. When I didn't wake up immediately, he opened the window and climbed in.

"Rain, Rain," he cried, shaking my shoulder. "What happened here? What's wrong?" he said gazing around the bedroom in disbelief. Even I was a little shocked, forgetting for a moment all I had done. A cake of perfumed body talcum was spread over some of the therapy machinery and the floor. A bottle of cologne was shattered, its contents spilled near the wall. Everything that had been on the vanity table was scattered and, of course, the mirror was cracked.

"I was doing so well," I began, my lips trembling. "I got myself in and out of the tub and I got dressed and I worked on my hair and...I left the water running."

"What?" He looked back and saw the puddle. "Oh." He went to the bathroom and looked in. "The faucet's off."

"I know. I did that, but I fell out of the chair and I ruined my dress and everything!"

I couldn't stop the tears, my body shaking with their flow. Austin tried to comfort me, laughing and pretending it was all nothing.

"Boy, now I know I better not get you angry," he said. "If you did this over a wet dress, who knows what you would do to me?"

I smiled through my shower of tears and he kissed some of them off my cheeks.

"We'll clean this up in a few minutes," he said starting to gather up the things I had flung every which way. "You'll change your dress, brush your hair, and we'll go," he added calmly.

"Oh, I can't go out in public, Austin. I'll look terrible and embarrass you."

"I doubt it," he said. "Go on. Choose something else while I do this. I'll mop up the water in the bathroom."

He left to fetch a mop and pail. I sighed and looked at myself in the cracked mirror. That's really me now, I thought. This image in the glass is really me. I've got a crack running through me just as deeply and as long. I can try to ignore it all I want, but that's the truth. That's what I am.

More out of a desire not to disappoint Austin, who worked so hard and quickly to repair my room, I found something else to wear. I brushed out my hair, but I was not satisfied with my looks. Nevertheless, I let him smother me with compliments.

"You don't need any makeup, nothing on those eyelids could make those eyes any prettier than they naturally are," he insisted. "You're fine. You look terrific. C'mon. I'm starving," he said and after I put on a light jacket, he wheeled me out of the house and into the van as quickly as he could, probably out of fear I'd change my mind. Moments later we were on our way to the restaurant, Austin acting and talking as if nothing unusual had occurred. He was so exuberant and happy, he almost had me believing it.

The restaurant he'd chosen was truly a beautiful place with thick dark wooden beams in the ceiling, eighteenth-century colonial art and furnishings, thick cranberry-red tables and chairs and brass candelabra on every table. He had reserved a table by the window that looked out over a lake. The lights of homes around the lake were reflected in the water, making it dazzle and glitter in the darkness. We had candlelight and wine and a delicious lobster dinner followed with a dessert of orange crème brûlée that was so good, it was sinful. Before long, my mood had indeed changed, and we were laughing, holding hands, occasionally exchanging kisses and just simply enjoying each other's company.

When a musical trio began to play in the lounge, however, I grew silent and moody thinking how wonderful it would be if I could get up and dance with Austin. He saw the sadness in my eyes and quickly decided it was time to pay the bill and get me home.

"You've had an exhausting day," he insisted.

I put up no resistence. He tried to keep my spirits up by talking continuously during our ride back, drawing up scenarios for fun days to come, places we would visit.

"We should consider taking a real vacation," he said. "I'll have two weeks off in a month. We could take the van and go someplace. What do you think?"

"Sure," I said. I would have agreed to anything, even a trip to the moon. He looked at me and saw that, too, but it didn't stop him from going on and on about it in a desperate attempt to restore my confidence and hope.

Back at the house, he helped me prepare for bed.

"Get a good night's rest tonight, Rain," he said.

"Are you going to leave?"

"I'll stay, if you want."

"Of course, I want you to stay. I'll never be the one to tell you to leave, Austin," I promised. He smiled, brushed back some strands of hair from my forehead and kissed me.

"Close your eyes. I'll be back," he promised and left.

I was so tired I didn't hear him return and get into the bed beside me. The phone woke us in the morning. For a moment I regretted forcing Aunt Victoria to have it installed.

"Hello," I said, clearing my throat.

"Is Austin there?" a man asked.

"What? Oh. Yes," I said.

There was a moment of silence and then he said in a very stern voice, "Please put him on."

I turned in the bed. Austin wiped his eyes and sat up.

"What?"

"It's for you," I said.

"Me?" He grimaced, then he got out of bed and came around to take the phone. "Hello?"

Watching him listen I saw his face turn crimson. His eyes flitted from my face to the floor. He turned his body so that I couldn't look directly at him.

"Okay. I understand," he said. "I'll be right there."

He hung up and for a moment just stood there in silence. "What?"

"That was my uncle," he said. "I've got to go."

He hurriedly began to dress.

"What is it? Austin?"

"I don't want to upset you," he said buttoning his shirt.

"What?" I demanded.

"Your aunt's attorney called my uncle and threatened to make a formal complaint to the state about me. That would mean my uncle would have to appear at a hearing and I would have to go, too." He hesitated and then he added, "If she goes through with it, he could lose his license and his entire business."

"Oh, Austin. I'm sorry."

"It's not your fault," he said. "I should have told my uncle about us. Naturally he wants to know what's been going on. I don't want to do anything that would hurt him. He's been more like a father to me than my real father."

"I feel terrible."

"That's why I was reluctant to tell you, Rain. Don't go blaming yourself now," he warned. "We'll straighten it out."

"In the meantime, stop worrying about me," I told him. "I'll be fine. I won't do anything stupid like last night. I promise. Just take care of your uncle and yourself."

"You are going to get someone else to help here, aren't you?"

"Yes."

"I'll see about helping you do that and..."

"Austin, I said for you not to worry about me right now. You told me to be independent so let me."

He nodded.

"You've got my pager number if you need me," he said shoving his feet into his shoes. "I'll call you as soon as I can."

He gave me a quick kiss and then hurried out. The pounding of his footsteps down the hallway was almost as heavy as the pounding of my heart.

As soon as I was up and dressed, I called my aunt. I was so angry, my hand trembled holding the receiver. Her secretary said she was away at a meeting in Richmond. She asked if there was any message for her should she call in.

"Tell her that any agreements between us, any compromises, are null and void and that she shouldn't bother bringing any paperwork of any kind to this house. Tell her not to call me about it either," I dictated. I could practically see her secretary writing furiously.

"Oh. Yes," she muttered.

"Tell her if she wants to talk to me she should call my attorney first," I said in a sweet voice, but a voice that also dripped with acid. I hung up.

"If she wants a war," I said to the phone, "I'll give her a war."

I didn't hear from Austin until midafternoon. From the tone of his voice, I knew immediately that things were even worse than we had thought.

"Your aunt isn't just threatening to start a complaint process with the state, she's threatening to release all the bad publicity and drive my uncle to ruin if I don't stay away from you. I've explained to him, that I really and truly love you, Rain, but for the moment, until this all calms down, it won't matter. I thought if I just resigned from his company, he'd be fine, but if I did I doubt that I'd ever work as a therapist again."

"Stop talking foolishly, Austin. You know how terrible that would make me feel."

"I know," he said, his voice so low and full of defeat it brought tears to my eyes. "I hate the thought of you being there all alone while all this is going on. This had to happen just after Mrs. Bogart's leaving."

"You don't believe for one moment that it's just a coincidence, do you?" I asked.

"What a cruel woman your aunt is."

"She'll be sorry," I said.

"I promised my uncle I'd stay away from you, but I'll be there after dark. It's just disgusting that I've got to sneak around."

"Maybe you shouldn't come back, even after dark, Austin. At least, not until things calm down."

"I wouldn't sleep a wink knowing you're all alone in that house at night, Rain. It'll be all right. She can't be having the place watched, can she?"

"She's capable of doing just that," I had to admit.

He was quiet.

"I'll be all right tonight," I assured him. "Just call me later," I said.

"We'll see."

"Austin, if I become the cause of just one more person's unhappiness..."

"All right," he said. I could tell he was frightened, not only for us, but for his uncle. "I'll phone you tonight. Tomorrow, we'll think of something," he said. "Maybe, we'll get you out of there," he added, his voice recuperating from its dark and defeated tone.

"Yes, maybe that would be something to do," I said.

"I love you, Rain. I really do. I wouldn't say it if I didn't mean it with all my heart."

"And I love you. It's because I believe you that I can say it, Austin."

"I'll call you in a few hours. Take care."

"You take care," I held the receiver for a long moment after he had hung up.

How dreary the world was again. As if to prove me right clouds rolled in and made the day dark and foreboding. I kept myself busy, cleaning and making dinner. The rain began just as I began to eat. It fell hard and heavy right from the start, pounding on the roof and windows. When the lights flickered, I held my breath. The thought of losing the electricity and making my way about in the dark was frightening.

Lightning slashed through the darkness right near my dining room windows and that was followed with a boom that made the whole building tremble. It rolled away like a dying growl, only to be followed by another flash and another crash of thunder. This time, the lights flickered and went out. I waited, my heart pounding, hoping they would come right back on, but they didn't.

It was as if a curtain had been pulled down in all the rooms and the hallway. Except for the occasional flashes of lightning, darkness ruled, turning each and every piece of furniture into a silhouette of itself, a shadow here and shadow there. I rolled back into the kitchen to look for candles and, feeling about the panty shelves awkwardly, I finally found some. I melted some wax at the bottom of a dish the way I had seen Mama do it and inserted the candle so it stood straight and firm. Then I lit it and placed it on the dining room table, but I had little or no appetite left.

Because there was not enough light, I decided to leave the dishes for later. I put anything that would spoil in the refrigerator, hoping that the electricity would soon come back on. Almost an hour passed and nothing changed. I decided to call the electric company to at least see if they were aware of it, but I was shocked to discover the phone was dead, too.

Truly shut off now from the outside world, I felt myself start to tremble. I tried to comfort myself, to calm myself down and finally decided that the best thing I could do was return to my bedroom and wait. These things could take hours, I thought, and there wasn't much else I could do. The storm didn't seem to be diminishing. In fact, the wind was whipping the torrents over the house, slapping the sides of the building and the windows so hard, the glass rattled and shutters knocked. I couldn't remember a storm as bad as this one during my time here. My luck, it had to happen tonight of all nights.

Suddenly, I heard what sounded like a small explosion and realized that somehow, the rear door had blown open. Perhaps I hadn't closed it tightly enough when my aunt had arrived. I heard the door slam against the wall and I rolled myself down the corridor as quickly as I could. The door was being blown so hard, it would soon be ripped off its hinges, I thought and reached for the handle. The rain seemed to have been waiting for me. A deluge of cold drops slapped my face and soaked my hair and clothes. I got hold of the door handle. Then, I had to struggle with the wind and hold onto the wheelchair at the same time. It was a losing battle. I didn't have the strength and I was getting soaked to the skin. Finally, I gave up and let go of the handle. The door flew back and then came back at me and slammed the side of the chair. I screamed. It had nearly smashed my arm and hand. Quickly, I retreated and then turned and wheeled myself away as fast as I could.

For a moment or two, I just fought to catch my breath. Shivering more from my own fear than the cold, I carefully wheeled myself into the bedroom and started to remove my wet clothes. I had to get a towel to dry myself off. After that, exhausted, I got into bed and there I lay, waiting, feeling miserable. Despite my fatigue, I couldn't sleep. Every time I closed my eyes, I heard more noise. The periodic boom of thunder echoed through the open rear door, up the corridor and into the house. My teeth chattered. I closed my eyes as tightly as I could.

Why did I convince Austin not to come? I should have been more selfish.

The thunder seemed to get lower and farther away finally. I stopped shivering and felt myself start to relax. The rain didn't seem to be falling as hard either. Maybe it was over at last and the storm had moved on. I waited and listened and hoped and then I was sure I heard the front door open and close.

Austin, I thought. He did come. Good. I couldn't wait to throw my arms around him and hold him closely to me. We'll do what he said. We'll run off together.

Quickened footsteps could be heard. I sat up in the darkness and looked toward the open door. A flashlight's beam appeared and moments later, Aunt Victoria appeared. The disappointment nearly caused my heart to stop.

"What is going on here!" she screamed. "The rain is

coming right into the house. Why did you leave the back-door open?"

She turned the flashlight on me and I covered my face.

"Why are you naked? Are you expecting him? Is he here?"

"No one's here," I cried. "Take that light off me."

She lowered it to the floor.

"You're a mess," she said. "It's lucky for you I've come just in time."

"I don't want you here after the trouble you have caused Austin and his uncle. I told your secretary to tell you. Now get out of here," I screamed at her.

"I did what any concerned and loving aunt would have done," she replied coolly. "Even that uncle of his agrees. We've reached an understanding," she added. "As long as he makes sure he keeps up his part of the bargain, it will be okay."

"You're horrible. I want you out of this house. It's mostly mine, after all. Grandmother Hudson wanted it that way and I understand why now more than ever. Get out. Did you hear me? I said get out!"

She brought the light up and grasped it with both her hands pointing the beam at her own face so I could see her eyes glowing, her smile like a mask with fire behind it.

"Don't be silly," she said in a voice so calm it made me shiver. "You can't handle this yourself and I have a great interest in all that happens. I'm here to help you for as long as it takes," she added, her lips practically dripping the sweet poison in her heart.

"For as long as it takes?" I gasped. "What are you talking about? What are you going to do?"

"What I should have done from the start," she said. "I'm moving in so you won't be alone."

"What? I'd rather be alone," I said.

"Of course you wouldn't, dear," she said. "And after all, with my poor sister so shattered and my poor brother-in-law with his hands full, who else can do what is necessary?

"Indeed, who always does what's necessary?"

"No," I said shaking my head. "I won't let you stay with me. I won't."

"You can thank me some other time," she said as if I hadn't spoken. "For now, let's just do what has to be done. Let's be family.

"After all, Rain, it's the least I can do for my darling sister isn't it?

"The least I can do is take care of her daughter," she said and flicked off the light leaving me once again in complete and utter darkness.

13

A Love Discovered

Forbidding her to move in with me was one thing, but enforcing that prohibition was another. If I believed my life before Aunt Victoria moved into the house was difficult, it now seemed those days had been nothing less than a picnic compared to what life would now be like.

At first I thought she can't really be serious about living here with me. It was just another idle threat, something else to get me to cooperate with her as far as Grandmother Hudson's will and our business interests were concerned, especially after I had threatened not to be cooperative.

However, I should have realized that the maddening light I had seen in her eyes the night of the storm was not similar to the lightning, a temporary flash of anger. Something evil and dark had been festering like an open sore in her ever since she had learned my mother was being released from the mental clinic and Grant was not only taking her back, but still trying to make their marriage a success, despite Brody's tragic death and my mother's secret past.

Of course, I had no concept of just what Aunt Victoria had been doing behind the scenes, how much time and effort she had invested in undermining my mother's marriage. I imagined she was like Iago in *Othello,* whispering tempestuous thoughts in Grant's ear, reminding him of my existence and the dark night of Brody's unnecessary death. Just as she had been talking negatively about my mother to me, she must have been filling Grant's mind with images of Megan as a spoiled girl who always had someone cover up her blunders and keep her from feeling any regrets.

"She never had to let go of her security blanket, not Megan," Aunt Victoria bitterly remarked to me and surely now to Grant.

Grant surely loved my mother very much, I thought, to forgive her for her past, to not blame her for the death of their son, to want her to recuperate and go on with their marriage. In the face of that determination, Aunt Victoria's insidious remarks and poisonous whispers must have been ineffective and discarded. Perhaps Grant had finally seen who and what she was and turned her away unceremoniously. If she mentioned him at all now, it was always bitterly, always with reference to the stupidity and selfishness all men shared, always depicting him as a willing victim of my mother's little deceits. For her descriptions of him to have undergone such a radical change—from the man of her dreams, the man she claimed she deserved and who deserved her, to the blithering idiot led by the nose that he had become—Grant surely had to have rejected her sharply and firmly.

Rebuffed, spun around and sent away, she now turned her venomous eyes on me, seeing me as the cause of it all. In her twisted logic, she went so far as to conclude that because I had returned and because Brody had been killed, my mother was able to win back Grant's love through his pity, a love Aunt Victoria otherwise might have won for herself.

"I know my sister well," she said bitterly. "She knew that if she pretended to be weak and sick and full of remorse, Grant would be blind to her basic weaknesses. She's happy you're here, happy you're crippled and even happier you've created all these problems. It gives her more opportunity to moan and groan and cry. I wonder how many times Grant's been made to kiss away her crocodile tears and urge her not to be sad, promising her a new day."

Aunt Victoria would rattle on and on like this the first few days after she had moved back into the house. I had sat in utter disbelief, watching from my wheelchair as two men she had hired carried in her things, which not only included trunks of clothing and personal items, but cartons of files that they brought to Grandfather Hudson's old office. She took it over completely and had business machines, faxes, copiers and her computer hooked up. Upstairs, she moved into what had once been her room.

I wanted to call my attorney and complain, but I was afraid of how angry that would make her and how she might take it out on poor Austin and his uncle.

The same day she moved in, she hired a new maid, but not a live-in. The new woman's name was Mrs. Churchwell and she was well into her fifties, a widow who was left after her husband's death with barely enough insurance to survive; she therefore hired herself out for part-time work. She was dour with brown and gray hair cropped short, the strands thin and hard like wire. Her beady gray eyes were always watery and the lines etched in her thin, pale face resembled scars more than wrinkles because they were deep and scattered over her chin and cheeks randomly, suggesting scratches and tears in her thin, sickly and almost translucent skin. She was as tall as Aunt Victoria, and when they stood beside each other in the dimly lit hallway, their nearly indistinguishable figures made Mrs. Churchwell resemble a shadow Aunt Victoria had cast.

It was clear from the start that Mrs. Churchwell was terrified of my aunt and wanted to please her and keep the job and what were apparently generous wages, generous especially coming from my aunt. However, Aunt Victoria had ulterior motives for providing such an ample salary. She wanted Mrs. Churchwell's complete loyalty and obedience, especially as it regarded anything to do with me. Unlike Mrs. Bogart who became a willing tattletale, Mrs. Churchwell was deliberately planted like some living bug device to report any contact I had with the outside world, especially any contact with Austin. Whenever my Aunt Victoria wasn't there, Mrs. Churchwell was there to watch where I would go the moment I wanted to leave the house. When I looked back, I saw her face at the window.

After the storm, the phones were repaired, but for some reason, mine remained out of order. I was told the wiring had to be completely redone and that had to wait for other repairs the company had to make in the area. So, if the phone rang in the house, Mrs. Churchwell usually got to it first, claiming it was someone soliciting. I couldn't imagine Austin not trying to call me and yet I didn't want to risk calling him and causing any more trouble. I didn't learn until nearly a week after she had moved in that my aunt had the number changed and unlisted. Neither Mrs. Churchwell nor my aunt volunteered the information.

Mrs. Churchwell, unlike Mrs. Bogart, had no experience with someone in my condition. She was truly only a maid and a cook. Once I learned her relationship with my aunt, I wanted her around me less and less anyway. The feeling was mutual. The sight of me displeased her, and not only because I was handicapped. It was pretty clear to me after only a day or so that she was quite prejudiced and was put off by my having a black father. If and whenever she spoke to me, she always looked away as if she could convince herself she wasn't really talking to me and definitely not working for me.

She was a mediocre cook. I told my aunt so immediately, but that didn't seem to matter. I started to cook for myself, which displeased Mrs. Churchwell.

"I was hired to do the cookin'," she told me the first time I went into the kitchen and started to prepare something.

I paused, looked at her and said, "That's not what you were hired for. And you weren't hired only to clean and maintain the house either."

"I'm sure I don't know what you mean," she said, but before I could elaborate, she left the kitchen. Somehow, despite my being in a wheelchair and relatively helpless most of the time, she seemed intimidated by me and couldn't face me down. I borrowed from the memory of my stepsister Beneatha's angry eyes for inspiration.

It turns out Austin had called that first week before the telephone number had been changed. My aunt told me later that she had answered so he didn't speak. She knew the silence on the other end was Austin's silence and later came to tell me so.

"It looks like that young man is not listening to his uncle," she said. "I know he's trying to reach you despite the warnings. As soon as he heard my voice, he didn't speak, but I knew it was your fortune hunter."

"Stop calling him that and anyway, you have no right to stop him from calling or seeing me," I told her.

"If I ever see him near this house or you, I'll reinstate the legal proceedings against his uncle and have his license revoked and you know I can do that," she threatened.

"Why are you doing this?" I cried.

"I'm only doing what's best for you. You're not capable of making these sort of decisions at this time. I'm looking for a new therapist for you and will have one shortly," she promised with that weak, plastic smile.

"I don't want another one. I won't cooperate with anyone else."

"Suit yourself," she said. "You're only hurting your own rehabilitation by biting off your nose to spite your face. Remember," she said waving her long, boney right forefinger at me, "the moment I learn he's been within ten feet of you, I call my attorneys." After her admonishment, she left me sitting there, fuming.

As soon as I could, I tried to take the van and drive away, but I discovered the keys to the van were gone and naturally, her precious Mrs. Churchwell knew nothing about them. When I asked my aunt, she told me doctors have advised her that I'm not ready for driving.

"But I already have driven!" I screamed. "I've done it many times and gone shopping and everything."

"That was a mistake, something that fortune hunter got you to do for selfish reasons," she told me.

"I want my keys. That's my van!" I shouted at her. She stared as if I had barely raised my voice. "I'm calling Mr. Sanger and tell him about all the things you've done and are doing. We'll sue you," I said. It was my turn to threaten, but she was always a step ahead.

The phone in my room was still inoperative. When I wheeled myself out to call from the kitchen, I was shocked to discover that now it didn't work either.

"Why are all the phones dead?" I asked Mrs. Churchwell. Whenever I asked her anything, she always acted as if she didn't hear me. I had to repeat myself and be louder and more demanding before she would finally acknowledge my existence.

"They're not all dead," she said dryly. "The one upstairs works."

"What? Only the one upstairs?"

"And in your aunt's office, of course," she said and I quickly whipped myself around and rolled down to my aunt's office because I knew she wasn't home. I should have saved my strength and realized that the door would be locked. I wheeled back and demanded Mrs. Churchwell open it. Again, she ignored me until I practically ran over her foot.

"I can't open it," she said. "I don't have the key and even if I did, I wouldn't open it without your aunt's permission."

"My aunt's permission. You can't breathe without my aunt's permission," I spit at her.

She glared at me and then she walked away and upstairs to clean my aunt's bedroom and bathroom.

In the evening after dinner, after Mrs. Churchwell left, I would go out on the portico if my aunt wasn't home and hope that Austin would just come driving up to rescue me. Usually my aunt returned before I saw any sign of him. I was sure once he saw her car parked in front of the house, he would simply turn away.

"Why are you out in the cold evening air?" she would ask. "Surely you know that can't be good for anyone in your weakened condition."

"I'm not in any weakened condition. You're treating me like some prisoner and I won't stand for it. I want my phone turned back on and I want the keys to my van."

"Just like your mother, not showing any gratitude. Here I decide to sacrifice my time and my energy for you and all you can do is threaten and complain."

"I don't want your help. How many times do I have to tell you?"

"Megan, Megan, Megan," she muttered shaking her head.

"I'm not Megan. Stop calling me Megan."

"You're getting yourself overly excited. Calm down. You'll end up in the hospital again," she warned, but at the moment, that sounded like a good place to be. I was actually considering complaining about severe pains just to get myself out of the house. But before I started my act, Austin showed up.

I had returned to my room after dinner. Aunt Victoria had called to say she would be late as she was at a meeting. She asked Mrs. Churchwell to remain a little longer. I knew she offered her time and a half for it because she put up no resistence. She sat like a sentry in the living room thumbing through magazines and watching the driveway, ready to leap up and run to the upstairs phone if Austin appeared.

Fuming, frustrated and enraged, I wheeled back to my room and sat there, mumbling to myself, trying to decide what to do next when suddenly I heard a gentle tapping a the window and turned to see his face in the glass. My heart leaped for joy. I quickly went to my door and locked it as he pushed up the window and climbed into my room.

I started to cry and he rushed to me, kneeling down quickly to embrace me.

"Rain, don't cry. What's happened?"

"Oh Austin, my aunt has moved into the house. She's hired the most horrible maid to be here during the day and spy on me constantly. She cut off my phone, too."

"I know. I tried to call and was told the number was no longer in service and there was no listed replacement. I wanted to come here days ago, but your aunt's attorney called my uncle and told him I had been trying to reach you. I had to lie to him. I felt terrible about it and then I just decided this was silly. I'm coming to see you somehow. I just knew you weren't doing well."

"Doing well? I'm a virtual prisoner here. She took the van keys and hid them, too, claiming doctors told her I wasn't ready for driving. She said if I violated one rule she would have her lawyers reinstate the complaint against your uncle and destroy him. She's capable of doing just that. I want to leave here, Austin. I want to leave here forever."

Tears streamed down my cheeks.

"I know," he said. "I know." He wiped away my tears and kissed my cheeks. "We'll do just that. I'll plan it."

"I have money, Austin. A lot of it. I just have to get to my attorney. I'll have him advance us enough money and we'll go somewhere else and I'll leave her here in her own hell. Then I'll have the house sold out from under her. I swear I will," I vowed. "I mean it, every syllable. Oh, Austin, I can't stand it another minute."

"Rain, just let me plan it out," he said in a soothing voice to calm me.

I shook my head.

"I can't stay here much longer, Austin."

"I know, I know. The problem is she might still go after my uncle. I've got to think about how we will manage this."

"No, she'll leave your uncle alone. I'll have my attorney negotiate with her and give her what she wants as long as she lets me go. You'll see. Just take me there tomorrow, okay?"

He nodded, but didn't look convinced. "Let's just take it a step at a time," he said. "I've got to plan where we will go and what I will do afterward."

"We'll have enough money, Austin. Don't worry about it."

"Money's not our only problem, Rain. You have greater needs. I've got to be sure you'll be well attended to," he said.

"I'll have you. What could be better?"

He smiled.

"I'm just a therapist, Rain. I can help you with your basic needs and get you strong, but we have to be concerned about your health needs, too. Let me plan," he repeated. "C'mon. Relax, Rain. Let's let things calm down."

I nodded. "Now that you're here, I'm calm."

He smiled and kissed me. I held onto his neck while he put his arm under my legs, lifting me out of the chair and setting me down gently.

"I really missed you," I said.

"And I missed you."

He knelt beside the bed and kissed my hand. His smile

was like sunshine, warming me all over, restoring my hope and my strength, like a rainbow after a storm.

"What have you been doing?" I asked him.

"Working with my other clients. Still, as always, all I could think of was your face." He laughed. "I even called someone else by your name and she got upset with me. The only way I could calm her down was to describe to her how much in love with you I was."

"Describe it to me," I urged.

As he spoke, he quietly and gracefully began to undress me and himself. For me it was hearing the fairy tale of fairy tales come true.

"It's like I don't have to eat anymore or sleep or do anything to keep myself alive; only think of you. I dream so vividly, I can actually feel your lips on mine. All day, every day, I see your face in someone else's face. I spin around and wonder if you've just gone by. My heart pounds. Every part of me is filled with longing and loneliness.

"I can't read, watch television, go to a movie, do anything. Nothing will take my mind off you. I wrestle with the temptation to come to you constantly. It's only knowing how much of his life and money my uncle has put into his company that keeps me from defying your aunt and her attorneys.

"But finally, the love raging in my heart burst and I couldn't stand being away. I drove here, parked my car far enough away, and ran through the darkness and the woods to sneak onto your property and to your window.

"And now," he said lowering his body to the bed and crawling in beside me, "I am here and I feel complete again."

We kissed. I clung to him.

"It will be all right," he whispered. "We will be all right."

It was our *they-lived-happily-forever-ending* for sure, I thought.

Contentment led to passion. I couldn't keep myself from crying out. That witch of a maid must have been hovering in the hallway. She came to the door and actually had the nerve to try to open it.

"Are you all right in there?" she asked. She wasn't asking because she was concerned about me. She just wanted to know what I was doing so she could make her report to my aunt.

"Leave me alone," I shouted.

We waited and then heard her walk away.

"My aunt must have gone to some prisoner of war criminal camp to find someone like her," I told Austin.

He laughed and kissed me again and again we made love. Then he lay his head between my breasts and we slept. Neither of us kept track of the time, nor did we hear anything or anyone outside my room.

I was sure about what happened next. My aunt returned and Mrs. Churchwell made her spy report. She told her how I had locked my door and chased her away. Full of suspicion because she herself was a veteran of deceit, my aunt located a room key and tiptoed up to the door. She stood outside with her ear to it and then slowly, quietly inserted the key and opened my door. She could see Austin beside me, bathed in the moonlight that streamed in from the window. How her heart must have skipped with pleasure at the discovery.

It was like an explosion. She snapped on the light and screamed, her right arm out, the finger pointed like a pistol at us.

"Rape!" she cried. "This is nothing less than rape.

The girl is a helpless cripple and you've raped her again!"

Austin was flustered and confused, he could barely speak. Neither of us expected her to do what she did next. All I anticipated was her screaming some more and then slamming the door after her threats. But she was like an executioner who loved her work, someone who wanted and needed to throw salt on wounds.

"Come here, Mrs. Churchwell," she ordered, "and bear witness to this lechery."

Suddenly, Mrs. Churchwell stepped up beside her. Austin had only raised his head in disbelief. I was about to scream back at Veronica, but she surprised us both by lunging at the bed and grabbing the blanket. She pulled it away so quickly and completely, I was shocked at her strength. There we were, both naked, exposed. Austin dropped his hands to cover his private parts. Her eyes widened and she smiled.

"Deny it now," she said through her teeth. "Deny what you've done with her. Bear witness, Mrs. Churchwell. Gaze upon this sordid, disgusting display."

Mrs. Churchwell nodded.

"Do you see it?"

"Yes," she said.

"Get out!" I finally was able to shout. "Both of you get out of my room!"

My aunt stood her ground, holding the blanket, enjoying her small victory. Then she turned to Mrs. Churchwell and they left slowly, my aunt dropping the blanket to the floor as she closed the door.

"My God," Austin said scrambling for his clothing. He scooped up the blanket and spread it back over me. "I've really gone and done it now."

"You see how terrible she can be?" I cried.

"Yes. There's no telling what she's going to do next. I'd better go."

He started for the door, then stopped and headed for the window.

"I don't want to face her again," he said.

"But Austin, you can't leave me here."

He stood there a moment, thinking.

"There's nothing we can do right now, Rain. I'll just have to come back for you."

"Don't forget," I said.

"I won't, but what will I tell my uncle when her lawyers call?" He shook his head, looking troubled, before crawling out the window, closing it behind him.

A moment later he was gone. I never felt as alone, even in the hospital after my accident when I had first been told of my plight. It was impossible to fall asleep again. I could only lie there, trembling, and like Austin, wait for the second shoe to drop.

It did drop, but not the way he or I would have imagined. My aunt didn't return to my room. Mrs. Chuchwell left and then my aunt went upstairs. I finally did fall asleep for a few hours. I woke up to the sound of my aunt's familiar heavy footsteps. I struggled to rise and get myself into my chair and to the bathroom to wash and then to dress for what I believed was going to be a terrible day.

I was sitting up in bed, the blanket wrapped around my shoulders when she opened the door and entered my room. She gazed around, listened and then nodded.

"He's gone, I take it?" she said in a sweet, almost pleasant voice.

She still wore her faded pink, terrycloth robe. Without makeup, her face wrinkled from her night's sleep and her hair unruly, she looked like one of those poor, disheveled homeless women who used to inhabit the alleys and dumps near the projects where I lived in Washington.

In her right hand, she clutched a light yellow folder.

"Yes," I said. "He left right after you burst in on us. You have some nerve invading my privacy."

"Invading your privacy?" She laughed and then grew stern. "You don't have a right to privacy. Not if you're going to conduct yourself like some street girl in my mother and father's house where only dignity and proper behavior were ever tolerated. I'm sure my mother would have changed her mind about you on the spot if she had been beside me last night. And after all the warnings and all the advice I have given you!

"Just like Megan, bringing disgrace to our doorstep. How many times did my father have to pay someone off or buy someone's favor just to keep our good name as high as it should be? More times than I care to count. I can tell you that much," she said, answering her own question quickly.

"Well, now that he was so brazen about his seduction of you, I have Mrs. Churchwell as a reliable witness."

"I wasn't seduced. I love Austin and he loves me," I insisted.

She wagged her head.

"Of course you do. What girl in your place, crippled, sentenced to be in a wheelchair her whole life, wouldn't grasp at the first good-looking face to turn his false smile to you and fill you with fictitious promises? Why, most girls who weren't in wheelchairs would fall for those lines and winks these days, much less someone like you."

"Stop it! You don't know what you're talking about. You could never understand," I yelled.

Aunt Victoria stretched her thin lips into a mean spinster smile.

"Why, child, there are few as well equipped to understand the craftinesses of men, their slyness and guile. Unlike most, I am not blinded by phony compliments. You might say I have a built-in lie detector. It rings here," she said putting her left hand over her heart, "and sends warnings immediately to here." She pointed at her temple.

"What did that fortune hunter tell you?" she continued, stepping closer. "Did he tell you that you were just as beautiful as before, maybe even more so? Did he tell you that you made his day, made his heart sing, brought such joy to him that he couldn't imagine himself without you? Did he tell you he saw you everywhere, constantly heard your voice and you were stuck in his mind forever and ever? Did he promise to always cherish and love you, too?"

"Yes, yes, yes, yes to all of that," I screamed at her. "And he means it and we will be in love and we will be together."

She nodded.

"We'll see," she said. "Maybe some day, I'll stop protecting you and you will end up with someone like him."

"I won't end up with someone like him. I'll end up with him," I vowed.

"Fine. But first you had better listen to me and do what I want you to do."

She opened the file and took out some documents, spreading them on the bed before me.

"I haven't just been sitting on my hands while precious Megan has been twisting and turning Grant in the wind, you know. Your mother gave up responsibility for you long ago. We certainly can't expect her to do anything for you now. Because of your incapacity, I have had my lawyers petition the court to appoint me your guardian. Yes, you can get your attorney to put up resistence, but I don't think you will.

"In the meantime, these documents here," she said taking out others, "are the documents to be sent to the state concerning your fortune-hunter's company."

"Stop calling him that," I said.

She shrugged.

"Call him what you want. These other documents," she continued, "constitute a lawsuit I intend to file against the therapy company. It will bankrupt him just to put up a defense. You know how lawyers can bleed you," she said gleefully.

"Here are the press releases I've had written as well."

My eyes were stinging with tears.

"Now," she went on, "none of this will go any further if you sign this."

She brought out another document.

"What is that?"

"It's the power of attorney I've been begging you to sign. Once I'm in complete control of the estate's business again, we'll all be better off, including you."

"This is blackmail. I'll tell my lawyer."

"You don't have to tell him. I'll just go forward with all the rest of this and you don't have to sign the paper if you don't want to. Suit yourself," she said gathering up the papers and putting them back in her folder.

"Listen," I said in a voice of calm reason, "I'll have Mr. Sanger contact you and your attorneys and you can work out whatever compromise you want and I'll leave."

"With that boy?"

"What's that matter to you?"

"If you think he won't go and make trouble afterward, you're an even worse dreamer than your mother. The moment he marries you, he'll hire an attorney to sue me and start all this over," she said.

"No, he won't. I promise."

"Promises. Do you know what promises made by women such as you are? Cotton candy. Dreams and illusions followed by dramatic proclamations peppered with *I swears* all over the place. I know. Megan has made me a thousand promises if she's made one and not one has ever been followed or come true."

"I'm not Megan!" I cried.

She stared a moment.

"Yes, you are," she said. She looked around the room and at the bed as if Austin were still beside me. Then she looked at my naked shoulders and into my eyes and repeated, "Yes, you are."

She put the power-of-attorney document on the bed with a pen beside it.

"Sign it and I'll put all these other documents on the shelf.

"I'll be back in ten minutes," she added and left.

I sat there, feeling as if all the blood in my body had drained to my feet. I was actually so dizzy I had to lower my head to the pillow for a few moments and take deep breaths.

Of course, she was wrong about Austin, I thought, but she was too paranoid and distrusting to believe in any guarantees I might make. I braced myself on my right elbow and looked at the paper she had left. This will never end until she gets her way with this, I thought. I was tired of fighting with her. Anyway, how could I let her destroy Austin's reputation and his uncle's business?

I took the pen in hand. I feared I was signing a deal with the devil.

I wrote my name on the line nevertheless.

Maybe now it would end, I thought.

I should have realized.

Now it would really begin.

14

Struggling for Freedom

Aunt Victoria returned to my bedroom, saw the paper had been signed, put it in her yellow folder and smiled.

"Good," she said. "You've made the right decision. Now, things will go so much better for the both of us, especially for you."

"I want my phone reactivated immediately," I said. "And I want the keys to my van."

"Anything else?" she asked. Her smile now cutting so sharply in her pallid face and her eyes turning so cold, she looked like she had become a wax replica of herself.

"Yes, I don't want Austin or his uncle bothered or threatened and I want you to keep that spy of yours out of my face."

"Actually," she said, surprising me, "I was thinking of dismissing Mrs. Churchwell. You've been correct about her. She isn't very much of a cook and I'm not pleased with her cleaning and maintenance of the house. She cuts corners. Mother would have fired her the day after she had been hired. For what I'm paying her, I can have two maids."

"Good," I said. I certainly didn't feel sorry for Mrs. Churchwell.

"There, you see how well you and I can get along if you're cooperative," my aunt said. She started out. "I'll have her prepare your breakfast for you and then leave."

"I don't want her to prepare anything for me. I can take care of myself."

"Fine," she said. "It will make it easier. I'll give her two weeks salary and send her on her way. For a while," she added, "it will just be the two of us."

No, it won't, I thought, because I'll be out of here myself today.

"Before you go to your office, please leave the van keys on the kitchen table," I asked as she started away.

She paused, nodded slightly with that same waxen smile, then left. I got myself out of bed and into the bathroom. I wasn't sure where I would go or what I would do, but it was exciting just contemplating leaving. I'd call Austin as soon as I could, of course, and let him know where I was. Then, I would drive to Mr. Sanger's office, and have him do whatever was necessary to set up funding for myself and Austin. He'd be upset I had signed the power of attorney paper, but I didn't care anymore about the house or the business anyway. Let her wallow in her victory and live in her dark loneliness, if she liked.

Maybe I could convince Austin to move to England with me. He could do whatever he had to do to become a licensed therapist there. We could set up a small flat together and start a whole new life away from all this trouble and unhappiness. We would see my father and his family often, go to the theater and spend nice weekend afternoons in the parks.

As I soaked in the tub, I dreamed of Austin and me along the Thames, going to a nice cafe, doing all the things I had done before my accident.

Practically all public places made accommodations for handicapped people now. We could go to museums, travel in the countryside, do anything we wanted. I envisioned all of us at Sunday high tea, my father and his family and Austin and me, talking, listening to music and simply enjoying each other's company. I could still have a life, I thought.

My aunt believed she had won. She considered all this a victory. Little did she understand that she was really freeing me from bondage. Actually, I should be the one thanking her. All I had really done, I concluded, was sign over my rights to a sinking ship, a depressingly dark and unhappy ship floating in a sea of tears.

Go celebrate your false victory, Aunt Victoria. Cherish your precious legal papers, brag to your friends and spend the rest of your life with a heart aching for a man you will never have. One day you'll wake up in this house or wherever you are and realize you've amounted to nothing. You'll have only your own shadow to keep you company and you'll hear only your own voice. You'll be more of a prisoner than I have ever been. Maybe you won't be in a wheelchair, but you'll be handicapped. Of that, I'm sure, I thought.

My musings were interrupted by the sounds of banging, a series of thumps echoing from outside. I even heard what sounded like a saw. I imagined it was the grounds people who came weekly to tend to the property and thought no more about it.

After I got myself out of the tub and dry, I dressed myself and then found a couple of suitcases in the back of my closet. I was too excited about leaving to think about getting myself some breakfast first. Instead, I spent most of the remainder of the morning choosing what I wanted to take with me and packing. Once that was all accomplished, I sat back contented and then finally decided I was hungry.

I wheeled myself out, realizing I hadn't heard anyone making any noise in the house all this time. I guessed Aunt Victoria really had given Mrs. Churchwell her walking papers, and she had already left without saying good-bye. That was good. I didn't cherish the idea of having to face her, even for one final time.

My first disappointment came when I saw that Aunt Victoria had not left the van keys on the kitchen table as I had requested. I looked everywhere, even on the floor thinking they might have fallen somehow. I checked the counters, the chairs, everything, but saw no keys.

Damn her, I thought. She deliberately didn't do it...or in her glorious haste forgot. I went to call her office and remembered the phone in the kitchen didn't work. A hive of frustration began to build rapidly in my chest, my anger buzzing and stinging until I felt hot rage.

I spun in my chair and wheeled myself rapidly down the hallway to her office. Of course, it was locked. I rattled the door and slammed it with my fist, crying and screaming my aunt's name. Then I sat back and tried to think calmly. I'll just wheel myself out and down the ramp and down the driveway to the road. I'll stop a passing motorist and ask him or her to help me get to a phone.

I turned my chair around and with renewed determination headed for the front door. It was a beautiful day, just a few clouds visible from the doorway. A warm breeze washed over my face, filling me with strength. I took a deep breath and wheeled myself out on the portico. This won't be difficult, I told myself. The first driver who sees me will surely pull over. It will be quite a sight to see a girl in a wheelchair hitchhiking. I laughed to myself and started for the ramp.

Then my heart fell as if it had been turned to stone. I stared in disbelief.

The ramp was gone!

That was the banging and sawing I had heard when I was in the tub. Why had she done this? Was it merely in anticipation of my leaving? Why didn't she wait until I had actually left?

Without the ramp, the steps looked foreboding. How would I get myself and my chair down? My frustration turned quickly to rage. I would not be defeated. As carefully as I could, I lowered myself from the chair to the floor of the portico. I decided I would push the chair down the steps as slowly as I could and then I would crawl, slide, do anything I had to do to get myself down and then climb back into the chair. It seemed like a good plan, so I began to carefully push the chair ahead.

It bounced down the first step and then the second and I held it as tightly as I could, but now I was at a very awkward angle. It was hard to inch myself forward and down and hold the chair at the same time. Finally, I decided to let it bounce down the steps on its own and then follow as quickly as possible.

As soon as I uncurled my fingers, the chair, carried forward by its weight, rolled down the remaining steps, only it didn't stop as close to the bottom as I had hoped. The momentum of bouncing forward kept it going and it rolled and rolled until it reached the driveway.

"Stop!" I screamed at the chair as if it was a living thing and could hear and obey.

It slowed down, but didn't stop. It rolled on until it reached the descending incline and then picked up speed again and rolled faster and faster down the driveway until I could see it no more. I stared after it in disbelief. I wasn't going to have to drag myself just down these steps now. I was going to have to drag myself quite a distance down the driveway as well.

I glanced back at the house. Even getting back inside and to my room would be a major endeavor.

What had I done?

Damn her, I thought, damn her for putting me in this horrible predicament.

"Help, someone!" I screamed.

My thin shout was carried away in the breeze. Who would hear me anyway? Maybe the grounds people would soon arrive, but what would I do in the meantime? I thought and decided I had little choice but to follow my chair. It might take me hours and hours, but I would get to it.

I turned and pushed my limp legs toward the stairs. Then, taking a deep breath, I pushed until my rear end bounced on the next step. It nearly bounced the breath out of me. I swallowed, closed my eyes and did another step and then another until I was down the stairway. My poor rear end felt raw and quite sore. I caught my breath again and then turned around, put my hands behind me and began to drag my body toward the driveway.

Gravel and dirt soon made my palms sting with pain. I had to stop often to wipe them off and rub them against my thighs. The noon sun beat down on my face and the warm breeze I had welcomed the moment I had opened the door now seemed like the tormenting hot breath of some giant creature hovering over me. I could feel the sweat beads trickling down my temples.

After another moment's rest, I pulled myself along again. My choice of clothing this morning wasn't exactly right for this exercise, I thought. The skirt didn't do much to protect the skin on my legs, especially about the calf muscles. I couldn't feel the pain at all on my left leg, but I could see the scratch marks and the red blotches. I did feel some stinging in my right leg.

After what must have been at least an hour, if not a little more, I reached the crest of the driveway and turned to look down the small hill. There was my wheelchair on its side near the road. It would probably take me another hour to drag myself down to it, I thought. My palms had started to bleed, too. It really was painful to put the full weight of my upper body on them and push along the dirt and gravel.

How was I going to do this now? I looked back at the house. It would be horrendous to try to return. I would have to get myself up those steps, too. I started to cry. The whole world conspires against me, I thought. The ground, the air, all of it is against me. Finally, nearly exhausted, I pushed myself up on my hands and in a moment of pure anger and frustration, turned myself into a ball by embracing my upper body and deliberately falling forward to get enough momentum to roll.

And roll I did, but my legs swung over like dead weights, bouncing me hard on my shoulders. I hit the side of my head on a small rock once and felt the warm trickle of blood under my hair, but I kept up my turning and spinning. The blue sky and clouds seemed to spin with me. Twice I felt as if I had knocked the air out of my lungs and gasped; finally, I stopped and lay on my stomach, looking up at my chair which was now only a few feet away.

I lowered my head to my arms and rested, feeling the stings of cuts and bruises from my hips up my arms to my head and my right ear. I was sure I looked a mess. My clothes were all stained and my blouse had ripped at the right elbow. I felt a scrape there and saw the blood.

Nevertheless, I had come this far. It was no time to stop and wail about it. I pushed myself up and struggled to get to a sitting position again so I could put my arms behind me and pull myself along until I reached the chair. I was nearly to it, too, when I heard the sound of an automobile and turned my head to see it coming at me. I shouted, for fear the driver hadn't seen me when he or she had come around the turn. It came to a stop in what was surely no more than a few inches from me. The bumper was so close I would hit it if I leaned back.

I heard the door open and I looked around hopefully, but the moment I saw her shoes and thin legs, I lowered my head like a flag of defeat. My aunt stood over me, her hands on her hips.

"What do you think you're doing?" she demanded. "What sort of a crazy thing is this? Have you gone completely mad? Look at you. Look at what you've done to yourself."

Through my tears I cried, "It's all your fault. Why did you have the ramp removed? Where were my van keys? Why didn't you leave them on the kitchen table as you promised?"

"Let's get you back into the house and cleaned up," she said. "How did you do this to yourself? Did you fall out of your chair? Why didn't you wait for me to come home? What was so important about you driving around now?"

She went for the wheelchair and brought it up beside me. Then she leaned down to scoop her arms under mine.

"Leave me alone!" I cried. "This is your fault."

"Stop acting like a fool and cooperate. I know you can move that right leg a bit, now help me to help you," she commanded.

I had no choice but to do what she asked and somehow, she had the strength to lift me high enough to drop me in the chair. I fell back against it, my arms so tired and weak, they dangled over the sides.

"Just relax," she said and struggled with pushing me up the driveway.

"Why did you have the ramp removed?" I asked weakly.

"We're selling the house, remember? How could I have real estate agents bring prospective buyers around with that ramp there? It would turn them off. People have to have a good feeling about a house before they'll consider buying it."

"Couldn't you wait until I left at least? How was I supposed to get down?"

"Who thought you would try to leave without someone helping you? You didn't have to go and try to leave on your own, foolish girl. You've always been so impulsive."

"What are you talking about? You hardly know me," I said shaking my head. "You shouldn't have had the ramp removed," I insisted.

I was surprised at how strong she was for someone so thin. Somehow, she managed to turn the chair around and pull it up with me in it, step by step until we were back on the portico.

"There," she said and took a deep breath. "You've

nearly exhausted me with your nonsense. "Now we've got to get you inside and cleaned up. You need to put some antiseptic on those cuts and bruises, too."

She turned the chair and wheeled me back into the house. I dropped my chin to my chest. My brave and determined attempt at escape had failed, heroic as it was, and I had been only moments from getting myself back into my chair and wheeling myself onto the road. Little did I know how important and precious those final moments were to be.

I would soon learn.

She got me back into my room and started to take off my clothing immediately.

"How do you think this would look if they came to visit and found you like this today? How do you think this would reflect on me? I'm capable of running a multimillion-dollar business, but not looking after one crippled girl? It would be a terrible embarrassment. Grant would wonder if I was as capable as I seem to be and he'd have every right to wonder.

"Your mother would run from the sight, of course. She would get so upset she would have to rest, and he would go to her and have to comfort her. We can't let something like that happen; we can't let that ever happen," she said.

I was too tired and in too much pain to stop her from babbling, but her words registered and I did feel shocked and a little terrified by the crazed look in her eyes when she rattled on and on.

I screamed when she washed some of the cuts and bruises, the soap cutting into me like tiny teeth.

"It's all your own fault, all the pain. Pain's good when it teaches you something. Hopefully, this time you'll learn," she said. As she worked, her eyes continued to widen and narrow like some telescopic lens being opened and closed.

"What do you mean, this time?"

She looked lost in a daze, her lips trembling softly above her teeth.

"We have to put antiseptic on it, Sister dear."

"I'm not your sister!" I screamed.

Her eyes blinked and then she pulled up stiffly.

"It's just an expression," she said curtly. "You don't have to get so uppity about it. We'd be better off if you now thought of me more as your sister and not some distant aunt anyway."

I closed my eyes and groaned. I've got to get out of here, I thought. Her mind is like some clock that stops ticking and then starts at a different hour or on a different day.

When she put the antiseptic on, she did it with a vengeance, enjoying my screams and cries. I know it was supposed to be good, but in her hands, it was like some Chinese torture invented nearly two thousand years ago. Finally, it was over.

"You'd better lie down for a while," she advised.

I sat there, breathing hard, struggling to regain my composure, but I was exhausted and the pain was coming at me from so many different places, I was on the verge of passing out. Too weak to oppose her, even with shouts, I did little to prevent her from lifting me and swinging me onto my bed.

"I imagine you didn't even eat," she said, standing over me and breathing hard, her narrow shoulders lifting and falling. Her eyes drifted and she blinked rapidly. When she looked at me now, it was as if she was looking through me.

"I don't understand how you continue to look so well

with the junk food you eat. You never even had a pimple problem and if you did have an occasional ugly little bump, you acted as if it was Mount Vesuvius erupting on your cheek or something," she said.

"What are you talking about, Aunt Victoria?" I asked in a voice that was barely a whisper.

"Of course you wouldn't remember. Anything ugly you block out immediately. Go to sleep. I have work to do," she said and started out.

"Wait," I called weakly. She didn't turn and a moment later, she was gone.

I'll rest, I thought. I'll rest and get back my strength and then I'll get out of here. She's going mad, drifting in and out of her own unpleasant memories. I let my eyes close and in moments, I was alseep.

I had been so exhausted from the ordeal, I slept hours and hours. In fact, when I awoke, the twilight had already begun and clouds made it even darker. Without a light on in my room, it looked so dreary. I groaned and pulled myself forward on my elbows, but the aches in my arms and in my hips were so great, I cried and collapsed on the pillow.

"Aunt Victoria," I called. "Aunt Victoria!"

I waited. Except for the sound of the wind, now stronger, brushing over the windows and the walls of the house, I heard nothing. Was she even here? My head began to pound and I realized I hadn't eaten a thing all day and not even sipped a little water. My lips felt like two strips of sandpaper.

"Aunt Victoria!"

How could she not hear me? I was shouting now at the top of my voice?

"Are you here?"

The hallway looked dark. She was probably not here, I thought. I looked at my wheelchair. She had left it too far from my bed. Back to crawling if I wanted to get into it, I thought, but just the thought of making that effort exhausted me again. I might as well decide to climb Mount Everest. I lay there, trying to think of what I could do. The pain in my head felt like a band of electricity stretching from one temple around to the other like a crown of static.

"Aunt Victoria, please answer me if you're here," I pleaded, but I heard nothing.

Maybe she was in her office on the phone and that was why she didn't hear me. I continued to listen hard, waiting for a sound to indicate I wasn't alone in the house, but the silence lingered and seemed even deeper.

I called again and again and lifted myself on my elbows and shouted as well. Still nothing.

Desperate now, I reached over and grasped my alarm clock. As best I could, I flung it out the door and into the hallway where it hit the far wall and bounced. It made a great deal of noise.

I listened.

Finally, I heard footsteps, but they were so slow and so weak sounding, more like an old person shuffling. I couldn't imagine them to be Aunt Victoria's footsteps. It seemed to take forever for her to reach the door, but she finally did. She was dressed in that ugly, faded pink robe and she was wearing what looked like man's leather slippers. She appeared more distraught and tired than I felt. Her hair looked like a pack of rats had run through it. Her eyelids drooped and her eyes were as dark as two pools of ink. Without her usual perfect, if not stiff posture, her sloping shoulders made her older, thinner. She moved as if her muscles and joints ached more than mine and for a moment I wondered if her efforts to get me off the driveway and back into the house hadn't exhausted her after all.

"What is it? What's going on now? I was asleep," she muttered.

"I want to get out of bed," I said. "I need my wheelchair and I want to get something to eat and drink. I'm parched."

She stood there, staring at me as if she hadn't heard a word.

"Aunt Victoria, did you hear me?"

"Guess what came in the mail this afternoon," she said instead of answering.

She smiled and dipped her hand into the big robe's side pocket to produce what looked like a picture postcard. She held it up and waited as if she expected I would understand.

"Who's that from?" I asked. Was it from England or from Roy?

"From them. Who else? Who else would have the audacity, the nerve, to send me such a card? I'll read it to you."

"Aunt Victoria…"

"Dear Vikki," she began and then lowered the card and looked at me. "She likes to do that sometimes, call me Vikki like we're loving sisters and she can use a nickname. She knows I hate nicknames and always have. I never let anyone call me Vikki in school. I wouldn't answer, but she got them to do it just for a joke. She began again:

Dear Vikki,

I just couldn't help but send you this card so you could see how beautiful it is here. We are having a very nice time. It's as if Grant and I are on our hon-

*eymoon. We're getting to know and love each other
all over again.*

> *I hope you're well.*

Love, Megan

She lowered the card and the put it back into her pocket.

"Love Megan," she said. "They're getting to know and love each other all over again. You see? She always gets what she wants in the end."

She laughed.

"Don't work hard. Cry at the first sign of unpleasantness, wilt in front of your man, bat your eyelashes, sulk and you'll get what you want in this life. That's the lesson to follow as long as men hand out the prizes.

"So why am I working so hard, right? Go on, ask me. Ask me," she commanded.

"I'm hungry and thirsty," I said. "Please push the chair up to the bed for me."

She smirked, shook her head and went for the chair. After she brought it to the bed, she shuffled out of my room and down the hallway.

"Got to get strong, got to get out," I chanted. My mantra gave me the strength to get myself into my robe and into the chair. As soon as I had, I wheeled myself out of the room.

I was truly surprised at how dark the rest of the house was. She hadn't bothered to turn on the hallway lights. I glanced at the office. The door was open and from the look of it inside, I imagined a single small lamp was lit and nothing else. I went to the kitchen, turned on the lights and began to prepare myself some supper.

As I worked and finally ate, I kept expecting her to appear, but she didn't until I had finished and put the dishes in the dishwasher. Eating and drinking restored some of my strength and energy. The cuts and bruises were at least only dull aches. I had just turned to start back to my room when I heard an unfamiliar click of heels in the hallway. The sound of the footsteps suggested someone full of energy. Who was here? I wished for my mother.

At first I didn't recognize her. My instant response to who is this was maybe she was someone from Aunt Victoria's office, maybe her secretary. It took a moment for me to get past all the changes and realize who it was.

I felt my own blood drain down toward my feet; a stinging sensation began behind my ears as my strength grew small, and I stared at the woman who seemed a stranger now, a distorted exaggeration of some fantasy.

Her hair had been rinsed in some coloring that had turned it into dry straw. Her face was caked in makeup to the extent that some of it flaked on her forehead. A bright red lipstick had been applied to those thin lips, making them look thick and wide, but clownish, too. The eyeshadow wasn't put on badly, but the false eyelashes just didn't fit and looked very artificial.

She wore high-heeled shoes which lifted her into the stratosphere. Drop earrings, gold with diamonds in their center, dangled to match the gold necklace. Her small bosom had been enhanced by one of those Wonder bras—or something—because she suddenly had cleavage, clearly visible in the low V-neck collar, tight dark blue cotton dress that was so snug it revealed her boney hips. The skirt of the dress was the shortest I had ever seen on her.

"Well?" she sang lifting her arms above her head and

turning slowly in a circle while she stood in the doorway, "how do I look?"

I couldn't find my voice. She was so bizarre, I was frightened. I tried to swallow, but the throat lump was heavy and large and wouldn't go down.

However, when she looked at me, disappointment flooded her face at my reaction, those eyes of excitement quickly turning cold and angry.

"What? What's wrong? I'm not as pretty? Even like this? Is that what you're thinking."

"No," I finally muttered. "No, I'm just surprised."

Her eyes remained narrow for a moment and then widened and she smiled.

"Of course you are. That's the fun of it though, surprise. Well, wish me luck," she said.

"For what?"

"For what? For my date. You always need a little luck on a date. You can't plan and plot every reaction, you know."

"You're going on a date?" I wanted to add, "like that?" but I didn't.

"Of course. I told you earlier. You just don't listen unless it involves you. Well, tonight is my night," she said. "And you have to stay home. You're the wallflower tonight, but I'll think of you when I'm eating something delicious and listening to the music and riding in the convertible and afterward. Yes, they'll be an afterward for me, too.

"Mind the store," she said with a wave and a laugh. "I'll fill you in on all of it tomorrow, if you're good."

She turned and started away.

"Wait. Aunt Victoria," I called after her and wheeled as quickly as I could into the hallway. She walked toward the front door. "Where are the keys to the van?" I called after her. "Aunt Victoria!"

She turned at the door.

"What? What?" she shouted, her face reddening.

I wheeled closer toward her.

"I need those keys," I said as calmly as I could. "You promised if I signed the paper. Please," I said. "We made a bargain."

"I don't know where they are. I'll look for them tomorrow. Don't tell me about papers and signing things. I don't want to discuss business now, you foolish little girl. Don't you have any sense of timing at all? My mind is full of jelly beans. I can't think seriously. You of all people should know that.

"Just try to be a good girl until I return."

"Aunt Victoria!"

She stepped out and closed the door. I sat there staring after her in disbelief. Then I spun around and wheeled myself down the corridor to her office, hoping she had forgotten to lock the door, but she hadn't.

She's mad, I thought. She's not going on any date. She's lost in some wild fantasy. I can't stay here a moment more, but I wasn't going to try to get down to the road again. That was for sure. I wheeled back to the staircase and contemplated it. Mrs. Churchwell had said the phone upstairs was working. The question was did I have the strength and the nerve to try to pull myself up all the steps? If I should slip and fall...At least I'll end up in the hospital and out of here, I thought. And then I thought, she might very well just pick me up and deposit me, broken bones and all, back into that bed.

Should I just wait and hope Austin returns as he

promised? Or has Austin and his uncle been sufficiently terrorized by Aunt Victoria's attorneys to stay away, especially after what had happened yesterday? I wondered.

My heart was pounding with indecision. How could I just return to my little prison of a room and simply wait? I'll take my time, I promised myself. Even if it takes me all night to do it, I'll go slowly and extra carefully and I'll get myself up these stairs and to that phone.

I'll get there if it's the last thing I ever do. That's just an expression normally, I thought, but for me, it might very well prove to be true.

Practically inching my way out of the chair and down to the first steps, I sat and took deep breaths. My heart was racing so, I thought I could possibly faint halfway up. Calm down, Rain, I told myself. Calm down or don't even attempt to do it.

It really wasn't all that difficult to go up a stairway, even with dead legs. I had the strength in my upper arms and shoulders, thanks to all my therapy with Austin. I sat on a step, put my arms behind myself and lifted myself up to the next step. I rested every two steps, holding onto the balustrade. To keep my mind from rushing into any panic, I counted the steps and then I became a little silly and sang, "Twenty-four steps on the stairs, if I do two more steps on the stairs, only eighteen left to go."

It took me the better part of an hour, but finally, I reached back to place my hands on the upstairs landing and lifted my body one final time. I was upstairs. My heart beat for joy now instead of in fear and trepidation.

I gazed down at my wheelchair at the foot of the stairs. I felt like I was looking over a cliff. Now, full of hope, I started down the upstairs hallway. All of the rooms had phones, as I recalled, but I felt most certain I'd find the working one in what had been her bedroom and where she stayed now.

As I moved down the hallway, however, I noted that the door to Grandmother Hudson's bedroom was wide open. Since it was closer, I decided to go for the phone there. After all, why would she have had that disconnected? Somehow it seemed right for me to make my desperate call for help from Grandmother Hudson's bedroom. Spiritually, she would be beside me as she had been when I needed her the most, I thought.

I turned into it and pulled myself up enough to flip on the lights.

What struck me first was the heavy scent of Grandmother Hudson's perfume. An aroma could linger, but certainly not as long as this nor as redolent as this. It seemed to have just been sprayed. Perhaps Aunt Victoria had used some on herself, I thought, but I didn't recall the scent downstairs when she spoke to me nor did it linger in the hallway, trailing behind her as she left. It surely would have.

Grandmother Hudson's phone was an antique, one of those brass telephones with the big receivers and mouthpieces. It was situated on her nightstand to the right of her bed. I decided I would use the side board of the bed as a brace and lift myself up and onto the bed. From there I would have an easy time using the phone.

I did it in two smooth motions, smiling to myself at how proud Austin would be if he saw me. With a final burst of strength, I lifted my body onto the bed and flopped backward to fall on the pillow.

Only, I didn't fall on the pillow. My cheek rested

against strands of hair instead. It was so unexpected, I froze for a moment and then slowly, I turned and immediately screamed such a shrill, long scream, it rattled every bone in my own body.

A wig the shade of Grandmother Hudson's hair had been put on a mannequin's head and rested on a pillow. The sight of it simply took my breath away like some vacuum cleaner hose sucking it all out of my lungs.

My head spun and then suddenly, all went dark.

15

Prisoner of Madness

I couldn't have been unconscious very long, but during the time I had taken to get myself up the stairs and into Grandmother Hudson's room, Aunt Victoria had traveled through the tunnel of illusion she had created for herself. She had gone on what I believed was her fantasy date and returned. I opened my eyes to see her standing over me.

She smiled.

"I'm not surprised to find you here. The moment I saw your wheelchair downstairs I knew that's what you had done.

"Of course, you want to be near her. Of course, you want to be here. How stupid of me not to have realized it from the start," she said.

I lifted my upper body and glanced again at the wig and mannequin head.

"What is this?" I asked.

"Shh," she said. "She's asleep. I bet you're tired, too.

What an effort it must have been to get yourself up here. We're all proud of you, proud that you finally decided to suffer a little pain and agony along with the rest of us."

"I want to leave," I whined. "Please help me go. You can have everything, all of it. I'll sign any document you want, only get me out of this house tonight."

"That's so silly," she chided me, "especially now that we're getting along so well."

"We're not getting along! Stop saying that!"

"Oh, you mustn't shout, Megan. You'll wake her," she added in a whisper.

"I'm not Megan. I'm Rain and you're ridiculous. You look absolutely ridiculous in that makeup and hair color. And there's no one to wake. Grandmother Hudson is gone, gone! Now you help me get up and out of this house or I'll report everything to my attorney. Understand?" I threatened.

She stared down at me and shook her head slowly.

"And here I thought you were improving and that you weren't going to be a spoiled brat anymore. What a terrible disappointment."

She turned away and started to leave.

"Don't you dare leave this room," I screamed.

She turned back.

"Maybe after a night's rest, you'll have a better attitude," she said. "Oh," she added, smiling, "I had a perfectly wonderful evening with Grant."

"You weren't with Grant. You'll never be with Grant!" I yelled as she closed the door slowly and clicked off the light. "Aunt Victoria!"

Her heels clicked away.

I turned and fumbled for the phone, but when I lifted it from the cradle, I heard only silence. There was no dial tone. Why did she have this disconnected? Did she imagine Grandmother Hudson was going to use it?

Madness.

I'm drowning in her madness, I thought in a panic.

I swept the phone off the night stand and it banged and bounced on the floor.

Did I have the strength to start back downstairs? And what would I do when I got there?

I groaned and lowered my head to the pillow. What had I done? I had separated myself from my wheelchair, my only way to move myself about and I had trapped myself even deeper in this pit, like someone in a straitjacket, turning and twisting and in doing so, making it tighter and tighter until I could barely move.

I slept through the remainder of the night. The moment I woke, I was overcome with the urge to vomit. Wave after wave of nausea kept me from lifting my head from the pillow. I took deep breaths and tried to keep myself calm. What was happening to me? Was it a result from my great physical exertion yesterday? I still had dull throbbing all over my body.

When I turned slightly to my left, my nipples tingled and then I felt a slight aching in my breasts. Why should that be? A terrifying hot fear shot up my spine like mercury moving up a thermometer. I shook my head to deny the possibility, however another realization flashed across my brain. I hadn't thought much about it because I had so many other physical concerns these days—but I had missed my period weeks ago.

All of this hit me like a punch in the stomach and I couldn't hold myself back any longer. I leaned over the side of the bed and vomited. As I did I screamed for Aunt

Victoria; I screamed for anyone. I thought I was dying on the spot. Every time I paused, I screamed again and again. Finally, she came to my door.

There was a radical change between what she had looked like yesterday and what she looked like this morning. As if she had woken from a dream, stopped her sleepwalking or snapped out of a coma, she was the more familiar Aunt Victoria again, at least in appearance. Dressed in one of her business suits, her hair brushed neatly, the makeup gone, including the lipstick, she stood in the doorway and stared in at me with a look of disgust emerging from within her boney face like a bubble of air rising to the top of some water.

That maddening mind of hers had slipped back into the present I thought. I hoped.

"What are you doing?" she asked.

"What am I doing? I'm sick," I said. "How could you leave me like this?"

"You're disgusting," she said and marched across the room to the bathroom where she plucked a towel off the towel rack and came back to throw it over the mess.

"You've got to call an ambulance and get me to the hospital," I said.

She stared down at me and shook her head.

"Everything has to be dramatic with you, doesn't it? Everything has to be an Academy Award performance. You always have to be the center of attention. Even today, even today you have to do this."

"What? Today? What are you saying?"

Wasn't she back to being herself? How was I ever to tell just looking at her? What was she talking about now?

"You know this is a big day for me. I might have put together the biggest deal our company ever had. How proud Father will be. You're afraid I'll steal your lime-light, is that it?"

"Aunt Victoria, stop and look at me. It's Rain. I'm ill. I think...I think I might be pregnant," I admitted, expecting her to go into a tirade about Austin, the fortune hunter, and how he had deliberately made me pregnant to get to my money.

She raised her head and squeezed her lips into her cheeks. Her eyes seemed to darken and then lighten as if some tiny bulbs behind them were turned down and then up.

"Really?" she asked dryly, her voice devoid of emotion or sympathy. "Why doesn't that surprise me, I wonder? Why doesn't it surprise me that your own personal plea-sures were once again put before any responsibility or any concern for your family and your family's reputation? Why aren't I shocked, Megan?"

"You're not listening to me. Please, listen," I pleaded. "I'm your niece, not your sister. It's very serious for me to be pregnant. I need medical attention. You've got to call for an ambulance and call my doctors immediately."

I reached up for her hand and she pulled herself back as if I was poison ivy.

"Oh stop it. You think you're the first girl to get herself in trouble? What do you think will happen? Do you think we can let the world know what a mess you've made of yourself? You want me to call an ambulance because you think you might be pregnant? That's ridiculous. Even if you really are pregnant, we'll handle this just the way we handle all of your mistakes, Megan, by ourselves, dis-creetly, without the rest of the world knowing just how bad you are.

"For now," she added, "a little suffering will do you

good. Perhaps it will help you to realize just how selfish you've been and why you should think about the rest of us next time you decide to throw caution to the wind and indulge your own fantasies and pleasures."

She turned away and marched toward the door.

"Wait!" I cried.

"What is it? I've got to go," she said turning. "I have a very, very important meeting today. It could be worth millions eventually. Can you imagine," she asked, her eyes wide with excitement, "can you imagine that I, a woman, have taken Father's company to heights even he couldn't imagine?

"Maybe now you'll appreciate me more. Maybe now they both will."

She gazed at the floor.

"Try not to make any more mess, will you."

She closed the door nearly all the way.

"Wait! Don't leave me here!" I screamed when she disappeared. "I'm not Megan!" I heard her descending the stairs. "Come back here and look at me! Listen to me! Aunt Victoria!"

Moments later the front door opened and closed below and she was gone. I was alone. The cramps continued, my nausea returned and I threw up again and again until I was too weak to lift my head from the pillow.

Rest, I told myself. Stay calm and rest and in a little while try to get yourself to the telephone in her room.

I drifted in and out of sleep. I could sense that things weren't going well with my bladder again. I was wet and my cramping became more and more severe. The waves of nausea moved into something else, something beyond. My body felt warmer and warmer and my mouth was suddenly so dry, I couldn't swallow. My tongue was a thick piece of sandpaper. Shouting for help was painful.

The pain between my temples, over my forehead became so intense it brought tears to my eyes. It felt like someone with a thumb and a forefinger made of steel was squeezing and squeezing me there. All I could do was moan and cry inside. I had no idea about time. There wasn't a working clock in the room. I know I drifted on and off for what had to be hours, feeling myself grow warmer and warmer until I thought I might set the very bed on fire. How I wished I had just a sip of water.

The movement of sunlight away from the east side of the house told me it was late afternoon. Drifting in and out of sleep I thought I had heard footsteps and the creak of the door being opened farther. Sure enough, when I opened my eyes again, I saw the door had been moved.

I tried to call. I thought I had shouted, but I'm sure it was barely louder than a whisper. Finally, after what must have been another hour or so, she came into the room. She was no longer in her business suit, but what I saw now was so weird, I thought I was surely still locked in a dream.

Aunt Victoria seemed to float past me. She was wearing only a thin negligee.

She was very slender and I could see her ribs outlined under the skin. She turned and raised her arms, holding them frozen in the air for a moment before dropping them to turn herself again in a strange dance. The smile on her face was so different. It looked more like a little girl's smile of joy.

She paused and looked at me as if she was pleased.

"Oh, Megan. I'm so excited. I couldn't wait to come in to tell you. Daddy loves me," she said. "Daddy loves me more than he loves you."

She did a little spin again and drew closer to me. My eyes felt locked, unable to turn an iota to the right or to the left. Her face was mesmerizing. When she spoke, she spoke in a little girl's voice.

"Daddy carried me up to bed. I had just finished my cup of hot milk and he said I should go to sleep now. I didn't want to. I wanted to stay up longer, but he said I had to go to sleep or Mother would be angry. She had left it up to him to take care of us tonight while she was at her charity ball meeting and he had better do it, he said, or he would get put in the doghouse.

" 'Do you want me to sleep in the doghouse?' he asked me.

"Of course, I shook my head, my face full of terror at just the thought of my getting him into trouble, and he laughed and looked at me with the softest face I have ever seen him have, even softer than when he looks at you. Yes, much softer," she happily concluded with firm nods.

I couldn't speak. Her face was so close to mine now that she frightened me and I was afraid of interrupting. I could see the tiny freckles under her eyelids and a light, small birthmark otherwise hidden under a corner of her nostril.

"Come along," he said and he reached out for me. His hand is so big, isn't it? My hand looked swallowed up when he closed his around it. I couldn't see my fingers.

" 'I can't see my fingers, Daddy,' I said and he laughed and said, 'Let's see if they're still there.'

"He opened his hand and touched my palm with his long, thick left finger and said, 'There they are.'

"I laughed and Daddy smiled at me and then he surprised me by pulling me closer and lifting me up as if I was made of air.

315

" 'Here you go,' he said. 'Upstairs to bed and don't go near Megan. She's got the measles and you will certainly catch them,' he warned.

"He carried me all the way up to my room and lowered me to my bed and then he caressed my face and ran his hand over my shoulders and down my chest to my stomach where he tickled me and made me laugh.

"Daddy never did that to me before. I know he did it to you, but never to me.

"Then he said, 'I bet you're catching up to Megan, aren't you? You're twelve. Girls catch up when they're twelve. Let's see,' he said and lifted my nightie to see below. 'Yes, you are,' he said. 'I've got two big girls now.'

"He made me feel good and kissed me on the cheek and his face was so red and hot that it almost burned mine when mine touched his.

"So he loves me," she concluded and did another little turn. "Daddy loves me too."

She stopped and looked at me. I had no idea what she was going to do next, but she lifted her hand slowly toward me and touched my face.

"Cool," she said, "but not cool enough even though your skin looks better today. Why, you almost look half alive, although you've lost weight, haven't you? All your boyfriends will be upset, won't they?"

She wiped her fingers on the bed as if she had touched something slimy.

"I'm very sick," I whispered, "very sick."

"I know. You feel terrible. It makes you feel terrible, but you'll get better," she said, her eyes small. "And then you'll be the pretty one again and Daddy won't look at me as much."

She knelt beside my bed. Her smile became vacuous, her eyes losing their light, flickering and going pale and distant.

"I watch him when he's with you. I heard him say you were so lovely you could bring love to anything. I see the pleasure in his eyes, the pride he has, the pride of an artist who created something so beautiful all the world would congratulate him."

She paused and then looked at me angrily.

"Why don't you stay sick a while longer? You won't have to go to school and worry about tests and homework. You'll continue to be waited on hand and foot, just as you like it. Huh?"

I shook my head.

"I know what. I'll help you stay sick," she said.

"Water," I pleaded in a whisper. "I'm so thirsty. Please get me some water."

Her eyes brightened.

"Water? You want a drink of water? That's good. I'll get you a drink of water."

She rose and went into the bathroom. I waited to hear the faucet running. Just the sound of water would give me pleasure, I thought, but I didn't hear that. Instead, I heard the toilet seat go up and then I heard her dip a glass in it and return.

"Here you go," she said. "Just drink this."

I shook my head.

"Please," I muttered through my dried lips. It was painful just to separate them.

"You said you were thirsty, didn't you?" she nearly barked, her voice so gruff. "Drink some of this water." She smiled. "Maybe it will keep you sick a little longer," she said. "Drink it," she commanded.

I shook my head and then she leaned over and brought

the glass to my mouth. I kept it closed as she poured the toilet bowl water over it, letting it run down the side of my chin and onto the bed and my neck. She squeezed my jaw, my mouth opened a little and some of the water got in. I coughed and spit. She watched me a moment and then got up and returned the glass to the bathroom.

I started to dry heave and did it so many times, my stomach ached.

"Good. I'll let everyone know you're sicker," she said gleefully. "Once again, it will just be me at the dinner table with Daddy. We'll have tea and toast brought up to you. I'll bring it myself, okay?"

She paused and tilted her head as she scowled.

"I don't know why I'm so nice to you. You're never this nice to me. You always avoid me in school and act as if we're not related."

Then she smiled again.

"But, I'm not angry. I'm not angry at all. Daddy loves me, too."

She walked slowly toward the door, gazed back to wave and then closed the door behind her.

My eyelids slammed shut almost simultaneously and I fell into a deep sleep, perhaps as a way of escaping a living nightmare.

There are times when we all want to rush back to our good dreams. My poor troubled brain was willing to turn itself inside out if it had to in order to take me away from my own painful, aching body. Happier memories blossomed like bright flowers in a dark garden, forcing back the cloak of dread and sadness and retrieving smiles and laughter.

I was a little girl again in that innocent time before I would be introduced to prejudice and hate, violence and poverty. I did not yet understand who I was, where I was and what storms and turmoil raged and awaited me just outside my precious world of lollipop fantasies and candy cotton promises. That would all come soon; that would all come soon enough, but for now, I could still feel safe.

What a time that was.

One memory vividly returned. I could smell Mama's good cooking and hear her humming and singing in the kitchen. Beneatha and I were in our room playing with some dolls Mama had gotten from the lost-and-found in the supermarket. We heard Roy come into the house, slamming the door too hard as usual.

"How many times I tell you not to slam that door, Roy Arnold?" Mama chastised.

"Ah Mama. I wasn't thinking about it," he said.

"Well, you should. You'll break it off the hinges and then where will we be?"

"In an apartment without a door," Roy said.

"What?"

We held our breath, waiting for her to raise her voice even more when suddenly she just laughed and laughed. We heard Roy laugh too and when I looked out the door, she was hugging him and running her hand through his hair. When he saw me looking at them, he pulled away quickly, embarrassed.

"Aw Mama," he moaned and hurried to his room.

"Whatcha lookin' at Sugar?" Mama asked me.

"Nothing, Mama. Is Roy all right?"

"Oh, he's fine. He just has to learn to be more of a gentleman. I'm just afraid he's not going to learn it here though," she muttered.

"Why not, Mama?"

"This ain't exactly the place for ladies and gentlemen," she said. Then she smiled at me. "But don't you worry about it, Rain. You're going somewhere good someday, somewhere special, I'm sure."

"Where, Mama?" I asked, wide-eyed with expectation. What secrets about my future did Mama know?

"I don't know right off," she said, "but I know it will be a wonderful place where people are dressed fancy and live in big mansions and have beautiful things like pianos and gardens and nice cars."

"Beneatha's going too, isn't she, Mama?" I asked looking back at my sister squatting on the floor by the dollhouse. She wasn't really listening.

"I hope so," Mama said. "I hope you're all going."

"What about you, Mama?"

"I'll be there, too," she promised. "Just leave the door open."

"What's that mean, Mama? Leave the door open?"

She laughed.

"I'm just funning with you, child. Come here," she said and held out her arms for me to run to. She held me close and kissed my forehead and stroked my hair.

"You're the coolness after the hot, burning sun, Rain. You're the hope."

She let me go and turned back to the preparations for dinner. When I looked toward Roy's room, I saw him peering out at me, his face locked in a soft smile.

Why was I so special? I wondered. In my house I felt like a star. Mama and Roy made me believe I could sparkle when I walked and talked. They made me think I was blessed and protected.

No wonder even the smallest cut, the tiniest bruise, the most inconsequential ache seemed so shocking. Gradually, with every passing day, I had to let go of the fantasy. Someone opened the door and let me see the world as it was around us and I knew that even Mama and Roy couldn't keep the pain away. But they tried, oh, how they tried.

Recalling all this, I know I was lying there with a cool, happy smile on my face even though my skin was so hot with fever I was practically radiating from the bed. The headache dulled. I breathed a little better and I slept on through the better memories, wrapping them around me like a cocoon in which I could safely and comfortably snuggle to wait for the burst of sunshine around me again.

Not long after, I heard Aunt Victoria coming up the stairs and waited, praying she had regained her senses and would realize that if she didn't do something for me soon, I might die and she would be blamed. Now dressed in a blouse and one of her familiar ankle-length skirts, she stepped through the doorway carrying a tray.

"Here you go," she said, "your tea and toast. That's all you're permitted to have for now."

She set the tray down on the night stand by the bed and stepped back.

"We're having a beautiful honey-baked ham and those little potatoes you love so much. I bet you can smell it up here, can't you? Does it make your stomach churn?"

"You're going to be blamed," I whispered.

"Excuse me? Are you trying to say something, Megan?"

I closed my eyes and struggled to speak. She drew closer.

"What was that? You're sorry about how you've been

treating me at school? It's too late for apologies. What's done is done, but not buried. It will always be here," she said pointing to her temple.

"You're going to be blamed," I said, louder. She heard one word at least.

"Blamed?" She laughed. "Me? What can I be blamed for? I've never been in trouble, never been sent to the principal, never had a dissatisfactory checked on my report card, never disobeyed my mother or father, never came home after I was supposed to or failed to call if I was going to be late. Who would blame me?"

"Drink your tea and eat your toast. If you're good, I'll bring you one of your silly movie magazines or beauty magazines. One of those I haven't thrown in the garbage, that is."

I shook my head.

"Stop," I muttered. "Call the doctor."

"Time for honey-baked ham," she sang and turned away. We both heard the sound of a doorbell and she stopped midway to the door. It rang again. She spun around and glared at me.

"Who's coming to see you? When I'm sick, no one ever comes to see me. You called one of your boyfriends, didn't you? Or are they all coming?"

Again, the doorbell sounded. It's Austin, I told myself. Thankfully, it's Austin. He's come for me, just as he had promised he would.

"Well, no one's going to answer it," she decided. "Whoever it is will go away if we just pretend no one is at home. It's dark enough downstairs and I won't make a sound."

"No," I moaned.

She walked out and closed the door gently. I heard the doorbell again and I waited and then I didn't hear it anymore. My heart shriveled with disappointment. It was as if someone had brought the blanket up and over my head. I closed my eyes and when I opened them again, it was so dark in the room, I thought I really was under a blanket. Overcast skies kept the stars and moon from shining any light through the windows. I had no idea about time, of course, so I didn't know how late it might be.

My fever hadn't broken. It lingered and drained me. My mind kept wandering. Images of different people flashed before me. I saw Randall Glenn in England smiling at me from his bed. I heard laughter and saw Catherine and Leslie, my French girlfriends at the School of Performing Arts, giggling.

Then I heard something on my right and when I looked, I saw my Great-aunt Leonora rocking in a chair in her bedroom, holding a large doll in her arms. Her shy maid, Mary Margaret, stood beside her, her head down and then looked up at me, tears streaming down her cheeks.

Off to my right, Mama began to sing.

I called to her and then, everyone popped like bubbles and left me in darkness.

Moments later, I heard the door open and saw my Great-aunt and Great-uncle's horrid butler Boggs approaching me.

"You overslept," he accused. "Get up and get to your chores. Get up or I'll turn your bed over with you in it. Get up!"

He reached out and I screamed and screamed.

"Stop it!" I heard Aunt Victoria snap. She turned on the lamp on the nightstand. "Why are you shouting? Now you want to get out of this room? Who brought you up here? Not me. I leave for a little while and you turn this house upside down. What a mess and I have no maid hired yet to keep after it and clean up after you.

"Oh my god," she cried looking down at the stale towel by the bed. "This place is disgusting and you stink. Where's your mother while all this is going on, huh? She's off at some Mediterranean resort basking in the sunshine, drinking cocktails, listening to music and dancing with Grant while I'm left here looking after you."

She turned on more lights. At least she's back to being Aunt Victoria again, I thought even though that was like being grateful that the devil was only Hitler.

"Well, what am I supposed to do with you now? I can't carry you downstairs, you know. I don't even want to touch you, you smell so bad."

She stared at me.

"What are you smiling about?" she asked.

Was I smiling.

"You think this is funny? You think you're hurting me? Ridiculous girl. First, you go and scrape yourself up on the driveway and I have to deal with that, and now, you get yourself up here and into my mother's bed and mess and I have to handle that, too."

She shook her head.

"Even I have limitations." She sighed. "All right, I'll do my best. I'll fill a tub and help you into it and then we'll see about getting you out of here."

"Get...me...to the hospital," I pleaded.

"Don't tell me what to do. You think I would allow anyone into the house the way you've messed it? First things, first."

She went into the bathroom and began to run the water in the tub. I shook my head.

"All right," she said returning, "I'll drag you in there, but you'd better help me. I can't do it all. I'm not some nurse's aide. None of this would have happened if you wouldn't have driven Mrs. Bogart away behaving like some tart with that fortune hunter."

I shook my head more vigorously as she pulled away the blanket. Then she squinted and squeezed her nose.

"Ugh," she said.

Just as she reached for me, the doorbell rang again. She froze.

"Who could that be at this hour?" she asked.

The doorbell was rung again and again. Whoever it was had decided to get results this time. A continuous stream of ding-dongs echoed below.

"Damn," she cried, returned to the bathroom to shut off the tub faucet and then stomped out of my room, this time leaving the door wide open. I listened as hard as I could. I could hear the front door being opened.

"What do you want?" she demanded.

"I want to see, Rain," Austin demanded in a stern, strong voice.

"You have some nerve coming back here. I'll be on the phone in minutes."

"She's not in her room. I looked in the window. She wasn't in there when I came here earlier either. Where is she? What's going on?"

"It's none of your business."

"Yes, it is. If you don't tell me, I'll go to the police," he said.

"Austin," I called as loudly as I could muster. "I'm up here. Austin. Come get me. Austin."

"Really? I think I'll call the police before you and

have them up here to arrest you for trespassing," she threatened him.

"Austin!" I cried. Why couldn't he hear me?

"What happened to the ramp? Why has it been removed from the front of the house?"

"We don't need it anymore," Aunt Victoria told him.

"Why not? She won't be able to get herself outside. I don't understand. What about taking her to the doctor when she needs to go? What about her wheeling out or being wheeled out for some fresh air?"

"She's no longer here. She's gone back to England to live with her real father," Aunt Victoria said quickly.

"What? How could that be?" he asked, astonished.

"Arrangements were made by him. She agreed and she's left. I think she made a good decision. She's better off there. We're selling the house anyway and that's that, so you might as well give up your pursuit of her and her money. You won't see a penny of it now and if you persist in bothering me or this family any further, I will ask the police to arrest you. As it is, I'm calling my attorneys first thing in the morning and starting all the legal procedures I promised I would start."

"No," I cried. "Austin, don't believe her." My throat ached with the effort and the strain, but I put all I had into another cry. "Austin!"

"I don't understand," I heard him say.

"Will you let me close this door or do I have to march back and phone the police?"

"I just can't believe it," he said.

"That's your problem," she told him.

Desperate, I braced myself on my elbows and tried to call again, but I could see that my voice was practically gone. Just a little more than a whisper emerged. What was I going to do?

I looked at the mannequin's head beside me and scooped it into my arms. Then, with all the strength left in my weakened body, I hurled it toward the door. It didn't reach, but it hit the floor hard a few feet short.

"What was that?" Austin asked.

"My stupid maid probably breaking something new," Aunt Victoria said. "Good night, young man and good riddance."

I heard the door slam shut below.

For me, it was like the lid being shut on my coffin.

16

Life Near Death

Aunt Victoria suddenly appeared in the doorway. She had come up the stairs like a ghost or else I was too weak and sick to hear any sound that came from beyond the room.

"How easy that was," she remarked with a slow smile that lit up her dark eyes with a sinister glow. "Why didn't I think of all that before and save us both all this aggravation? Now that he believes you have left, he'll stop coming around and our problems are over.

"For a while you'll just have to stay inside, stay away from people so no one can tell him otherwise. Don't worry. I'll make sure there is plenty here to amuse and occupy you. What would you do out there anyway? Tomorrow, I'll find us a new maid, a more dedicated one who can keep her mouth zipped shut.

"Actually, what I should do is try to win back Mrs. Bogart," she continued. "Once she learns that he's gone for good this time, she might consider returning. I know what.

I'll offer her more money, lots more money and she will return. How's that sound? Good? Good. I knew you'd agree with me."

Who agreed? She heard only what she wanted to hear.

"What's this?" she asked, seeing the smashed mannequin's head on the floor. "How did this get here? Oh, was that the noise we heard?"

She shook her head.

"You were trying to get his attention, weren't you? How foolish. What a foolish little girl you can be. Well, we'll clean this up later.

"Now," she said, pausing, "what was I about to do before we were so rudely interrupted? What was it? Oh yes, get you cleaned up. Then, we'll dress you in a comfortable nighty and if I can reach Mrs. Bogart tomorrow, I'll have someone strong enough to get you back downstairs where you belong.

"Doesn't that all sound wonderful? Don't bother to thank me. I know you're appreciative," she said and went into the bathroom to start filling the tub again.

"My mother has so many nice bath salts. I'll pick one out for you," she shouted back to me. "Mother was crazy about her baths. She wouldn't go a day without taking one, whereas I prefer showers.

"Megan, on the other hand, is more like my mother. She likes to soak and soak, especially in those special skin oils. She once took a bath in milk, you know, because she read that Cleopatra would do that. Can you imagine?"

She came out of the bathroom and stood there looking toward me with a grin on her face.

"Once, I snuck into the bathroom while she was having one of her wonderful so-called skin soaks. I tiptoed in and came up behind her and pushed her head under the water before she had a chance to resist. I held it there a few seconds and she came up sputtering and coughing and crying. She was so angry. I said it was just a joke. You like to laugh with your friends. Now you can tell them about it and laugh about it, I said. Tell them I thought you should soak your whole head. She was pretty angry at me and she didn't speak to me for days, but that didn't matter because we usually didn't have much to say to each other anyway.

"You wouldn't get angry if I pushed your head under for a joke, now would you?" she asked, followed by a cold, thin laugh.

I stared at her. I felt so helpless, as if my body had been poured out and was in a mold, forming but still loose—unconnected, not yet installed with any energy.

"Now how do we get you out of that bed and into the tub?" she asked, tilting her head as she considered the problem. "How did Mrs. Bogart do it so well? I won't ask you how that fortune hunter of a therapist did it. I hope he never did and if he did, don't tell me.

"I guess I'm going to have to lift and drag you, is that it? I'm certainly not going downstairs to get that chair and carry it back up here. I'd still have to get you in and out of it anyway, which is extra work. You could cooperate and make it easier. Are you going to cooperate?

"Of course you are," she said with a smile. "We're friends now that I've solved all the problems like our business arrangement, your annoying therapist, all of it. When Megan and Grant do come here to visit, they'll find the two of us chatting pleasantly in the living room and they'll be very impressed. At least, I know Grant will. If I know Megan, she'll try to make it seem like nothing at all.

"You've never really had a nice talk with her, have you?

I know you haven't because there's so much about her and about me that you don't know, things you would know if she had ever bothered to really make you part of this family. She sent you down here to be a servant and then they sent you to England to be a servant. At least, I'm not making you a servant, am I? I'm making you a partner and I'm looking after you, protecting your interests.

"Why is it that everyone likes her so much? You still like her, don't you?" she asked in a accusatory tone. "After all she's done to you, you still care for her. Why? She fails at everything important and still people love her. He loves her. What's her magic?

"And don't tell me it's her good looks," she said quickly. "A pretty face is a dime a dozen, especially for a man like Grant who could have his pick of beauty contestants."

She looked back at the bathtub.

"All right," she said. "It's time."

She went in and shut off the water.

My heart began to pound as if it had a brain of its own. Don't let her put us in that tub it was chanting with every thump. "Don't, don't, don't," it thumped as she approached the bed.

"Let's get these clothes off," she said and began to undress me. I wasn't cooperative, but she pulled me roughly and turned my arms at will. In moments I was naked.

She stood back and gazed down at me.

"You know, despite all your trouble, you're still a very attractive young woman. Maybe some day you will find a suitable man.

"But don't depend on it," she instantly added. "There are so few suitable men out there today. No one knows how difficult it is for women with half a brain."

She sighed as if she carried the burden of all the intelligent women in the world on her narrow, frail shoulders.

"Let's get this done," she said. "I have to get back to work. There are deals, deals, deals to make and that requires much time and intelligent analysis, you know. You'd be surprised at how many scam artists are out there, just waiting to prey on women like us, women they think are weak.

"Won't they be surprised every time they try? They sure will," she said laughing. "They sure will."

She reached down for my wrists. I shook my head.

"Please," I said. "Leave me alone. Call the doctor. Get me to a hospital."

"After you're cleaned up, you'll feel better," she replied, but hesitated. "How does one move a crippled body like yours without doing any more damage?"

She shrugged.

"Oh well, I'll do the best I can."

She turned me so she could slip her hands under my arms and then she tugged, dragging me off the bed. My legs fell like logs to the floor, nearly pulling her over, but she steadied herself and then straightened with surprising strength.

I don't know where I found the strength, but I turned and twisted, trying to break out of her grip. She held on firmly and began slowly, but steadily to back up toward the bathroom, my feet bounced limply over the floor as she dragged me along.

"No," I cried.

"Now, now, now, you have to be cleaned up. What a mess you are? You don't want anyone seeing you like this, do you?"

"Please, stop."

My panic grew frenzied when we passed through the

bathroom doorway. She had developed strong momentum now. In a desperate move to keep her from putting me in the tub of water, I reached out for the edge of the sink and grasped it firmly, far more firmly and rapidly than she had ever anticipated. Her rearward motion continued, but the abrupt stop broke her grip under my arms and I felt her fall backwards, away from me.

My upper body, now unsupported, dropped to the floor hard and the back of my head slammed on the tile, nearly knocking me unconscious. I heard her short scream, which was more like a muffled curse and turned my head just in time to see her go over the edge of the tub, slap the side of her head sharply against the long, decorative brass faucet and then seemingly slide gracefully into the water with barely the sound of a small splash. From my angle on the floor, I couldn't tell what she was doing, but her legs lifted and then fell over the outside of the tub as the remainder of her body disappeared below the tub's edge.

I groaned and turned on my stomach. My head spun, my eyes feeling as if they were falling back into my skull. I fought losing consciousness and reached up for the toilet bowl. I was running on pure determination. Every iota of energy had seeped from my broken, languid body with its bones barely holding it together. Yet, I managed to somehow pull myself up so that I could gaze over the side of the bathtub and look down at her.

I saw her floating just under the water, her eyes closed, small bubbles evacuating her nostrils and her lips like sailors fleeing a sinking ship. There was a thin but steady flow of blood from her right temple and I saw blood on the faucet as well. Strands of hair rose toward the surface as if they wanted to pull the rest of her up. The blow had obviously knocked her unconscious.

Suddenly, my arms collapsed and I fell back to the floor. My stomach tightened and the tightening climbed up to my chest, making it almost impossible for me to breathe. I reached out limply for her left ankle, grasped it and made a vain attempt to pull her up and out of the tub. I had barely enough energy to lift the ankle a few inches. My fingers slipped off her skin and my arm dropped to my side.

The struggle to prevent her from dragging me in and the effort it had taken to lift myself to look at her in the tub had taken all my remaining energy. I groaned and then sucked in a deep breath just before all went black.

It seemed like the floor beneath me was rattling the way it would if the house was caught in an earthquake. It continued for another moment until I was able to open my eyelids, which felt stuck together. My vision was cloudy, but slowly a silhouette took shape. I could hear a muffled distorted voice and then the silhouette cleared and became Austin and I heard him calling my name. He had been shaking my shoulders.

"Rain, wake up. Rain, c'mon, sweetheart. Wake up, baby. Wake up."

"Austin," I whispered.

"What went on here? There's an ambulance on the way," he said before I could even try to respond, "and the police, too. I had to run all over this house to find a phone that works."

As he spoke, he wrapped a blanket around me snugly and then he lifted me off the floor and held me in his arms. I dropped my head against his chest and closed my eyes. I must have passed out again because when I opened my eyes this time, I was in an ambulance. The attendant was hovering over me after just having inserted an IV.

"Hey," he said. "How you doin'?"

"What's happening to me?"

"You're on the way to the hospital. Just relax and let us do all the work. That's why we get all those big wages," he said and someone behind him laughed.

I closed my eyes again, lulled by the sense of movement and the comfort of the stretcher. For the moment I couldn't think; I didn't want to think. When we arrived at the hospital, I felt myself being moved and didn't open my eyes again until I was in an examination room.

"She's completely dehydrated," I heard someone say.

"Infection," someone else added.

"Get her upstairs," the first voice said.

My body felt like a sack being turned and moved, rolled along and lifted until I was snug in a hospital bed, the blanket up to my chin. I slept on and off, finally waking and holding my eyes open for an extended time. Sunlight basked the white walls and tile floor. I turned my head to the right and saw Austin asleep in a chair, his head down until his chin touched his collar bone.

"Austin," I called. "Austin."

Slowly, he raised his head and opened his eyes. When he realized I had called him and I was awake, he literally leaped out of the seat and to my side.

"Rain, how are you?"

"I don't know," I said. "What happened? I can't remember much."

"After your aunt turned me away, I realized I had spotted your wheelchair in the hallway, behind her. It didn't come to me immediately. At first I actually believed what she had told me. I mean, the ramp was gone. It seemed to make some sense. I imagined you wanted to just run away from all this and knowing you, I thought you wouldn't call me because you didn't want me to stop you. I was planning on contacting your father in London and flying over there.

"Driving home, suddenly, the chair loomed in my mind and I thought how could you have been taken out and put on a plane without your wheelchair?

"I turned around and went back to the house. This time I didn't go to the front door. I went to the window of your room, our window as I liked to think of it," he said smiling, "and I pushed it up and crawled in. I could see your things were all still there in the drawers and closets, confirming that you hadn't left. Why was she lying to me? I wondered, but most of all, where were you? What had she done?

"I went through the bottom floor quietly, listening. At first I thought you might be locked in that office because I couldn't open the door. I tapped on it and listened and then decided I had better check the rest of the house first. It was puzzling that even she wasn't around downstairs.

"I tiptoed up the stairs and listened. I thought I heard you groan and then I charged into that bedroom and found you on the bathroom floor and your aunt in the tub."

"What happened to her?" I asked.

"She drowned. The police will be coming to ask you questions, but no one in his or her right mind would think you had anything to do with it. From the way I found you, I imagined she was helping you into a bath and probably fell, hitting her head. Is that right?"

"Yes. I didn't want a bath. I was afraid of her, Austin.

She was so cruel to me and she was out of her mind half the time, talking to me as if I was my mother."

"Is that why you have all those scrapes and bruises? She beat you or something?"

"No. I tried to get away from the house, tried to get to the road so someone would take me to a phone. I was going to call you, but when I wheeled out, I discovered she had gotten the grounds people to remove the ramp. I tried to get down to the road anyway and lost control of my chair. I crawled for hours and that's how I got all bruised. She found me and afterward when she was gone again, I climbed up the stairs to get to a phone there.

"Then, it really got bad. I've been very, very sick, Austin."

"I know. They've got control of your fever and the infection."

"I think there's something else going on beside another infection."

"What?"

"I think I'm pregnant," I said.

He stared for a moment and then his lips softened and his eyes brightened.

"That's possible," he said. "We were a little too passionate and threw caution to the wind too many times."

"I'm afraid, Austin."

He nodded.

"I'll have the doctor check you," he said.

"We once discussed the possibility of someone in my condition getting pregnant, Austin. You told me about another client of yours."

"Yes."

"What are the dangers for me?" I asked.

"Let's talk to the doctor. I'm not really any sort of expert about it," he said.

"Should I have an abortion, Austin?" I asked.

He studied me a moment.

"Let me start by telling you this, Rain. I'm going to marry you no matter what you decide to do."

I smiled back at him.

"You're crazy," I said.

"Crazy in love," he replied.

The nurse came in to check my medications and my temperature and shortly afterward, the doctor arrived. Austin stepped aside, waiting near the door.

I was surprised to see my doctor was a woman who looked to be no more than in her late thirties. She had hair almost as dark as mine and a very soft, friendly smile. Her glasses were in an attractive pearl-colored frame. She didn't look to be much taller than five feet one, yet she did carry herself with authority and confidence.

"I'm Sheila Baker," she said. "How are you feeling?"

"Numb," I replied. She laughed, check the charts and then began to examine me. As she listened to my heart, I spoke.

"I think I'm pregnant," I said.

She stopped listening, studied me for a moment and then glanced back at Austin.

"Oh? And why do you think that?" she asked.

I told her my symptoms.

"Okay, we'll see if that's the case," she said.

"If it is, what sort of complications would I experience?" I asked. "I mean, in my present condition?"

She lowered her glasses, which she kept on a jeweled tie.

"Well, I've got your charts and your history, so I can tell you some things. There's a chance you'd experience what

338

we call autonomic hyperreflexia, uncontrolled reflex motion. This syndrome's effects range from mild, annoying symptoms to the fatal possibility of intracranial hemorrhage. Usually, bouts of hyperreflexia don't harm the fetus. A little more care must be taken to be sure the fetus doesn't suffer hypotension or hypoxemia, which is lack of oxygen in the blood. It's best you give birth in a hospital equipped to handle the complications.

"The site of your spinal injury makes it less likely that this would occur," she added with a smile.

"But not completely unlikely?"

"I hate to say never, ever," she replied.

"What else?" I asked. There had to be more, I thought.

"Premature delivery is more common for women in your condition. You'll be able to perceive the beginnings of labor and you need some education about what to look for. You'll have to have weekly cervical examinations and late in the pregnancy, you'd have to be in a hospital setting.

"However, I would not expect you to require Cesarean section. Sometimes forceps delivery or vacuum extraction are used through the final stages.

"In short, nothing is as easier for you now as it is for someone without your injuries, but I wouldn't tell you not to get pregnant."

She looked at Austin.

"Is this your husband?"

"Soon to be," he said. "Soon to be, husband and, I hope, soon-to-be father."

We locked our eyes so intently, Doctor Baker felt uncomfortable being anywhere in between.

"Well, okay. You're doing fine for now. I'll see you later," she said and left us.

"Are you sure about all this, Austin?"

"When I leave here, I'm going right to the printer to start on the invitations," he said as a response.

I laughed.

And then I thought a wedding.

What would that be like?

Late in the afternoon, two police detectives came. One was so short and overweight, I couldn't imagine how he could be a policeman. In my mind I envisioned television detectives and saw him trying to chase a thief or killer. The other detective was tall with very short dark brown hair and a very businesslike manner and seemed more like an FBI agent.

I described what had happened. The tall detective took notes and then they left, giving me the impression they were just going through procedures and weren't looking for any surprises. They both seemed very uncomfortable talking to me in my hospital room anyway and looked grateful for my cooperation. I was just as eager to have it all over. I didn't want to ask any questions or hear any gruesome details about Aunt Victoria's death.

Four days later I was released from the hospital. Austin was there to take me home, and when we drove up to the house, I saw that he had arranged for the ramp to be reinstalled. I knew that he had also already moved his clothing and accessories in.

"There's another surprise waiting for you," he told me.

After he wheeled me up the ramp and into the house, I saw what else he had done.

"Your attorney and I discussed it and we decided to make an executive decision," he said.

He had gotten a mechanized chair installed on the stairway. All I had to do was transfer myself into it, press a button and it would take me upstairs to a second chair.

"The mistress of the house no longer sleeps in the maid's quarters," he declared.

"Oh Austin," I cried, "you really are going to look after me."

"Til death do us part," he said. "Which reminds me. Under the circumstances," he continued, patting my stomach, "I thought a wedding as soon as possible would be in order. I have another surprise for you," he added with an impish grin from one ear to the other.

"Austin Clarke, what else have you done?"

"I took the liberty of contacting a certain English professor in London."

I shook my head.

"You don't mean to say..."

He nodded.

"Yes, he's coming with his wife. He sounded very excited about it, too."

My heart began to pound in anticipation.

"Austin, you've done so much."

"It's just a small, church ceremony with a little reception here afterward. My mother has been a great help. Actually, she's taken care of all the arrangements," he said. "I hope you don't mind."

"Mind? I'm overwhelmed. I feel like I might faint," I said.

He laughed.

"I probably should have waited until you were settled in and comfortable before unloading all this news, but now that I've gone this far..."

"What?"

"Your mother wants to come to see you tomorrow."

"My mother?"

"She and her husband came down for your aunt's funeral yesterday and they stayed to handle the legal work."

"Why didn't they stay here?"

"I don't know," he said. "Maybe they just weren't comfortable with the idea. They're at a hotel. Your attorney has been talking with Grant and he passed all the information to me to give to you.

"If you're not ready, I could call and have her postpone her visit to another time. Grant has given me an indication they will attend our wedding."

"Really?" I thought for a moment. "But do they know that my father is coming from London?"

"Not exactly," he admitted. "I thought I'd leave that to you to tell her."

"Maybe we should have just eloped," I muttered.

"We could still do that, of course, but your father would be disappointed, I think. I know my mother would."

I nodded.

"Let's try this contraption out and get you upstairs. I didn't think you'd want to go back to what was your grandmother's room, so I had the room you told me you originally used to use set up for us. Is that all right?"

"Yes, but someday soon, I'd like to move back into Grandmother Hudson's suite. I know she would want that, Austin and I can't let what Aunt Victoria did stop me from doing so."

"I understand," he said and helped me out of my chair and into the mechanized lift.

He laughed as it carried me up.

"You look like a queen rising above your subjects," he kidded.

I insisted on making the transfer to my upstairs chair myself.

"You're not going to be hovering around me day and night," I explained.

"Fine. You're doing a good job of it."

"I'll rest now," I said permitting him to wheel me into our bedroom, "but if this is going to work, I have to be trusted to do my share."

"Trusted? Expected is a better word for it," he said, feigning sternness. "When I come home from work, I will require a hot dinner ready and waiting. Especially now that I know how good you can cook," he added with a smile.

"I can't wait to do it," I said, meeting the challenge.

"For now though, you are to rest and regain all your strength. You will need most of it for the days ahead. We are going on a honeymoon, you know. A wedding without a honeymoon is like a birthday without the cake."

I laughed at his over-the-top lusty eyes, but I also agreed. Getting into bed and resting was important. I slept like a baby until I woke to find Austin bringing in a tray of food.

"That all smells very good. How did you make that?" I asked looking at the chicken, potatoes and vegetables suspiciously.

"I used an old recipe my grandmother passed down to my mother. It's called, 'Calling for take-out'," he replied.

How we both laughed and how good it felt. He held my hand and smiled at me and kissed me softly.

"All our days will be days of joy," he predicted. "We won't ask for very much, just the chance to enjoy each other."

"Are you sure about all this, Austin, really, really sure? You can still back out," I said.

"Remember when you threw yourself into the lake and I told you I felt I had gone in with you? Well, when I watched the ambulance taking you away, I felt I was in there, too, Rain. We're connected. It's forever," he said with such intensely firm and determined eyes, I could barely breathe. "I hope you're happy about it."

"Of course, I am. I never thought I'd ever be this happy again, Austin."

He kissed me.

"Eat and get strong. You're going to be a mama soon, you know," he said.

My mother arrived late in the morning. I thought she looked remarkably well for a woman who had been through all the turmoil and sorrow she had experienced. Her face was lightly tanned and her hair was radiant.

I was in my wheelchair just gazing out the window of my bedroom, looking toward the lake and beyond, reminiscing about my horseback riding and how free and happy it used to make me feel. I had just written another letter to Roy, practically begging him to contact me. I hadn't heard a word from him or about him since his army attorney's call, informing me of Roy's courtmartial.

I don't know how long my mother was in the room. Suddenly, I had that warm feeling on the back of my neck, that sense of being watched from behind and I turned my chair around to face her.

Her eyes flooded quickly with sadness and pity as soon as she saw me turn the chair and not rise out of it to greet her.

"Hi," she said. "How are you?"

"I'm fine. How are you?"

She shrugged.

"I take it day by day now. Some days go faster than others. Some seem to take weeks."

"That sounds familiar," I said and she nodded.

She glanced around the room.

"This was my room, you know."

"I know."

"It doesn't seem possible now."

"What?"

"That I lived here once, that I had a life here once. Maybe that's good. Maybe that's the way our minds protect themselves from really going mad. Forgetting is not such a bad thing sometimes."

She laughed and crossed to the bed.

"I used to think it would be wonderful for every day to really be a new day. I mean, to be born again each day. You reach a point in your life when you've grown as much as you will and then you start these multiple existences. Today, I'll be Megan. Tomorrow I'll be...Diane. The day after I'll be Clara, and it will be more than just a change of names. I'd have a different history each day and a different personality, too. That would be more fun, don't you think?"

"If that happened, how could you ever fall in love or be part of anything significant or become anything?" I asked.

"That's the point. You'd just start something and never finish and never, ever be disappointed. It would all end too soon for defeat and sadness.

"We become different people before we die anyway, Rain. I'm certainly not the person I was when I lived here, and I'm not the woman I was in college. I'm not even the woman I was last year, not now, anyway.

"You'll see," she said.

"Maybe I already have," I replied.

"Yes," she said, staring at me and nodding. "Yes, I think you have. Anyway, I'm glad you're okay. I can't even imagine what it must have been like with Victoria. She could be very cruel. She was never a happy person, never. I know she hated me."

"She envied you," I said.

"That's the same thing in the end. You get so you hate the things you can't have or can't be. It's true for me now," she nearly whispered. Then she shook her head as if that would shake out the bad thoughts and smiled. "So, what's this I hear about a wedding?"

"He's a madman," I said, "but I love him and I'm pretty sure he loves me. No one else would want to do this."

"Fiddlesticks," she said. "You're a very pretty girl and a bright girl, too."

She sighed, looked at a picture of Grandmother Hudson that was on the dresser and then turned back to me.

"I want you to know I really never blamed you for Brody's death. I mourned hard because I knew I was totally to blame not only for his death, but for your sense of guilt. I felt I had destroyed two of my children."

"Neither of them can hate you, Mother," I said.

She smiled, softly.

"No. I'm the only one now who can do that, I suppose. I have no right to expect anything of you, Rain, but I'd like to come back and I'd like to try again to be your friend."

"I never wanted anything else," I said.

Her smile widened.

"I'm looking forward to your wedding."

"I have something to tell you. Actually, two things you

ought to know. I'm determined to shut secrets out of this house and my life from now on," I added.

"Good," she said. "I'll try to do the same."

"My father's coming to the wedding," I said.

"Larry?"

"Yes, and with his wife Leanna."

"Oh." She was silent a long moment. I expected she would say she couldn't attend now, but she surprised me. "Well, I'll deal with it."

"And Grant?"

"He'll have no choice," she said with surprising assurance. "What's the other revelation? The famous second shoe?"

"I'm pregnant?"

"What? Pregnant? But how...can you be pregnant?"

"Yes, Mother, I can and I am," I said, laughing.

"Oh," she said, her smile fading.

"What's the matter? Will it bring more disgrace or something?"

"No, no," she said, shaking her head. "That's the last thing I fear about it."

"Then what?"

"Don't you realize what this means?"

"Well, I know what I realize. What do you realize?"

"I'll be a grandmother," she said. "I'm too young to be a grandmother," she wailed.

We stared at each other.

And then we laughed.

And laughed until she hugged me tightly.

I felt her tears on my face when she kissed my cheek.

They were already mixing with my own.

Epilogue

My wedding was a great success, in a large part due to Austin's mother's enthusiasm. She was, as he described, a real Southern lady who in many ways reminded me of Grandmother Hudson. Her name was Belva Ann Clarke and her attention to detail was impressive. She had an arch of white and pink roses created for us in the church and one of Austin's little nieces was the most adorable flower girl. Belva Ann took care of the printing of the cards and arranged for the ushers at the church.

My mother helped me choose my wedding dress and then decided she wanted to work with the caterers to do the reception. There was such a storm of excitement around me because of the speed with which everything had to be done that I found myself spinning with new information and decisions every day.

Mother and Belva Ann got along famously. They both possessed a reverence for those small details that made an occasion like this extra special. They marched up and down the hallways together, thinking of things to do to dress up the house for the reception. On and on it went, a discussion about forks and spoons, napkins, colors, ribbons and even festive balloons to be hung on the trees and bushes. Austin and I soon felt like outsiders, observing someone else's marriage. When they were gone for the day, he performed imitations of both of them.

"Now let's see, should we use the hand-painted imported porcelain dishes or the everyday china, and what about the champagne glasses? Isn't it uncouth to use those plastic things, even though more and more people today are doing so for receptions like this? Do you favor bright red napkins? I just hate paper napkins. We need at least cotton ones, don't you agree?"

Sometimes, he was so accurate, he had me bent over with laughter.

"Now you see why we should have eloped," I teased Austin.

"But they're having so much fun," he said. "Of course, we could let them do it all and then not show up. We'll get on a cruise or something and leave a note behind."

"And be responsible for a two suicides? No thank you," I said.

The only sour note in all this was my half sister Alison. My mother finally had told her all there was to tell about me, and Alison had a predictable reaction. She went from denial to anger and then to indifference and rebellion. My mother told me she didn't think Alison would attend the wedding.

"We've been having a lot of problems with her even before all this," my mother said. "I don't want to get into depressing things at this time, but she's being quite a handful, hanging around with the wrong people, drinking—even, we fear, doing drugs. Grant's very concerned and is trying to do everything possible, including private counseling."

"I'm sorry," I said. "Maybe some day we can be friends," I added, but that was about as realistic in my mind as walking again.

My mother nodded without any confidence in her eyes and we stopped talking about her.

Two days before our ceremony, my father and his wife arrived from London. We insisted they stay with us. I wanted them to get to know Austin well and it gave me more time to get to know them better too. We had invited my great-aunt and great-uncle, but they claimed it was impossible to break a previous engagement involving the royal family, which was fine with me whether true or not.

After my father had arrived, and up until the day of the ceremony, my mother avoided coming to the house. Of course, their meeting was inevitable. Everyone was very civil when it finally happened. Grant actually got into a long conversation concerning politics in England with my father. My mother walked about the house and grounds with Leanna, talking about the flora and the indigenous trees. Still, I felt as if we were all tiptoeing over thin ice and it would take only a longer glance, an unfortunate word or memory to sink us all.

Thankfully, nothing like that occurred and the wedding itself went off like a space launch every single part of it conducted without the smallest mistake, even my being wheeled down the aisle to the altar. What a thrill it was for me to have my real father there to give me away! Austin had thought ahead and had my place raised so that he and I were practically eye level with each other during our vows.

The ceremonial kiss went well, too, and everyone was pleased.

It seemed so strange to have so much festivity in grandmother Hudson's house afterward. For so long it had been the scene of dark and depressing events, but with the decorations, the music, the happy guests and the good food, it was easy to push the shadows back, make them retreat below where I hoped they would be shut up forever and ever.

Nevertheless, when it was all over, and I had to say good-bye to my father and his wife, promising to visit them as soon as we were able, I had a dreadfully deep foreboding that all this happiness and joy would dissipate like smoke in the wind and leave us with the cold reality to remind me that I was still a paraplegic, that I still had a difficult birth ahead of me and that I would have even a more challenging time trying to be a mother. The rose-colored glasses had to be lifted from my eyes. Gray skies were also a part of our world, and not all the music, flowers, fancy dishes and wonderful food could change any of it for long.

We were able to hold it off a while longer because of our honeymoon in the Bahamas, but when we returned, we did have our dark days, our depressing moments as we adjusted to our new lives together. However, Austin never showed any strain or regret. How perfect he was for me because he was so familiar with what someone who had my handicap experienced. He was still my therapist, even during my months of pregnancy, chiding me if I was too lazy, reminding me that the stronger I made myself, the easier the delivery would be for me and for our baby.

Now that Aunt Victoria's threats were gone, Austin and his uncle continued to develop their company. He hated leaving me every workday, but I insisted he not give up any of his life nor his career.

"If to make this marriage work, your sacrifice is so much bigger than mine, Austin, I will be weighed down with too much guilt to ever be happy," I warned.

He understood, and assumed his full duties. In my third trimester, we hired a part-time nurse to be with me. Austin found a delightful woman in her fifties, Mrs. Meriweather, who had actually assisted in two pregnancies and post deliveries of paraplegic women. She agreed that after I had given birth, she would move in with us for as long as I needed her. She had never married and had no immediate family to consider. It seemed perfect.

As the clock ticked toward the day of my delivery, I grew more anxious. Fortunately, the more serious complications Doctor Baker had described never occurred, but I kept thinking what if after all this effort and preparation, something terrible happened? If I lost this baby, I would surely never even think seriously about trying to have another.

At the beginning of what was to be my final week of pregnancy, they took me to the hospital. As Doctor Baker had predicted, I went into a normal delivery with assistance of vacuum extraction. Austin and I had decided not to learn our baby's sex beforehand. We wanted the surprise and the fun that came with predicting. He was there in the delivery room and the moment I heard my baby cry, Austin leaned over to kiss me and say, "It's a girl. I win."

We had already chosen names. Our choice for a girl was Summer. It was when he and I had grown to know and love each other and it was the season we both loved the most. Austin, showing off, quoted Shakespeare's Sonnet 18 and recited, "But thy eternal summer shall not fade."

"She will always be summer to us, warm and full of life," he predicted when I held her for the first time in my arms.

"I hope I can be a full mother to her, Austin," I said, worrying aloud now that she was born and actually breathing and sleeping against my breast.

"Of course you will, Rain. Who else knows more about how important that is than you?"

"That's why I worry," I said, rocking her gently.

"That's why you won't fail her," he insisted.

My wonderful, optimistic husband, closing the door on any dark thoughts, stood beside me, smiling, making me believe in myself and our future together as a family.

It wasn't until the spring of the following year that I was to hear from Roy. He had been in an army prison all that time and was too ashamed to let me know. When I spoke to him on the phone, I had no idea how close he was.

"I wanted to see if you hated me for not writing or calling you before this," he admitted.

"Roy, I could never hate you, but you shouldn't have kept me from knowing how you were."

"I'm sorry," he said. "About a lot of things."

"Where are you?"

He hesitated and then said, "About ten minutes away."

"You're not! You're here! Oh, Roy, I can't wait to see you. Hurry," I cried. "We have tons and tons of stuff to catch up on."

He laughed and hung up.

Summer was outside with her Glenda, a twenty-four year old unwed mother whose little boy Harley was a year older than Summer. Austin had found her. She was the daughter of one of his clients and he was impressed with how loving, thoughtful and responsible she was with her own child. She needed the work. I agreed because I needed the help, at least for now; but it was always my hope that I would soon not. Austin thought it would be good for Summer to have a playmate, even at this young age. It all did seem to be working out well.

I wheeled myself out of the house and down the ramp to wait for Roy. Glenda and the children were under the large old oak tree about two hundred yards east of the driveway, where Austin had put in a sandbox and small outdoor gym under the shade of the tree. I waved to Glenda and shouted that I was waiting for someone, not to worry. She turned her attention back to the children.

My heart raced with expectation. It had been so long since I had seen Roy. Of course, I had trepidations, too. After all, he had tried so hard to convince me we should become husband and wife.

He drove up in a rented car and got out slowly. I saw immediately that he was a good deal thinner than usual, but still held himself tall and confidently. When he saw me sitting there, waiting, he paused. I could just imagine how hard it was for him to confront me in a wheelchair.

He was dressed in civilian clothes, a light blue short sleeve shirt and jeans. His hair was a little longer than he customarily wore it, especially when he was in the service. I wheeled myself toward him. Still, he stood staring at me.

"Don't I at least get a hug?" I said.

He smiled and moved quickly to hug and hold me.

"How you doing?" he asked.

"I'm fine, Roy. Really. I'm okay."

He nodded, skepticism bright in his eyes.

"Wow, this is a big place," he said, looking up at the house. "How do you manage?"

I laughed.

"I have lots of help," I said.

"I bet you do."

"What happened to you, Roy?"

He looked down and kicked a small stone with the toe of his sneaker.

"When I heard about your accident, I wanted to come right back, but because I had gone AWOL in London when I went to see you, they weren't charitable. My request was denied. I decided to go anyway and made it to the airport where the military police picked me up. They sentenced me to three years, but it got cut back and I was given a dishonable discharge. That's the worst of it," he said.

"I'm sorry. I feel it was all because of me."

"It wasn't, no way. I made my own choices, Rain and I don't regret any of it. Only thing I regret is not getting to you."

"You're here now," I said. "That's all that matters."

"Yeah."

We heard the kids laugh and Roy turned. His eyes narrowed and then he looked at me.

"Who's that?"

"That's my mother's helper, Glenda, and her little boy, Harley, playing with my daughter, Summer."

"Your daughter?"

He looked so shocked a strong breeze could knock him over.

"Yes," I said, smiling. "I'm married, Roy."

"Married?"

"My husband's name is Austin Clarke."

He continued to stare in disbelief.

"How could you do all that and be..."

"Handicapped, a paraplegic? I lucked out, Roy. The man who fell in love with me and whom I fell in love with was my therapist. There's a lot to tell. C'mon, push me up the ramp and let's go inside and have some lunch."

I turned my chair, but Roy didn't move.

"It's all worked out well for me, Roy. I hope you'll be happy for me. I want to know all about you, your plans, how I can help you."

"Wow," he said. "I feel like I just got punched in the face."

He shook his head and blew through his lips.

"I want you to be close to us, Roy, be part of my family. You're all I have left of those old days," I said. That, at least brought back a small smile.

"Same for me," he said. "But I was hoping for more."

"It just wasn't meant to be that way, Roy. I don't love you any less or need you any less. I inherited a major portion of a big business that's run by a bunch of strangers for me. Maybe you'll help with that," I suggested.

"I don't know."

"I mean, I don't want to interfere with any of your plans, but..."

"Interfere with my plans?" He laughed. "Looks like someone already did that."

He looked like he might cry. Suddenly, Summer ran toward me, laughing.

"Look how well she can walk and run at fourteen months, Roy," I said.

He turned and she stopped to look up at him.

"Hi, honey. This is your Uncle Roy."

She moved cautiously toward me.

"She's beautiful," Roy said.

She smiled at him and he beamed. She clung to my leg.

"You want to give him a hug, Summer? Go on," I said.

She looked up at him expectantly and Roy knelt down and opened his arms.

Without any more hesitation, she ran to him. He held her close and kissed her and looked at me.

"She could have been our baby," he said.

"You'll have plenty of your own, Roy, but she'll always be close to you and so will I. Welcome home," I said. "Go on. Carry her into the house for me. I'll follow," I said.

Pausing only for a moment, he started up the stairs and I wheeled myself behind him up the ramp. Glenda started back to join us.

In a few hours Austin would be home. We would all be together and somehow, I hoped, we really would become a new family, driven by all our mutual needs for love and hope. I was afraid to look too far into the future. There were still so many unanswered questions.

Would I ever be close to my half sister? Would I continue to develop a new relationship with my real mother and my real father? Could Roy manage to find himself and create a life for himself if he was near me, the woman he had dreamed would be beside him as his wife forever and ever? Would Austin remain as strong and optimistic as he was?

And Summer, what of all this would she inherit? Would the world be a friendlier place for her than it had been for me? She certainly had a more advantageous beginning. I couldn't help but hope that Grandmother Hudson's spirit and Mama's had joined to hover over us and especially over Summer, to whisper good thoughts in her ear and fill my daughter's nights with sweet dreams.

At the doorway I paused and gazed out toward the lake. The wind was holding the dark clouds back, pushing them toward the horizon.

"Keep them away forever," I prayed.

Like a promise, my blackbirds swooned over the water soaring toward the blue skies and the coming of tomorrow.

POCKET
BOOKS

The Orphans Series

BUTTERFLY

Book 1

For as long as she could remember, Janet's life had been the orphanage, full of cruel jokes and silent wishes for the day she'd have a family of her own. She hardly believed it when Sanford and Celine Delorice chose her to be their daughter, whisking her away from her tragic past.

Her new father is handsome and kind, and though Celine is confined to a wheelchair, she is the most beautiful and elegant woman Janet has ever seen. Celine is convinced Janet will one day dazzle audiences as a ballerina, just as she did before her accident. Eager to please her new parents, Janet tries with all her might, but she is dancing on a fragile web of happiness, never knowing what might happen if one glittering strand should break...

ISBN 0 6710 2197 4

PRICE £2.99

POCKET
BOOKS

The Orphans Series

CRYSTAL

Book 2

When the Morrises choose Crystal from all the girls
and boys in the orphanage, she is full of optimism - at
last she has a home to call her own. Karl Morris, her
new dad, likes maths as much as she likes science, and
he's already proud of her being a good student.
Thelma, her new mom, makes her feel truly wanted
for the first time. And though Thelma seems more
interested in her television soap operas than in real
life, Crystal feels that their tidy little house will
become a real home.

Crystal is especially pleased when the Morrises
approve of her first boyfriend. But she will soon
discover that in her new home, sadness is banished to
the back of a closet... and that means no one is
prepared when a shocking tragedy comes rattling at
the door.

ISBN 0 6710 2197 4

PRICE £2.99

POCKET
BOOKS

This book and other **Virginia Andrews** titles are available from your book shop or can be ordered direct from the publisher.

☐ 0 671 85392 9	**Pearl In The Mist**	£5.99
☐ 0 671 85462 3	**All That Glitters**	£5.99
☐ 0 671 85572 7	**Hidden Jewel**	£5.99
☐ 0 671 85573 5	**Melody**	£5.99
☐ 0 671 00535 9	**Heart Song**	£5.99
☐ 0 671 00539 1	**Music In The NIght**	£5.99
☐ 0 671 02197 4	**Butterfly**	£2.99
☐ 0 671 02198 2	**Crystal**	£2.99
☐ 0 671 02195 8	**Brooke**	£2.99
☐ 0 671 02196 6	**Raven**	£2.99
☐ 0 671 00538 3	**Unfinished Symphony**	£5.99
☐ 0 671 02200 8	**Olivia**	£6.99
☐ 0 671 02201 6	**Runaways**	£5.99
☐ 0 671 02199 0	**Orphans**	£7.99
☐ 0 671 02964 9	**Rain**	£5.99
☐ 0 743 40914 0	**Lightning Strikes**	£6.99
☐ 0 743 20844 7	**End of the Rainbor**	£16.99

Please send cheque or postal order for the value of the book, free postage and packing within the UK; OVERSEAS including Republic of Ireland £1 per book.

OR: Please debit this amount from my:

VISA/ACCESS/MASTERCARD ....

CARD NO...

EXPIRY DATE...

AMOUNT £ ....

NAME..

ADDRESS..

....

SIGNATURE...

www.simonsays.co.uk

Send orders to: SIMON & SCHUSTER CASH SALES
PO Box 29, Douglas, Isle of Man, IM99 1BQ
Tel: 01624 83600, Fax 01624 670923
www.bookpost.co.uk
Please allow 14 days for delivery
Prices and availability subject to change without notice.